A LOST PARADISE

A LOST PARADISE

JUN'ICHI WATANABE

Translated by
Juliet Winters Carpenter

KODANSHA INTERNATIONAL
Tokyo • New York • London

Translator's Note: This novel first appeared serially in a national newspaper. Since serialization can result in a measure of repetition (the reader needing to be reminded of certain facts), a few passages in the original have been shortened in translation. These minor cuts are in no way bowdlerizations, nor do they take away from the thrust of the novel.

Originally published in 1997 by Kodansha Ltd. under the title *Shitsurakuen.*

Distributed in the United States by Kodansha America, Inc., 575 Lexington Avenue, New York, New York 10022, and in the United Kingdom and continental Europe by Kodansha Europe Ltd., 95 Aldwych, London WC2B 4JF. Published by Kodansha International Ltd., 17–14 Otowa 1-chome, Bunkyo-ku, Tokyo 112–8652, and Kodansha America, Inc. Copyright © 1997 by Jun'ichi Watanabe. English translation copyright © 2000 by Kodansha International Ltd. All rights reserved. Printed in Japan.

ISBN 4–7700–2324–3
First edition, 2000
00 01 02 03 04 05   10 9 8 7 6 5 4 3 2 1

Sunset

"I'm scared…"

The moment Rinko spoke, Kuki stopped moving. He looked at her, there in his arms, her small-boned, shapely body nearly folded in two in the shadow of his broad back. In the glow of the bedside lamp he could see frown lines between her brows. Although shut, her eyelids fluttered as if she were weeping. She was at the very point of orgasm, body and soul soaring high, shedding all restraint. Nonetheless, on the brink of release, she pulled back.

She had cried out during sex with him before: "Nooo," or "I'm going to come," or even, softly, "Help…" The words tumbled out just at the point where she felt she'd burst. Yet never before had she spoken of fear. He held her tight, saying nothing, while her writhing turned to rippling shudders and then to stillness. She had climaxed.

Kuki waited in silence for several minutes.

Before their lovemaking, she tended to be fairly reticent, as seemed only appropriate in another man's wife. Now, as if embarrassed by her sheer abandon, she lay on her side in the fetal position, knees drawn up, the sheet covering her body from the breasts to below the hips.

He put his chin on her round shoulder and whispered from behind, "Just now, you said you were scared…"

She twitched slightly, as if his breath had tickled her ear, but said nothing.

He tried again. "What did you mean?"

In the languorous tone of one basking in recent sexual fulfillment, she murmured, "It was as if all the blood in my body had started flowing backward, and was going to gush out of me…"

He couldn't quite understand the sensation. "It felt good, though, didn't it?"

"Of course, but more than that…"

"Tell me."

She paused, reflecting. "When I lose myself, climbing higher and higher, my skin tingles all over, like goose bumps. My womb feels as big and hot as the sun, and pleasure floods through me…"

Listening, Kuki was awestruck, fascinated and a bit jealous that a female could experience such a spectrum of erotic sensations.

"Here…?" he murmured, resting a hand lightly on her belly where he imagined her womb to be.

Eyes still closed, she went on. "You can't possibly be reaching so far inside me, but I feel you in me deep and strong, as if you've gone straight through the top of my head … and I don't care what happens then…"

She turned suddenly and clung to him. He held her radiating body in his arms, sure that she'd just reached her highest level of pleasure yet.

After sex, they always nestled together for sleep. Lately, he would lie on his back with her facing him on her side, her head on his left shoulder and her hips close to his, their limbs entwined. They lay that way now; but soon he slipped his right arm out and began to rub her back. She lay motionless, eyes shut, her former abandon gone, tame as a puppy while he gently massaged her, from the nape of her neck to the base of her spine.

Her skin was soft and smooth. When he told her so, she said drowsily, "It's gotten softer since we started doing this."

He had never thought about it, but it made perfect sense that a rich sex life improved the circulation, stimulating hormones and softening skin. Pleased at having such an effect on her, he went on stroking her; but gradually he tired, the motions of his fingers slackened, and Rinko too, in a state of satiety and comfort, slowly drifted off.

As usual, they settled in comfortably for the night. Sometimes he would wake up, his arm numbed by the weight of her head, or they might have pulled apart from the waist up, but still be lying in a tangle of legs. They never knew what position they would awaken in, but they both treasured this time after sex when they lay together in indolent disarray, neither touching nor apart, floating together naked on the bed.

Still wide awake, he glanced over at the curtained window. It must be nearly six, time for the sun to sink beyond the gentle arc of the horizon.

They had arrived at this hotel in Kamakura the evening before, a Friday. Kuki had left work after three and met Rinko as arranged at Tokyo Station, where they caught a train straight to Kamakura. The hotel was on a slight rise alongside Shichirigahama Beach. In summer the road along the beach was crowded with young people, but now in September traffic was light; the taxi ride had taken less than twenty minutes.

He'd chosen this spot for their tryst because here, only an hour from the city, they could imagine themselves at some far-off romantic hideaway. Their room overlooked the ocean, and they could savor the quiet of the ancient capital. As a bonus, the hotel was new, with few regular patrons. There was little likelihood of their being spotted.

Of course, their privacy could not be guaranteed. The publishing house Kuki worked for, Contemporary Books, was relatively open-minded, but being caught staying in a hotel with a woman not his wife would not do his career any good. He dreaded complications, and by maneuvering had always averted confrontations. In the past, he had taken great pains to keep his dealings with women under wraps; but with Rinko he felt different, almost reckless. She was the most desirable woman he had ever known, worth whatever risk he had to take.

His new defiance also had to do with his demotion the year before from head of his company's editorial department to a dead-end job in the reference section. The change had come as a kick in the gut. Until then, he had assumed he would one day take his place in the company's center of power. At fifty-three, he had been touted as a candidate for the next executive opening, a challenge he felt ready for. Then, instead of stepping up, he found himself booted downstairs to reference. A new president had taken over, resulting in a redistribution of responsibilities that Kuki never saw coming.

All he knew was that now, having let slip his chance to become an executive, he would soon be fifty-five with zero prospects for promotion. Any subsequent transfer could only mean a still more lackluster job in the main company, or a trip to a subsidiary. That insight brought something else into focus: from now on he would cease to be a drudge and live more freely—life, after all, was short. This simple shift in perspective had a dual effect, diminishing the importance of what had always seemed crucial and making what had once seemed unimportant invaluable.

Since the demotion, his official title remained "editorial director," but it rang hollow. As a member of the reference section, his job only involved gathering an assortment of material and now and then putting together some sort of feature article for submission to an appropriate magazine. Nor were there any hard and fast deadlines.

Finding himself in an unchallenging job with time on his hands allowed Kuki the disquieting discovery that in all his life he had never fallen completely in love, never loved anyone from the bottom of his heart. Certainly he'd been attracted to many women, beginning with his wife, and had even had an occasional secret fling; but no relationship had been truly satisfying. Never had he felt consumed by passion. He was afraid that he was going to miss out on one of life's most intense experiences.

And then Rinko Matsubara came into his life.

Romantic encounters are, of course, always accidental, and his meeting her was no exception. Toward the end of the previous year, his old friend Kinugawa, head of a newspaper-sponsored Culture Center, had asked him to give a talk on writing. Nearly thirty students had signed up, and he was supposed to say something about style.

Kuki was no writer, only someone who made books. He demurred, but Kinugawa told him it was no big deal; all he needed to do was say a few words from his own experience, as someone who had taken on a number of authors and helped get their work into print. "Besides," Kinugawa added, "things are a bit dull for you now, aren't they?" That persuaded Kuki. Apparently the offer had less to do with needing this particular lecture than with offering him encouragement at a difficult time in his life.

The two of them had been college classmates, graduating from the same literature department, then parting company as Kinugawa took a job in journalism and Kuki went into the book business. They still got together for an occasional drink. Six years back, when Kuki became head of the editorial department, Kinugawa had quickly followed suit by becoming chief editor of his newspaper's cultural section. Then, three years ago, he'd suddenly been appointed head of the paper's downtown Culture Center. Whether the change was to Kinugawa's liking or not Kuki never knew—though a wry comment that he was "on the way out" seemed to indicate he would have preferred staying with the parent company after all. Anyway, his own experience of falling off the promotion ladder must have made him sympathetic to Kuki's current plight. Hence the call.

Appreciating his friend's solicitude, Kuki had accepted the offer, and set out on the designated evening. After his ninety-minute talk, he and Kinugawa went out for dinner in the company of a young woman whom Kinugawa introduced as a calligraphy teacher on his staff: Rinko.

Had he not accepted Kinugawa's invitation, had Kinugawa not invited her to dinner that night, they might never have met. Whenever he thought back to their first meeting, Kuki couldn't help feeling the strangeness of love. There was a sense of destiny about it.

From the moment they were introduced Kuki felt a rush of excitement, as if his heart had grown wings. Since marrying he had drifted into involvements with various women, not only when younger but also in middle age; one had been drawn to his "detached" quality, she said, another to the "little boy" in him. He had found their choice of words mystifying, but as he looked back over his dealings with women, it seemed they might both be right. With Rinko, he had been disconcertingly single-minded in his approach. Might that be his boyish side coming out? He had taken it on himself to call the number on her business card barely a week after their chance introduction. Other women had attracted him before, but never with such intensity. Though amazed at his own temerity, he couldn't restrain his longing for her. He called her almost daily, seeing her secretly again and again until finally, this spring, they had made love.

He was enthralled by her, just as he thought he would be. He tried pinpointing what it was about her that had so captivated him that first evening. Her face had nothing exceptional about it, but was small and sweet. Her slim, well-proportioned figure had been sheathed in a smart, sedate suit appropriate for a married woman. Though thirty-seven, she looked younger, but what had attracted him above all was her ability as a calligrapher, particularly her speciality—*kaisho*—the square, precise style she'd been hired to teach on a short-term basis. At that first meeting, she personally seemed to possess all the dignity and neatness of *kaisho*. And later, little by little, she had melted, showing him more tenderness and warmth, eventually giving everything over to him, becoming ever more passionate, more wanton. He found the process of this gradual breakdown intensely appealing.

Now they lay naked together, each one attuned to the other's slightest movements. The moment he raised his head to look at the curtained window, her left hand clutched him in seeming alarm. He put his hand over hers and checked the bedside clock: ten minutes past six.

"The sun's about to go down, I bet."

Through the floor-to-ceiling windows, the view took in the ocean stretching out from Shichirigahama, and the little round island of Enoshima. Now, beyond that window, the sun should be setting. The day before, the two of them had arrived moments before sunset, just as the blazing red sun was sinking behind the hill at the end of the long bridge to the island.

"Want to take a look?"

Getting out of bed, he put on the robe that had fallen on the floor and opened the curtains. The moment he did so, slanting beams of sunlight came pouring into the room, spilling across the floor all the way to a corner of the bed.

"We're in time…"

The sun was above the mountains beyond Enoshima, sinking slowly as it reddened the lower half of the sky.

"Come and look," he said.

"I can see it from here."

She was dazed by the sky's sudden brilliance. Still naked, she kept the sheet wrapped around her as she rolled over to face the window.

"It's bigger and redder than yesterday." He opened the curtains all the way, then went back to the bed and stretched out beside her.

Summer haze still floated in the air, making the setting sun seem to shimmer and swell. Then, just as its lower half neared the hills, the sun suddenly shrank, turning into a crimson ball like a clot of blood.

"I've never seen such a sunset," she declared.

Kuki remembered that a bit earlier she had compared her womb to the sun. Like the sun slipping from the evening sky, was her body that had blazed so hot now fading into stillness? Imagining this, he drew close to her from behind, sliding one hand across her lower belly.

As the sun disappeared behind the mountains, it radiated crimson shafts of light. Soon the sky turned purple, and then darkened as evening spread over all. Till then a sparkling gold, the ocean suddenly went as black as ink, and the distant silhouette of Enoshima stood out against it, with lights along the shore.

The day before, after arriving at the hotel, Kuki had learned for the first time that there was a lighthouse on the island; now its slender band of light swept across the sky.

"The sun's gone."

As Rinko murmured the words, Kuki nodded; then it occurred to him she might be thinking about home, and his breath caught in his chest.

According to Kinugawa, her husband was a medical professor at a Tokyo university. He was supposed to be some ten years her senior, which would make him forty-seven or forty-eight. "His seriousness is his only virtue," was all she said about him, half joking, but a mutual acquaintance had disclosed that he was tall and good-looking. With a catch like that for a husband, Kuki wondered why she was interested in a guy like him. But asking wouldn't get him a straight answer; he also felt that finding out now wouldn't change anything, either.

Their time together was too precious to spend worrying. Far better if they each forgot about home and concentrated on each other. That was how he wanted it, but now as she watched the darkening sky an unmistakable shadow fell on Rinko's profile. They'd been together since the afternoon of the day before; this was day two of their tryst. Staying another night would mean two nights in a row away from home. Rinko had understood that from the start, but he worried that as she watched the sunset fade to night, thoughts of home might fill her with misgivings.

Carefully, as if to probe the secrets of her heart, he placed his hand under her left breast. Rinko's breasts weren't big, but they were round and firm to the touch. He cupped his hand over the breast, feeling its softness and warmth, and wondered what she was thinking. He meant to ask, but all he said was, "Shall we get up?"

They were still lying in bed, eyes fixed where the sun had sunk into the sea.

"Close the curtains, will you?" she asked, and obediently he did. Still covering herself with the sheet, she groped around on the floor for her scattered underwear.

"We seem to have gotten day and night mixed up," he said.

They had driven around Shichirigahama Beach and Enoshima Island in the afternoon, getting back to the hotel at about three, he remembered. From then until the sun dipped and went down, they had been together in bed. Suddenly appalled by his own lechery, he went into the next room and took out a beer from the refrigerator.

He sat drinking his beer and watching the dark ocean while Rinko showered. She came back wearing a white dress, her hair tied up behind with a white ribbon.

"You want to go out for dinner?" he suggested. The previous evening, they had eaten at the hotel restaurant on the second floor, overlooking the ocean.

"Didn't you promise we'd be back, though?"

The manager had stopped by their table to say hello, and when they mentioned they would be staying a second night, he had promised to save them some abalone from the day's catch.

"All right, let's eat here again, then."

Her body still exuding the languor of lovemaking, Rinko seemed happy to remain in the hotel.

"Tonight I might get drunk," he said, and she smiled, all trace of any shadows gone.

Kuki reconfirmed the reservation by phone, and together they set out for the restaurant on the second floor. It was Saturday night, and there were a number of families there, but the manager led the pair to a table by the window reserved for them. The square table was turned at an angle to the window; they sat down on each side of one corner, and gazed out the window in front of them.

"You can't see a thing now," she said.

In daytime and early evening there would be a view of the ocean, but now it was swallowed up in darkness. Only the outline of a great pine showed indistinctly at the window's edge.

"We can see our reflections," he said.

The night window was a dark mirror, reflecting the two of them at their table and, behind them, the other customers and the chandelier. It was as if another restaurant loomed beyond the window. Kuki searched in the reflection for a face he might recognize. On his way in, he'd kept his eyes downcast as he followed behind the waiter. He realized he hadn't looked around because of the guilt he felt being with a woman not his wife.

Let someone catch them together, he thought defiantly—what the hell. He had thought he'd laid this issue to rest, yet here it was again, nagging at him. Was it because they were in Kamakura? In Tokyo, he could always say she was a business associate, even a friend. But to be dining together in a Kamakura hotel so late at night was clear evidence of a greater intimacy. He had both relatives and old friends in the area. Who was to say none of them would turn up?

Torn between bravado and cowardice, Kuki settled the matter by deciding to say, if confronted, that he'd had errands here in town and had simply taken the opportunity to meet a friend for dinner who also happened to be in Kamakura.

Having settled the matter in his own mind, he looked back at Rinko. She was sitting erect, gazing out into the night. Her profile was serene, filled with a certainty and calm that seemed unlikely to waver no matter who saw them together.

Before the food arrived, the sommelier came over and asked what they would like to drink. Kuki chose a light, fruity white wine for starters. As they were eating their marinated appetizers, the manager brought them a large plate of fresh-caught local abalone.

"We'll serve it both lightly steamed and grilled in butter," he suggested.

Kuki could tell immediately that the fish was so fresh it would also make excellent sashimi, but decided to go with the man's recommendation.

The restaurant's interior was so clearly reflected in the dark window before them that they could easily make out the faces of the other dinner guests sitting nearby. Kuki took a sip of wine and asked Rinko, "Anyone here you know? After all, this isn't far from Yokohama..."

Her father ran a well-established furniture import business in Yokohama, and she had gone to college there. It was likely that she had quite a few acquaintances in the vicinity. Still, she made no move to look around, and only answered nonchalantly, "I doubt it."

"You looked a little sad before, when the sun was going down," he said. "I thought you might be feeling homesick."

"Me?"

"Well, you've been away from home two days now..."

Fingers around her wineglass, she smiled. "I was worried about my cat."

"Your cat?"

"When I left, she didn't seem quite herself, so I was wondering how she is."

He already knew that Rinko, who had no children, doted on her cat. Still, it took the wind out of his sails to think that, as she gazed at the darkening sky after making passionate love, a cat had filled her thoughts. What crossed his mind next was an image of a man putting out food for a cat: was Rinko's husband alone with the animal now, in their home?

Though curious about her husband and their life together, Kuki usually restrained himself from asking. Deep down, he was more afraid of knowing too much than not knowing enough. On hearing that after two days away from home what weighed on Rinko's mind was her cat, his curiosity was piqued anew.

"Who's feeding it?"

"I left some dry cat food out for her, so I think she'll be okay."

He wanted to ask what her husband would be eating, but knew that such prying would likely spoil the mood of their romantic tête-à-tête.

The sommelier refilled their wineglasses, and, on his heels, the waiter served the abalone: lightly grilled, and steamed with a slice of lemon alongside.

Kuki's taste in French cuisine was definitely "nouvelle," light fare that brought out the flavor of the ingredients. Rinko apparently shared his preference. "It looks wonderful," she declared enthusiastically, and dug in. Their energetic afternoon had clearly given her an appetite; but even with gusto, she handled her knife as neatly and gracefully as ever.

"Mm, delicious."

Rinko concentrated simply on her food. As he gazed at her, Kuki's mind traveled back to the scene in bed a while ago. It was hard to put into words, but the truly delicious morsel was Rinko herself. The subtlety of her firm and succulent flesh was a delicacy among delicacies.

She continued to eat her abalone, little suspecting what he was thinking, and Kuki joined in, conveying steamed abalone to his mouth.

They finished dinner a little after nine. They had been drinking both white and red wine. Rinko, not much of a drinker, had a light crimson flush from her cheeks all the way down her throat. Perhaps the lingering echoes of their lovemaking had intensified the effects of the wine, for the corners of her eyes, too, were languid. Kuki also felt the alcohol affecting him more rapidly than usual, but he wasn't yet ready to turn in.

They walked out of the restaurant and looked into the bar at the far end of the lobby. It was too crowded, so they turned to go back to their room.

"Shall we go outside?"

At her suggestion, he slid open the door leading outside and found it led directly to a garden ending in some shrubbery about thirty feet on. Spread before their eyes was the night ocean.

"Just smell the sea," said Rinko.

A light wind ruffled her hair as she stood with her shoulders thrown back and drank in the ocean air. The sea seemed to loom even closer.

"Enoshima is surrounded by lights."

True enough, the shoreline drive, lit up by streetlights and the lights of cars, led in a gentle curve to Cape Koyurugi, and past there to the island, jutting out into the sea, lit up like a battleship by seaside lights. The beam from the lighthouse, atop the hill midway on the island where the sun had gone down, had increased in brightness as the night deepened, now slicing cleanly across the dark sea.

"It feels nice…"

He drew close to her as she stood facing the wind, but the glass in his hand prevented him from folding her in his arms. He bent down and kissed her. There in the ocean-scented breeze, the only one who saw the kiss was the light in the lighthouse.

"I'll bring you a drink," he said. "Scotch and water?"

"I think I'll have a brandy."

Placed invitingly in a corner of the breeze-swept garden was a white table and chairs. When they left the restaurant, he'd thought he had reached his limit, but here in the salt air he felt renewed capacity.

"A private bar with a view of the sea," was Rinko's way of putting it, and it was true: except for the starlight, and the beam of the lighthouse out at sea, there was nothing else to come between them. As they sat in their secret bar sipping their drinks, it was as if this one corner of the world were detached from reality, afloat in a dream.

"I don't want to stir from here, ever," she said.

"You'd stay here forever?"

"Wouldn't you?"

"Yes, if *you* did…"

They looked up together at the stars, but after a pause she said softly, "It wouldn't work, though, would it."

Unsure what she meant, Kuki thought back over his own obligations. No one knew he was here. The day before, he had told his secretary he was going home early, and to his wife he'd said that he needed to do research in Kyoto and would be gone for a couple of days. She had asked no questions, probably assuming that she could call his office, if need be, to find out how to reach him.

After their only daughter married and left home, his wife had grown absorbed in her work as a design consultant to a ceramics maker, a job she got through a friend. Often she arrived home after Kuki. Husband and wife they might be, but their conversations were businesslike, and they neither dined nor traveled together. All the same, he had never thought of leaving her. Though they were unaffectionate together, with no sex or excitement in the marriage, he had convinced himself that, at their age, this was normal. Until meeting Rinko he had believed himself content.

So ran his thoughts, revolving around his home and wife, until a new breeze off the ocean whisked them off to the distant sky, making way instead for renewed concern about Rinko's home life.

"Will it be okay, your staying away for two days?"

"I've been away before." She went on looking up at the stars, as if addressing them. "My calligraphy work takes me to different parts of the country with my teacher, and there are exhibitions and things, too."

"So that's what you said this time, too?"

"No, I'm supposed to be seeing a friend tonight."

"For two whole days?"

"Well, I have a close friend in Zushi, and it's the weekend…"

Would that be enough to fool her husband? Even if it were, what if an emergency came up and he tried to contact her?

"Does your friend know you're here?"

"I did tell her, but it's all right."

What was all right, he wondered.

She said flatly, "He won't look for me. He's in love with his work."

As a medical professor, he might well spend most of his time in his office, but wasn't she being a little incautious? "Isn't he suspicious?"

"Are you worried for me?"

"I thought it might be unpleasant if he found out."

"Would that be a problem for you?"

Kuki let out a big breath and thought about it: a woman asking a man, "If my husband finds out about us, would that upset you?" On one level, a simple question—or, possibly, a revelation of her own determination to ride out whatever might happen in that case.

"Does he know about us?"

"I wonder…"

"He hasn't said anything?"

"Not in particular…"

That was a relief, he thought, but in the same moment she murmured nonchalantly, "Maybe he does know."

"He hasn't asked you directly, though, has he?"

"Maybe he doesn't ask because he doesn't want to know."

The wind off the ocean suddenly stiffened, picking up her last words and trailing them out into the distance. As he traced the path of the wind, Kuki thought to himself: *Doesn't want to know because he's afraid to know.* Was that it? He might sense she was cheating on him, but prefer not to face the fact. Better not to know at all than to know and suffer the consequences.

Again the image of a tall man in a doctor's white coat rose in his mind's eye. Her husband had no apparent flaw in either social status or looks. Despite suspecting his wife of having an affair, this paragon kept silent. Did he keep from cross-examining her out of love? Or was he feigning ignorance, watching coldly as betrayal piled on betrayal? Pondering, Kuki found his inebriation quickly slipping away as the image of this mystifying couple emerged.

"You must think we're strange…"

He started to nod in agreement, but caught himself. What was really so strange about couples out of love? There were any number of examples, the world over.

"It's not only you two. Most couples aren't all that happy."

"I wonder…"

"Knowing something must be wrong, they go right on keeping up appearances."

"And what happens when that doesn't work any more? Then what?"

As she looked up at the stars, light from indoors cut across her face so that only the left half shone palely. With his eyes on her bisected profile, it struck him that here was a new question: Was she saying that she herself had already reached that point, or that she soon would? Either way, she seemed to be waiting expectantly for an answer.

"Well, does he—" For whatever reason, he couldn't bring himself to say the words "your husband"; he could only refer to him in the third person. "Does he still try to have sex with you?" The moment he said it, Kuki knew that this was what he'd wanted to ask all along.

She was quiet for a while, considering, and then murmured to the stars, "No."

"He never…?"

"I won't have it."

"He accepts that?"

"I don't know, but he has little choice," she said matter-of-factly. Her profile had the set look of a woman unwilling to put up with something she found distasteful.

At some point, love reaches an impasse.

It begins with two people who meet and discover a mutual attraction. In surprisingly little time, they draw close, establish intimacy. The process is astonishingly smooth even to the lovers, who yield to each other in a blaze of careless passion. But the moment they imagine they have scaled the heights, a deep valley often yawns in their path; they surrender greedily to their delight in one another, but what they fancied was a garden paradise turns out to be a weed-grown wasteland, as they look around them in silent dismay.

Rinko and Kuki had now gone beyond the first, smooth stage of love to arrive at an impasse of sorts. The future of their affair hinged now on their ability to find a way through.

Meeting in secret several times a month, going off together on an occasional overnight jaunt: as long as they were satisfied with this level of intensity, they didn't need to pass through the valley. But should that cease to suffice—should they feel the need to see each other more often, sense one another's presence more strongly and intimately— they would have to muster the courage to plunge ahead.

Courage to follow their desires whatever the cost, that was what they needed. Given enough determination, they might then be able to revel in their time together all the more, indulge their passion still more freely. Yet to do so they had to pay a price. Rinko had to earn the mistrust of her husband, Kuki that of his wife, leading inevitably to conflict and perhaps, depending on how things turned out, the final breakdown of their marriages. To fend off potential disaster and yet satisfy their longing to be together: striking that balance was their biggest challenge.

From what Rinko said, her marriage was on the verge of breakdown: if she steadfastly refused her husband's sexual advances, why should the two of them go on being husband and wife? But then, as far as that went, Kuki's relationship with his wife was equally sexless, his own marriage in no better shape. What made it harder to bear for Rinko than for him, however, was the difference between the sexes— she being in the difficult position of having to rebuff her husband's every advance, while Kuki only had to refrain from making any to his wife.

With the wind off the ocean in his face, Kuki felt more confident now. It was time to be frank. He would sound Rinko out directly, and together they could find a way.

"Tell me something. Does he know *why* you won't sleep with him?"

"Yes, I think he does."

Once again, an image rose in his mind of her husband, the scholar. He had never met the man, but always pictured him as even-featured, wearing glasses. Even though they were rivals, for some reason he couldn't work up much of a dislike. Kuki was having a love affair with the man's wife. The man was a cuckold. Perhaps that pathetic fact aroused his sympathy, or perhaps it was hard to feel antagonism toward a man so placid that he bore in patient silence the indignity of a wife who consistently turned him away.

In any case, there was no question that he, Kuki, now had the edge. But the greater his advantage, the greater his responsibility.

"I know you're in a hard position." Inwardly, he bowed his head to her. "Knowing you are in pain hurts me as well."

"But *you're* all right. Men can always manage, can't they?"

"That's true in a way, but sometimes we can't."

Another breeze came in from the ocean, turning into a scudding gust. As if in response, Rinko murmured, "I'm about at the end of my rope."

"It's that bad?"

Slowly she nodded at the night sky. "And I don't care what happens now."

"But..."

"It's not easy for a woman."

Rinko had her eyes closed, feeling the wind on her face. As he looked at the set expression on that face, tenderness flowed over him, and he took her in his arms.

They kissed and went back inside. He was stroking her hair, damp from the ocean air. The next thing they knew, without either of them having asked or answered the question, they were in bed together. Talking about their marriages had become more and more painful. Stifled, unable to find a solution, they could only find comfort in one another's warmth.

Impatiently, Kuki lunged at her, yanking open her top, tearing off her clothes, pulling down his shorts. She made little whimpering noises, all the while pulling off her own underwear, matching his rhythm and urgency.

Her desire was as torrid as his.

Naked at last, breathing hard, they embraced. Now between her flesh and his there was nothing to separate them—not her husband, not the lighthouse beam or the ocean breeze, not even the air in the room. They held each other so tightly that their bones dug into each other, as they sucked at each other's mouths.

Perhaps because of the drink, their feverish passion was soon spent. Rinko found a quick and shuddering release, and after making sure she was satisfied, he fell still. The only witness to the storm unleashed in their bed was the light from the bedside lamp, falling faintly across the pillows.

After turning in an instant into wild animals, attacking and devouring one another, they now lay as tame and docile as a pair of house pets, legs lightly overlapping. The combination of inebriation and passion had left Rinko's body warmly aglow. Absorbing the lingering heat with his full length, Kuki thought of the expression "body language."

Just now, their bodies had certainly shared a kind of communication. Words were not enough; talking only confused and tangled an issue. At such times, their bodies were their sole means of communication. It was as if to be aroused, be locked together physically, and so find fulfillment and release, made all their problems, however intractable, fade away.

As proof of this, the two of them lay now in a delicious lassitude, the oppression of a short while ago forgotten. Nothing was resolved, yet allowing their bodies to communicate had enabled them to reach a mutual understanding and acceptance.

For a man, knowing that his partner was sexually fulfilled brought great peace of mind and renewed confidence.

"Was it good?" he asked.

Not that he needed to ask: he had only to think back to the way she'd been a few minutes ago—and yet he wanted to hear her say it. She defied his expectations, though, by nestling up to him and lightly pressing her forehead against his chest without a word. The answer had to be "Yes," but she was embarrassed to say so. Perhaps that was it.

"Do you like me?"

No need to ask this, either. She was betraying her husband to be with him; she certainly couldn't dislike him. Even so, he asked again.

This time she answered simply, "No."

He turned and looked at her.

She said categorically, "I hate this."

"This?"

"Having you make love to me."

What was she saying? It made no sense.

In a husky voice she went on, "I don't like it when we're together like this and I stop being myself. It feels awful to lose all control."

Lose all control? Wasn't that another way of saying she'd found complete satisfaction, that her body had experienced joy and release? Delicately, he said, "But if it's getting better for you..."

"It's as if I've fallen into a mantrap."

"I'm the one who's fallen—for you."

"Anyway, shame on you for doing this to me."

"Sorry, it's your own fault."

"My fault?"

"You're too delicious."

She seemed taken aback to hear herself spoken of like a piece of cake.

"If you weren't, I wouldn't be so crazy about you."

"It's all new."

"What is?"

"Being ... like this."

He checked the clock by the bed and found it was after eleven. Whatever she might want from him, he had no strength left; yet it was too early for sleep. He wanted to drift a while longer as they were, naked in one another's arms, enjoying the moment. Thinking this, he asked her again, "And you do like me, after all?"

"I told you, no."

She showed no sign of stopping this verbal sparring.

"Then why...?"

"Why did I fall for you so easily, you mean?"

She sounded so grim that he said lightly, "I never thought anyone as nice as you would look twice at me."

"You're nice too."

"Liar. You want to know the truth? I had no confidence at all."

"That was just what I liked, your lack of confidence. Most men your age are so full of themselves. They show you their business card, and all they can talk about is how important they are in their company, what worldly power and prestige they have. You never said anything like that..."

"Believe me, I wanted to, but there was nothing to brag about."

"Women don't care about things like that. They want someone who has tenderness and a certain aura..."

"Aura?"

"Yes, you seemed a little weary, somehow, and lonely."

Whatever aura he might have conveyed, there was no denying he'd been mentally exhausted back then.

"You had some time at your disposal, you said, so you'd decided to study memorable women of the Showa era, and that was interesting, and besides…"

"Besides what?"

"You were so incredibly good." Gazing off into space, she said it lightly.

No woman had ever said such a thing to Kuki before. Mostly he managed to satisfy the women he was with, he supposed, but never had he thought of himself as having prodigious sexual skills. Not that it was for a man to say. There, a man could only defer to a woman's opinion—but it had to be a woman who had been with a certain number of partners. It was certainly not unpleasant to be told he was "incredibly good." That it was Rinko who said it, this woman he was so in love with, was an even greater boost to the ego … if he could take her words at face value.

"You're not joking? You mean it?"

"Of course. Why would I say it otherwise?"

In his delight, he said, laughing, "So I pass?"

"Absolutely," she answered without hesitation, then added, "You must have been with lots of women before."

"No."

"You don't have to hide it, especially since it's worked out to my advantage." After two full days with him, Rinko seemed completely relaxed.

"You said just now this was all new to you—what about before?"

"What do you mean?" She must have known, but she made a point of asking.

"I mean sex with … him."

"There were times when I would start to feel something, but not often."

"Then it wasn't really…?"

"That's why you're a bad man, teaching me all this."

"Believe me, you were a quick study. You have 'natural aptitude.'"

"Is that what it takes, aptitude?"

Asking him this with a serious air, she seemed suddenly young and adorable. From behind, he grabbed her breasts.

Nothing makes a man happier or prouder than to see the woman he loves awaken to the joy of sex. Her body starts out young and inexperienced, tight as a bud, gradually loosening and becoming more pliant until one day it bursts into bloom like a gorgeous flower. By participating in that process, enabling a woman to blossom, a man sees confirmation of how deep a mark he has left on her. Knowing this creates a satisfaction that can give his life a new meaning.

Rinko said unequivocally that he, Kuki, had taught her, and no one else. This meant that he alone had awakened her capacity for pleasure. It was also an admission that until now she had felt nothing, that marital sex had given her no joy.

"I'm glad," he whispered in her ear. "Now I know you won't forget me." He felt as if he'd driven a wedge into her body—a thick, stout wedge, running through her from the hips to the crown of her head. Now she could never get away, struggle as she might. "I'll never let you go."

"What if I never do go away? What will you do?" When he made no immediate answer, she persisted. "Doesn't that frighten you?"

Her question reminded him that, just before sunset, she had murmured that she was afraid. Then, she'd been referring to the hot intensity of her sexual response; now, it appeared, she was talking about cold reality.

"We'll go to hell for this."

"We will?"

"I don't know about you, but I will, definitely." She clung to him. "Hold me, don't let me go…"

Echoes of their passion still throbbing within her, she was troubled by a deep divide between body and mind.

As he comforted her, saying gently "There, there," Kuki thought again about the mystery of human sexuality.

He believed that sexual pleasure was weaker in the male than in the female. Because of this, instead of being preoccupied with his own simple response, the mature man found it ultimately more satisfying, more gratifying to guide his partner toward full arousal and orgasm. By Kuki's age, when the young man's need for rough-and-tumble sex had started to fade, switching to the role of active pleasure-giver made a man feel most alive. Some women might find it hard to accept that a man could be satisfied by giving one-sided pleasure—but there was deep delight in taking on that active role, in reminding oneself that the woman's pleasure was the man's responsibility.

Rinko, for example, had started out as neat and circumspect as the *kaisho* style of calligraphy she practiced. Once freed from all sorts of restrictions, she had blazed into life as she discovered the secrets of pleasure, and proceeded to enjoy herself as a mature sexual woman, free of inhibitions, until she became addicted to it—to sensuality. It was at once a process of disintegration and a return to her innermost nature as a woman. For a man, nothing could be so exciting, so electrifying, as to witness that transformation firsthand. To observe it in detail was to gain a visceral understanding of what it meant to be human, to be a woman, with a myriad physical resources and ways of changing.

Yet the enjoyment of an observer or bystander was clearly limited. However much a man might define his role as that of sexual instigator and observer, as long as sex involved the connection of two bodies, no one partner could be solely passive, the other active. The man might devise artful new techniques, but as the woman responded to them, ever more aroused and passionate, he in turn grew excited too and chased after her until before they knew it both were lost in the depths of sex, tumbling together into the abyss.

Their paths to rapture might differ, thought Kuki, but as long as they stayed together, there was no way either of them could fall alone into hell. Stroking Rinko's back as she clung to him, he mulled over the fear she'd just expressed. Certainly, if the two of them went on indulging their passion this way, they might find themselves tumbling into an abyss. That abyss, to Rinko, was hell; and to keep from winding up there, she thought they ought to call a halt to this love affair.

But Kuki didn't consider what they were doing to be a mortal sin. True, for a man with a wife and child to carry on with another man's wife was a violation of moral law, a breach of ethics; but then, where was the harm if two people in love acted on their desires? Common sense and ethics might change with the times, but there was an absolute and universal justice in the sexual union of two lovers.

Whatever Kuki might feel, though, as long as Rinko remained unconvinced, their love couldn't last. Any intimidation she felt would keep them from taking their love to the next level.

"You aren't going to hell," he said, stroking her round hip, the skin still flushed with heat. "We're not doing anything bad."

"Oh, yes, we are."

Besides the compunction she felt as a married woman, she was troubled by a sense of sin that was traceable, perhaps, to her graduation from a college founded by a Christian missionary.

"But we're in love."

"It's still wrong."

No logic he might offer would persuade her, he thought. If she was bound on going to hell, all he could do was follow quietly along.

"I'll go with you, then."

If they went on indulging in illicit sexual pleasure, they might very well end by falling into their own private hell; but neither was abstention any guarantee of heaven. In which case, Kuki thought with defiance, they might as well give themselves up entirely to this passion, and damn the consequences.

Autumn Sky

From his office window, the facade of the building opposite shone cheerfully in the sun. The typhoon three days earlier had finally brought the long summer to an end, ushering in a spell of bright, crisp fall weather.

Leaning back in his chair, Kuki finished reading his fourth newspaper of the morning and looked out the sun-drenched window. It was almost eleven, but the room was quiet and peaceful. From near the door, the faint but rhythmic clicking of the secretary's word processor was the only sound.

This, the reference section, was on the sixth floor, at the end of the hall and to the right of the elevator. As one entered, there was a small reception area. Other than that, there were only six desks arranged face to face in the room's center.

Kuki came here every morning at ten.

Currently, four men were assigned to reference, and one woman who doubled as a secretary. Kuki's three male colleagues were Suzuki, the section chief, who was three years senior to him, and was editing a social history; Yokoyama, who was one year senior, and doing a business-related statistical survey; and Muramatsu, who was two years junior, and developing a new dictionary. Kuki's own project was to be a history of the Showa era. The scale of each man's project, and the time allotted for it, were alike indefinite. All four had landed there by getting bumped off the promotion ladder. They now belonged to the "window-seat tribe"—employees with little or no real work to do who could sit and look outside all day if they liked. In this office, with no need to push oneself, time passed slowly.

At first, Kuki had chafed at the unaccustomed leisure, but after six months he settled in, giving less and less thought to his loss of reputation. Today, after getting to work and finding nothing on his desk demanding attention, he'd started, as had become customary, by reading the morning papers. He then lit a cigarette, looked out the window past the sunlit building across the way, and stared at two slanting clouds and a large TV antenna. The clouds were like giant streaks of paint, and looking at them in the tranquil sky brought thoughts of Rinko. The image of her soft white skin came into his mind, and his ears began to ring with the sound of her urgent cries in bed.

He realized that on this calm, bright autumn morning, he was probably the only person in the building with nothing to do but think of a woman's soft skin. Suddenly, he again resented his enforced idleness; in his old job, with frequent meetings to attend and texts to prepare, he wouldn't have been so haunted.

Staring for a few more moments at the clouds, Kuki abruptly stood up, as if remembering something he had to do. His colleagues went on reading or looking at their computer monitors, paying him no attention. With a swift glance around, he walked out of the office and past the elevator to the stairway door, opened it, and stepped onto the landing. While daydreaming earlier, he had decided to call Rinko at home. At this time of day, she would be alone.

He closed the door behind him for privacy and took out his cell phone, a relic of busier days that now came in handy for secret calls to Rinko. He pulled out the short antenna, punched in her number. Her voice promptly answered, "It's me." It was as if somehow she'd known he was going to call. He double-checked that no one was around and then whispered into the receiver:

"I had to hear your voice."

"Aren't you at work?"

"Yes, but I started thinking about you, and something came over me…"

"What?"

"The clouds in the sky started looking like you…"

"Oh? It isn't even lunchtime yet."

"… and I wanted you."

"You're not to make me think about that."

"Want to go back to Kamakura?"

It was nearly two weeks since their tryst in that Kamakura hotel. Afterward, Kuki had been frantic with worry about what might happen when she arrived home. What would her husband say after she spent two nights away? The next day he had called to check, only to have her reassure him calmly that everything was fine, sounding like her normal self. A strange marriage those two must have. Either the husband was gutless, or somehow she managed to outmaneuver him. It was a relief to know nothing serious had happened, but he nonetheless knew that the next time he and Rinko spent the night together, he would worry all over again.

"There's a firelight performance of Noh this Thursday." He had long known about the Kamakura event, but had never gone. "If you like, I'll get us tickets. It ends late, so we'd need to stay overnight again."

"I'd like that."

Her reply came so abruptly that he paused. "Are you sure it's okay?" he asked.

"I don't know. But I want to go."

She was unequivocal. Going off with him was apparently not a morally charged issue for her, but something she did because she wanted to.

"Great. Then I'll get the tickets."

"But that's three whole days away…" Once the words slipped out, she seemed anxious to retract them. "Never mind. I can wait. That's what you do, isn't it?"

Intimacy with his wife was a thing of the past. Kuki murmured his assent.

"It's you who made me like this, you know," she said reproachfully. "It's all your fault."

When he returned to his office, the secretary told him he had just had a call from a Mr. Kinugawa. In his circle of friends, the only Kinugawa was the head of the Tonichi Culture Center. Kuki called him back from the office phone, not using his cell phone this time. Fortunately, Kinugawa was in. He had business in the city that evening, he said, so how about getting together for dinner? Kuki arranged to meet him at six in a little tavern in Ginza, and hung up.

Things at the office were as slack as ever. Suzuki gave a huge yawn, and the four men exchanged glances as if on cue. "What a fabulous day," said Suzuki. "Not too hot, not too cold. Perfect for a little golf." The rest all nodded in agreement, but Kuki wasn't much into golf lately. Before, he used to go once a week, but now that he had more time, he actually went less often. No more clients to entertain, for one thing—but more than that, the game held little attraction for him now. Perhaps recreation was most fun when squeezed into a busy schedule. Of course, there were also men like Suzuki who took advantage of their enforced idleness to take up the game. "Just because you don't have so much to do, you can't let it get you down," Suzuki would tell him, not knowing of his torrid affair with Rinko. Love beat golf at keeping a man young, any day. That was Kuki's opinion, at least, but he didn't dare say so out loud.

They continued chatting till noon, when everyone got up and left the room as if unable to wait a minute longer. Mostly they went to the company cafeteria, but Kuki liked to go to a buckwheat noodle place a short walk from the building. Other company employees went there too; sometimes he ran into young staff members from his former section, which was rather awkward for him, and apparently for them as well. They seemed to have some difficulty in saying hello to a former boss fallen from grace. In the beginning, Kuki would exchange silent greetings with them, but lately he felt relaxed enough to call out a casual "How's it going?"

That evening, Kuki met Kinugawa at the little tavern. Kinugawa had been there before, but since his last visit the place had been renovated, and he'd had trouble finding it. "God, it's completely different," he said. "I thought I was in the wrong place." The interior was no larger, but there was more seating space, and the old gleaming black counter and tabletops had given way to plain unvarnished wood. The difference was quite dramatic.

"A little too bright now, isn't it?" said Kinugawa.

Old familiars like them would mourn the loss of the former atmosphere, but young people probably liked this better. The manager only grinned.

"Definitely a change for the worse," agreed Kuki.

This was what he really liked about the place, being able to sound off over a drink. They ordered what the manager recommended: parrot fish sashimi and a savory mixture of shiitake mushrooms, some white fish, shrimp, and ginkgo nuts steamed in a clay pot. Then they clinked glasses and downed their beer.

"Haven't done this in a while," said Kinugawa. "Gone out drinking in Ginza, I mean."

"It's on me. I owe you."

"I guess you do! I won't be letting you forget it, either."

Kuki had been referring to the fee for his talk at the Culture Center, but Kinugawa evidently meant his encounter with Rinko.

"How's she doing anyway, the calligraphy teacher?"

Asked flat out, Kuki took a quick swallow of beer.

"Still seeing her, are you?"

"Now and then."

"You're a fast worker. You had me fooled."

Since it was Kinugawa who had introduced them, Kuki had quietly let him know that they were involved, a couple of months after their relationship took off.

"She dropped by the Center the other day," Kinugawa went on. "There was something different about her, a kind of sexiness."

The course in *kaisho* calligraphy was over. Perhaps she'd gone there with another calligraphy instructor.

"Better ease off a bit. If you lead someone like her on too far, you'll be a sorry son of a bitch."

He made it sound as if Kuki had taken some innocent, unsuspecting housewife and made a fallen woman of her, crazed with love. One could see why he might think like this, yet the implication was that Rinko had been completely at Kuki's mercy from the start. It was exactly the sort of comment that pretends to be protective of women while actually treating them like children.

Kuki had not exactly pursued Rinko one-sidedly, dragging her kicking and screaming into infidelity. Love came about only when the attraction between two people was mutual—when one was fish and the other water, as the proverb said. He wasn't trying to justify himself, yet back when he first met her, she must have been looking for something. Nothing as well-defined as an affair, perhaps, but there was no question she had felt somehow unfulfilled. The tight-lipped comments she'd made about her marriage were a dead giveaway; when the conversation veered in that direction, she would only say that being at home "wasn't pleasant." After that, he had taken the initiative in pursuing her, yes, but she had responded willingly. Now they were equally passionate, and she seemed more defiant of convention than he could ever be.

Kinugawa knew nothing of these details.

When a flask of hot saké arrived, Kuki poured some out for his friend.

"Did she say anything when you saw her?"

"No, she was with the other teacher, so we didn't talk much, but she looked as if she's been having a hard time."

"She did?"

"Could be my imagination, but she seemed to be brooding about something. I have to say, it made her look even sexier."

It gave Kuki an unpleasant start to realize his friend saw Rinko in that way. He changed the subject. How was business?

Culture Centers were popping up everywhere, it seemed, and competition was intense. Having been around longer gave Kinugawa's outfit a certain edge, but at this rate, management practices would have to be revamped from the ground up. That was why he was in this area today, to talk over strategy with the main office. "Anyway," he finished, "no matter what I do, it's not easy. Believe me, you have it made."

"That's not true..."

A soft job like Kuki's had its own difficulties. Still, no use unloading his troubles on Kinugawa. Better let it go.

Kinugawa sighed enviously. "In a company job, whether you work your ass off or sit around and take things easy, you get paid just the same."

True enough. Kuki no longer received the extra pay he'd been entitled to every month as a department head, but overall his paycheck was little diminished. "I didn't ask for this much time on my hands," he said.

"I know. I'm about ready to do like you, though—give work the heave-ho and enjoy myself with a real doll."

"Hey now, you've got it wrong."

"A man works his ass off so that in the end he can find a good woman and make her his own—it's the same wherever you look in nature. Males do all they can to find food and defeat rivals, and what they get in the end is a female body, and some affection. That's what drives men out into mortal combat, again and again."

Kuki felt uneasy, wondering if others in the restaurant might overhear this little lecture, but Kinugawa kept right on.

"I'm not saying you've put ideas in my head, but lately I've been dying to have an affair. Have a romantic fling with a spectacular woman. Kind of ridiculous at my age, I guess."

"No, you've got it backward. That's typically how men feel as they get older. It's a cliché."

"I don't know. The way things are going, I'm scared I'll end my life having missed out on something really important."

Until now, Kinugawa had lived for his job. While in the newspaper's local news division, he'd talked heatedly about politics and social problems, with scarcely a word about romance. To Kuki, from his vantage point in the publishing business, he had seemed a bit straitlaced and unbending. Now, hearing him say he wanted an affair, Kuki looked at his friend as if for the first time. Could Kinugawa have changed because of daily encounters with women at the Culture Center, or was it a factor of growing older, as he himself had said?

"But maybe I'm past it." Already he seemed to shy away from the notion. "Love takes energy and a lot of guts."

It certainly did, as Kuki could attest.

"Anyway," Kinugawa said, "a job like mine is no picnic. It's okay for you to play around, now that you've been bumped off the promotion track, but frankly, I'm not out of the game yet. I haven't made the top, or anywhere near, but I'm still a player. If anyone found out I was fooling around, God help me. Our whole goddamn society is riddled with jealousy and backbiting."

"Maybe so: the higher up you are, the less freedom you have," said Kuki.

"Anyway, the first thing I'd need is money and free time. Without money, I'd never feel at ease. You're lucky, you've got it." This last remark he threw out a little too carelessly.

Kuki might try to deny it, but he probably was somewhat better off than his colleagues. His annual income was nearly twenty million yen; the house in the upscale residential area of Setagaya was an inheritance from his parents; and his only child was already married. Besides, his wife's working part time for that ceramics company meant he had a fair amount of pocket money to throw around. Certainly he didn't begrudge whatever money he had to spend for the sake of his relationship with Rinko.

While he was thinking this, Kinugawa poured him some more saké. The little cup was made of thin white china, so the liquid in it shone like amber. Gazing into the cup in his hand, Kuki thought again of Rinko's pale skin. What would she be doing now? As he wondered, Kinugawa seemed to read his thoughts.

"You're so full of energy—God, I envy you." The tone of raillery made it clear he was talking about sex. "You two do it every time you're together, right?"

No need to answer that. Kuki ignored the question, but Kinugawa kept on.

"I hate to admit it, but I'm completely out of practice."

"What about at home?"

"Zilch. Not for a long time. You?"

Kuki also shook his head.

"That happens," said Kinugawa. "When you get to be our age, a wife's more of a friend. Makes it hard to get in the mood."

"So you turn elsewhere."

"I'd like to, but no such luck. There's no Rinko out there for me. Even if there were, frankly, I don't know if I could handle it."

"Sex is different with a different person."

"Fine for you to say—you get it all the time. When you've been on the sidelines as long as I have, it's not so easy."

"'All the time?' Give me a break."

"Anyway, maybe I'm getting old, but I find I can get along without it okay. Just tell yourself that's the way it is, and after a while you don't mind so much."

"Come on, stop talking like an old fart."

"No, it's like any habit. Once you give it up, you can live without it. But the longer you do, the less of a man you are, definitely." He downed the rest of his saké. "Maybe it *would* be different with someone else, I don't know."

This wasn't Kinugawa as he usually was. Whether because the stress of his job was getting to him, or because he had no one else to talk such things over with, tonight he kept harping on the opposite sex. Kuki was anxious to call it a day, but Kinugawa ordered a fresh bottle of saké.

"So, what's her husband up to?" he asked intently. "He must know what's going on."

"I'm not sure that he does."

"What's wrong with the guy?" Kinugawa took another drink. "You watch, one of these days he'll go storming into your boss's office, yelling for someone's head to roll. Did you know he's a doctor?"

"You're the one who told me."

"You'd think a doctor would know how to please a woman, but maybe not. You never know. Maybe he's the timid type. Knows his wife is cheating on him but looks the other way because he doesn't dare bring it up. Maybe he's no good in bed, either."

"Okay, okay, enough."

"No, you'd be surprised. A lot of men in top jobs are like that. They make the grade everywhere but where it counts."

"Think so?"

"He'll catch on to you two eventually, though. Then there'll be hell to pay." After this dire prediction, he added, "That's why with someone like her, you want to keep it light."

"Just an affair?"

"Yeah; nothing too heavy. Like light music."

Possibly out of pique at his own lack of a lover, Kinugawa refused to let the subject drop.

"Then again, maybe the guy's a smart player."

"Meaning?"

"Meaning she's definitely cheating on him, so okay, maybe he's cheating on her, too. Meaning maybe they both know about the other one, and they go right on being married without batting an eye."

To close the conversation, Kuki looked at his watch and called for the check. Prolonging this encounter would only allow Kinugawa to go on probing.

Three nights later, Kuki met Rinko at Shimbashi Station and set off with her for Kamakura. It was the rush hour, but he still managed to get them adjoining seats in a new luxury Green Car. They were surrounded by commuters, mostly older men who looked like company CEOs. No one he knew, thank God. He and Rinko were the only couple on board. As he was imagining what one of his colleagues would think if they got caught like this, Rinko, in a wine-colored suit with a scarf at her neck, snuggled up contentedly and confided, "I'm so glad to be going away with you again."

He thought she was excited about seeing the firelight Noh, but it was for a different reason.

"I told you before about my girlfriend Henmi, the one who's an industrial designer, remember?"

"The one you've known since high school, who went to college in the U.S.?"

"Yes. She was seeing the president of a famous blue-chip company, but recently they broke up."

"What happened? Did his wife find out?"

"Oh no, he was too careful for that. They took trips together to places like Kyoto and even Hong Kong, but always traveled separately. On the super-express they'd ride in separate Green Cars, one in car 9 and the other in car 10, and when they went overseas they took separate flights. She said flying first class was a waste, that she'd much rather have flown economy and sat together."

"He was trying to avoid attention."

"Yes, but wouldn't it be lonely to travel everywhere separately? You'd hardly know why you were traveling. She loves him, she said, but she just couldn't go on like that…"

"And so she broke up with him?"

"I saw her a week ago, and she swore she'd never love a man like that again."

Kuki could understand this, but the company president's feelings made equal sense to him. Both last time and now, he and Rinko had sat side by side on the way to Kamakura. It did bother him a little to sit together so openly, but he rationalized that it was only a short ride, and if anyone did see them, he could always say she was an acquaintance. In the back of his mind was the awareness of his permanently derailed career. He had little to lose.

But were they to go all the way to Kyoto, or even fly overseas, he might well exercise greater caution. Not to the same extent as the man they were discussing, insisting on different train cars and different flights, but he might want them to be more indifferent to one another in public, or perhaps pretend not to know one another at all.

What choice did anyone really have? Society frowned on illicit love affairs. Meddling was the word. To suffer because you'd put your foot in it at work was one thing, but the possibility of being demoted or passed over for promotion just because you loved a woman other than your wife made falling in love a real risk. Everyone from the mass media to company insiders was on the prowl, snooping for scandals, so men had to be constantly looking over their shoulders. However steady and sober people might appear to be on the outside, on the inside they were forced to repress their desires until any freewheeling, open-hearted qualities were lost. As Kinugawa had said, society itself was turning treacherous, with rampant scandalmongering and jealousy.

Calls for economic détente filled the news, but perhaps there was a greater need for détente in the area of romance. As his thoughts spun on, Rinko's right hand stole over his left hand. "I'm so glad we go

43

together everywhere we go." She wound her fingers in his. "It's one of the things I like most about you."

Gratifying as it was to hear the woman he loved say such things, there were far too many eyes on this train for them to keep holding hands like this. Furtively he extricated himself, marveling at the way she didn't seem to care.

The train pulled into Kamakura Station at a little past seven. They caught a taxi in front of the station and headed straight for Daitogu Shrine, where the firelight Noh performance was already under way on a temporary stage set up in the rear of the compound.

Kuki handed their tickets to the usher and they set off behind him, walking hunched over as they made their way between other members of the audience toward their seats in front to the right. On stage was a scene from the Kyogen farce "Kiyomizu" in which servant Taro Kaja, unwilling to fetch water, dresses up as a demon to intimidate his master.

It was still early autumn. From time to time a light wind stole through the trees encircling the shrine compound, while the bonfires ablaze on either side of the stage emphasized the depth of the surrounding darkness. The figure of a demon appeared again on stage, but by this time the master had his suspicions and stood his ground; and eventually he tore the demon's mask off, sending his servant scrambling off as he followed in hot pursuit.

The storyline was easy to follow, and Rinko smiled and put her hand in Kuki's again. Since they were outside in the dark, he squeezed her hand back. She brought her lips close to his ear and whispered, "Will it be the same room tonight?"

"I think so…"

"You be a demon tonight."

"A demon? Me?"

"Yes…"

He was at a loss for a reply, and the next performance began. This time it was the Noh drama "Cormorant Fishermen." First, a wandering monk came on stage and asked a villager for a night's lodging. Kuki watched the spare, evocative movements of the actors, so different from the earthy humor of the Kyogen, and thought about Rinko's whispered command.

Recently, she had begun to show an interest in acts that weren't exactly perverted but somewhat out of the ordinary. The addition of a slightly sadistic touch seemed to excite her. Had the demon mask conjured up some such scene in her mind? Kuki stole a look at her. In the light of the bonfire falling aslant on her face, her profile glowed a fiery red.

The performance ended shortly after nine. The stage lights were extinguished, and when the fires burned out, the shrine was swiftly engulfed in deep blackness.

As if to escape the sudden quiet, Kuki stepped out into the street, hailed a taxi, and headed with Rinko for a little place he knew, an establishment that a couple of famous literati had once hung out in. Kuki used to go there with an editor friend who had lived nearby. The door opened on a long counter. In back were tatami rooms, but the best way to enjoy the place was sitting and drinking at the counter with like-minded friends.

Kuki had not been there for three years, but the manager remembered him, and they raised glasses of beer in a convivial toast. Kuki ordered slices of raw stonefish, fresh-caught shrimp, and grilled sea bream. As before, the food was wonderful, simple yet delicious.

Secure in the knowledge that they were staying the night, Rinko switched to saké after only a sip of beer.

"In the old days, wasn't firelight Noh performed only by the light of the bonfires?" she inquired, having noted that electric lights were also in use that night.

"They've had about forty performances of firelight Noh in Kamakura now," he said, "but it must be pretty different from what people saw in the old days, before electricity. Same with the Daimonji ceremony in Kyoto, where they set fire to the mountain every summer to see off the souls of the dead. Imagine it: no streetlights or neon signs, the city dark and still, only the great mountain ablaze with red flames. It must have been a solemn and beautiful sight, the kind that makes people instinctively press their palms together in prayer. And with outdoor Noh, say if there was a pond near the stage, and the performance was lit only by the fire leaping with the wind and reflected in the pond, it must have been far more dramatic and mysterious than now. The effect would be magical."

"And the demons would be that much scarier."

Kuki nodded, remembering her whispered command.

By the time they finished eating, it was past ten. Kuki ordered a cab and paid the bill. Outside, after the bright, cheerful atmosphere of the restaurant, all at once the hill-enclosed darkness pressed in on them— a vivid reminder, along with the piney fragrance in the air, that this was, after all, Kamakura. The shrine grounds, so enlivened by the recent Noh drama only a short while before, lay shadowy and still.

On traffic-free roads at night, the ride to the hotel took barely ten minutes. On arriving, they checked in and were given keys to the same suite as before, as requested. As soon as they walked in, Rinko fell against him and he swept her up in his arms, half carrying her to the next room where they collapsed together on the bed.

"Finally, alone," she breathed.

In the train, at the play, then in the restaurant, they had been under constant constraint, surrounded by others' eyes; now she felt relief and liberation.

"I'm a teeny bit drunk," she said.

"Good."

"Why?"

"More erotic."

She gave him a reproachful look, and he pulled her to him and kissed her, all the while deftly unbuttoning her suit jacket and unzipping her skirt.

"The light…"

Obediently he reached out with one hand and switched off the lamp on the bedside table. Then he removed her jacket and smoothly pulled off her skirt. Next he opened her blouse, but just as he was moving in to kiss her breasts, she suddenly shook her head.

"Wait. Let me shower first."

"You're fine."

46

"No, I'm all sweaty."

"Who cares."

He felt an urge to make her do the very things she found embarrassing, force her to do his bidding. There was a touch of cruelty in his insistence, a trace of masochism in her reluctant compliance. His right arm fast around her shoulders, he laid his other hand on the top of her pantyhose.

"Don't…"

Again she resisted, but it was too late. Her pantyhose slid down easily, along with her underwear, until all at once her round, soft bottom popped out. He only needed to tug the front down a little further, and she was his. At this point she seemed to resign herself.

"You shouldn't…"

This served to make him redouble his efforts. He tugged again at her stockings, and this time she cooperated by bending her knees and bringing her feet together. She was now under his command. Or was he under hers?

With all her clothes off, completely naked, Rinko clung fast to him, seemingly shy. As he felt the smooth warmth of her, he whispered into her ear, "Tonight I'll be a bit rough."

"No, don't."

"You told me to be a demon."

She went on shaking her head. "I'm not myself these days…"

Nor was she the only one, he acknowledged silently in the faint darkness.

Demons must first take their prey captive. With one arm firmly around her shoulders, he wrapped his legs around her lower body, then began gently caressing her smooth back. Freed from long restraint, she relaxed at his touch, drifting along happily, enjoying the soothing sensation. Let her enjoy it while she could. Slowly his demonic nature was coming out; he wouldn't leave her long in this untroubled state.

His left arm still holding her tight, his right hand moved steadily down from her nape to her back, over the hollow at the base of her spine to the roundness of her hips. Little by little, keeping his touch so gentle she could scarcely feel it, his hand crept down her spine. The gentler, more furtive the touch, the more acute the response.

As his fingertips kept up their light caressing, working their way back down to the cleft of her hips, she finally let out an agonized cry: "Stop…" What had been pleasurable was now an unbearable tickling. But one cry wasn't enough for him to relent. He wanted to rule over her, not as a lover but as a demon.

She squirmed in his grasp, trying to escape, but he tightened his hold, continuing to stroke her back. The sense of tickling, once aroused, was relentless. She turned and twisted, desperate to get away, but he ignored her efforts and went on moving his fingers as lightly as feathers.

When his attention shifted from her back to her belly, she gave a final shriek of protest. Then she pleaded for mercy, panting for breath, grasping dimly at last that this man holding her really had become a demon.

As the tickling went on unabated, she writhed and moaned in torment, but the devil in him wouldn't let up. Again and again she begged, now sobbing, until he finally released her. After a huge gulp of air, she stretched out her arms and legs and then began to pummel his chest with her fists.

"How could you, how could you!"

It was her idea, he thought. All he did was fulfill her wish. To voice the desire and then turn on him for fulfilling it made no sense.

"How could you do that to me?" she said again more softly, and rolled away from him, the sheet up over her head as if she wanted nothing more to do with such a horrible man. But as long as she was naked in bed with him, there would be no escaping.

Having exacted satisfaction for the moment, the demon inched up to her again from behind as she lay quiet, her breath returning to normal, and whispered in her ear: "It's only going to get worse."

She scrunched up her shoulders, but he reached out from behind her and cupped her breasts, then lazily began tracing light circles around the nipples with his fingertips.

"No…"

She tried to cover herself, but her nipples were already taut and erect, as if newly awakened. He continued caressing their tips tenderly with his fingers, then bent his head down closer.

"What now?..." she said with a quaver in her voice, but the answer was obvious. He burrowed under the sheet until his lips found the nipple he'd been fondling with his right hand.

Kuki's style in bed had slowly evolved over the years. Till his thirties, he thought only of possessing a woman with every ounce of strength and vigor at his command. In his forties he had eased up a little, becoming more gentle, and now, in his fifties, he finally had the staying power to be patient, seeking not to be passionate and violent but to take his time, show how tender he could be. In part, the change reflected a natural decrease in physical strength; but also he had discovered that women thrilled more to his touch this way. Muscle and power were not the whole story. Better to come on gradually, softly, sometimes so quietly as to drive her nearly insane. It was a lesson he had taken twenty years to learn.

Now, her nipple in his mouth, he reached down blindly and found her tiny, quivering bud. Only the tip of his tongue brushed her nipple, only the tip of his finger grazed against her bud. No strength was called for. The softer and gentler he could be, the keener would be her reaction.

Women claimed to prefer "gentlemen." It might be literally true, less a matter of external manners, perhaps, than of this lightness of touch. With women, gentleness was a potent weapon.

Rinko was now steadily surrendering to his gentleness, dissolving into the welter of sensations it aroused in her. Sensing this, Kuki wrapped his tongue around her nipple again and continued, tantalizingly, to let his finger play with her bud, brushing it ever so lightly until she began twisting in frustration.

"Ahh...," she moaned.

There was irritation in her voice, and exasperation, but still he made no further move. For a while longer he kept agitating her with his soft touch, waiting for her to beg.

Her moaning increased. She seemed now to be at the peak of exquisite anguish: one minute more and she would go up in flames.

Pushed to her very limits, she cried out in entreaty, wheedling, then sobbing, begging him to hurry. Caught in a seething cauldron of sensations rising up thick and fast inside her, she groaned and writhed like someone in a death agony.

He realized how desperate she was, but still he held back. "I want you, let me have you": these simple words were all he needed to stop what he was doing and slide willingly inside her eager, waiting flesh. He would hold off a bit longer, just for the thrill of hearing her say it.

A man's pleasure from sex being comparatively weak, his interest tends to focus less on the act itself and more on the richness of response it evokes in the other person: the way his lover throbs, moans, and gasps, the blissful or tortured look on her face, all changing from one moment to the next as she rises ever higher. Only by knowing and savoring these responses can a man find emotional and physical satisfaction in sex.

"Please, please, please…"

She was wild with desire, near the edge, but he confronted her with a cruel demand. "Tell me what you want!"

So far he'd had the upper hand, but the moment he gave in, he would become her victim, just an object to be devoured and absorbed, nothing more. This knowledge was another incentive for him to prolong her torment while he could.

Her body was now a sea of flames; her round shoulders and breasts were moist with sweat, the slit between her legs as wet as a spring. Only now, when she was more than ready to receive him, did he enter her slowly, with a slight fumbling and seeming hesitation.

This too the old Kuki would never have done. Before, if a woman was at all willing, he would have taken her immediately, possessed her urgently and exclusively on his own terms. Intensity had been his only strong suit. Whether that had satisfied the previous women in his life, he couldn't say: he had never asked. It was beginning to dawn on him they might well have been unsatisfied, even frustrated.

Kuki no longer had the stamina for such fierce maneuvers. Now he took his time, pacing himself slowly and gently to suit his partner. At this very moment, in this union with Rinko, the wisdom of his experience came into play. As a young man, at this point he would have plowed ahead to a one-sided satisfaction. Now, he chose instead to lie close alongside Rinko, facing her on her right side so that he could continue to fondle her, sustaining himself at will, his other hand stroking her beautiful body while he watched her every move.

He liked it even better lately if she lay with her hips slightly raised, so that once inside her he could properly stimulate the sweetest spot of all, on the anterior wall. Right now he was doing just that, with her letting out tiny, secretive love-cries as she steadily ascended the ladder of pleasure.

Kuki could tell with near certainty when she would climax, not only from her cries and movements, but from subtle changes deep within her. As she became more aroused, her feminine core, normally soft and warm, became hot and sticky, gripping him fast. Finally, at the last possible moment, the folds of her flesh surrounding him would break into waves, then endless little rippling spasms as she came and came and came.

"No, no, no…"

She was trying to hold her emotions in check even though her body was taking off, or to rein in her body, hold it back with words. Yet once her body began to soar, there was no turning it back.

At last her core, now molten, burst into a cascade of tiny spasms, over and over, as her flesh wrapped his penis round in folds of velvet. This was it: the culminating moment for a man—the moment for which he would willingly devote himself to a particular woman, treat her with every courtesy, pay her every expense. An investment of time, money, and effort all aimed at this shared moment of physical ecstasy.

Yet Kuki held on for all he was worth, battling to control himself. Why let slide this God-given opportunity? Some might shake their heads; but the sight of one's lover melting in pleasure can give a man a stronger sense of accomplishment and satisfaction than wallowing in his own delight. The raw power of Kuki's youth might be gone, but in its place he had acquired this ability to hold himself in check, stay calmly in control. This was a man's compensation for growing older, a fair tradeoff for whatever loss of vigor he might sustain. Thanks to this new ability, Kuki had just given Rinko an orgasm while his own erection remained intact within her, firmly in place.

Youth was not the main thing. The mechanism of a man's arousal was so intimately connected with the workings of the brain, so psychological in nature, that the least timidity, anxiety, or loss of self-confidence could interfere. Young men had physical strength in abundance but were apt to lack self-confidence, as Kuki himself knew. Around the time he joined the publishing company, he had been seeing someone five years his senior, a woman studying to be an actress while working in a Shinjuku bar. Her former lover was a theatrical producer known even in that flamboyant world as a supreme playboy. When Kuki got to take her to bed, he'd found himself haunted by the ghost of that long-gone competition.

Men have an unfortunate tendency to obsess about their sexual performance, to see it as a matter of pride or face. When making love, most of them want to hear that they are better than any predecessor, that sex was more enjoyable with them than with anyone else. But the more they exert themselves to that end, the more impatient they become, until all too often their strength fails. Here lies men's primary claim to being the more "delicate" sex. Rather than youth, a far more important and effective elixir for men is a sense of ease and confidence around women.

That was what had gone wrong between Kuki and the older woman. Try though he might, his strength had failed him, leaving him unable to perform. In effect, his own youthful energy had been undermined by the playboy of his imagination. The woman's reaction, however, couldn't have been nicer, even from his current middle-aged vantage point. As he became increasingly nervous and edgy, she had reassured him that all was well, and generously continued seeing him until he recovered his self-confidence. Had she ever looked the least bored, or said anything cutting, he might well have suffered a permanent loss of confidence and developed a lifetime complex. In a very real sense, men are created by women. Trained by them as well. The driving force behind his ability to satisfy Rinko now could be traced back to all the women who had come before her.

To climax at the same time as a woman was fine, but to watch her come first, sharing in her orgasm as it happened, was also fulfilling. The former was the pleasure of losing oneself in sexual rapture, the latter, the pleasure of leading one's lover into the garden of earthly delights and seeing *her* find fulfillment there. For Kuki, the first was now slightly anticlimactic, the other, richly satisfying. What made it even better was that, this way, he had a reserve of strength with which he could lead her back to the garden time and time again.

Rinko, unaware of his thoughts, lay dreamily on the bed, savoring the last reverberations.

A woman never looked so relaxed or sexually appealing as when she lay naked in the aftermath of sex. Gone was all tension, affectation, and rebellion. She lay in a state of quiet intoxication, enfolded in the remnants of rapture. How could any man not respond tenderly at such a time? Her abandon was a sign of trust, a signal to him that she was in his hands. Who wouldn't feel a surge of affection?

Kuki laid a hand on Rinko's shoulder and drew her gently near. In her numbed state she nestled up docilely, pressing her full length against him, damp with sweat and flushed with heat. He cradled her in his arms and whispered, rubbing her back, "Was it good?" There was no need to ask, yet he had to hear.

She nodded.

"Was it?" he pressed.

This she ignored, as if to say she would never tell. Provoked, he laid his hand between her legs, and she wriggled slightly in response.

"Stop…"

She tried to pull his hand away, but he ignored her. He continued stroking her with his fingers until she started to respond again—only a short while after coming. The resurgent powers of a woman's body were amazing: one moment she was like seaweed drifting in the waves, the next she was pure vitality, hungry again for new pleasure.

A man's sexuality is finite, a woman's, nearly infinite. You don't need an advanced degree in math to understand that against the infinite, the finite is powerless. Fortunately, Kuki hadn't yet given his all; he had managed, just barely, to restrain himself. That reserve of strength was just enough for him to respond now.

He rallied to her newly flaming desire with a different approach. He came up from behind, cupping his hands over her breasts, teasing her nipples. Having already come once, she was in a state of heightened sensitivity, responding to the least stimulation.

Every time he touched her breasts, she twisted away as if it tickled, and tried to cover herself with her hands. The time had come to give those wicked hands a fitting punishment. Holding them behind her by the wrists, he reached for the cotton sash on the edge of the bed.

"Don't do anything silly, now," she said.

When she saw what he was up to, she tried frantically to wriggle free. She squealed in protest, chafed her hands together, but the knot was fast and wouldn't come undone.

Her apprehension grew. She rubbed her wrists together harder and squirmed, struggling to free herself, but succeeding only in pulling the sheets awry and exposing her own nakedness. "Please untie me," she pleaded, but the man-turned-demon showed no mercy, only revealing his intention to impose another, even crueler punishment: "I'm turning on the lights."

She turned her head and looked at him, shaking her head emphatically.

He had the upper hand again—he could do as he wished, force her to comply. The demon-man brought out a hand-towel from the bathroom and announced in a tone of firm authority that he was going to blindfold her.

"No!" she burst out, and fought hard, but he tied the towel anyway, cutting off her vision. "You're scaring me!" She almost screamed the words, but it was done.

As she continued to struggle, the demon solemnly intoned his last demand: "And now, the lights."

"Oh God...," she said, faintly now, but again the demon ignored her, clicking the switch so that every light in the place came on at once.

In the center of the room was a big double bed, and in the middle of that bed lay a naked woman, blindfolded and defenseless, her hands bound behind her. She lay with her body curved, her legs bent and pulled close to her chest as if to hide herself from sight. Lovingly he traced the contours of her body from the rich shoulders and swelling breasts to the narrow waist and the flare of the hips, then the white, round curves of her protruding bottom.

A woman's body is full of mystery. That the sight of a beautiful body should be arousing is only natural, yet the slightest bit of adornment adds a twist. The mere addition of undergarments or stockings, say, greatly enhances its allure. All Rinko had on now were a cotton sash and a thin hand-towel—items of no beauty in themselves, yet the moment they were added, her body took on a voluptuousness and fascination that set something in him aquiver.

Why should a naked body in itself be less provocative than the same body fettered and restrained? Was there a kind of toxin it produced that gave rise to fantasies and stratagems?

A woman abandoned on a bed, stark naked, hands bound behind her, blindfolded: confronted with such a scene, men were drawn to her vulnerability, felt a quickening of excitement as they imagined her inner sense of shame. Not even a demon was proof against the power of this.

As he gazed at her, the center of Kuki's body felt molten. Impulsively, he swooped down on the bed and swept her into his arms, the demon in him becoming a mere human being again, filled with lust.

Even so, a devil's influence lingers on. As proof, he pulled her ample bottom so that it thrust straight out from the bed, then walked around admiring it from every angle, whispering about the size of it and the color of her nipples, comparing her to some luscious fruit...

Unable to cover her ears, Rinko seemed anxious for him to enter her; and Kuki also knew by this time that he couldn't wait, much as he wanted to go on gazing at her. Positioned behind her jutting buttocks, he plunged in one swift stroke straight into the red, fully opened flower that they enclosed.

The moment he did so, she gave a little scream and arched backward, but then, feeling him firmly inside her, slowly slid her hips closer. Having entered her from behind, he could easily reach the sweetest, most sensitive part of her anatomy. The more she arched her back, the more snugly they fitted together.

He drove deep inside her and then relaxed a little, pulling slightly back, repeating this sequence over and over while he held onto the knot tying her wrists and swung it back and forth like the reins on a horse. He was the undisputed master at that moment—but it was a position he was doomed to lose.

The cloth over her eyes seemed to increase her focus on her own bodily pleasure. At first, Rinko responded to the alternation of fast and slow movements shyly, but soon her ardor increased, and before long she took off like a runaway mare. From then on he was hers, to be stirred up, toyed with, and whipped on until he forgot he'd ever been in control. He came hugely, exploding inside her.

Now they were equal in their sense of abasement. Driven initially to shame, Rinko now shifted to defiance, throwing aside every shred of modesty. A man might begin by fancying it was he who was "taking" the woman, but in the end, after both had found release, it was always he who lay drained and exhausted, flung across the edge of the bed like a dead body.

Out of the utter stillness that fell upon them, Rinko was first to speak. "Untie me…"

Only then did he realize her hands were still tied behind her at the wrist. The blindfold had slipped off in the heat of their lovemaking. He got behind her again and undid the sash. The moment he did so, she unleashed a fury of slaps at his face and chest.

"You bastard! How could you do that to me!"

She was livid that he had tied her up. He let her go on hitting him until her anger played itself out. Then he said, "Wasn't it good, though?" She said nothing, only sighing, the slight movement conveying itself to him through the roundness of her breast.

"Remember, you were the one who wanted a bit of demon treatment."

"But I didn't think you'd ever really do it."

"Next time it will be worse."

"Why? What makes you want to do that?"

"Because you like it so much."

The moment he said this, she pressed her forehead flat against his chest and said without moving, in a low voice, "I really have been getting strange."

"You have?"

"Imagine having you do a thing like that to me, and *liking* it..."

"More than usual?"

"Being blindfolded and tied up ... like a prisoner ... just the thought of it was exciting..."

"Maybe you are a masochist."

"But I don't want you to hurt me!"

"It's all right. I never will, because I love you."

She knew their passion was firmly based on love, and that he was not "abusing" her. Nor did he really think she was a masochist. Neither felt "abnormal," just unbridled by their love.

"I wonder if everyone does this."

"No. Other people don't love each other as much as we do." He had never watched other people making love, but he spoke with conviction. "It's only us."

After such an exhibition of mutual, uninhibited passion and release, they felt closer than before. Each knew they had shown the other their most natural, most uncontrolled self.

Kuki lay nearly flat on his back, Rinko on her side with her head on his shoulder. Out of the blue, he said without stirring, "Can I ask you something?"

"What?" After lovemaking, her voice was a little husky.

"When you're with him..." He still couldn't bring himself to say "your husband." "... is it like this?"

"What are you talking about?" All at once, her voice was clear and crisp. "I told you, we're never together."

"What about before, though?"

She said nothing, as if loath to reply. He knew he was probably treading on forbidden ground, but he couldn't help asking.

"It never felt this good?"

"No." Her voice was low, her answer curt.

Again, Kuki pictured to himself her husband the brilliant doctor. It was hard for him to accept that such a man was unable to satisfy his wife. "I wonder."

"He's not the type. It wouldn't interest him."

"He's a brilliant man, though, isn't he?"

"What has *that* got to do with it?"

He couldn't get over her husband's being a professor of medicine, but perhaps that really did have nothing to do with it. Men of high social status and financial clout have a natural advantage over other men, and wield greater influence. Everyone recognizes and accepts the dominance of such people, those attributes being externally verifiable. But sexual dominance, also a matter of huge significance among men, can't be judged by external appearances—leaving everyone to draw his own conclusions. The best way to measure oneself against another man would be to ask a woman who had been with both, but there would still be no guarantee of getting a straight answer. In the end, everyone was suspicious of everyone else, with nothing to go on but their own imaginations.

Just now, however, Rinko had been unequivocal. She mentioned nothing specific, but it was plain that in one way or another, he, Kuki, had the edge.

"I'm glad." He might have guessed as much from Rinko's behavior lately, but it was still a relief to hear her say it out loud. "At first, you know, I never thought I stood a chance."

"Why not?"

It was hard to explain, but from the time he first heard about her husband, Kuki had figured the odds were against him. He lacked her husband's status, his wealth, even his youth. The reason he had plunged ahead anyway, knowing himself to be outclassed, was first because he was so drawn to Rinko, and second because he figured with some defiance that he had nothing to lose by trying.

But his gamble had paid off. He might not be a match for her husband in some ways, but in bed he definitely had the advantage. To be blessed with status and wealth but have one's wife stolen away, or to lack both money and prestige but be the one to charm the man's wife out of his arms—which was better? That was not altogether easy to say; but Kuki was perfectly content with his lot.

What a strange business sex was! The things men and women did together must be universal. Given the physical structure of the species, it had to be the same for everyone—the process by which the male entered the female flower, was enveloped in the softness of her petals, and found sexual satisfaction. Yet within that act was endless variation. People's sexual likes and dislikes were all different, as well as their patterns of response. The variety was truly infinite, sex being never the same twice even for the same two people.

The higher the animal, the more complicated and wide-ranging the variation, no doubt. Put humans at the top of the evolutionary heap, and it was only natural that there should be all manner of differences in individual styles. Flirting, kissing, undressing, physical coupling: for each step along the way—including how lovers spent the rest of their time together, and how they parted—every man would have his own particular style of doing things, every woman her own particular preferences.

Everything about a man and a woman was laid naked during sex: their birth and childhood, their breeding and cultivation, even their experience and sensitivity. What made it all even trickier was that no amount of reading or going to school could enlighten anyone about it. Manuals might provide clues to structure and function, but between book knowledge and reality stood an enormous gulf.

No, the only way to learn about it was to experience it, feel it with all one's powers. When it came to sex, the number of exams one had passed, or the quality of the university one had attended, were totally beside the point. By the same token, even a fellow with no education at all could easily excel in bed. In that sense, maybe nothing was so free of class distinction, so purely democratic, as sex.

As his thoughts spun on in this vein, Rinko spoke up softly. "A penny for your thoughts."

"Just thinking how lucky I am to have met you."

He drew her closer, burying himself again in her infinitely sweet, rich flesh, and so dropped off to sleep.

Moonlight

The last Saturday in October, Kuki was at home watching TV. There was nothing on he particularly wanted to see, but he sat through a summary of the week's news and a golf program until three in the afternoon.

Then he jumped up, turned off the TV, and went to his room to get dressed. In the old days, his wife would have helped lay out his clothes; nowadays she left him alone. He dressed in brown slacks, a checkered coat and matching tie, and went back into the living room with his golf bag in tow. His wife was at the table using her calculator to check the cost of sets of china in preparation for the gift-giving season at the end of the year.

"I'm off," he said.

At the sound of his voice, she took off her glasses and turned around as if noticing him for the first time.

"And you're not coming back till tomorrow, is that right?"

"After the prizegiving party I'll be at a hotel in Hakone—I'm playing a round of golf tomorrow."

He went to the doorway, and she followed at a little distance.

"I have to meet someone in Ginza tonight at six," she said, "so I'll be home late myself."

He nodded and went out, shouldering his golf bag.

Kuki was in fact on his way to a secret meeting with Rinko. The golf bag was camouflage. Not everything he'd told his wife was bogus: the part about the prizegiving tonight was true, as was the bit about staying overnight in Hakone. But the prizes were sponsored by the calligraphers' association that Rinko belonged to, and the two of them would be going to Hakone together.

Basically it was all true; he was simply keeping it quiet that he would have a companion. Deceiving his wife. Not that full disclosure would be any more appropriate. Between a husband and wife no longer young whose marriage had cooled, the occasional deception seemed to him an actual kindness.

The drive to the hotel in Akasaka where the awards ceremony was to be held would take him the better part of an hour. As he drove, Kuki thought about the woman he'd just left behind. She had no imperfections to speak of. Forty-eight years old, six years younger than him, with a round face that made her look even younger. When first starting work, she had reported with glee that junior male colleagues took her for at least five years younger than her actual age. Average looks. A cheerful disposition. Housework and the rearing of their daughter, all managed with aplomb. To top it all off, she had gotten along beautifully with Kuki's mother, dead these ten years. As a wife she deserved high marks, but sometimes that very aura of sensibleness and security could translate into a dismaying lack of excitement.

For nearly a decade now, he hadn't slept with her. He never had made frequent overtures, and desire gradually fell off over the years until now he saw her as less a woman than a companion in daily life. Among Kuki's colleagues, some espoused the curious philosophy "Never take work or sex home with you," and Kuki's relationship with his wife had gone somewhat along those lines.

Sheer male self-indulgence it might be, but after twenty-odd years of living with the same woman day in and day out, knowing all there was to know about her, he was convinced that sexual excitement was no longer possible. Eventually, a wife evolved into something like a close relative—and, as some wag had said, sex with close kin is taboo.

In any case, after their twenty-five years of marriage, romantic flutters and quickened pulses were things of the past. The one good thing about their relationship now was its solidness. It came down to this: with women you could have serenity or you could have excitement, but not both at the same time.

Yet excitement was definitely what Kuki now sought, what he was up to his ears in.

Even for a Saturday night, the roads were surprisingly crowded. He had left home a bit early, but at this rate he would barely make the five o'clock awards ceremony. Once past the tie-up at Shibuya he relaxed, and glanced at the golf bag propped up in the seat next to him with a rueful smile. Overnight trips with Rinko were nothing new, but in the past he had always headed for their destination straight from work, which was frankly easier on the nerves. Today's being a day off made it harder to get away, so he had invented the story of an over-night golf trip with friends.

When he told this to his wife last night she had betrayed no sign of suspicion, and when he left just now, she had acted the same as always. She didn't know. He believed this, yet he wondered: suppose she saw straight through him?

Not that she was the type to fly into a jealous rage or show anger on the surface, anyway. Hers was a serene and unruffled approach to life. Or so it appeared to him. He had certainly presumed upon her calmness before, taken advantage of it to be unfaithful more than once. Something in her unwavering composure had always made him suspect that she did actually know, and assumed he would come back to her.

But this time was different, he couldn't help thinking. Despite the intensity of his feelings for Rinko, she remained as calm as ever, too immersed in her job, perhaps, to notice. Or what if it was another man? Hard to believe anybody would bother pursuing his nearly-fifty wife. Still, he himself was past fifty. Stranger things had happened. If she were having an affair, he wouldn't exactly like it, but neither was he in any position to go pointing fingers.

Kuki pulled up to the hotel at 4:50, just ten minutes before the cere-mony was to begin. He parked and went straight to the second floor, where calligraphers and guests were clustered at the entrance. He threaded his way among them and went to the reception table. As he was writing down his name, Rinko came over as if she'd been looking out for him.

Pale lavender kimono, white embroidered obi. Hair piled on her head and fastened with a pearl clip. As she drew nearer, he made out a scattering of tiny chrysanthemums on the breast of her kimono. The lavender steadily deepened in the skirt of the kimono, and along the hem was a design of orange blossoms.

As he stared, admiring, she frowned in seeming concern. "Is something wrong?"

"No. You look gorgeous."

She looked completely different: sweet and trim in Western clothing, crisply elegant in kimono. She epitomized the fascinating yet unattainable married woman.

"You took ages. I was beginning to worry."

"Traffic was bad."

He followed her in, and she led him to a seat in the center and slightly to the rear.

"Wait for me here, all right?"

"Where will you be?"

"Up front. Afterward there's a small reception in the room next door. Please stay."

Kuki nodded. She turned away, revealing a pattern of two open fans on her obi as she moved to the front of the room.

Rinko had won an honorable mention for her entry in the exhibition. The work was a three-foot-square sheet of paper bearing four Chinese characters: *shin-shi-kei-shu.* "Discreet beginning, dignified ending."

From his male perspective, the sentiment was a bit too proper and staid. He had been on the verge of saying so to Rinko earlier, when he caught himself, realizing that it was something she herself believed in seriously.

Kuki was here at her urging. What about her husband, he wondered. Could he be here, too? The idea nagged at him. Hard to believe she would invite both men to the same event, though.

The ceremony began promptly at five, with almost two hundred people in attendance. First came opening greetings by a representative of the sponsoring newspaper and a representative of the calligraphers' association. Kuki learned that the competition was national in scale, with a history of nearly thirty years. Next came the awards, beginning with the grand prix, each award-winner mounting the stage in turn to receive a certificate and prize. Warm applause greeted them all, from a dignified old man splendid in formal *hakama* and *haori*, every inch the master of his craft, to a budding young woman calligrapher.

As winner of an honorable mention, Rinko was among the last to mount the stage, taking her place with the other two honorees—a fiftyish man and a woman still older. Sandwiched between those two, Rinko, in the prime of womanhood, looked more glowingly beautiful than ever.

One by one, the names of the three were called out, and they stepped forward. The moment Rinko accepted her prize, the room burst into applause that seemed louder than for either of the other two.

Watching her bow respectfully and take her prize, Kuki felt a surge of pride. The attention of the audience, and of the other award-winners as well, seemed focused on Rinko. She looked nervous and a little pale, but her pallor only set off the lavender kimono all the better, tempering the sumptuousness of her dress with a quiet grace. What other women might be thinking as they looked at her, Kuki couldn't say, but most men in the room, he was willing to bet, were weaving fantasies about her involving the body beneath the kimono.

But none of them knew. Only he knew the shape and heft of her breasts, the warmth of her innermost parts, the abandon of her love-making when they were alone. He realized that he now shared in the secret pleasure and sense of superiority that a man married to or sleeping with a renowned actress or geisha must feel.

Little suspecting the drift of Kuki's thoughts, Rinko stepped off the platform to a fresh burst of applause. After that came the judges' comments, and then it was over. A reception was scheduled immediately afterward in the spacious room next door, and everyone stood up and began moving in that direction.

As Kuki was trying to make up his mind whether to go, Rinko came up.

"You won't mind if we stay a little while, will you?"

"How long?"

"I can slip out in thirty or forty minutes."

"I'll stick around for a bit, then go down to the coffee shop on the first floor."

Rinko nodded and went back to her calligrapher friends.

The reception was attended by even more people than the awards ceremony—some three hundred or more, he guessed. After another speech by one of the sponsors, an elderly, evidently respected calligraphy master proposed a toast, after which everyone began talking among themselves.

Kuki drank beer at a table by the door, his eyes roaming the room until they lighted on Rinko. She was near the main table at the front of the room, exchanging greetings with an older gentleman. Apart from the designated masters, the calligraphers were predominantly female, but Rinko easily outshone them all. Neither large of build nor flashy in appearance, she had a quiet dignity overlying the sensuous glow of a woman in her prime.

Everyone seemed to feel her spell. Men clustered around her, smiling and talking. Until now Kuki had never known it, but she might be a rising star in this world. As he was studying her in this way, someone clapped him on the shoulder from behind.

"So you made it."

He turned around to find Kinugawa standing there.

"She asked me to come. You know how it is."

"I wasn't planning on coming either, but I got out of work early, so I thought I'd pop in." Kinugawa shifted his gaze to the front of the room. "It must give you a kick to see how popular she is with men."

Running into Kinugawa like this would make it difficult to slip away with Rinko as planned, but on his own, Kuki had found time hanging heavy, and he was glad of the company. "I never thought there were so many female calligraphers," he commented.

"A lot of women paint, too, but even more do calligraphy. It's a bit of an issue…"

"I don't see why. Women add color."

"Sure, they're colorful, but you'll notice the masters are invariably men. Surround one of them with women, young and old, and what do you think happens? Naturally, he's partial to the young, pretty ones." Swiftly, he raised a hand. "Mind you, I'm not saying this applies in *her* case. But with a pretty young thing at his feet, a master automatically eases up, isn't so strict. Some call it favoritism; I'd call it male instinct."

Kuki nodded in agreement.

Lowering his voice still more, Kinugawa added, "Some of them win by copying out something their teacher picked and wrote out as a model."

"Are there competing groups, schools, whatever you call it?"

"Absolutely. Students stand to gain if their teacher is from a powerful faction. If he's not, they lose."

"Sounds like the same pecking order stuff you see in schools of traditional Japanese dance and flower arranging."

"Basically, there's not much difference."

Kinugawa seemed to know the ropes in calligraphy circles, probably from his newspaper experience.

"Who buys the calligraphy at these exhibitions?"

"Except for works by famous masters, or a few calligraphers in the mass media, they're almost all bought up by the students, friends, and family."

"What do they want them for?"

"It's a way of showing their loyalty."

So this was the world Rinko lived in. Kuki felt a pang of sympathy; at the same time, he was impressed by her resilience.

Rinko seemed to have noticed that Kuki and Kinugawa were talking. Catching sight of her, Kinugawa waved a hand. As she came over, he smiled and said, "You look especially lovely tonight. From the minute you came in, all eyes were on you."

Kinugawa was always moaning that he was too shy to speak to women, but today was apparently an exception.

"I've been hearing all about the secret world of calligraphy," Kuki said, changing the subject.

Rinko seemed bothered. "What do you mean?"

"Don't worry, it's got nothing to do with you," Kinugawa said with a shake of his head. Just at that point, a middle-aged man who appeared to be a reporter handed Rinko his card, a photographer came up from behind, and a flash went off.

She hadn't won the grand prize, or even second or third place. Why were they treating her like a star? Was it her beauty? Kuki stepped back to observe.

"What are you doing afterward?" asked Kinugawa.

Caught off balance, Kuki mumbled something or other, and Kinugawa quickly caught on. "Never mind, you two need to go somewhere and have a drink in celebration." He followed this show of tact by asking, "Anyone from her family here?"

Kuki had been wondering the same thing. He glanced around the room again.

"You're pretty gutsy, actually. What if her husband shows up?"

He was there only at Rinko's behest, thought Kuki, suppressing the desire to say so.

"I guess *she's* the bold one," said Kinugawa with a touch of irony. "Anyway, you aren't going to start a war over her, are you?" He was enjoying the baiting, but as Kuki failed to respond, he began to lose interest. Ten minutes later, he announced he was leaving, and was gone.

Kuki found himself alone again, the party at its height. Rinko was back over by the main table, laughing and talking and having her picture taken with colleagues. Following her with his eyes, he thought over Kinugawa's last comments. As far as he knew, her husband was not expected, but even if he should show up, they were total strangers. How could there be a problem?

Telling himself this, he had another beer, and checked the time: over half an hour now since the party started. He walked out and went down to the first-floor lobby. Entering the coffee shop on the left where they'd promised to meet, he took a seat by the wall at the rear and ordered a cup of coffee. On this Saturday night, the place was full of couples from a wedding reception. When his coffee arrived, he checked his watch again. Past six-thirty. At this rate, it might be close to nine by the time they reached Hakone.

He sipped his coffee, leafing through his appointment book to pass the time. He had just lit his second cigarette when Rinko appeared at the far end of the lobby. After exchanging bows with an older woman, she came over by herself, carrying a large paper bag. "Sorry that took so long. Shall we go?" She seemed anxious to leave, as if concerned about being seen.

They went out through the lobby to the underground parking lot. Not until they were safely inside the car did she recover her usual poise. Softly she apologized for dragging him around.

"Not at all. I enjoyed the peek inside another world." He started the engine. "Is it all right if we head straight for Hakone now?"

"There is another party after this, but I said all along I wouldn't be going, so it's all right."

"Will you be comfortable, dressed like that?" She still had on her kimono.

"I brought a change of clothes with me. I'll change after we get there."

The car rolled out of the hotel parking lot, and instantly they were surrounded by the neon lights of Akasaka.

"You look ravishing. No wonder you had all the men eating out of your hand."

"That's not true." She turned bashfully toward the window, and took out her compact.

"You must get lots of invitations."

"Even if I do, we're always in a group."

"Still, it looked to me as if most of the teachers and the advanced calligraphers are men."

"*Old* men. And there's nobody as energetic as you are."

"You never know. A man is a man."

"They're all perfect gentlemen, so stop worrying."

They were at the Kasumigaseki interchange, about to turn onto the municipal expressway. His eyes on the traffic light ahead of him, Kuki said, "Kinugawa thought we were taking quite a risk."

"He did? Why?"

"What if your husband had shown up tonight, he said."

"Him? He'd never come."

71

"Is he out somewhere?"

"No, but he said he wouldn't come, and he wouldn't." Her voice was firm.

The car left the Kasumigaseki ramp and swung onto the express-way, heading southwest from Shibuya toward Yoga. From there, they could get on the Tomei Expressway and head straight for Gotemba. Foot on the accelerator, Kuki probed further.

"Does he know the awards ceremony was today?"

"Even if he did, it's got nothing to do with him." She kept her eyes fixed on the streaks of flying light in front of them.

"He never said he wanted to go?"

"No, nothing like that."

"And what about after the party?"

"I'm supposed to be out with some friends."

"But you won't be going home. Won't he mind?"

"I don't know, maybe he will."

At this unexpected answer, Kuki asked inquisitively, both hands on the steering wheel, "You mean you don't care?"

"No, it's just that he's not the type to ask a lot of questions."

Kuki still couldn't get a clear idea of their marriage. "He must have his suspicions, though."

"He's too proud for it. He'd rather not know anything unpleasant. If he poked around and found out the truth, he might feel as if he'd shot himself in the foot."

"But if he cared about you…"

"There are all kinds of men. Maybe some would want to know, but others are like him, more afraid of injuring their pride, getting hurt."

"But that means…"

"I know. Endless pain for him and for me." She had a faraway look in her eyes.

For a Saturday night, outbound traffic was surprisingly thin. At the Yoga interchange, they entered the six-lane Tomei Expressway and picked up even more speed. The lights of the city quickly fell away, replaced by silent apartment buildings and stretches of dark woods that sprang up in the car windows and as quickly disappeared.

Whatever he thought of Rinko's marriage was irrelevant. For the wife-stealer to be concerned about the wronged husband was hypocritical in the extreme. He put it out of his mind, and asked about her calligraphy.

"Tell me, when you sit with a brush in your hand, facing a clean sheet of paper, does that have the calming effect they say it does?"

"Oh, yes. Even if I'm upset about something to begin with, grinding the ink draws me in, and by the time I pick up my brush, I feel much more peaceful."

Kuki had never yet seen Rinko in the act of writing, but he could imagine her grinding the ink and sitting with brush poised over the surface of the paper, the picture of dignity and concentration.

"And is it true that the calligrapher's personality comes out in his work?"

"If you're referring to the saying 'Calligraphy is character,' yes, I think it's true."

It made sense to him that a person who wrote precise, upright characters should be precise and upright by nature.

"What happens when you're in love?"

"They say it adds a certain shine."

"What about this time?"

"Sorry. Not very shiny or romantic, I'm afraid. I purposely tried to hold my feelings back, to keep them from showing."

"You can do that?"

"Yes. If all I'm writing is a single character, or a four-character phrase like this time, no one would know."

Kuki thought about this, remembering her four characters: *shin-shi-kei-shu*. Begin with discretion, end with dignity. "I don't know about shine, but there was freedom and grace in the lines, I thought."

"Well, thank you. That's a very nice thing to say."

"But I wish you'd written *shin-shi-ran-shu*, 'Begin with discretion, end with abandon.'"

"Don't be silly."

She made a face, but it was true: at night, she showed a wild abandon undetectable from her external primness and self-possession. In

73

fact, it was in quest of that unlikely transformation that he was now tearing along the dark expressway.

When they pulled up to the hotel, it was eight-thirty. Before leaving Tokyo, he'd pegged their arrival at nine, but traffic had been light and they'd made unexpectedly good time.

They checked in and were shown up to a room at the end of the hall on the third floor. Rinko had wanted to change her clothes before dinner, but decided it was already so late that she would go down as she was.

The dining room was on the first floor. Outside, all was shadowy and dark, but through the large window they could see the pool, lit from below so that the blue surface of the water floated up in the darkness.

"Like an oasis," said Rinko.

The ceremony and reception had evidently been a strain on her. Away from the city, she was finally relaxing. Kuki ordered beer, and again they toasted her success; then, having only snacked at the party, they ordered a light meal.

"It's as if somehow, now that we're here, everything will be all right," she said.

It was true. There by the mountain Hakoneyama, Kuki too felt a sense of relief at being cut off from the workaday world. Was that a sign of mutual feelings of guilt over this illicit affair?

Their hors d'oeuvres arrived: rainbow trout from Lake Ashinoko, garnished with sour cream. Filling their glasses with red wine, Kuki thought again of her prize-winning work.

"I noticed you sign your work with a sobriquet," he said. "Suigyoku … Green Jade. Is that something you have to think up yourself?"

"Some people do, but that name was given to me by my teacher."

"Suigyoku Matsubara. A nice name. You should sign it on something romantic."

"How about an old love poem?"

"I know one: 'You do not touch my skin, hot with pulsing blood / Are you not lonely, you who preach the Way?'"

Hearing him recite this celebrated *tanka* by the passionate Meiji poet Akiko Yosano, Rinko commented dryly that it was just the sort he would choose.

Kuki then softly recited a poem by Fumiko Nakajo, a lesser-known female poet who made her debut shortly after the Pacific War, and died at the early age of thirty-six: "'Owls and tadpoles, flowers and love / She makes them all come dwell with her, my woman.'" Kuki thought it nicely captured the power of a woman to attract. Didn't she agree?

"Yes," was the simple answer.

They had gotten a late start on dinner, and by the time they finished, it was after ten. After her long day, Rinko was tired. They went straight back to their room and closed the door. For the first time, Kuki felt they were truly alone. He pulled her to him. As if she too had been waiting for this moment, she pressed up against him, and they kissed.

The hotel in the mountains at night was absolutely silent. No sound came to his ears but the rustle of her kimono as she swayed slightly in his arms. After a long kiss, she smoothed her hair and went over to the windows. They were floor-to-ceiling, opening on a little veranda set with a white table and a pair of chairs.

"Is it all right if we go outside?" Wanting a breath of cool night air, perhaps, Rinko slid open the door and stepped outside, Kuki right behind her. "The air has a chill to it, doesn't it?" she murmured. A wind had sprung up, sweeping across the fall highlands. "Look, such a big moon…"

He raised his eyes. Shining in the middle of the sky was a nearly full moon.

From inside the room, everything beyond the veranda had appeared pitch-black, but out here in the moonlight they could see the wide grassy plateau and part of a golf course, with the peaks at the edge of the crater looming in the distance like a scene painted on a screen. Perhaps it was the purity of the air that made the moon appear so much bigger and brighter here than in the city.

"Isn't such a full moon thrilling?" she asked softly, her eyes still looking skyward. "It's as if the light goes right through me, as if every inch of my body is exposed…"

"All right, then, how about if I undress you in the moonlight tonight?"

"That's all you can think about."

She looked modestly away, but Kuki was thoroughly turned on by the erotic vision that had entered his head.

"I'm getting cold," she said. They went back inside, the enveloping warmth of the room making the drafts of night air feel even chillier.

Moon-gazing had filled Kuki with amorous thoughts, but Rinko was anxious to get out of her kimono and into a shower. He settled down to wait for her, first changing into a robe and then stretching out on the bed while Rinko turned off the overhead light at the switch by the door.

Instantly the room went dark, only the windows remaining bright where the moonlight came streaming in. As he gazed in fascination at the tranquil light, Rinko began to remove her kimono.

She was standing bent over slightly, next to the wall on the left side of the bed, toward the bathroom. She removed a number of silken cords around the folded material at her waist. With the smooth whisper of silk on silk, her obi slid down.

The dim moonlight seemed to gain in strength as his eyes grew accustomed to it. Standing in the moonlight with her back to him, Rinko looked as if she were wearing a light robe over her head, the sort ancient noblewomen of Japan used to cover their faces with when they went out: the illusion came about because she was bent over with the kimono draped across her shoulders, removing her underthings.

Ordinarily, one would first remove the kimono, then the under-kimono, then the undergarments, layer by layer. Yet even in the presence of her lover, Rinko chose to undress with her back turned, keeping the kimono draped about her. This was what appealed to Kuki, her innate modesty and dignity.

She must have finished disrobing, for her figure disappeared into the bathroom, still with her back turned and the kimono over her head.

Inside the bathroom, she would now be completely naked.

Inhaling the lingering scent of her cast-off silken garments, Kuki thought again how it was the transformation that turned him on; one minute she was a woman of modesty and restraint, the next a creature of wild abandon. Wild lovemaking from someone who was wild to begin with would just be predictable.

He wondered if Rinko understood this aspect of her appeal. She had apparently stepped into the shower: the sound of washing came faintly to his ears.

In preparation for her return, Kuki made sure the room was warm enough for her to be comfortable. He left the curtain open, allowing transparent moonbeams to pour into the room.

Now all that remained was to await the entrance of his lovely prize.

When stepping out of the bathroom, Rinko paused by the door and made no move to come closer. He sat up.

"Why is the curtain open?" she asked.

No need to explain. He said nothing, and she went over to draw it. That very moment, her figure was caught in the rays of moonlight coming through the window. Her body, fresh from the shower, was wrapped in a white silk under-kimono, the too-long sash hanging down in front; above her graceful neck, he could see the silhouette of her hair piled atop her head.

After gazing entranced for a moment, Kuki slipped out of bed, went over, and caught her by the hand. "I said I would undress you by moonlight, remember?"

"Well…"

Folding her hand in his, he led her back to the bed.

She was still concerned about the light streaming in through the windows, but when he took her in his arms and gently laid her on the bed, face up, she lay quiet, seemingly resigned.

"Now I shall dissect you, by moonlight."

"Don't do anything scary."

"Lie still and you'll be fine. Lie still, and imagine that you're giving yourself to the moon."

With that, he untied the sash of her under-kimono and pulled it out from under her. Then, using both hands, slowly he pulled open the top of the garment, as far down as the gentle swelling of her breasts.

Whether obeying his instructions, or mesmerized by the moonlight, Rinko lay face up on the bed with no sign of resisting. He wasn't expecting such compliance; after spreading open the top of the under-kimono, he pulled open the lower half.

Rinko twisted her hips slightly, but she had nothing to cover her, nowhere to hide. She soon relaxed, and Kuki removed the garment with the determination of a thief. Now she was totally naked, lying still on the bed bathed in streaming moonbeams.

Her head was turned to one side, as if to avoid the light from the windows, and her eyes were shut tight. Her body was perfectly supine, her two hands covering the space between her legs. Her naturally white skin appeared still paler in the moonlight, waxy-white amid the shadows.

"So beautiful…"

It was Kuki's belief that even the most cold-blooded of humans couldn't help but be moved by great beauty. He was aware that he'd been prepared, once she'd been laid bare, just to assault her from on top. Now he found her loveliness so enthralling that he couldn't violate it. He wanted only to go on drinking it in. He remembered that when he was younger, getting off quickly with a woman had been his sole concern, but now he took deep pleasure in possessing her first with the eyes. He felt one with the trailing moonlight, infiltrating her white body with his gaze.

Without his skin ever touching hers, Rinko could feel his hot, pene-trating gaze traverse every part of her body. Finally, as if unable to bear it, she turned her back on the moonlight and began to curl into a ball. Kuki stopped her with both hands, whispering in her ear, "Don't. The moon will take offense."

Her pale body was like a live sacrifice to the moon.

The taking of this woman in the clear moonlight required finesse; he couldn't simply give free rein to his desire. He began by stroking her gently from the breasts to the hips; then, pretending his fingertips had brushed accidentally against them, he eased her hands away from the space between her legs.

The moment he did so she resisted, only to yield to his strength and withdraw them. Her body was exposed defenseless to the invading moonlight, the tuft between her legs a patch of utter darkness.

Oddly, the instant her pubic shadow showed against her alabaster skin, her body shed its former purity and now looked wanton.

At the sight, he longed to go beyond the thrill of looking at her. Leaving one hand on her round breast, with the other he parted the tuft below, finding the tiny bud hidden within. Used to his caresses, it quickly came alive, and her soft flower became drenched with dew.

If he took her now it would be still be much as it always was; but tonight he wanted to try something slightly different.

Having ascertained that she was fully moist, the man took the woman's right hand and drew it slowly to the black tuft. As soon as her fingertips touched it her hand stopped moving and, after a moment's consternation, pulled back as if afraid.

The man paid no attention. He placed her finger on her own bud and made her move it slightly. After doing this a few times, she murmured in evident distress, "No, no more…"

Say what she might, tonight he wanted her to learn for herself the sensuality hidden deep within her own body.

"That's it…"

"I can't…"

When her hand fell still again, Kuki took over. Lightly, his fingertip moved rhythmically from side to side, and the woman's bud grew moist and swollen.

Rinko gasped and twisted, finally turning her head to one side and reaching climax faster than ever before.

He waited for the fine tremors to subside before asking, "Was it good?"

"No, it was too strange."

His question arose from the quickness of her climax, but she evidently was speaking of the novelty of touching her own secret place.

"Well, now sometimes you can do it yourself…"

"No, please…" She shook her head and murmured, "I'd much rather you did it."

He drew her to him again, saying, as he took her right hand in his, "You know Kawabata's novel *Snow Country*? In it, a man travels from Tokyo to see a geisha named Komako, in a town up north that lies buried in snow."

"I know," said Rinko, quoting the book's famous first sentence: "'When the train left the long tunnel, they were in snow country.' Something like that."

"Anyway, you remember when he sees her again after a long absence, he holds out one finger in front of him and says, 'This remembered you'? She's embarrassed, but she takes hold of his finger and softly bites it."

"I remember that scene from the movie."

"Which finger do you think he meant?" asked Kuki, holding Rinko's right hand up to the moonlight. Hard to imagine these soft, slender fingers, so white and graceful, at work inside her hot, dark cleft just now. "In the novel it's his index finger, and in the stage version, too, the actress playing Komako always bites the man's index finger."

"What's wrong with that?"

"To touch her down there, it should be this one." Holding her middle finger, gently he placed her hand below. "This finger moves better, and is more gentle."

"You mean that Kawabata was wrong?"

"I don't know about that, but this way seems far better to me..."

He went on moving her middle finger around her bud, lightly and playfully. She didn't want to start again. "No..."

He kept his finger where it was, struck by a strange notion.

The novel *Snow Country* was written around 1935. From then until now—no, from the distant age of the *Man'yoshu* poets until this very day, men and women had been doing the same things over and over again. Since time immemorial, men and women had lain as naked as when they were born, touching one another's skin, sharing one another's warmth, seeking out the secrets of one another's bodies. Just as Kuki lay now with his middle finger on Rinko's bud, so had all those other men done the same—whether using their index finger or another one, alike in their determination to give pleasure to a woman. And women in turn had responded to their efforts. For thousands upon thousands of years, human beings had behaved in exactly the same way, sometimes taking great risks if necessary for the privilege of doing what he and Rinko were doing now. The thought made him feel

80

a bond with those unknown ancestors, whose blood now pulsed in his veins.

"This is something everybody learns to do naturally," he said, feeling her grow moist again.

"But it's not the same for everybody."

No, it certainly wasn't. What else could be at once so universal and so individual, so mysterious, as sex? People did the same things today as in bygone millennia, yes, but with infinite variation—not only in their ways of doing them, but in the range of sensations they felt and in their ways of gaining satisfaction.

Sex was a world without progress or regression. Coming from a technologically advanced society did not make modern man any better at it, nor was ancient man necessarily clumsy at it. Everyone learned little by little from their own experiences and sensations, trying out what seemed good to them, alternately pleased and disappointed with the results.

Truly it was a world where science and civilization could not intervene, a culture and a wisdom gained anew by each generation as living men and women came together.

With this at the back of his mind, Kuki entered the warm wetness of her body.

After the long caressing of her vulva, his solid embrace set her instantly ablaze. Where earlier it had lain submissive in the moonlight, her body now became a pillar of flame. Suddenly, with her eyebrows raised and a look of grief on her face, she reached orgasm.

How he loved her look at such times! It was as if she were tearful, angry, and coquettish, all at once. Contained within that elusive, ever-changing expression was all the passion and allure of a woman.

Again, after their lovemaking, an incredible stillness descended on them. As he lay there unmoving, pressed against her still-glowing body, she murmured, "It was different again…"

From the way she said it, shyly, face hidden, he understood her to mean the moment of climax.

"It always is, every single time."

"Deeper?"

She nodded, then said as if to herself, "Maybe there's something weird about me..."

"No."

There was nothing for a woman to be ashamed of in being overly passionate; rather, it was a sign of ripeness and richness.

Suddenly curious, Kuki touched in turn her still-throbbing flower and her bud.

"Is it different here, and here?"

"Yes, there it's deep and strong..." She closed her eyes lightly. "It's as if you're penetrating me all the way to the top of my head..."

However she explained it, for a man it was a world beyond imagining. Next he touched her bud, and she said, "There it's shallower, and sharper..."

That was probably more like the feeling in a man's anatomy.

"But when you rub me there the way you did before, it's like electricity, harsh and intense."

As he listened, Kuki began to feel jealous. How could a woman's body contain so many sensations, of such variety and depth? By doing all he could to arouse Rinko and give her pleasure, maybe he'd been encouraging something that would grow into a monster

Compared with a woman, a man was fairly flat and simple. Where women had many erogenous zones, a man had only one. A man's orgasm was like the tide, building up until it reached the point of overflow and then receding, vanishing with hardly a trace. Compared to that, a woman's sensuality was rich and many-hued: as Rinko said, her sensations ran the gamut from shallow and sharp, like a bolt of electricity, to deep and strong, as if she were being penetrated right the way through. There was really no comparison. A woman must feel easily two or three times the pleasure of a man, he thought, and maybe ten times more.

"Women are greedier than men," he said, in a tone of mixed irony and envy.

She shook her head. "It wasn't always this way."

True enough. In the beginning she had been timid, and her ability to express pleasure, weak. As they made love more often, gradually she had awakened sexually, becoming more assertive. As her sexual guide

Kuki had felt a sense of superiority, as if he were dominating her; but before he knew it, she had absorbed all his lessons, and her satisfaction had become his natural duty. He was no longer the guide who ruled and directed her, but the devoted servant, bent on serving her needs.

"I never thought you'd come so far so fast."

"It's all because of you."

To be told this by a woman was any man's crowning achievement, but there was no denying that Rinko's blossoming also owed a lot to her own amazing self. However skilled the gardener, without good seeds he could never bring beautiful flowers to bloom.

"You have the gift."

"It's a gift?"

"I don't really know, but this much is certain: *this* is wonderful." Gently he laid his hand on her still-warm flower.

Rinko seemed undecided as to how to take this praise. She must have sensed herself changing, deepening in sensuality; but to be told this about herself straight out, his hand touching her as he said it, was understandably disconcerting.

Kuki went on anyway. "It's the best. The best in all Japan!"

"Now you're being silly."

"No, I'm not. I'm saying it because it's true."

"I don't know what you mean."

He searched for words to explain it to her. "It's so warm inside, and it clings so fast to me, all around…"

"Aren't women all made the same?"

"Certainly not. They're all different."

She looked unconvinced.

"Women don't realize it, but what they have comes in all shapes and varieties. Some are wonderful, like yours, and others aren't."

"Doesn't it depend on the man a woman is with?"

"To some extent, yes. But sometimes a man is accepted, and plunges in, only to find it isn't so nice after all. And then he wants out, in a hurry."

Rinko suppressed a laugh. "That's too bad for him. He's being unreasonable."

"Is he?"

"Well, he's only there in the first place because he's attracted to her, isn't he?"

"Yes, but you never can tell about a woman till you actually sleep with her."

"I've never heard of such a thing."

"Men know about it, but you see they can't say anything to women."

While Rinko pondered this, Kuki brought up an example from a much earlier period in history.

"Take Lady Rokujo, in *The Tale of Genji*. I have a feeling hers wasn't very good."

"Really?"

Since his demotion, Kuki had had time to do a lot of reading. Mostly he read modern history, gathering material for his intended social history of the Showa era, but sometimes he went back over books he'd read in the past. One of these was the eleventh-century classic *The Tale of Genji*. Once he began rereading it, he found it hard to put down.

Demotion had its advantages, he concluded, impressed by aspects of the novel that had escaped him before. His view of Lady Rokujo had changed, too. She now intrigued him.

"She was highborn, beautiful, and well-educated, and she had superb taste. She's portrayed as an ideal woman, lacking nothing on the outside. But inside, she was inadequate."

"I still don't know what that means."

"It could mean lots of things. Too loose, or too slippery, or not warm enough, for example."

"Is that really possible?"

"Yes, unfortunately, in some rare cases."

"Isn't there any cure?" She sounded anxious.

"If someone who really loved a woman was willing to make the effort, and so was she, things might improve; but there are limits to what most men can or will put up with."

"Even for love?"

"You could love her, but you would always feel sexually frustrated.

And if someone else came along, you might easily stray."

"You're saying men are selfish, then, after all."

"Let me ask you this: don't women hate 'bad sex'—to have a lover who is terrible in bed?"

"Well, yes."

"There you are. Men don't want to go to bed with a woman who's unsatisfactory, or apathetic and inert, either."

Stretched out on a bed in the moonlight, a man and woman lay naked, discussing the mystery of sex. In a famous scene in *The Tale of Genji* known as the "judgment on a rainy night," Genji and his best friend have a frank discussion about women. By the same token, perhaps this could be called the "judgment on a moonlit night," thought Kuki. Or the "naked judgment," since they were both undressed.

One hand still on her tuft, he said, "Lady Rokujo's tragedy has to do with pride and jealousy, but her own sexual inadequacy may have been the biggest factor of all."

"Does the novel say that?"

"Not in so many words. The author was a woman; she couldn't have written such a thing outright. It's definitely implied, though. You have to put two and two together."

Rinko fixed her eyes on Kuki in wonder, and he proceeded to explain.

"Genji falls in love with Lady Rokujo the first time he sees her, and he goes after her with a vengeance. Finally his wish comes true, and they spend the night together. But suddenly after that one night he acts coolly toward her, as if he's lost interest."

"He's faithless."

"Yes, that's the female consensus. Female commentators all say that Genji is fickle." He laid a hand gently on Rinko's back, as if to soothe her feelings. "Lady Rokujo is so affronted at his change of heart that in her jealousy she becomes a malevolent spirit, a living specter who stalks his wife, Aoi no Ue, and another woman he loves, Yugao. Because of her, they both eventually die."

"She is pretty vindictive, isn't she?"

"On the surface she's reticent and quiet-spoken, but she broods over things, and God help anyone who comes in her sights."

"But wouldn't you say Genji's treatment of her is the explanation?"

"Yes, but you have to realize the difficulty of his position. No man would want to go on sleeping with a woman so dysfunctional. Yet she's always after him, demanding to know why he fell out of love."

"Women have no idea men think that way." She seemed troubled by the idea that Lady Rokujo might have lost Genji's love because her sexuality was somehow deficient. "To be told that about yourself would be a devastating shock."

"No man would be caught dead saying such a thing to a woman. Genji is dissatisfied with Lady Rokujo but never says why, and goes on sending her tender little poems and letters from time to time. And when she leaves for Ise, he goes to Nonomiya to see her off."

"Even though he doesn't like her?"

"She idolizes him, so he can't very well ignore her. Whatever complaints he may have about a lady, on the surface he always treats her with proper respect, and does all he can for her. That was the chivalry of the Heian nobleman. It might be the source of Heian elegance, too."

"And yet Genji goes on being put down by us ladies, poor thing."

"He does his best, but his efforts go unappreciated. Women don't see his underlying kindness."

"How can we? He does things by halves, so of course we don't. If he doesn't like a person, he shouldn't deliberately act in ways that invite misunderstanding."

"All right, what then? What if he slept with someone once or twice, and never had anything more to do with her? You'd be harder on him than ever. You'd say he was a cold, unfeeling bastard."

Rinko was silent for a moment. Then she said, as if reconsidering, "You said she wasn't … satisfying. Is there any way a woman could know that about herself without asking?"

"Well, if the guy sleeps with her once or twice and doesn't try again, that could be a sign."

"There's nothing she can do?"

"I wouldn't say that. Maybe the two are just incompatible."

Talking about such things in the moonlight seemed out of place. Beneath this pale, pure light, some other, loftier topic of conversation would have been more suitable; and yet what was more fundamental and important than sexual problems?

"This sort of thing is never really discussed by men and women. The sexes have gotten by without ever understanding each other."

She nodded, then leaned forward and said, "May I ask one more thing? Lovers or married people often start out wildly passionate and then somehow it wears off. They don't make love as often. Would that be another sign?"

"No, that's just waning interest, not the woman's inadequacy."

"How can a person tell the difference?"

Her question hit on the crux of the matter. "Well, in Lady Rokujo's case, as I said, they slept together only once or twice. They had other opportunities, but Genji chose never to take advantage of them. Most couples go on sleeping together all they can until their interest fades, and the man stops trying. It's completely different."

"As long as they've made love enough times, it's no reflection on the woman?"

"Of course not. Otherwise, there would be something wrong with every housewife in the country."

Rinko seemed relieved, until a new question occurred to her: "Why do men tire of the same partner?"

"That's a whole different issue."

"I've heard a man doesn't really let himself go when he makes love to his wife. That he doesn't want to teach her things, or he's just not very enthusiastic. Why is that?"

Rinko's increasingly astute questions had Kuki more and more on the defensive.

"That's a hard one, but maybe men are afraid that if their wives begin demanding sex all the time, they'll be worn out. It could be that men are afraid of that happening, and hide their fear by joking about it."

He had never had such a deep conversation with Rinko about sex before. To talk so honestly about a man's real feelings was a little embarrassing, as if he were somehow giving himself away; but then being able to talk such things over together was surely yet another sign of their mutual trust. As he was telling himself this, Rinko moved on to a new question.

"Prince Charles was seeing an older woman before his marriage…"

Kuki was taken aback at the sudden leap from *The Tale of Genji* to modern British royalty.

"… and even after marrying, he kept on seeing her. His wife said it was like having three people in the marriage. Now, what could that be about?"

"What do you mean?"

"Well, with all due respect to the other woman, Princess Diana was younger and far more attractive. Why wouldn't he leave his mistress for her?"

"That's another tough one. Again, there could be some sort of sexual incompatibility."

"How could someone as gorgeous as Princess Diana not be good enough?"

"I agree. But probably the prince felt more comfortable with the other woman, and that applied to sex as well, so he couldn't bring himself to say good-bye."

"But she's so much older, and not at all good-looking!"

"Now, wait a minute." Kuki put a hand on Rinko's shoulder. "Sex has very little to do with age or appearance. Lots of women her age have terrific sex appeal, and some young, pretty women are complete duds. There's nothing as private and idiosyncratic as sex. You just can't tell about people from the outside. That's partly what makes it so fascinating and strange and fun."

"Fun?"

"It wouldn't be fun if the young, pretty girls *always* won out, now, would it? To keep that from happening, God created the mystery of sex."

It was time to end this "judgment on a moonlit night" and get some sleep, but Rinko was still struggling with something.

"After all you've said, I'm starting to think it's a serious disadvantage to be a woman. Men don't have the same sort of problems, do they?"

"We have troubles of our own, don't worry. There's impotence, premature ejaculation, all kinds of dysfunction to worry about. A lot of it is psychological, too, which only makes it harder to deal with."

"How does one overcome a psychological hangup?"

"The key is to build confidence. Having your partner praise you is the best way to do that. But no matter how attractive a man is on the outside, if he's no good in bed, what woman wouldn't be let down?"

"True," Rinko unhesitatingly agreed.

"And just like women, men hate having their sexual performance criticized, too."

"What woman would do such a thing?"

"Not in so many words, maybe, but her attitude after sex gives it away. And during a quarrel, some women can be pretty nasty."

"Would this be the voice of experience?"

"Not much, I'm glad to say."

"Not *any*, I'm sure you mean," she said ironically, then added thoughtfully: "But I see now that couples face all kinds of problems."

"When you come down to it, not many are compatible both physically and emotionally."

"*We* are, though, aren't we? We've lasted this long."

"Of course. Remember what I said? You're the best in all Japan."

She snuggled closer, and there in the moonlight he took her smooth, lissome body in his arms, and fell asleep.

That night, sometime toward dawn, Kuki had a dream.

In a vast field of pampas grass, a man stood looking his way. Somehow, he knew it was Rinko's husband. Rinko was also nearby, walking blindly through the grass toward a wide road in the distance. Left behind, Kuki and the man stood facing each other amid the feathery plumes.

That was all. He could recall neither the man's expression, nor when or where he went away, but he awoke with the lingering, chilly sensation of having been seen right through. He looked beside him at Rinko, lying turned slightly away in her sleep. She must have gotten up sometime in the night to put on this cotton yukata, the neckline of which was drawn modestly together.

The bedside clock said five-thirty. It must be close to dawn; the bottom of the curtain was dimly white. Kuki looked at the brightening window and thought back to his dream again.

Obviously the pampas grass in the plateau on the way to the hotel had left a deep impression. Thoughts of Rinko's husband were never far from him, which explained the man's appearance in the dream, but as Kuki had never laid eyes on him, his features and expression were vague and unformed. Most curious of all was the way Rinko had walked straight between them in profile, and gone on.

After trying unsuccessfully to recapture other shreds of the dream, he got up and opened the curtain. Outside, everything was still shrouded in mist, only the crests of the old crater rim faintly visible, like a monochrome ink painting. Sunrise was still a way off, he judged, but the mists over the plain were beginning to stir.

Kuki went back to bed. When he woke up again it was past seven-thirty, and the morning sun was poking under the curtain with considerably more strength.

Rinko was still asleep. He slipped out of bed alone and went to peer outside. Beneath a bright fall sky, the ring of hilltops appeared close at hand. Midway down their flanks was a white oval of mist, floating suspended in midair. Plainly, it marked a round hollow surrounded by hills.

The last time he came to this hotel it had been fall, too. Gradually, as the morning mists broke up, the plateau came into view. Part of the golf course was now visible. Around the starting hole he could make out the figures of several golfers. Looking at them, Kuki remembered telling his wife he would be golfing in Hakone today. Had she believed him? He felt a twinge of conscience, but quickly banished it by closing the curtain again. The movement woke Rinko.

"Up already?"

"I couldn't sleep any more." He went back to bed without telling her about his dream. "Let's not get up yet."

A round of golf on a bright fall day had its appeal, but nothing could compare with the warmth and smoothness of the woman beside him.

"What are you doing?" she murmured when he touched her sash.

"It's still early." He sensed even as he spoke that their time together was growing shorter by the moment. There was no time to waste. He pressed his lips to the breast half showing where the front of her yukata had come open, and drew her hips closer with both hands. Outside, the morning mists were thinning, but here it was still night.

He couldn't remember the face of Rinko's husband from the dream, but a sense of the man's chilliness clung to him, which at the same time seemed to stir up a certain excitement in him. There in bed, shielded from the morning sun, Kuki was more aggressive with Rinko than he usually was, keeping her just on the edge, forcing her to wander in no-man's-land until, at the limit of her endurance, she began to make inarticulate, pleading noises. Even then, he kept her hanging. That his grim detachment was connected to his dream, he could only speculate. After she finally came, she scolded him in a resentful murmur. But the look on her face was so endearing that he hugged her close, and the two of them fell asleep again.

As before, she fell into a deeper sleep than he did; and when he finally woke up, she was still asleep.

It was already nine-thirty, the sunlight coming in under the curtain more strongly than ever. Outside, birds were singing. By now the mist would have lifted, the skies would be clear, and the golfers would be out chasing their little white balls around. In sharp contrast to such a wholesome activity, he, Kuki, lay in bed savoring Rinko's warmth. The knowledge that he alone was luxuriating in this indolent, immoral life was rather pleasurable. He drew closer to Rinko, and she stretched her neck, slowly opening her eyes.

"Mm. I went back to sleep."

"That's because you wore yourself out, ma'am."

"Stop that talk." She laid her hand on his mouth, laughing, then looked at the bedside clock. "Oh no, it's almost ten o'clock!"

Their plan was to see Lake Ashinoko and go back to Tokyo in the afternoon. These stolen moments were drawing to an end.

"Shall we get up?"

The second time she prodded him, Kuki left off toying with her breast and got out of bed. With the curtain drawn, it was still dark in the room. Rinko slipped out of bed, went into the bathroom, and started to take a shower. While she was gone, Kuki switched on the television set to see if anything significant had happened in the rest of the world while they were engrossed in each other.

Soon she re-emerged and sat down in front of the mirror, and he went in to take a bath. He had lain naked beside her almost the whole night, yet so far as he could tell, her scent had left no trace on him. That was another thing he liked about her body; it had no clinging odor to speak of.

When he came out after a brief soak, he found the curtain open and Rinko seated at the dressing table by the window, doing her hair up on the back of her head. Seized by an impulse to touch that white, graceful neck, he said to her reflection, "You're a handsome woman."

"For some reason, after I've been with you, my makeup goes on more smoothly."

"It's the hormones. This feels nice and smooth, too," he said, leaning over and patting her on the bottom.

She twisted aside. "Stop it, you'll muss my hair."

"Who cares." He kissed her lightly on the nape. "Fabulous sex makes a woman glow, but it just shrivels a man."

"That's not true."

"The female devours the male in the end, you know. It's fate."

The word "fate" struck her as funny, and she laughed in the mirror. "You poor doomed male, hurry up and get your clothes on."

Kuki sheepishly took off his robe and began to get dressed.

After brunch in the hotel restaurant, they went outside. The air was cool but not cold, the day piercingly bright. They decided to take the excursion boat around the lake. This being a Sunday, it was rather crowded, so they got off at Hakone Garden and took the ropeway from there up to Komagatake, where they could see all the way to Mount Fuji and Suruga Bay.

From the 4,400-foot summit, the surface of the mountain was a brocade of autumn colors reflected perfectly in the blue waters of the lake below, both mountain and lake ablaze with crimson and gold. They enjoyed the autumn wind and the scenery to their fill, went back down the ropeway, and were back where they'd started by four o'clock. If they were going to return to Tokyo, they would have to leave soon or the roads would be impossibly crowded.

"What do you want to do?"

Her failure to answer one way or the other suggested that she didn't want to leave.

"You don't mind getting back a bit late?" She shook her head, so he decided they should stay a while longer. "Over by Komagatake there's a restaurant overlooking the lake."

They made their way back along the road, now starting to get crowded, and up the mountainside to the restaurant. It was less than halfway to the top, which meant they had a close view of the crater lake below.

As they finished their early supper and looked back, they could see the sky glowing red behind the distant rim of the crater. The sun seemed to set early at this height: slanting beams of late-afternoon light fell from rifts in the darkening clouds across the mountain and down upon the surface of the lake. Kuki stepped out onto the balcony and whispered to Rinko, his eyes on the hills silhouetted against the crimson sky: "It would be nice if we could stay."

She said nothing, but he thought she gave a barely perceptible nod, so he went ahead and asked the question: "Shall we? Stay another night?"

Gazing at the darkening lake, she nodded slightly. "All right…"

He had only been half serious, extending the invitation lightly, fully expecting her to say no. "Really? You're sure?"

"What about you?" she asked in turn. "Is it all right?"

For a second, he was stumped. Certainly he could stay another night if he wanted to, but he would have to call his wife and make up an excuse. Also, there was work tomorrow, and even though there was no pressing business on his desk, he was due at the office by ten.

More worrisome than that was Rinko's situation. Easy enough for her to say she'd gone celebrating with friends after the calligraphy party, but did she dare stay away from home two nights running?

Tomorrow was Monday; her husband would be going to work.

"I can manage, but what about you?" *Don't you have to worry about your husband?* he almost said, but swallowed the words. He glanced at her.

Staring at the lingering red in the sky, she said quietly, "If it's all right with you, it's all right with me."

After the sun went down, the mountain-cradled lake quickly lost its sheen, the surface of the water darkening moment by moment as they watched. Looking at the dark, lonely lake, Kuki remembered the face of Rinko's husband in his dream. By this time it was quite fuzzy and uncertain in his mind, but the general impression of chilliness remained strong.

Was Rinko planning to stay the extra night deliberately in order to make trouble with her husband?

"It's definitely okay, then?" He pressed the point, but the words were less an expression of concern for her than a question directed at himself: was he prepared to accept responsibility for Rinko, if it proved impossible for her ever to go home again?

"You're sure?" he asked a third time, but she only kept her eyes trained on the darkening skyline, unmoving.

Understanding that she was determined to stay another night come what may, he went to a public telephone just outside the restaurant and called the hotel where they had stayed till noon. This being Sunday evening, the hotel was fairly empty, and he was able to book the same room for another night.

After that he called home with some trepidation. Luckily, the answering machine was on, so he left a brief message: "My friends have invited me to stay on another night, so I'll be at the same hotel tonight. I won't be back till tomorrow." Then he hung up.

So much for his affairs, at least for the time being. Now, what about Rinko? He went back inside the restaurant and told her he had gotten a room.

"Do you want to make a phone call?"

She stared into space as if thinking, then got up, and was away for a few minutes.

"Everything all right?" Kuki asked with some anxiety when she returned.

"I don't know," she said with apparent unconcern.

"Tomorrow's Monday, after all. If you have to go back, just say the word. I'll understand."

"Do *you* want to go back?"

Hearing her turn his question back on him again, he hastily shook his head. "No, I just thought it might be difficult for you."

"I'll manage."

He was unconvinced, but who was he to argue the point? "In that case," he said, "we're spending every minute of this night together, just the two of us." If Rinko was that determined, he certainly didn't want to show any signs of faltering. Anyway, whatever the outcome of this decision, as long as they were together, they shouldn't have anything to fear. "Shall we go?" Suddenly exhilarated, he caught her by the hands and murmured, "Thank you." In a sense, the gratitude he felt was less for her decision to stay than for the courage she had given him.

It felt a little odd, coming back to the same hotel where they had checked out just before noon, but the management seemed to take their reappearance in stride, assigning them without comment to the same room as before.

Dusk had fallen. When the porter opened the door and turned on the lights, the same bed, table, and chairs were there waiting for them. Even after the porter had deposited their luggage and gone out, they remained standing in the middle of the room; but the moment they looked at each other, they were in each other's arms, locked in a tight embrace. No words passed between them, yet each knew exactly how the other felt. *You didn't go back, after all. You're going to be with me one more night.* The words were unspoken, but for each one the nearness of the other said it all.

Kuki hugged her still tighter, his lips seeking hers while in his heart he murmured, *You don't care, then, even if your husband makes a scene?* Rinko responded to his kiss, asking him silently in turn, *You don't care, then, even if your wife is angry?* Mouths pressed hungrily together, each one gave the answer: *I don't care what my wife may say... I don't care what my husband says, either.*

Kuki released her lips, cradled her head in his hands, and rested his cheek on hers, knowing as he did so that they had crossed a line. It was a line he had never thought to cross, however much they loved one another. It was the last line of defense, and they had gone past it together. Now there was no turning back: they were at the battlefront, where bullets flew thick and fast, and where at any time they might be hit.

"You're sure...?" He said the words aloud, to make doubly certain, and suddenly Rinko's cheeks were wet with tears—whether from anxiety over the possible consequences of her decision, or from heightened emotion at the commitment she had made. Whichever, to ask now would be pointless.

Kuki wiped her cheeks with his hand. Then he stood in front of her, took off her coat, and opened the front of her blouse. As she stood there, eyes closed, her coat and blouse dropped to the floor around her feet, followed in turn by her skirt. She remained as motionless as a doll. When she wore only bra and panties, Kuki undressed himself, picked her up, and carried her to the bed.

The night before, moonlight had stolen in from the veranda all the way to the edge of the bed, but tonight there was a thick layer of cloud, the veranda cut off in darkness. The width and bounce of the bed were the same. They collapsed together onto it and held fast to each other. As they embraced, his chest against hers and her hips against his, arms and legs in a tangle, gradually the warmth of her body permeated his, sending thoughts of home, wife, work and everything else receding far into the distance.

Now softening and melting into Rinko's warmth, Kuki was swept by an illusion of being sucked into a deep, incoherent space: a sense of isolation, abandonment.

To stay here was self-destructive. He would become an outcast at work, get stuck in a place from which there was no way back. He knew it, and murmured a warning to himself in a corner of his mind; but he was used by now to the sensation of falling, body and soul intoxicated by the pleasure of this depravity.

The words "Watch out..." flashed across his mind, before the two tumbled greedily into the garden of delights again.

Shorter Days

The days remained warm on into December. Mornings and evenings were chilly, close to freezing, but in the sunny afternoons soft light bathed the city streets, and office workers on their noon breaks went to the palace grounds to soak up the sun.

The monk Yoshida Kenko had remarked on just such mild weather as this in his *Essays in Idleness*, thought Kuki, recalling a line from the old classic: "*Jugatsu wa koharu no tenki*. In the tenth month, the weather is springlike." As far back as the fourteenth century, in other words, a late spell of warm weather had been normal—the tenth lunar month being equivalent to modern November. That word *koharu*, "little spring," was appealing. "Little" because the springlike weather of fall was shorter-lived, more fleeting than actual spring. Leave it to the ancients to come up with such a charming word, reflecting their closeness to nature. People nowadays had inherited the word, anyway. Could be the timing now was a bit off compared with Kenko's day— traditionally, December was the month of *kogarashi*, wintry blasts, yet here "little spring" was still going strong. Had Japan's climate warmed over the centuries?

His thoughts rambling idly, just as Kenko's brush had wandered wherever his fancy took it, Kuki made his way through the noon sunshine to the coffee shop where he and Goro Mizuguchi had arranged to meet. His friend was there already, waiting for him.

"Did you eat?"

"Not yet, but no hurry," said Kuki. He sat down across from Mizuguchi and ordered coffee.

"Thanks for coming."

Mizuguchi was Kuki's senior by a year, though they had entered the company at the same time. He had gone from magazine editor to company director, the most successful of their bunch. Today he appeared rather subdued.

"What's on your mind?" asked Kuki.

Before answering, Mizuguchi lit a cigarette and inhaled deeply. "As a matter of fact, they're moving me to Marron next year."

The company he named was a struggling subsidiary with headquarters elsewhere in the same Kanda district of Tokyo. Since the new president's arrival, there had been a general reshuffling of personnel, but Mizuguchi had not been a director very long, nor had he seemed to have any difficulty getting along with the new boss. This was a surprise.

"The boss told you so himself?"

"Yesterday, in his office. Amano's health problems have left them short-handed, and would I please step in." A year or two older than Mizuguchi, Amano—the head of Marron—was a diabetic, prone to absences from work.

"As president?"

"Not exactly. Amano stays. I'll be vice president."

"It must be just a matter of time, though."

"I don't know. Being president of that outfit wouldn't amount to much, anyway."

Marron employed some twenty people and dealt mainly with practical how-to books not handled by the main company. Financially, it wasn't doing well. For an ambitious man like Mizuguchi with a bright future in the main company, the prospect of becoming president there would be less than enticing.

"Did you say yes?"

"Why should I? What did I do to deserve this?" Mizuguchi took another drag on his cigarette in evident irritation. "I told them I'd think it over. But the new president seems to have his mind made up."

"'Autumn does not come when summer has gone,'" said Kuki ruminatively.

"What?"

"It's from Yoshida Kenko's *Essays in Idleness*. It's been on my mind lately. It means autumn doesn't start all at once at the end of summer—signs of it are there throughout the summer, all along."

"Yeah?"

"To us, the seasons seem full of sudden, drastic changes, and so does life—but that's only because we miss the constant, subtle changes going on behind the scenes." Kuki thought of his affair with Rinko. If this was the hot midsummer of their love, then were signs of autumn chill already present? Were they poised to start a downward spiral?

Unaware that Kuki's thoughts were on the woman he loved, Mizuguchi clucked his tongue in vexation. "I'll tell you one thing, you and I are a dime a dozen. When they're through with you, they toss you out like used Kleenex."

"Nobody's tossing you out. Marron can still get back on its feet, if it's handled right."

Mizuguchi shook his head firmly. "Too late. Now I know how you felt when you got the boot."

"Leave me out of this."

"Hell, if I'd known this was going to happen, I'd have slacked off a bit and had more fun."

Mizuguchi had climbed straight up the corporate ladder. He had a gift for editing large magazines, combined with a managerial knack. Sharp and articulate, he was a go-getter—the very qualities, perhaps, that had made the new president decide to hold him at bay. Kuki, by contrast, had spent his entire career in the arts, devoted to books and their authors. While not averse to career moves, neither had he ever had any objection to staying immersed in the cultural side of things. He was an artisan, content to remain one editor among many.

"I should be more like you." Mizuguchi sounded subdued, but no man of his caliber would give up without a fight. Sure enough, he went on to declare he had no intention of folding up quietly, though most would.

It could go either way, thought Kuki. A person could be either energized or dispirited by the position he was assigned.

"You've got lots of life in you yet."

"Right. Maybe I'll find myself a good-looking woman and make the most of it!"

The jest put Kuki off. To Mizuguchi, love was a stimulant to boost job performance—one of life's little pleasures, at best—whereas for Kuki it had become something far deeper and more significant. Lately, the thought of Rinko brought not so much joy as a kind of pain that left him sometimes breathless.

"I must say, I envy you," Mizuguchi went on. "Even down in reference, you're the same as ever. You never let it get to you. If anything, you've got more energy now than before." Naturally, he had no inkling of Kuki's current mental distress. "Anyway, nothing like this ever happened to me before. You were the only one I could talk to."

"It's better not to brood about it." Kuki had gone through hell after his demotion, but agonizing did no good. You had to make the adjustment and get on with your life.

"Can we talk again sometime?"

"Any time. Just say the word."

Talking it out had apparently put Mizuguchi more at ease. They discussed two or three other personnel changes, then parted. Kuki stopped off and ate a solitary bowl of noodles before going back to the office, where he soon got a call from Kinugawa.

"How's it going? Life treating you okay?"

He hadn't seen Kinugawa since Rinko's calligraphy party, nearly a month before.

"Sure, how about you?"

"Oh, you know—busier but not richer." Increasing the number of courses at the Culture Center had brought no corresponding rise in students. After complaining about it, Kinugawa abruptly changed the subject. "Tell me something. How would you feel about a change of jobs?"

The suddenness of the question left Kuki momentarily speechless.

Kinugawa explained, "My old outfit wants to beef up its publishing division, and expand the literary section, too." He had worked for a major newspaper company. The newspaper itself was the company's main cash cow, of course, with all other divisions, especially books, mere appendages. From the perspective of an ordinary publishing house, it offered little competition. "But newspaper publishers today have to diversify to get ahead. These people want to launch a major drive in book publishing and eventually put out their own paperback line."

"It could be too late."

"That's why they want you. They think you're the man for the job."

So this was Kinugawa's offer, to transfer to the publishing division of his old newspaper. Quite a coincidence, the invitation coming just as one of Kuki's oldest colleagues was being farmed out to a subsidiary.

"Why me?"

"Can you talk about this now?" Kinugawa seemed nervous about Kuki's being at work, but no one was in the office now except Suzuki, from whom he had nothing much to hide.

"Why not?"

Relieved, Kinugawa launched into a fuller explanation. "Okay. The current head of publications is a guy named Miyata. I met with him the other day, and when I mentioned your name, he asked me to sound you out."

"Look, I appreciate this, but I need time to think about it."

"You don't have to answer right away. It won't be until next April anyway, if it does work out, so there's no hurry, but Miyata is definitely interested. Wants to talk to you in person."

"Has he been there long?"

"No, he transferred from the city room. The guy's a real whiz. He'll make something of the place."

Given the emptiness of his present job, Kuki was genuinely grateful for this chance, but he was not in a position to snap it up. "As I say, I appreciate it, but I'll have to think it over."

"Fine." Kinugawa lowered his voice. "By the way, how's *she* doing?"

Kuki spoke to Rinko on the phone nearly every day, but lately he'd seen less of her. After their two nights together in Hakone, it seemed harder now for her to get away. When they did meet, she hurried off at nine P.M. "Be patient," was all she would say. There might have been trouble of some sort with her husband. Kuki's worries were not allayed by Kinugawa's mysterious tone.

"She's all right. Why do you ask?"

After a short silence, Kinugawa said, "You don't think she'd walk out on her husband, do you?"

"What do you mean?"

"It's probably nothing, but three days ago she came to see me at the Center." Kuki had talked to her on the phone just yesterday, but she'd said nothing about it. "At first she hedged a little, but it turns out she wants us to give her a steady teaching job."

"Can she do that?" Rinko had been sent to the Center originally on a temporary basis, to teach square *kaisho* calligraphy in her teacher's stead. She would obviously need the latter's permission to continue working there. "I mean, has her teacher said anything about wanting her to take over?"

"No. I think that's why she came around by herself. She hasn't said anything to you, eh?"

Kuki mumbled something noncommittal.

"According to her, she wants to take up teaching full-time. If you ask me, she's after the money."

"Money?"

"Yeah. A regular paycheck."

As far as Kuki knew, she had no money problems at present. If she did, he was sure she would tell him.

"I just don't know…," was all he could muster.

"Well, I don't either, but something about her manner gave me the feeling she's trying to become self-supporting. She'd only need to do that if she had plans to end her marriage."

The words hit Kuki hard. The idea had never crossed his mind that she might be contemplating anything so drastic. Nor had it occurred to him that she wanted to continue teaching.

"Does it look like you'll have a job for her?"

"Well, hiring is up to us, so theoretically we could ask her to handle all the calligraphy classes, yes."

"Surely she wouldn't accept without her teacher's permission."

"I don't know, I wouldn't put it past her, would you?"

"What do you mean?"

"No offense, but she seems like the type to go straight for what she wants."

There was indeed a rather daunting, do-or-die side to Rinko, though Kuki didn't much like having Kinugawa point it out. Kuki remained silent, puzzled that she hadn't confided in him.

"You really didn't know, did you?" Kinugawa said inquisitively.

"No, I didn't." He didn't see any point in lying.

"So are things cooling off between you two?"

"Not a bit." They weren't spending the night together, but he saw her once or twice a week. Her time was at such a premium that they would feast on each other hungrily the moment they were together, often parting without time to linger and savor the experience.

"None of my business, I know." After a pause, he added, "Anyway, if she's really determined, I'll okay it, but I thought I'd better check with you first."

"I'm glad you did."

"Talk it over with her." Then, as an afterthought, he said, "She seemed very ... preoccupied."

For no reason, Kuki pictured Rinko's face at the moment of physical ecstasy, her brows knitted in apparent anguish. Clutching the receiver in his hand, he shut his eyes.

After Kinugawa's call, Kuki badly wanted to get in touch with her, but he couldn't very well do it from the office. Smoking a cigarette, he thought of what he would say to her. Above all, he had to know why she had asked for a teaching job at the Culture Center.

For money, Kinugawa had said. Could it be so simple? He'd also said she seemed preoccupied, as one would be if planning to abandon a marriage. But why wouldn't she have told him? He had to find out, but only face to face. He opened his appointment book. The month of December was always busy with year-end parties of one kind or another. He was tied up tonight and tomorrow night, both. Of course, if she were free, he could slip away from any other commitment, at least long enough to have a talk.

Having decided what to do, Kuki left the room with his cell phone, going, as usual, to the stairwell by the elevator to place the call. After making sure no one was around, he punched in Rinko's number. Two-thirty P.M. Unless she was out on an errand of some kind, she would be home.

On the fifth ring, someone picked the phone up. Rinko, he thought, but the voice that came on wasn't hers: "Hello?"

Instantly Kuki held the phone away from his ear, holding his breath. It was the voice of a man.

"Hello? Hello?" The same male voice could still be heard, but as if far away.

Shocked, Kuki clicked off and thought hard. Rinko had no children, she and her husband lived alone. It must be him. A man in his late forties, supposedly, but the voice had sounded brisk and youthful. What the hell was he doing home at this time of day? What business did a medical professor have being home now? Maybe he'd gone back on a sudden errand. Or maybe he'd come down with the flu and canceled his classes for the day. Not that he'd sounded sick. There must be another explanation.

Anyway, her husband, assuming that's who it was, had picked up the phone only after it rang a while, so presumably she was out. Or unable somehow to answer the phone herself. The more he thought about it, the more anxious he became, scenario after scenario presenting itself to his worried imagination. What if they'd been fighting? Her husband might have been grilling her about her infidelity, or her string of absences from home, the scene escalating into a shouting match until she collapsed, sobbing, in the middle of the floor. She was too distraught to answer the telephone, so he took the call instead—but then the caller made no reply, hanging up without a word. Suspicions mounting, her husband began to abuse her all the more.

Kuki's guilty conscience painted one awful picture after another. He needed desperately to get in touch with her, but the possibility of her husband answering a second time gave him pause. *Better hold off a little,* he told himself, trying to stay calm, but he was in no shape to go back to the office. Instead, he went down to the basement cafeteria and ordered a cup of coffee.

The lunch hour was over, the place almost empty, but a few

acquaintances nodded before getting up to go. He imagined them whispering among themselves that the poor slob had nothing better to do, seeing him sit down for coffee at this hour. His paranoia was quickly checked by thoughts of Rinko, and other more important things.

Half an hour went by. This time, she might pick up the phone. If her husband answered instead, all he had to do was hang up. With this in mind, Kuki walked out of the cafeteria and back toward the stairs, and punched in the number. Poised to hang up in a split second if need be, he stood with his ear pressed to the phone, listening to it ring. Before, the man had answered on the fifth ring, but now the sixth ring went by, and the seventh, and the eighth. After ten, Kuki hung up. He waited one minute and called back, but again after ten rings there was still no answer. Had her husband gone out? Had they gone out together?

Half relieved, half disappointed, he leaned against the wall and reconsidered. Where could she be? He had always taken it for granted that he could talk to Rinko whenever he wanted to. The fact was, however, that they only had the telephone to connect them. The moment that link was severed, he had no idea what might be happening to her. She might be ill or missing, but unless she contacted him, he had no way of locating her.

He'd thought the bond between them was as strong as it could be, yet here they were, cut off from each other in a heartbeat. Was this the defining quality of an extramarital affair, this fragility of connection? The idea filled him with an even deeper ache, an insistent need to see her right away. His longing was made painful by his feeling of help-lessness in tracking her down. He could try her again in the evening; otherwise, he had to wait for her to call him on his cell phone.

In resignation, he headed back to his office and turned his attention to his work on the social mores of the 1930s. He was finding it quite absorbing. Particularly from around 1935, along with increased restrictions on freedom of speech and thought, there had been a rise in vio-lent protest, including the attempted coup d'état of February 26, 1936. Also, several sex scandals had shocked the nation during the same period. The most notorious of these was the case of the murderess Sada Abe.

Abe, a live-in waitress in an establishment in Tokyo's Nakano Ward, strangled her employer with a cord from her kimono and then cut off his private parts. Kuki's interest was attracted not only by the admittedly gruesome facts, but also by the sentence handed down in this unprecedented case. The prosecution had originally asked for a sentence of ten years, but the judge reduced it to six, and as another year was lopped off for good behavior, she served only five years in prison. The judge had apparently ruled the incident not a simple murder but an attempted double suicide carried out at the peak of sexual ardor, or in a fit of postcoital madness, brought on either way by an excess of passion.

The incident had occurred just after the failed army rebellion of February 26. The military was on the rise, the nation as a whole beginning its dark slide into war. Why, at a time of heightened tension and growing militarism, would the perpetrator of such a bizarre sex murder receive so lenient a sentence? The question intrigued Kuki. He meant to explore the issue by examining arguments for the defense as well as contemporary reactions from the man in the street, hoping that way to re-examine the Showa era from a previously unconsidered angle.

Kuki had all sorts of plans for the project, without having any fixed completion date. Now, he just kept on reading, stopping intermittently to think of Rinko, then read some more. Before he knew it, it was five o'clock, the short winter daylight already at an end.

Editors' office hours were pretty flexible. People might stop off on their way to work to conduct an interview or pick up a manuscript and not get in till the afternoon, while a proofreading job could last till late at night, or straight on till morning. What mattered was not the amount of time spent in the office, but the quality of the work that got done.

In Kuki's section, which was somewhat removed from the main action, it was common to arrive at ten in the morning and leave around six. Tonight, however, was different. This was the night of their annual year-end party, so after five they all knocked off and prepared to go out on the town. Kuki put away what he was working on, and left with his colleague Yokoyama.

The party was at a Chinese restaurant in Shimbashi, so they caught a taxi from in front of the company building. The closer they got to Ginza, the worse the traffic became. The city streets were always grid-locked in December, every restaurant and café packed. The economy having not yet recovered from the lingering recession, people were perhaps more eager than ever to go out drinking and forget their woes.

They arrived at the restaurant a little ahead of time and went on up to the second-floor room reserved for their group, but nobody else was there yet. Kuki went back downstairs to the public telephone by the entrance and redialed Rinko's number. It was almost six. If she'd been out shopping, she ought to be back by now. Even so, wary of getting her husband on the line again, he held the phone at a slight distance from his mouth.

No answer. After the tenth ring he hung up and tried again, with no better luck. They were both out, then. Where could they have gone? Hard to imagine the two of them setting off somewhere together. Kuki stood by the phone absorbed in thought until the others arrived and he had to go back upstairs.

Technically, the reference section was part of general affairs, so they could have joined their year-end party, but for the last year or two they'd been celebrating on their own. Since there were only the five of them, including the secretary, the cost was fairly steep, at ¥8000 a head.

Section chief Suzuki stood up and said the usual sort of thing: "The year is almost over, everyone. Thanks for all your hard work." He wound up by urging them each to continue to develop the field they specialized in, and to work with renewed zeal in the coming year. This was Kuki's first year-end party with the reference section, but Suzuki's way of putting it made sense, since they all worked on different pro-jects.

After that, glasses were filled with beer, toasts were drunk, and the meal got under way. Conversation centered at first around company politics and recent office gossip, but gradually the topics got more personal. Some people started griping about their own situations. As the drink began to take effect and the party grew livelier, attention focused on the lone female secretary. Though not especially pretty, she was good-natured, and there was quite a lot of light banter going on around her.

Since she was thirty-five and divorced, the men all wanted to know if she'd found a new boyfriend. From there, the conversation moved on to a consideration of each one's ideal type of woman. Even the normally staid Suzuki joined in, asking her: "Which one of us has the most sex appeal, d'you think?"

"Oh, dear!" The secretary examined each man's face in turn, and then said, "I don't know about that, but I do think the one most likely to have a lover right now is Mr. Kuki." This remark drew an instant chorus from the other men.

"No way, not me," he quickly protested, but the others began to tease him, not without some envy.

Suzuki was first. "You know, I *thought* it was funny the way he carries that cell phone around everywhere he goes! Now I get it."

"That's right," Yokoyama chimed in. "He never leaves the room without it."

Even Muramatsu, the youngest of the men, got in on the act. "He's been looking awfully happy about something lately."

Kuki did all he could to deny the charge, but his protestations only made things worse. What had been idle rumor became accepted fact. They began asking his advice on dating.

"I should take some tips from you," murmured Suzuki.

Where was the best place for a rendezvous, Yokoyama wanted to know. He seemed to have someone in mind. "Do you go to love hotels?"

"No, those are passé," Suzuki said in a knowing tone of voice. "To impress a woman, you have to take her to a classy city hotel."

"Yes, but doing that every time could run into big bucks," complained Muramatsu.

"It's worth it, if it makes her happy," said Suzuki, then glanced at Kuki. "Anyway, Kuki here has already paid for his house, his only child is married off, and his wife works as a consultant, if I remember right. He's got money to burn." As section chief, he was certainly well informed. "He's not like the rest of us, struggling to pay our mortgages. He's loaded, trust me."

"You certainly can't have fun if you're worried that stopping in one more bar is going to clean you out," said someone.

"Right. To enjoy a love affair properly takes money and time."

"Well, everyone here has plenty of *time*, anyway!" said Yokoyama sardonically, and they all laughed.

Just then, Kuki realized his cell phone was ringing. Usually when he was with colleagues he turned it off, but tonight, concerned about Rinko, he'd stuck it inside his bag with the switch on. He could hardly take the call here in front of everyone. Quickly he stood up and rushed out of the room, taking his bag with him. The stairs were just ahead, but without waiting, he took out the phone and finally answered it. The moment he heard her voice, he felt the sting of tears. For some reason there was distant static, but it was unmistakably her. "Thank God!" On the point of colliding with a waitress carrying a tray of food, he drew back.

"Where are you?"

"Yokohama."

"Wait a minute." The party room was too close for comfort, the passageway too narrow. Holding the phone pressed against his ear, Kuki went down the stairs till he came to a fairly large space by the entrance. Standing there, he said again, "Hello?"

"I'm here."

With relief, he said intensely, "I've been trying to find you all day. I called your home, but you weren't there."

"I'm sorry. My father died."

"No!"

"Word came this morning, so I hurried back to my mother's house." Her family home was in Yokohama, where her father had run a furniture import business.

"What was it?"

"A heart attack, they think. He was fine yesterday … it happened early this morning."

So there'd been a death in the family. Kuki had imagined something completely different. "I had no idea…" Unsure how to console her, he mumbled, "I'm sorry."

"Thank you."

"But it's wonderful to hear your voice." This was the truth. He stumbled on, knowing it was inappropriate to say such things on the very day her father had died yet unable to stop himself. "I have to see you." Discomfiting news from Mizuguchi and again from Kinugawa had been topped off by hearing her husband's voice over the phone. One thing was certain: talking to her by phone wasn't nearly enough to quell his anxiety. "Today or tomorrow."

"That's not possible."

"When, then?"

"Maybe the beginning of next week."

This was only Wednesday. That was another four or five days.

"I have to talk to you about something," he said.

"What is it?"

"I can't say over the phone. Will you be at your mother's for a while?"

"At least till the day after tomorrow. Tomorrow is the wake, and the day after is the funeral. I'll call you."

"Wait." Kuki gripped the phone tightly. "Tell me your number there."

"What for?"

"I might need to get in touch with you."

Reluctantly, she told him. He scribbled the number in his appointment book, and then asked casually, "Is your husband there with you?"

As if taken aback by the question, Rinko was silent for a moment before answering in the affirmative.

"Is he staying the night, too?"

"No, he's going home," she said flatly.

Somewhat relieved, Kuki said good-bye and hung up.

It was a relief to know she was safe, but now he was uneasy about her husband. That definitely must have been his voice on the phone before. She had told him the news, and he had come home from the university to change into mourning. The two of them had then rushed off to her mother's, where now they would be accepting condolences, side by side. Rinko would look beautiful in black. With her brilliant husband at her side, also in black, people would be looking at them and thinking what a fine couple they made.

In his thoughts, Kuki came up hard against the security of marriage. A lawfully married man and woman could go anywhere and see anyone in each other's company. Lovers, especially illicit lovers, dared not be seen together on public occasions, and even had difficulty going out in private. Once, a woman had complained to him that she'd never been out in public with her lover, and now he and Rinko were in the same boat. No matter how much in love they were, their relationship had to be kept secret, and they could never be seen together. The insecurity of an extramarital affair was now heavily brought home to him. Of course, he had only himself to blame.

To break the mood, he put away the cell phone and went back to the party. As soon as he walked in, everyone burst into applause.

"Hey, congratulations!" Yokoyama teased. "She called, eh?"

Kuki resorted to the same feeble denials. "No, you've got it wrong. I had some family business to see to, that's all."

"I doubt it—you should have seen the happy look on your face when you ran out of here with that phone."

It was no use. Resigned to becoming the butt of everyone's jokes, Kuki drained the beer in his glass.

The party went on till just before nine. Suzuki, Yokoyama, and the secretary announced they were going to a karaoke bar afterward, but as Kuki didn't like singing, he and Muramatsu set off instead for a Ginza bar. It was a snug little place with a long counter that would barely accommodate ten.

"So tell me," Muramatsu said seriously, "is there someone new in your life?"

Kuki nodded.

"And you're sleeping with her?"

"No use pretending it's platonic, is there?"

"Matter of fact, I'm seeing someone too, but you know, I'm not half the man I used to be. I figure it's age. What about you?"

Asked point-blank, Kuki was unable to answer. Muramatsu went on, clearly encouraged by the drink. "So do you come every single time you have sex?"

"Probably not every time."

"I try to hold myself back too, but it's rough. I'd never breathe a word of this to anyone else … but once she and I are alone, I just don't feel like I'm getting in as far as I once could..." Despite the frankness of all this, his tone was straightforward and inoffensive.

"Stronger and deeper isn't everything," Kuki replied.

"No?"

"There's a more accessible place that women find pleasurable."

"Isn't putting a pillow under her hips supposed to help?"

Kuki hardly felt qualified to give sex tips, but was still willing to share what he'd learned himself. "Yes, or try coming in from the side."

Muramatsu nodded. "Maybe we've just seen too much hard porn."

"What matters most is how you feel about her, anyway."

Muramatsu nodded again.

Maybe all men had their questions and worries about sex. Kuki felt a sudden affection for Muramatsu, and poured him another whiskey.

It was after eleven when they parted and he headed for the station. The evening's unusually frank discussion of sexual matters may have had something to do with it, but as Kuki walked along he found himself consumed with longing to see Rinko. It would be nearly a week before they could meet again, she'd said on the phone, but he couldn't wait that long. Knowing he couldn't possibly ask her for a date on the day her father had died, he decided to call just to hear her voice.

Seeing a phone booth on the sidewalk, he felt inevitably drawn inside. He took out his memo of the Yokohama phone number and called it. He had to do it now, while he was still drunk, or not at all. Telling himself this, he waited, ear to the phone, until the voice of an older woman came on the line. Kuki identified himself and then asked politely for Rinko Matsubara.

"I'll go and get her," said the voice.

In a few moments, Rinko's voice came on the line: "Hello?"

The sound filled his chest with heat. "It's me."

"What's the matter?" She sounded flustered at this late-night call to her mother's house.

"I went out drinking after we talked, and I missed you so much I had to call, no matter what." Then he blurted out the question uppermost in his mind. "Can I see you now?"

"But this is the day my father—"

He knew he was being unreasonable. "Tomorrow?"

"Tomorrow is the wake."

"Come after it's over. I'll wait in a hotel in Yokohama."

She was silent.

Kuki went on, "Tomorrow night, I'll call you again from the hotel. Just give me one hour, that's all I ask. Thirty minutes." He pleaded with her over the telephone, unable to explain even to himself why he was saying such wild things.

The next day, Kuki came to work an hour later than usual, rather hung over. He hadn't been all that drunk after the party, at least not when talking to Muramatsu. The problem was his calling her and insisting on seeing her. What could have gotten into him, saying such things to the woman he loved on the very day her father had died, when she was in both shock and grief? He was appalled at himself. It must have been the thought of her being there with her husband that had set him off. After saying good-bye to Muramatsu, he'd gone on drinking alone, not getting home till after one in the morning.

At his age, it was no surprise if a drinking bout affected the next day's work. Realizing he'd seriously overdone it, he was genuinely thankful he had such an undemanding job.

He sat down at his desk and glanced at a few papers, but soon got up to light a cigarette and drink a cup of tea. He then persuaded himself to sit back down, but in twenty or thirty minutes he was ready for another break. After continuing all day in this fashion, half working and half loafing, at dusk his head finally cleared and he felt up to going out.

The evening before, Rinko had not promised to see him. Still, having said he would be in Yokohama, he felt he had to keep his word. He had a light meal at a little place near work before heading for

Tokyo Station and boarding a train for Yokohama.

What hotel to go to he hadn't yet decided, but it might as well be somewhere easy to locate. After some thought, he settled on a high-rise hotel overlooking the bay, where they'd once had dinner. He had planned to wait for her in the bar, but the wake would go on for hours yet, and he felt like resting a little. He made up his mind to take a room.

The bellboy led him up to a room on the bay side of the sixty-fourth floor. A spectacular night view spread out before his eyes: he could look down on the Bay Bridge, connecting clusters of lights. This wouldn't be too far from her house. He stood by the window and gazed at the scene below, imagining what it would be like to make love to Rinko here if she managed to slip away from the wake.

More worrisome than the length of the wake itself was the hour of her husband's departure. Naturally, she couldn't get away until he was gone.

At ten o'clock he picked up the receiver, but decided it was still too early to call. At eleven, he took the receiver off the hook again, and dialed her number.

Summoning another man's wife to the phone on the night of a wake: you couldn't get much lower than that, he knew, but along with his sense of guilt was a slight thrill at the thought of his own depravity.

The phone was answered by a male voice—not her husband. More calmly than the night before, Kuki asked to speak to Rinko. "Would that be the daughter?" inquired the voice, evidently belonging to someone who worked at her father's company. As Kuki was telling himself this, Rinko came quickly on the line.

"It's me," he said. "I'm in a hotel in Yokohama."

"Really?"

"I said last night I'd be here, didn't I?" He told her the name of the hotel and the room number. "Come right away, would you?"

"Now? But—"

"The wake must be over by now. What about him?" He meant her husband.

"He went home a little while ago."

"Then come. It's not far." If she said no, he would have taken the room for nothing. "Please. I have to talk to you."

"All right. But that's all."

"Of course. I understand."

Would she show up still dressed in mourning, or would she take time to change? It didn't matter, he thought. Once he saw her, he wouldn't be able to keep his hands off her.

Kuki sat down on the sofa, watched TV, and waited. From her mother's house on the bluff, the drive shouldn't take more than fifteen minutes. Of course, if she did change her clothes, it could take her an hour. These random thoughts tumbled through his mind as he stared at the screen. Unable to focus, he rose, took a brandy from the mini-bar, and sipped it alternately with some water. It was almost midnight. The late-night talk show was wrapping up, and the other channels were flashing previews of the coming season.

Kuki turned off the TV, walked to the window, and stood staring out at the night. It occurred to him that the year had begun and ended with Rinko. Since they first had sex last spring, their mutual desire had consumed them. Like oppositely charged particles, they became inseparable; like hungry animals with their prey, they devoured each other.

It had been the most passion-filled year of Kuki's life. It was like reliving his distant, all-but-forgotten youth. As he poured himself another brandy, he looked down from his sixty-four-story aerie on the glimmering streets below. He felt light-headed as he imagined her wending her way toward him. Every light below seemed to glow with her presence. He could feel her approaching, between darkened buildings, past blinking traffic lights. Soon she would pass the hotel's front desk, ascend in the elevator, and be in his arms.

At the very moment he rested his forehead on the window's thick glass, the doorbell rang. Kuki sprang to the door and opened it. Rinko stood before him in a black silk mourning kimono with matching obi. Over her arm she held a black coat. Her hair was in an upsweep, a collar of immaculate white encircling her throat.

"You came!" he said, gripping her hand and ushering her inside. "You really came," he whispered, almost unbelieving. She fell against him, her knees buckling as he crushed her in his arms. In his desperation to fulfill his own needs, he forgot why she was in mourning, forgot whose wake she'd come from, forgot it was her father who had died. He covered her mouth with his, wanting only to indulge his passion.

When the long kiss finally came to an end, their bodies parted. He looked her up and down admiringly.

"Mourning becomes you," he said finally.

"What an awful thing to say!" She was right, of course.

"I was afraid you wouldn't come."

"But you insisted! Come immediately, you said." Fingering her obi, Rinko walked over to the window and gazed down on the glittering scene outside.

"You've never been here before?"

"Never upstairs, in a room."

He joined her at the window. "I was staring down at the lights, waiting for you." As he took her cold hand, he again appreciated the fact that she had hurried through the frosty night just to be with him. Warming her hand between his own, he asked huskily, "He went home?"

"Him? Yes." Her tone was detached, indifferent.

"I was jealous."

"Really? Why?"

"Imagining him with you at the wake, at the funeral, at your side, greeting one and all, with everyone saying, 'Oh, what a lovely couple.'"

"That's what hurts so much."

"What?"

"The endless comments. My aunt was fishing around, asking 'Is everything okay between the two of you?' And my uncle was dropping not very subtle hints about it's being high time we started a family. They think it's their business."

"But it isn't."

"Of course it isn't, but it seems everyone is concerned. They sense something isn't right."

"What if they found out you were here with me?"

"I can't imagine—I'd never hear the end of it."

He looked past her shoulder, from which a faint scent of incense arose, to the spangled city lights. Feeling giddy with excitement, he pulled her toward the bed.

"No." She shook her head adamantly, trying to wriggle from his grasp.

"I won't do anything. Just lie down next to me for a bit."

"I can't. My hairdo; it would be noticed."

Though she resisted, he tugged on her arm as he sat down on the bed. "Then let's just sit here together." Reluctantly, she yielded and sat, patting some stray hairs into place.

"Do you really have to go back?"

"Of course. I told you, thirty minutes at most."

From the edge of the bed, he could still see the city lights stretching out to the ocean.

"The other day I got a call from Kinugawa. He said you came in asking to teach full-time at the Center."

"Oh, he told you, did he?" Rinko nodded, not seeming surprised.

"Why didn't you tell me first?"

"I didn't want to worry you."

"But can you do that? Leave your own teacher, and work a full schedule?"

"If they could use me, I'd certainly try to get permission."

"He also mentioned he thought you wanted to leave your husband."

She stared ahead at some point in the darkness outside, her face like stone. "I mean to if I can."

Mesmerized by her profile, his right hand found her knee.

"I'll leave my wife then, too, shall I?"

"You don't have to do anything."

"Of course I don't have to..."

"Anyway, you couldn't."

"That's not true," he said vehemently, his right hand pushing aside the black outer fabric to touch the white silk beneath. Just as quickly, she brushed his hand away, but it fell between her knees and remained there.

Obviously unrepentant, he continued the conversation. "You really intend to work full-time and leave him?"

"I can't live alone with no income."

"I would never let that happen." He slid his hand in deeper. Flustered, she clamped her knees together. A struggle ensued, with her locking her legs, him probing with his hand. Finally, she yielded. His fingertips reached her inner thigh. "This is all I want," he said, soothed by the warmth of her skin.

They sat side by side on the bed, apparently gazing out the window at the nighttime view. Anyone taking a close look would have seen the disarray of the kimono, and the man's arm thrust up amidst the silken folds.

She knew what he wanted, and despite the indecency, if not depravity, of such behavior on the night of her father's wake, she felt herself giving in. Sensing her acquiescence, he ran his fingertips back and forth along her inner thigh. This, of course, was his strategy, his clever way of lulling her into a state in which her flesh would respond to his touch, despite her mind's resistance. She grew moist.

Then his hand reached her most private place, still covered in soft white silk. She gave a little cry, then leaned forward, hunching her shoulders. First his palm cupped the whole flower; then the tip of his middle finger gently touched the tiny bud. Because he had proceeded so slowly, so gently, she felt herself growing soft and wet.

Neither of them stirred, their eyes fixed on the window. Softly, in circular motions, his fingertip brought forth her juices. He then moved from bud to lips, lightly parting them, exploring between them gently and then with more force. His fingers entered and withdrew in an ever increasing rhythm until it was more than she could bear. Her body froze, and her voice managed a hoarse "Stop."

His fingers moved for a few more moments, then stopped in seeming resignation. "I want you," he whispered urgently, entreating her. She didn't answer. Again he pleaded. "Just a while longer?" With that, she seemed to awaken from her trance. Suddenly aware of her situation, she shook her head.

"No. Not now!"

"It'll only take a minute," he said feebly.

"I have to go."

His manner changed. "Turn around," he commanded coolly.

She looked at him, uncomprehending.

Softly he said, "If you turn around and pull up your skirt, your hair won't get mussed."

Finally she understood what he wanted.

"Be quiet and turn around," he repeated.

He had long known that some people made love this way, and had tried to imagine what it would be like. Now the dream lay before his eyes.

Rinko was supporting herself on the bed on her arms, head down, back rounded. From the front, she would simply have looked as if she was crouching on hands and knees. From his vantage point, however, he could see that her feet were still on the floor. She was leaning, knees bent, against the edge of the bed. Her kimono skirt was hoisted up past her waist, her round, white mounds enveloped by a fantail of black and white silk.

He took a deep breath. It was a supremely erotic vision, and it stirred him to the core. Almost every man in Japan must have had this fantasy at one time in his life. But to take a woman in the most formal of kimono, to force up her skirt and take her from behind, was so blatant and brutish that few men would ever act it out, or even talk about it.

But the fantasy *was* talked about, for it belonged to legend. In bygone times, such a position was a necessity, when a popular geisha during the holiday season would entertain at one engagement after another dressed in formal, crested kimono and with elaborate, lacquered hair piled high with great ornamentation. Often, she had only the odd moment to steal away with her lover between bookings. Such a posture would be the only one possible to satisfy the lover's lust without spoiling the woman's appearance. So it was on this night of Rinko's father's wake: with limited time, and to avoid ruining her hairdo and costume, they could unite no other way.

She was ready for him, unfurled like a peacock.

When she had turned around she'd still been reluctant, but as she assumed the posture he had told her to take, she began to succumb to real desire. He repeatedly praised her beauty, her sexiness, watching her become more and more excited: "You're wonderful, so beautiful, fantastic..." His voice became dry and hoarse, but he kept up a litany of praise.

Suddenly he stopped. He looked with wonder at the white bottom exposed by the upturned kimono, and fondled the warm, smooth skin. Then, unable to restrain himself, he thrust himself inside her full tilt, forcing from her a sharp cry that was close to a scream. He held her hips steady with both hands as she lurched forward, binding them together like two animals.

The position felt at once bestial and natural. Because it was primitive, without pretense, it seemed all the more conducive to pleasure. Now they were just a pair of animals, male and female, nothing more. Morals and ethics, reason and education and all the other accretions layered on mankind since the dawn of history and pervading the human body head to toe, were cast aside.

Their writhing continued until finally—like the slow dying away of an animal's howl—it ended in stillness.

For a while they lay heaped on the bed like corpses, male and female, motionless as stone. A total stillness enveloped them, the shadow of death hovering just beyond love's extremity.

Then he roused himself from his stupor, just as she too began to return from the realms of pleasure. He came back quickly, but she remained in a lingering trance, face down, her body still collapsed in the pose of abandoned passion. When she finally rose and went into the bathroom, the enormity of what she'd done began to dawn. She remained there, obviously upset by what had just occurred.

Five minutes went by, then ten. Before fifteen had passed, the door opened quietly and she emerged. Worried, he asked, "Are you going?"

He couldn't catch what she murmured back, but she nodded slightly. He had insisted that she come here, and now it was clear that she regretted doing so. What ought he to say? Kuki was at a loss.

They stood face to face at the door. He lowered his head, saying simply, "I'm sorry." A beast only moments before, he now reassumed his ordinary human form, and acted shocked and ashamed at what he'd done. "It shouldn't have happened, but..." He drew a breath and finished softly and honestly, "I wanted you so much."

Rinko shook her head slowly. "It's my fault," she said.

"No, that's not true."

"To do this on this night, of all nights. I deserve to be struck by lightning."

He folded her in his arms. "Then I'll be struck right along with you." If their love was mutual, so was their sin.

She straightened her kimono collar, impervious to his tenderness. She opened the door, her face deathly pale. He sought another brief kiss, but she stepped straight into the corridor, precluding any further physical contact. She walked off without a backward glance. He watched her back recede down the corridor until she turned to get on the elevator and disappeared.

Kuki closed the door and returned to the bed, where he lay face down. She had left without so much as a good-bye. Was that her way of saying that she regretted the entire act, or just its timing?

Musing, he flung out an arm, his fingertips touching something small and metallic. It was one of her hairpins. Only a short while ago, she had crouched here on this bed, hands gripping the bedclothes as he entered her. Her head must have been where his was now. He recreated the scene in his mind, but the room remained deathly still, her fallen hairpin the only reminder of their earlier passion.

Holding the hairpin in his hand, he realized that at any moment Rinko would be arriving back home. Where would she say she had been? She'd stayed in this room the better part of an hour, and including travel time she'd been away an hour and a half. What possible excuse could she give? Her kimono and her hair looked perfect, but nonetheless tongues would wag.

More important was the question of Rinko's attitude. Those who feel guilty often act guilty. If she suffered pangs of conscience, she might arouse suspicion. He hoped she would behave normally, but the memory of her tense, pale face worried him.

He prayed that she would be all right. As he did so, a surge of renewed tenderness passed through him. Unconsciously, he kissed the tiny hairpin in his hand.

A New Year

From the last day of December to the day after New Year's, Kuki never left home. This didn't mean, however, that he spent all the time alone with his wife, since his daughter Chika and her husband came to stay for the holiday, filling the house with lively chatter. When they left, it was as quiet as the grave. As they got older, couples supposedly spent less and less time talking, but this silence was unnatural. Kuki had neither the energy nor the will to bridge the gap, and his wife, clearly sensing his remoteness, made no attempt to change things either.

In spite of all this, on the afternoon of the third, they set out together for *hatsumode*, the customary New Year's visit to a shrine to pray for happiness and prosperity in the year ahead. They went because they had always done so.

The shrine was tucked into the corner of a residential area not ten minutes from their house by car, and the other visitors were all locals like themselves. Kuki stood next to his wife in front of the shrine with his hands pressed together, as hers were. He prayed first for peace of mind and good health throughout the year, then that his and Rinko's love might be deep and long-lasting.

He imagined that his wife was praying for health, success at work, and perhaps even the birth of a grandchild. He wondered briefly if she might have other secret prayers, things unknown to him. Then they drew sacred lots. Hers was *daikichi*, great good fortune, and his, *shokichi*, small good fortune. She smiled with pleasure over what was apparently her first *daikichi* in a long while. Kuki was unconcerned about what he'd picked. He felt simply that he had done his duty, and after they returned home, he got ready to go out again.

"I'm going to pay a call on the boss," he told her, changing into a new suit. Despite his declared intention, which he meant to fulfill, his real aim was to go on to see Rinko afterward; they'd arranged to meet at six at the Yokohama hotel for their first date of the new year.

Having just lost her father, Rinko had decided to spend New Year's with her mother. Her brother was now the official head of the family, but she wanted to keep her mother company and help her through this difficult time. As he'd listened to Rinko explaining this over the phone, Kuki had wondered about her husband. As if reading his mind, she volunteered only that she was alone. It was possible that he was off visiting his own parents, but Kuki really didn't care where he was: the simple fact that he wasn't around helped put him at ease.

At first, Rinko was evasive about meeting him so early in the new year. She said she was too busy, but he knew this was just an excuse: she still felt guilty about what they'd done on the night of her father's wake.

He apologized repeatedly. Finally, after he had said "I was wrong to do that" for the umpteenth time, she agreed to meet him on the third. Later, he worried that she wouldn't actually show up, and fought the urge to call for reassurance. Nonetheless, he cut short his New Year's visit to his boss and got to the hotel well before six. He wouldn't really allow himself to think that she might stand him up.

The lobby had an array of women decked out in bright kimono milling about. Several families with children had apparently stayed there over the holiday and were in the process of checking out. Everywhere, people were coming and going. Kuki sat on a sofa off to one side, keeping a watch on the front entrance out of the corner of his eye. It was getting toward six, the promised hour. What would she be wearing? Restlessly, he scanned the entry. Then suddenly there she was, just beyond the revolving doors, which were in almost constant motion. He leaped to his feet just as Rinko entered, moving in his direction.

She was in a white kimono with an auburn obi, and carried a fur stole over one arm. As she came nearer, he saw that the kimono had a floral pattern: from top to bottom were flowering sprays of plum and scattered blossoms. He strode up to her.

"Happy New Year."

She dipped her head lightly. "Happy New Year to you, too."

"You look beautiful."

She looked down in pleased embarrassment, with no trace of the pale and haggard look she'd had when she walked away after their last encounter.

"Let's eat upstairs here, shall we?"

Not knowing Yokohama well, he had made reservations at the hotel restaurant on the top floor. They went straight up and sat down facing one another at a window table. The restaurant was full, with several large families celebrating the last of the holiday by eating out, but Kuki felt relaxed in the crowded room. Rinko, too, seemed totally at ease. They were getting used to being together in public, he thought, getting more daring all the time.

He ordered from the menu for both of them, and after drinking a toast of sherry, he gazed at her again.

"I was afraid you wouldn't come."

"Why?"

"Just a feeling." The memory of what he had put her through last time weighed heavily on him. "Did you spend the whole of New Year's with your mother?"

"Yes." Apparently, she had been away from her husband the whole time, too.

"Have things settled down a bit?"

"Oh, yes, except Mother's very lonely."

The death had come so suddenly, it was no wonder her mother was having a hard time. "It might be a good idea to stay on with her, then," he suggested.

The issue was a delicate one, but Rinko answered easily, "I wouldn't mind…"

Their first course was a dish of steamed oysters, smelling faintly of champagne. Kuki had eaten almost nothing at his boss's house. He raised his glass of white wine, and they drank another toast.

"We go back a whole year now," he said. It was at the same time the previous year that they'd become acquainted, having met at the

Culture Center. They had gotten together for dinner now and then after that, but hadn't yet fallen in love. He was amazed at what a difference twelve months could make, that they could go from being virtual strangers to feeling this close.

He was thinking out loud. "A year can mean such different things." Some years were branded on the memory and others slipped into oblivion, notable only for making one that much older. The past year, he felt sure, would prove to have been the most unforgettable of his life.

"After it warms up, shall we go back to Atami?" It was after a trip to see the plum blossom there that they had first made love. He had always wanted to go, and when he invited her along on an impulse, she had said yes. Together they had enjoyed looking at the blossom in early spring, and then returned to Tokyo, eaten dinner, and gone to a bar for drinks. Unwilling to say good-bye, he had asked her to go with him to a hotel. Whether it was because they had already spent so much time alone or because the cocktails had lowered her defenses, Rinko agreed after only the feeblest of objections. Remembering her sweet innocence that night, he looked at her again.

"That kimono looks wonderful on you." From the left breast down to the obi was a scattering of open plum blossom. He realized that the quiet dignity of the plum suited her much better than the brighter, more showy flower of the cherry tree.

"I had it made for this, for our first meeting of the new year."

It was in the plum blossom season that they'd first made love, and it thrilled him that she had chosen to commemorate the occasion with this piece of beautiful silk.

The soup arrived. Rinko sipped it slowly from her spoon. She sat erect, her elbow slightly bent as she carried the spoon to her mouth; a model of comportment. Kuki gazed in fascination. After a moment he said aloud, "You really are more like plum than cherry blossom."

"What do you mean?" she asked, spoon in hand.

"Cherry blossom is beautiful, but it's too loud, almost overbearing. The plum is quieter, not as pushy."

"A bit too quiet, perhaps?"

"Not at all. It's got dignity ... and freshness."

She reminded him that long ago the word for flower—*hana*—was understood to mean plum blossom.

"That's right, it was. It wasn't till around the tenth century that the cherry started hogging all the attention. Another nice thing about the plum is the shape of the branches—they're just as interesting as the flowers themselves."

Rinko nodded, and glanced down at her kimono sleeve. "See, here the pattern has only bare branches, without any flowers."

"The old masters used to say, 'With cherries, the blossom, with plums, the tree.' There's something so graceful about the branches." A haiku occurred to him. "There's a good haiku by the Meiji poet Hakyo Ishida: 'Flowering plum branch—the body laid out perfectly straight.'"

The moment he said it, he knew he'd made a mistake, that it would make her think of her father.

He tried to explain. "It's not that the flower has any special connection with death, but there's a certain quality … of—what?—clarity, solemnity, about it. In that poem, cherry blossom wouldn't work: too sentimental. Plum blossom conveys a kind of stillness…"

"I think I know what you mean."

"But it's funny…"

"What?"

"Nothing, I was just remembering something."

A vision of Rinko in a moment of unbridled passion had flashed into his mind: like a branch of plum blossom being shaken wildly, waving about, as if dancing in a windstorm..

To wipe this distracting image out of his mind, Kuki made a start on the main course, carving the roast duck with his knife.

"Did you go somewhere for *hatsumode*?" he asked, changing the subject.

"No, not while we're in mourning. What about you?"

Omitting the fact that he'd gone with his wife, he told her he'd drawn a *shokichi*.

"The same as last year!" she said.

"You remembered." Last year, they had gone together to Hie Shrine in Akasaka. It had been January 10, a bit late. Praying and drawing sacred lots together had seemed to bring them closer.

"So you won't be going?"

"I'd like to, but I probably shouldn't."

He nodded, and asked casually, "What about your husband?"

"Certainly not."

Kuki stopped cutting up the duck, surprised. "Why? Because he's in mourning, too? Surely it matters less if it's your father-in-law who's died."

"He doesn't care about that. He thinks it's pointless, that's all."

"He does?"

"Shrines, fortunes, all of it. To him it's all a big waste of time."

"The voice of a true scientist."

"Is that what you call it?"

Catching a sharpness in her tone, Kuki changed the subject again. "How long will you be in Yokohama?"

"I'm supposed to go home tomorrow."

"So soon?" He had thought she might stay for at least a few days. "His university hasn't started classes yet, has it?"

She gave a barely perceptible shake of her head, then said lightly, "My cat needs me."

Rinko's cat was a Himalayan, he remembered. "You mean your husband hasn't been home, either?"

"He spent New Year's Day with his parents, but he's probably been back since yesterday."

"Alone?"

"He's not happy unless he can be in his study. He likes to sit in there, surrounded by his books."

"A scholar."

She made no comment. After a sip of wine, he ventured, "With him there, the cat will be all right, won't it?"

"No. He has absolutely no interest in living things."

"But he's a doctor."

"All the more reason. Last year, Zsa Zsa had trouble urinating, and I took her to an animal hospital. He said it was a waste of time, that they would just make some random diagnosis and prescribe something that would do no good anyway. I shouldn't even bother taking her. But I did, and she got better. Then he complained it cost too much."

"It's true that veterinary care can be expensive."

She frowned. "But my cat was in pain. I couldn't just do nothing."

"Of course you couldn't. Pets are family."

"If it was up to my husband, he'd probably use her in a medical experiment."

"You're joking."

"He lives in a different world."

The sommelier refilled their wineglasses. Kuki watched, then turned his gaze toward the pattern of lights outside the window. Behind each one were living people, men and women in couples. The notion struck him with uncanny force. Naturally, some were well matched, others not. Rinko and her husband obviously fell into in the latter category.

As he stared at the lights, something else began to become clear to him. He'd never really understood why Rinko had gotten involved with him; he had assumed she'd simply been bored with her husband and looking for a fling with someone. But now he realized it hadn't been like that at all. He knew little about this man who rejected tradition as a waste of time, and pets as a waste of money; but he was obviously a cold fish, and made no attempt to understand Rinko's feelings for her cat, or probably anything else. Such differences, unimportant only to the naïve, go to the very heart of who a person is. With Rinko, they obviously weighed heavily. Logic had nothing to do with it; it involved values and feelings, which made compromise hard, mutual acceptance harder. It was obvious that Rinko's husband, despite his good looks, his brilliance, and his full-professorship, was totally wrong for her. Dissatisfaction, loneliness, and a sense of the emptiness of her life must have driven her to find comfort elsewhere; to open up to him.

As he was thinking these things, looking down on the night scene outside, Rinko also leaned lightly against the window and gazed below. He wondered fleetingly if she had read his thoughts. When he looked back inside, she did the same.

"Life is complicated," he said, trying to sum things up.

She nodded slightly and apologized for spoiling the conversation.

"No, I'm glad you told me." He couldn't take pleasure in her unhappiness, yet something in her account had given him a sense of slight relief. "Anyway, here's to the New Year," he said, picking up his glass and clinking it gently against hers. "May it be a good one." They drank to that, and then he said reflectively, "I wonder what sort of year it will really be."

"For us, you mean?"

"I want to see you more often, do more traveling together." She nodded enthusiastically, and he pressed the point. "Can we?"

"Yes," she said, then seemed to pause. "But if we go on this way, what's going to happen to us?"

"Us?"

"Yes, us."

The simple, pointed question caught him off guard. He could have made any of a dozen casual or facetious replies, but none of them, he knew, would do. Reveling in their secret love was heady and exciting, but face to face with the hard question of where it was leading them, he felt the world and all its complications beginning to close in again.

Although for the romantic, the timing of the question was terrible, he knew avoiding it would be turning a blind eye to the future. It was clear a woman like Rinko, when in love, could never accept living in limbo. She was the type who liked to lay things on the table and see them for what they were. She deserved an honest response.

What indeed *would* happen to them if they fell even deeper and more passionately in love? After spending more and more time together, traveling more, spending less time at home—what then? Would the bond between them become as firm as it could be? Would their affair end in shambles? Or would they end up tumbling together into the void? He had neither the strength nor the courage to think that far ahead. Whether through cowardice or irresolution, he changed the subject.

"You can spend the night, can't you?"

She was silent.

"Let's spend the night here."

This was no sort of answer to her question, but he told himself that after a night together there would still be plenty of time to explore what their future held in store.

They finished the main course. Next came salad, then cheese. Usually at this point in the meal he grew apprehensive, wondering about his chances later, but not tonight. She hadn't accepted his invitation, but neither had she said no. Apparently she was torn, part of her wanting to stay. Best in that case to say no more, and take matters into his own hands.

Without another word, he got up and went to the phone by the register to reserve a room for the night. He asked for a double room with an ocean view. The last time they were here, Rinko had left before him, and he hadn't stayed the night, either. They had missed the sight of the sun coming up over the water. Tonight he wanted to stay till morning.

He went back to their table, sat down, and reported, "I got us a room."

"I didn't ask you to."

"I did it anyway." He couldn't let her go home now. "This is our first time together in the new year." Gently, he picked up her hand from the table and held it. "I'm glad you're wearing a kimono again." She looked away in embarrassment, no doubt remembering what had happened the time before. "But I won't do anything like that again." On the night of the wake their time had been limited, but tonight was different. "Let's go to our room."

"Must I spend the night?"

"Of course. I'm not letting you go."

"Ah. Caught again, am I?" He couldn't be sure whether she was saying it to him or to herself.

He ordered tea and brandy. Over her protests, he insisted on pouring her some. "You can handle this much," he said. Rinko wasn't in fact much of a drinker; a small amount of alcohol was enough to make her tipsy, and this brandy was sure to have a powerful effect. But since they were staying the night, he felt it didn't matter, as long as she was up to taking off her kimono by herself.

"Is that Chiba, in the distance?"

Unaware of the drift of Kuki's thoughts, Rinko had been looking out the window again. Beyond the harbor illumination lay the black waters of the ocean and, beyond that, a narrow band of light.

"I think the sun comes up there," he said. Chiba was east of Yoko-hama. "Have you seen your first sunrise of the year?"

"Unfortunately, no."

"Then we'll see it tomorrow." He pictured the two of them in each other's arms, watching the sun come up. "I'll bet we can see it from our bed."

"Won't that make the gods angry?"

Maybe it *was* sacrilegious to think of watching a special event like the first sunrise of the year from their adulterous bed. But there was also an appeal to the prospect, a decadent appeal.

"Shall we be going?" he prompted her, excited by his thoughts.

"Just a minute," she said, and went over to the phone by the register. Would she be calling her mother, or her house in Tokyo, he wondered. In either case, she must be making some excuse for staying out all night.

She was back shortly, looking a little distracted. "Is this absolutely necessary?"

"Of course." He was firm.

She thought a moment. "Then could I leave at five A.M.?"

In that case, they would miss seeing the sunrise together, but he'd worry about that tomorrow. He got to his feet.

She lagged behind slightly as if still struggling with her decision, entering the room just as the bellboy slipped past after putting down the key. Kuki saw him out, then put his arms around her.

"It's been so long..." He had seen her at the end of the year, but only for an hour. Tonight they would make up for lost time.

As they kissed, he felt for her obi. He didn't really know what he was doing, but somehow, as they embraced, it came loose, one end falling to the floor. "Wait," she said, and went into the bedroom to take it off herself. Kuki breathed more easily. Now there would be no more talk about going home.

He sat down on the sofa. Rinko put her kimono away in the closet and went into the bathroom. He changed into one of the cotton yukata supplied by the hotel, and checked his watch. Not yet nine. Even if she did leave early tomorrow morning, they had plenty of time.

He looked around. It was a two-room suite, sitting room and bed-room. In the sitting room, there was a long sofa against the wall, a cof-fee table, and a writing desk by the window. On the wall over the sofa was a mirror reflecting the contents of the room. In the bedroom was a king-size bed, facing the window. Outside, the ocean was a black void, but at dawn the sun would come up there.

He had taken a suite precisely in order to watch the sunrise with her. She had to stay. He turned off all the lights in the bedroom except for the soft glow of a bedside lamp, and in the sitting room he left on only the light on the wall by the mirror. As excited as a boy at the thought of taking her to bed, he absorbed himself in setting the stage.

Finally he heard the bathroom door open and Rinko emerge. Eagerly he waited for her, wondering what she would look like. She had on a white silk under-kimono, and her hair was neatly combed and twisted up in a knot.

"Ooh, I had too much to drink," she said, walking carefully toward him as if afraid of losing her balance. Perhaps while showering she had realized she was more drunk than she'd thought. He got up and put his arms around her.

"You're fine."

Her slight inebriation, and the shower, made her more desirable than ever. He took her by the arm and led her carefully over to the wall beside the sofa. Squinting in the light, she turned away and buried her face in his arms, unaware that her figure was reflected from behind in the mirror. He said nothing, enjoying the view. Below the thick coils of hair on her head was her slender nape, then the curves of her shoulders, tapering smoothly to her narrow waist and flaring again at the hips. Beneath the sheer under-kimono, every line and curve of her body showed plainly.

As he gazed, a wicked thought came to him. Taking advantage of the way she was leaning against him, he eased one hand in under her slip and around to the small of her back. He kept his hand there a while, savoring her warmth, and then slowly began to caress her in widening arcs. Little by little, the hem of the garment worked its way up, revealing the backs of her knees and thighs.

She had nothing on underneath.

He inched the hem up further, until just above her long, slim legs he glimpsed the round swelling of her buttocks. He couldn't take his eyes from the two mounds showing beneath the hem of her under-kimono in the half-light of the room.

Even through her mental haze, she sensed something. She looked up, started to turn around. He let the hem drop, but it was too late. She gave a cry of dismay.

Tearing herself from his arms, she turned around and saw, for the first time, the mirror on the wall. Her anger exploded as she realized that his stroking had been calculated to expose the reflection of her naked bottom. She scratched at his face with both hands.

"Wait, wait…"

One minute she was leaning contentedly against him, the next minute, wild with fury. Overpowered, Kuki retreated to the doorway between the two rooms and propped himself there, catching her firmly in his arms as she hurled herself at him.

"You sneaky bastard!"

She beat her fists against him but, paying no attention, he picked her up and carried her to the bed. He watched her land on the sheets with a little bounce and settle into place. Then he held her down, covering her body spread-eagled with his. "Let me go!" she cried, but the outcome was a foregone conclusion. The more she struggled, the more she felt the effects of the wine and brandy, flailing uselessly and exhausting her strength.

"Surrender," he whispered in her ear, and then in one swift motion he untied her sash and pulled open the top of the under-kimono. Suddenly, there were her breasts, not large, but round and firm. He saw a look of bewilderment on her face.

Exposed like this, she tried frantically to pull together the front of her garment, but he grabbed her hands and put them back at her sides. She tried again, and he did it again. After several rounds of this, she finally lay still. Her outburst had spent what little energy the alcohol had left her; now her entire body was languid, heavy and helpless to resist.

It was a crude way to have behaved, but he sensed Rinko had

wanted him to take over. It began after dinner, when she asked if she really had to stay all night, then said she would have to leave before dawn. She hadn't spelled it out, but he knew she had mixed feelings. After sneaking out from her father's wake for a secret meeting with him, after allowing him to make indecent love to her, here she was seeing him again. She must still have felt ashamed. The only way for her to forget was to get drunk and carry on, tiring herself out both mentally and physically. Maybe then she could justify things by thinking "I said no, but he wouldn't take no for an answer."

"It's the first time this year for both of us," he whispered to her as she lay there perfectly quiet, no sign of resistance now. "Do you know what that's called?"

Silence.

"*Himehajime.*"

For both of them, their first sexual partner of the year was not their spouse. Along with guilt, they felt also the thrill of betrayal. And, having yielded, she now surprised him by quickly becoming more passionate than ever. Her moaning and writhing, her undone hair and flushed body belied her opposition a few minutes earlier.

Inflamed by the sight, Kuki had to struggle to hold back. "No!" she cried as she climbed higher, reaching peak after peak of pleasure, frightened by the intensity of it. Finally, consumed, she sank back onto the bed. Sporadically, her body gave little twitches, reverberations of the pleasure she'd attained.

He wrapped her body, now damp with sweat, in his arms. He felt elation at the intensity of her orgasm. He marveled again at the mystery of the female body, that it could experience richer, fuller transformation every time they were together. But now there was something else as well. The violence of her passion struck him almost as disturbing. It seemed to worry her, too.

"I meant to stop seeing you this year."

"No."

"I'm always meaning to, but my body has a mind of its own." He found it strange to think that he owed this night with her only to her body. "I know this is wrong. I know I have to stop—I'm constantly telling myself so—yet here I am again." Which side of her was speaking to him he wasn't sure. "I vow never to see you again, but then I always give in…"

Kuki also knew how powerful the magnet of physical attraction could be, but he couldn't help asking her, a little meanly, "It was never like this for you before?"

"No."

"With your husband?"

She turned and faced him. "Are you sure you want me to talk about it? You won't hate me for it?"

"Go ahead."

"You're sure? All right, we did have sex sometimes. Not often, but enough so I got the basic idea. And just as I was thinking, 'That's it?' along you came. And I changed."

"And since then…"

"I haven't slept with him again. I told you."

"How does that sit with him?"

"I don't know, but that's the way it is, and there's nothing he can do about it."

It was rude, he knew, but again he couldn't help asking what it was about her husband that repelled her sexually.

"I don't know. His voice, his skin… I can't put it into words."

"No matter how much he wanted you, it wouldn't matter?"

"Women aren't made that way. A woman's not like a man."

What she seemed to be saying was that, insofar as sexual fidelity was concerned, women's bodies were more principled than men's.

"What does your husband do, then?"

"I have no idea," she said, adding: "It's all your fault for teaching me so much, anyway."

He had no ready answer to that accusation. But if a man and a woman grew close to one another, sex was only natural, and he saw no reason why the responsibility should be laid solely at his feet. "We were made for each other," he said.

She nodded. "I think from about the second time we were together, I knew I was in for something big."

"Something big?"

"Yes. I felt as if I were taking a leap into the unknown, getting in deep. It was scary."

For better or worse, Kuki didn't feel he had changed as much as she had. Gently he touched her breast. Its nice, round shape was no different from before, but her response to his touch had changed enormously. He mentioned something about this.

"I never thought it would be this much, though."

"Is it bad?"

"Yes! I didn't know anything until I met you, and now just look at me."

"But it's all for the better."

"I can never go back." She pressed his hand, which went on fondling her breast. "What are you going to do about it? You've got to take responsibility."

"For what?"

"For making me so that I can only have sex with you. You're the only one who can satisfy me now." She gave his hand a savage pinch, and he yelped.

Comments of this kind were flattering, but being told to take responsibility deflated the flattery considerably. A sexual relationship was something a man and a woman created together, so how could either one be held solely responsible? Besides, he too was addicted to sex with her. He couldn't honestly claim that no one else could satisfy him, men's sexual urges being by nature different, but even so, he found sex with Rinko a consuming passion, a craving.

Weren't they equally to blame, then?

He started to make that case, and stopped. Perhaps, after all, the man should bear the lion's share of blame. A woman's sexual feelings were triggered and nurtured by the man. Without his providing the necessary stimulation, most women would not awaken to the delights of sex. During male puberty, it seemed that male flesh moved of its own accord, so responsive to touch that boys naturally masturbated to bring about the sharp pleasure of ejaculation. No woman's help was needed, nor was the pleasure experienced all that different from being with a woman, and it was certainly preferable to a clumsy experience with one. The spiritual aspects of love were, of course, a different matter.

Viewed in that light, maybe Rinko's claim that he was responsible for making her need him was justified.

Kuki made a show of rubbing his hand where she'd just pinched it. "What was that about?" he said. "You're mean."

"No, I'm not." She ignored it. "You're *glad* I can only be with you now, aren't you. You think it serves me right."

"No. But it does make me happy."

"Not me—it makes me feel manipulated."

"You're no such thing."

"Yes, I am. At this rate, I'll be your slave." Suddenly she sat up and thrust her fingers at his neck, the manicured nails pale pink. "What about you? Say it. Does it have to be me or nobody?"

"Of course."

"You're lying." She wrapped her fingers around his throat. "Lying is not permitted."

"I'm not lying."

The moment he said it, her fingers tightened.

"Okay now…" He thought she was joking, but she paid no attention, pressing harder. She wasn't strong enough to strangle him, but even so, her grip was tight. He began coughing. "Leggo."

"No."

"Cut it out!" He finally managed to pry her hands away, but for a few seconds he coughed uncontrollably. "What the hell? You could kill a person that way!"

"You deserve to die."

Gingerly he felt his neck. There were unlikely to be any marks, but he could still feel the constriction.

"What got into you?" he muttered hoarsely, rubbing his neck and trying painfully to swallow. Then he began to feel a strange excitement. Rinko had lunged at him, tried to strangle him. He thought at first she meant it playfully, but she was half serious. He'd been alarmed that she might accidentally do him in—but there'd also been a small but undeniable lure in the thought. Beneath the fear of strangulation, he'd felt a tiny undercurrent of compliance, a sense that he wouldn't *mind* if his consciousness just faded out. What was that all about? He turned it over in his mind, puzzled.

Rinko said softly, "I hate you."

"But you said just now you loved me."

"I do. I hate you because I love you. Do you have any idea how miserable I was the other night?"

"The night of the wake?"

"Yes, and you know why."

"Did anyone guess?"

"My mother knew something funny was going on. But nobody could have guessed how badly I'd behaved. It makes me cringe to think what my father would say."

Kuki could find nothing to say.

"How I could have done such a thing on the night of his wake I'll never know. He loved me so much. I deserve to be punished. I deserve to go to hell..." Her back turned to him, she choked up. "Why did I do it?"

"It was my fault."

"It doesn't matter about you. I'm just so appalled at myself for allowing it to happen."

He struggled to find words to comfort her. "If you regret it that much, your father would forgive you. But there's no use in overdramatizing it. Besides," he said laughing, "it was good, wasn't it?"

"Stop it. How could anything like that be good?"

He remembered it well. Her sweet, round behind shaking hard as she reached climax. "You were incredible."

"Don't say it."

The more embarrassed she was, the more he had to tease her. "Want to try it again?" he whispered in her ear, his breath warm on her neck. She scrunched up her shoulders.

"Don't be silly."

"I am silly, though." Too late now to worry about what had happened the other night. On a sadistic impulse, he bit her lightly on the shoulder. "I want to eat you up."

"Behave yourself."

As she shook her head, he put his hands on her, pulling the soft roundness of her hips toward him with both hands. In response, her body arched so that her hips jutted out in an inverted V. Her conscious words and actions said no, but her body struck a provocative pose on its own. Slowly he laid his hands on the soft flesh.

"So smooth…"

"Stop…"

"Your skin is so smooth, it feels wonderful."

"Does it?" As if more confident, she thrust her hips further out.

Kuki had struggled desperately to control himself the time before this, and here was the payoff: once again he was stiff and ready to go. To satisfy a woman as passionate as Rinko, he couldn't let himself reach climax every time or he would never keep up with her. The only way to keep a woman like her excited and satisfied was to exercise strict control over his own urges.

Some men would say it was absurd to go to such lengths, that sex was supposed to be fun, and sex without climax was meaningless. Kuki had a different view. Sex for purely procreative purposes was one thing, but sex was also an expression of affection, a shared joy, something cultivated by two lovers over time. For a man to simply satisfy himself wasn't right.

As she became more aroused, his fingers moved in response.

"No, no…" She continued to protest in words, but her secret place was already fully moist.

Sometimes the body betrays the mind. The mind may think that a certain erotic act is wrong, but the body yields and indulges in it nonetheless. There are people who condemn such lapses. Some women have nothing but scorn for their weak-willed sisters, believing that rational and controlled behavior is their only defense against corruption. Their argument has some merit, but human behavior is not governed by logic.

Rinko was usually a model of intelligence and composure, yet once aroused she was gone. Did this mean she was really just undisciplined, or that the joy of sex was more rewarding than any satisfaction gained from self-control could ever be? The latter, definitely. Second thoughts aside, she was always eager to smolder and burn. Reason was abandoned as the deepest instincts of the human body boldly reasserted themselves.

What use were ethics or common sense to a woman of such hidden fire? A woman who allowed herself to fall, in full knowledge of the consequences, entered into a garden of delights unknown to those who lived by reason alone. "I know a dazzling joy that they know nothing of." The moment she said that to herself, her attitude shifted to one of defiance and, with it, a sense of pride at becoming a new member of a sexual elite.

Rinko had that defiance, and yet she continued to murmur "No, no," as if delirious. This was the last pocket of resistance, though, and surrender was inevitable. Rinko knew now that her body had won out over her mind, and the moment she accepted that, she was free.

But the excitements of love, once experienced, tend to lose their novelty, and one craves the next level. That was where Kuki and Rinko were now. After the shameful night of the wake, when she'd still been wearing her mourning kimono, there was little that could now surprise her. And so, despite her initial opposition, Rinko ended by thrusting herself at him hungrily until Kuki, stroking her, murmuring words of praise, finally entered her.

She had reached orgasm only a short time earlier, and that perhaps made it easier for her to re-erupt so quickly now and come again with a long, low moan. Kuki hugged her tightly to his chest.

Few women would not be disappointed by a man's turning his back on her the moment the act is finished, pushing her away as if to say he has no more need of her. Considering all the ardent coaxing that leads up to sex, what could be more of an anticimax than to have the charm switched off so suddenly? Fortunately, Kuki had just managed yet again to hold himself back, so he still had a tiny reserve of strength in him. Instead of turning away, he held her close, waiting for the last ripples of passion to subside. He wasn't sure, but he thought possibly this was one reason she was so attached to him—his attentiveness during the afterglow of sex.

As he waited for her to quiet down, she suddenly opened her eyes, like a lotus flowering in a pond. Eyes on his neck, she said in a half dream, "It was different again."

"Better?"

"No, just different. New."

Kuki couldn't fathom the extent of these sensations.

"How do you know so much about me?" She seemed to be talking about her most erogenous spot.

"Lucky guesswork." His hand was on her flower. "It's here in front, isn't it."

Which part was most sensitive he knew in general, but in Rinko the area of heightened sensitivity seemed to be steadily enlarging.

"You pulled back there just a little, didn't you? It was amazing. I didn't think I could stand it..."

Before, he had always tried mainly to drive in as deeply as possible, but after finding the sweet spot just inside, he would linger there, now and then drawing gently back and forth.

"When you enter me, I'm just helpless. I feel so strongly connected to you, and I feel your presence all in me and around me, and nothing else matters..."

Inside that secret place, so warm and soft and clinging, were count-less buds of pleasure that must all stand up in turn and make them-selves known.

"Then what happens?"

"I don't know..." She added in a low voice, as if to herself, "I could die, just like that..."

At the pinnacle of sexual fulfillment, many women cry out that they want to die. Obviously, few mean this literally, but rather as a descrip-tion of the intensity of their pleasure, or possibly the expression of a subliminal wish to die at this high point. For most men, such grada-tions of feeling are out of reach. Addicted as he was to Rinko, Kuki had never once fantasized about dying during sex with her. The closest he ever came to a sensation of death was when he lay drained and exhausted beside her, every resource spent. At such times he felt a sense of pervading loss, his entire body shriveling, all hopes and attachments fading away to nothing.

As he thought about it, he realized that it was indeed possible that both men and women might entertain visions of death during passionate sex. The difference was that such thoughts came to women on a rising, spreading wave of pleasure, and to men in just the other way. He was stung by jealousy.

"You could die, really?"

"Absolutely." She didn't hesitate.

"But sex alone won't kill you."

"Then strangle me."

"You want me to?"

"Yes." Again, she was matter-of-fact. "What about you? Will you die too?"

"I could." He was remembering the sensation of her fingers on his throat a little while before. "But if I strangle you, only one of us can die."

"No, it has to be together."

"Then we'll just have to strangle each other."

Rinko laid her forehead slowly against Kuki's chest. He kissed her wide forehead lightly and closed his eyes, yielding to drowsiness...

In the night, he had a dream. Someone, he couldn't tell who, was choking him with white hands. Slowly but surely, the pressure intensified until he had to do something, and quickly, or he would die. At the same time he felt a kind of resignation, a willingness to cast everything aside and accept it.

Clearly, he thought when he awoke, her pretending to throttle him and their subsequent conversation about death just before drifting off lay behind the dream. But whose white hands were those? Rinko's, one would suppose, but in the dream she had been in a big parlor-like room, watching with a smile on her face. So perhaps they belonged to some other woman. In any case, all he had seen of his attacker was a pair of disembodied white hands.

Still more mysterious was the reason why the hands had released their hold. He hadn't struggled against the pressure, but given in to it. Might it be that, as they slept, Rinko's hands had somehow wrapped themselves again around his neck, however briefly? With an uneasy feeling, he rolled over and looked at her, but she was peacefully asleep. He tried to trace the rest of his dream, but it was impossible. He checked the bedside clock. The dial read six-thirty.

All of a sudden it hit him—she had wanted to leave early. Should he wake her up? She was sleeping so soundly that he decided against it. He slipped out of bed, put on a white cotton yukata, and went over to the window.

When he parted the curtains, below the ink-black sky stretched a band of faint white. The sky wouldn't grow light for some time yet, but the moment of daybreak was close at hand. He went back to the bed, touched her on the shoulder, and whispered, "It's six-thirty."

Instantly she turned her head away, as if to avoid the sound of his voice, but soon turned back, half awake. Her eyes still closed, she said sleepily, "What?"

"It's six-thirty."

Now she opened her eyes. "Is it really?"

"You said you wanted to get an early start."

"I do." She looked at the clock. "Oh my God." She swept back her hair. "I forgot to set the alarm."

After twice making intense love, coming again and again, she had fallen into a deep sleep. It was hardly surprising that she forgot about the alarm.

"Is it dark out?" She looked anxiously toward the window.

"It's just starting to get light."

"Then I've got to go."

"Hang on, now." As she started to get up, he grabbed her by the arm. "You can't leave now."

"But I want to get back while it's still dark. Otherwise the neighbors will see me."

She was bound to stand out, going home in a formal kimono at this hour. But he stood firm.

"It's too late." Sunrise would be at six-forty or six-fifty. Even if she hurried, by the time she got home it would be light out, anyway. "Better wait and go home at ten or eleven."

"I can't do that," she said, and tried again to get out of bed. He caught her shoulders from behind and pulled her to him. "Stop it..." Ignoring her protests, he pulled open the front of her gown and cupped one of her breasts with his hand.

"You might as well, now you're this late."

"No."

"It's all right."

He started caressing her breast, and soon Rinko sank back in seeming surrender. Relieved, he pulled open the curtains. The white band of light across the horizon had gotten bigger, its center now swollen and red.

"It's almost time for the sun to come up," he whispered, putting his other hand on her secret place.

"I have to go home," she repeated, but the movements of his fingers were too much for her. Even while urging him to stop, she clung to him.

The half-light of dawn was perfect for lovemaking. Kuki threw off the sheet and, after making sure she was moist and ready, put one hand under her buttocks and entered her slowly from the side. By now she had lost any urge to resist, instead cooperating by parting her thighs slightly to accommodate him. He lay on her right side, able to see the slight rise of her bosom each time he penetrated her, and the slight fall as he withdrew. While he continued the slow, rhythmic motion, the increasing light from the window showed her creamy, sinuous body with ever more clarity.

As she became aroused, thoughts of the rising sun and of plans to go home were alike forgotten, and she began responding vigorously. Just then the sky turned a brighter red, as if heralding the sun's imminent arrival. She gave a soft moan and then immediately twisted her upper body toward him, crying out, "Do it..."

He was confused for a second, but quickly realized she wanted him to come at the same time she did.

"Please, I want it..."

As she cried out a second time, every membrane in her entwined around the tip of his stiffness, drawing to the surface all that was in him, all that he'd been holding back, until it burst forth all at once.

She gave a shuddering sound like a death cry as she came in a series of little spasms. It was also a cry of satisfaction at having squeezed him dry—at not allowing him any last restraint.

They had reached orgasm simultaneously as the sun rose. The window, pale white when they began making love, now sparkled red in the morning sun, growing brighter by the moment.

In contrast to the sun's energetic, upward motion, Kuki lay on the bed like a piece of floating timber, his energy consumed. Outside, a new day was under way, but inside their high-rise suite all was still. Kuki lay motionless on his side, Rinko's knee barely grazing his thigh. At that one point of contact, they felt all the warmth of each other's flesh and blood.

He lay in full surrender to the lull that held his body. Rinko moved nearer and whispered "Thank you," her face close to his. At the lilt in her voice, he opened his eyes. She was smiling. "You came too, didn't you?" He made no reply. "You couldn't help it this time, could you?"

The look on her face told him he had lost. All last night he had exercised strict self-control, but this last time he couldn't. The old strategy no longer worked. She had counterattacked, and outmaneuvered him.

"Good!" She was jubilant. "Now you don't want to move either, do you." It was true. Even if ordered to get up, he felt too heavily languid to move. "Then I won't go home." She snuggled up to him like a kitten.

Feeling her soft warmth, it struck Kuki again how much she had changed. She said nothing, but inside she must be thinking it: from now on she wanted no more of the clinically controlled sort of sex whereby he brought her to climax, watching at a slight remove. It was as if she had made an announcement that from here on, she would switch from a passive role in bed to an active one.

They fell asleep together.

When Kuki next awoke, the sky was still brighter, and the bedside clock indicated nine-thirty. They'd slept another two hours. What to do now? As he lay there thinking, Rinko stirred beside him. What time was it, she wanted to know. He told her, and she glanced at the window.

"Oh dear." Broad daylight. "What are you going to do?" she asked.

Kuki considered. Yesterday he had told his wife he was going out to pay New Year's calls and that he would be home late, but he'd said nothing about staying out all night. He was definitely AWOL, but after one night his wife was unlikely to raise a fuss. Sure of himself, he hadn't bothered to call, but the thought of having to go home now and make excuses was irksome.

"I really do have to go." Telling herself this, she sat up.

"Sorry I detained you."

"You should be!" Then she turned back to him. "But it's all right. I'm glad I stayed."

"Will everything be all right at home?"

"I don't know. You must have some explaining of your own to do, too." He nodded, and cheerfully she said, "I forgive you then, since you're in trouble too."

"I'm in trouble?"

"Yes. It'll be hard for you to face your wife, won't it? So we have that in common. Makes it easier to bear." With that, she slipped out of bed and went into the bathroom.

After a love-feast, there was always a lingering emptiness. He was sorry he hadn't called it a day sooner. What made him act like this? He felt a surge of compunction, helped only by the knowledge that Rinko felt the same way. They were accomplices. The time was long past when one or the other of them could suffer alone while the other remained unaffected. Her pain was his, and his, hers.

The bathroom door opened; Rinko came out and began to dress.

"I ran a bath for you," she said, and he moved in that direction. As she wound her obi around her waist, she said, "I've decided something. From now on, I don't care what anyone says."

"Your family?"

"Or my husband," she said flatly. "Otherwise, I can't go on seeing you. So you've got to ignore what your wife says, too."

If she was that determined, he had to agree.

"From now on, I'll think only of being with you," she said.

At the end of December and again now, he had forced himself on her in many ways. He was glad that she had ended by accepting him, but in the meantime she had grown more resolute, acquiring a defiance and strength of will she hadn't shown before.

"All right?" she pressed.

Nodding, Kuki sensed in his bones that the coming year would be a crucial proving ground for their love affair.

Winter Waterfall

Just as it is generally felt that the new year is a time of renewal, Kuki and Rinko felt their relationship undergo a distinct shift. For one thing, Rinko was beginning to take the initiative. She had usually been a willing participant in their assignations, but it was he who generally did the inviting. Since New Year's, however, she insisted that he call once a day. When he did, she'd ask to see him. Considering how restrained her behavior normally was, this new assertiveness was a major change.

It went back to her declaration that January morning in the Yokohama hotel: "From now on, I'll think only of being with you." She had apparently made a New Year's resolution to deal with their relationship head-on, whether it was morally wrong or not.

Her new attitude was reflected in their new meeting place. At first they had met in medium-sized hotels in and around Tokyo. Occasionally they would meet at a "love hotel" where, for obvious reasons, clients paid by the hour, but they both felt uncomfortable in such surroundings. The alternative was to use first-class hotels, but then not staying the night seemed a shame, while checking out after only a few hours was decidedly awkward. Also, being in a different room every time they met was unsettling. The biggest practical consideration, though, was cost: Kuki had spent a small fortune on hotel bills since they had begun their affair.

Renting their own apartment would allow them to meet whenever they wished, and economize at the same time. When Kuki proposed the idea to Rinko in such terms, she readily agreed. The idea had actually occurred to him much earlier, but both his own ambivalence and his fear of her reaction to such a plan kept him quiet about it. But soon, with her complicity, he was ready to take the big step.

Since he lived in Setagaya, and she came from Kichijoji, they decided that Shibuya, being fairly central, would be the best place for their love nest. For 150,000 yen a month, he took a two-room apartment. Only a ten-minute walk from the station, it was a bit pricey, but still a bargain compared to hotels.

By mid-January the lease had been signed, and they began shopping for the usual amenities. As they made the rounds of department stores and supermarkets, Kuki felt buoyant, as if he'd rediscovered his youth and was on his honeymoon. Rinko shared his excitement as they made careful purchases of everything from a bed to linen, from curtains to dishes.

It was the last day of January by the time they had their first real "date" in the now habitable apartment. According to the calendar it was the coldest time of the year, but the weather was an unseasonably mild 50°. The apartment was warm and cozy, and their lovemaking had even more sizzle than usual. Afterward Rinko made a hotpot with crab, tofu, and vegetables that she'd picked up on her way there. They ate at the little table feeling like newlyweds, so happy they couldn't keep from smiling.

"I know what," she said jokingly. "I'll just stay here from now on."

He nodded. "Okay, and tomorrow I'll come here after work."

"Make sure you come straight home, now."

It was only banter, but as their eyes met, Kuki for a second was thrown off balance, feeling a flicker of anxiety that, with his former dream now a reality, he might end up stuck in a situation he had longed for.

"Or I could arrange to be here any time of day," she said.

"Now there's a brilliant thought."

Kuki was lucky: his time was his own during the day. One perk of being an editor was that you didn't punch a clock. If he needed to meet with an author, he might not make it to the office until after lunch, and he was just as likely to leave early. Like a salesman, he was not tied to a desk. Although his current job gave him fewer pretexts to get out than his old one, his light workload meant that he was rarely missed. United by having been demoted, the reference staff covered willingly for one another. Playing hooky was easy.

After getting the apartment, Kuki began to leave work early on a fairly regular basis. Technically, he had to leave word of his whereabouts, but the Showa history project made that easy: all he did was write "National Library" on the board.

Rinko could also leave home in the daytime, so they would arrange to meet at two or three in the afternoon. Each had a key, so either one could arrive first. As soon as they saw each other, they would embrace, full of unspoken emotion … and then go to bed.

Though he was seeing a married woman in broad daylight, Kuki was able to be unguarded, with no fear of what others might think. They both felt guilty yet somehow excited by these workday trysts.

But having the apartment made things perhaps too easy. The string of visits to the "National Library" was bound to attract attention at the office, since he'd never gone out much before. One day he was taken aback when the secretary, Ms. Kinoshita, made a pointed remark about how much busier he seemed. He quickly, too quickly, protested, and his fluster alone more than likely betrayed him. He relied on her to take messages in his absence and explain his whereabouts to others. It wouldn't do to have her suspecting the truth.

After that, they decided to meet in the afternoon only once a week; the rest of the time Kuki went to the apartment straight from work. Usually Rinko was there before him. Sometimes she made dinner, sometimes they went out to eat nearby. Occasionally they'd run into the building manager, a man about Kuki's age, who would look at them suspiciously. Kuki had rented the apartment in Kinugawa's name, to hide his identity, and although the manager had no way of knowing that, he did seem to know that Kuki actually lived elsewhere.

Kuki, of course, said nothing, having no need to defend himself. Being called "Mr. Kinugawa" was a bit nerve-rattling, but he felt far more at ease than he had in the hotels, and that led straight to the second problem: being with her now was so cozy that he could hardly tear himself away. It was always tempting to spend the night together, yet to do so would only make life more difficult for them both, and wind up causing more pain.

They both felt now as if they were married, or at least living together, a feeling reinforced by all sorts of little everyday events. When Rinko was washing her things, for example, she would rinse out his handkerchief and socks. And although he never asked her to, she bought him a new set of underwear. One morning, after they'd spent the night there, she casually said "Here, use these," and laid them out for him. The thought went through his mind that his wife would notice, but realizing Rinko had bought his usual brand, he decided it didn't matter.

Part of his insensitivity was due to the fact that, during this time, he and his wife were in a state of cold war, with little to say to each other. The fault, of course, was his. His heart now belonged to Rinko, which made treating his wife with affection impossible. She, sensing the change, kept her distance.

It was not really a war, but a lack of passion—neither seemed able to gear up for a fight. Under the circumstances, Kuki felt that an occasional night out would cause no trouble, but as he stood in the vestibule about to leave for work one morning, his wife came up and said bitterly, "Go ahead and have your fun. Just try not to make a complete fool of yourself." He spun around, unsure how much she really knew, but she disappeared into a back room without another word.

It was, of course, possible that she knew about Rinko, but he couldn't bring himself to ask her. He simply left the house, putting off the inevitable once again. One thing was certain: his marriage had steadily deteriorated, most noticeably since the beginning of the year.

If there was a deepening fissure between him and his wife, Rinko and her husband were also drifting further apart. Although she never actually said as much, Kuki inferred so from both her comments and her attitude. In the old days, when she was going to be away all night, she would call her husband privately to let him know. She never said what she was doing, but it was obvious. Lately, however, even when they decided on the spur of the moment to stay together, she made no move to call home. It would be on the tip of his tongue to remind her, but he never did. It wasn't his place to say anything. He did wonder if she was being openly defiant, or if they had arrived at an "understanding." Although he couldn't help but be concerned, he knew it wasn't really any of his business.

The change wrought by having their own place was evident in little things Rinko said. Once as they sat at their table eating, she sighed and said, "Food tastes so much better when you eat it with someone."

Kuki was puzzled. "What about when you're at home?" he asked.

"I almost always eat alone. He gets home late, and I don't want to eat with him, anyway." Her matter-of-factness was chilling.

"He's there on weekends and holidays, isn't he?"

"Then I pretend I have work to do, so I won't have to eat with him. When I do, it takes my appetite away." She did look thinner. "I hardly know which is my real home any more."

It sounded as if her marriage was over. With both of their marriages in meltdown and the two of them spending so much time together, the obvious solution was for each to get a divorce and marry each other. Kuki still found it hard to envision such a future, found it hard to justify pulling the plug on her marriage. Perhaps he could tolerate the thought of borrowing a man's wife but not stealing her. It made little sense, but he had decided that her husband seemed hardworking and decent enough.

Also, what did Rinko herself want? Her lack of interest in her husband was plain enough, but did she have the courage to walk out? In terms of social respectability and income she was better off as she was. She might well choose to stay that way.

Divorce would mean a host of new problems for Kuki, too, since the cause of his marital troubles was his own infidelity. He and his wife might be in a cold war now, but eighteen months ago they'd been an ordinary married couple, and for many years had been very close. Theirs had been a love match, after all, not an arranged marriage. Their present hostilities began with the entrance of Rinko into his life. It was he who was to blame for the shambles their marriage was in. Yes, he was in love with another woman, but was that reason enough to abandon the woman who for years had been a good and faithful wife?

Also weighing on his mind were the words his daughter Chika had said to him at New Year's: "Be good to Mother, okay?" Why would she say such a thing, unless she sensed that something was wrong? Would he be able to just ignore his daughter's feelings and leave her mother?

With more than twenty years invested in this marriage, divorce was not something he took lightly. However, neither was it impossible. It all came down to a question of willingness—a question Kuki was far from having settled in his own mind.

February 14, a month after he rented the apartment, was Rinko's birthday. At six that evening he picked up a bouquet for her at the flower shop by the station. It was made up of white roses, tulips, and orchids. When he reached the apartment with it, she was there waiting for him.

"Happy birthday," he said, handing her the flowers.

She buried her face in their fragrance. "They're beautiful. This is for you." She handed him a small package wrapped with a red ribbon. It was a box of Valentine chocolates. On a small card she had written, in a hand flowing with affection, the simple words, "To the one I love most in the world."

"I'm sure you got chocolates from lots of women at work today..."

"Yours make me the happiest." He had also gotten chocolates from Ms. Kinoshita and from the women in his former section, as was customary on Valentine's Day, but none of their gifts could match hers. "Now, what shall we do to celebrate your birthday?"

"You already gave me flowers! That's plenty."

Once before, when he'd asked what she wanted, she had pointed out that the apartment already used up more than enough of his resources. She had insisted that he not buy her anything.

"There must be something you want."

"I'm thirty-eight." Her age seemed more of an issue to her than presents.

"A birthday's a birthday, no matter what."

She considered, then said, "All right, here's something."

"Fire away."

"Take me away from here. Someplace where we can be all by ourselves."

Fair enough. After a month of being cooped up in their tiny place, it was time for them to have a short getaway. "Where to?"

"How about up north, somewhere cold? We could sit all day and look at the snow."

He imagined a lingering visit in a white landscape.

The following Saturday Kuki and Rinko set off for Nikko by train. He had tried to find the sort of place she'd described where they could be alone and look out at the snowy scenery. The northern Tohoku and Hokuriku areas were too far away, and in case of a major snowfall, they would have trouble getting back. Heavy snow warnings had been issued for the whole Hokuriku region over the weekend. In the end, he decided on Lake Chuzenji in Nikko, a relatively short hop from Tokyo. He had been there once in midwinter over a decade ago, and had never forgotten the hushed beauty of the blue lake surrounded by snow-covered mountains. It would be wonderful just to relax with her in such a peaceful place.

She had never been there in the winter. "I've only been to Nikko once, and that was toward the end of summer."

"When?"

"Ages ago. In high school."

What had she been like? He imagined a lovely young girl with the same poise and intelligence.

"We drove to Oku-Nikko, but the road was so crowded we had a terrible time."

"At this time of year, there won't be anybody there."

She nodded, then asked suddenly, "What time will we get back to Tokyo tomorrow?"

"In a hurry?" He had left the return trip open.

"Not really."

"If we check out around eleven, I guess we could be back home early in the afternoon."

Rinko seemed to turn that information over in her mind, but she said nothing more, just giving a small nod.

From Asakusa to Nikko took nearly two hours by express train. When they pulled out of Tokyo the weather was clear, but along the way the sky clouded over, and just past Tochigi it started to snow. Kuki had a sweater on under a black overcoat with a dark red muffler. Rinko had on a black turtleneck sweater and black pants, a wine-red half-coat, and a gray hat. Kuki thought they must look like lovers rather than man and wife, because Rinko was so carefree and gay.

The wind picked up, slanting the falling snow. It piled up on fields, on farmhouse roofs, and on tree branches until the scene from the window looked like a monochrome ink drawing.

"It's as if we've come far, far away," Rinko murmured, her eyes on the enveloping whiteness. Kuki felt the same.

They arrived in Nikko after three and took a taxi to Lake Chuzenji. As they climbed up the Iroha Driveway, full of steep hairpin curves and named for the first three letters of the curving Japanese syllabary, the flanks of the mountains pressed in on them through the continuing snowfall. The higher they climbed, the colder the air became, and the more powdery the snow.

"Is it snowing up by the lake, too?" Kuki asked the driver.

Looking straight ahead through the swishing of the windshield wipers, he replied, "Conditions are different at different elevations." Winds sweeping in from the Japan Sea dumped moisture on the mountains north of Lake Chuzenji, he explained, while to the south the amount of snowfall was far less. "It won't amount to much," he predicted.

Kuki nodded and squeezed Rinko's hand. She gave a squeeze back.

From the right, a mountain suddenly came in closer, as if trying to peer in at the lovers. This was Mount Nantai, "male figure"—a name well suited to its rugged shape. As they stared up its steep slopes, the winds at the summit seemed to blow off the storm clouds; by the time they reached the top, the snow was thinning, and then all at once the sky cleared and the sun was out.

It was just before four o'clock. There was still time before evening set in.

"Since the weather's cleared, why don't we go see the falls first, and then go to the hotel?" Kuki instructed the driver to take them to Kegon Falls.

"Might be frozen, mind you," he warned them, but the idea of a frozen waterfall had an appeal of its own.

To see all 318 feet of the falls, they had to take an elevator down to an observation platform. Just as the driver had said it would be, the top of the waterfall was a cascade of icicles, partly covered with snow and partly shining blue in the sun like a magnificent ice sculpture. Closer examination revealed that underneath all that ice the falls was still alive, a trickle of water still dropping down the face of the rocks into the gorge hundreds of feet below.

"There's something magical about a waterfall in winter," said Rinko, her hands thrust into the pockets of her coat. She gazed at it for a while and then pointed to some poles sticking out of the rocks to their right. "What's that?"

"A kind of life-saving device, I'd say, to catch anyone who falls from above." Netting was strung across the poles in a fan shape. "This is a famous suicide spot." So many people had once made their way to the top of the waterfall and flung themselves down toward the basin below that a barrier had been constructed on top, too, to discourage would-be suicides.

"A long time ago there was a high school kid, just eighteen years old, who said, 'Mark my words, it's a mystery,' and jumped to his death here."

"What did he mean? Life?"

"Life, or the human heart, or himself. Or maybe all of it, all of the imponderables."

Rinko nodded as she stood there before the frozen falls, her face shining in the slanting rays of the sun.

At four-thirty they arrived at their inn. They were shown to their tatami rooms, consisting of a large sitting room with a smaller room attached, and a wide, enclosed veranda directly overlooking the lake. They stood by the window, drawn by the lake, as the sun prepared to set.

To their right was the rugged form of Mount Nantai, its cryptomeria forests and snow-covered flanks bathed red in the sun's waning light. The Shirane Mountains far in the distance and the range of mountains stretching off to the left were completely covered in snow, and nestled in their bosom lay the hushed and wintry lake. There was no sign of a boat on the water, nor any human form on the land. It was a world of utter peace and silence, scarcely changed from what it must have been like in ancient times.

"It's awesome," said Rinko softly. Kuki shared the feeling. The scene was one of awe-inspiring grandeur. No word like "beautiful" or "lovely" could do it justice.

They stood mesmerized as the lake transformed itself before their eyes. Just moments before, the mountain had been red, but slowly the sunset color faded until the world before them was starkly monochromatic. The surface of the lake went from razor-sharp indigo to dark navy blue, subsiding into a gray against which the snowy shores of the lake shone even whiter under the darkening sky.

Slowly but surely, the lake was engulfed in the oncoming darkness.

His eyes never leaving the sight, Kuki put his arm around Rinko's shoulders and waited for her to turn to him before kissing her quietly and deeply. To kiss before the gods inhabiting the lake seemed at once a sacrilege and a solemn vow of love. They sat side by side on veranda chairs until the scene was wrapped entirely in darkness, the lake sunk into the black of night. Only a necklace of lights around the rim suggested its round shape.

"This place used to be off limits to women," said Kuki, remembering something he'd read. "Women couldn't climb Mount Nantai."

"Why not? Because they were considered unclean?"

"Partly that, but if you ask me, I think men might have been afraid of them—of their black magic."

"Women have black magic?"

"Probably."

"Are you afraid of me?"

Suddenly faced with the question, Kuki slowly nodded.

She gave him a solemn look and said, "All right then, maybe I'll drag you off."

"Drag me where?"

"To the bottom of the lake."

She looked back at the window, where tiny snowflakes were falling aslant against the dark glass. It was amazing how quickly the weather could change at this altitude. In the few minutes they'd been talking, it had started to snow again.

"The snow falls the same everywhere, whether on the mountain or on the lake, doesn't it?"

Kuki nodded absently, mulling over her threat to drag him off to the bottom of the lake. She couldn't possibly do that in real life, he knew, and yet, deep down, it seemed to him she had in her the kind of passion that was capable of doing exactly that: dragging a man down and down, till he touched the very bottom.

"It must be snowing on that waterfall, too," she went on. "What a cold place to die that would be."

"Yes, but they say dying in the snow is actually quite painless." He passed on a piece of information a friend from the northernmost island of Hokkaido had told him. "When they find a body lying face down in the snow, the expression on the face is always calm and beautiful."

"That's nice. If death is inevitable, it might as well be beautiful."

Going on in this vein would cast too strange a spell over the evening, he thought, and he moved away from the night-filled window back to the sitting room. They had arranged to have dinner at six-thirty. Before that, they changed into cotton yukata provided by the inn and went downstairs for a bath.

Their room had a private bath, but since they were at a hot spring Rinko wanted to try the large communal bath, and Kuki went, too. They went down to the first floor and followed a turning and twisting corridor to the end. The maid showing them the way made the comment that they had so few guests they might as well bathe together in the family area if they wished. They declined, going separately to the men's and women's baths.

Ordinarily these would be crowded at this hour, a little before six, but there were no other bathers. Kuki stretched out full length in the steaming water, luxuriating in the spaciousness and privacy. When he had finished, he went back upstairs and was watching TV when Rinko returned.

"It was nice and quiet and relaxing," she said. Apparently the women's bath had also been deserted. Her damp hair was twisted on top of her head, her cheeks and neck slightly flushed. "I went in the outdoor bath, too."

There had been a small side door at one end of the men's bath leading to an outdoor bath, but as it was snowing, Kuki hadn't ventured out.

"I walked barefoot in the snow."

Imagining her tiptoeing naked through the falling snow stirred something in him.

"But when I went in the water, it was warm and wonderful. It felt so strange—snow falling all around, yet I was snug and warm."

"Maybe I'll try it later."

"When I looked up, I could see snowflakes falling out of the black sky, landing and melting on my eyelashes."

The maid appeared with their dinner. "We haven't anything special at this time of year, I'm afraid," she said apologetically, but it was a feast: appetizers followed by sashimi and assorted fried things, plus a bubbling hotpot and even roast duck. "Just ring the bell if you need anything."

After she left and they were finally alone, Rinko poured out some hot saké and Kuki leaned back in contentment, enjoying the cozy ambience of a Japanese inn in winter. For a while they continued sipping their saké, keeping one another's cups filled and letting the comfortable warmth spread through them. They had shared meals before in their Shibuya apartment, but doing so here in the snowy inn so far away from Tokyo made them feel they had entered another world.

"I'm so glad we came," sighed Rinko. It had been her idea, her birthday present. "Thank you." Her eyes were slightly red at the corners, an effect of the saké. There was fire in her sweetness.

Embarrassed by her gratitude, Kuki got up and took a small bottle of whiskey from the refrigerator. "Shall we have some of this over there?" He moved to the veranda chairs, making them each a Scotch and water while Rinko phoned down that they were finished with dinner.

"It's still snowing, isn't it," she said, joining him. The wind seemed to have got stronger. The snow was blowing sideways now, forming little piles under the eaves. "I want it to go on all night," she murmured as if to herself. She bent forward to put ice in her glass, and from the loosened neck of her cotton robe he could see the roundness of her breasts.

Kuki was strongly tempted to slip his hand inside her yukata, but then the door opened and the maid came in. "We've come to clear the dishes," she said, and set to work assisted by a young woman. When every trace of the meal had been whisked away, a man came to lay out the bedding.

Waiting, Kuki sipped his drink and looked out the windows at the falling snow. The moment they were gone, he murmured "Finally," in relief.

Two sets of futon were laid out side by side on the tatami mats, with a small lantern at their head. He wondered fleetingly how the inn people had them categorized? He took another sip of his Scotch and water. Beer and saké at dinner, and now whiskey. He was fairly drunk, but he felt good. The prospect of a night here with her made all the difference. Being far from Tokyo in this snow country made it easy to forget work and home, and relax.

"How about one more?" he said, taking another small bottle of Scotch from the refrigerator.

"Are you sure that's a good idea?"

"Probably not." He poured whiskey over the ice cubes in his glass. "I might not be much use tonight."

Understanding, she said huffily, "That's all right, I certainly don't care."

Amused by her show of anger, he started to refill her glass, but she stopped him with her hand. She wasn't a drinker and never had been, but through him she had come to appreciate the pleasure of mild intoxication.

"Let's go over there," he suggested. That glimpse of cleavage was as tantalizing as ever, but as long as they sat across from each other, there was no way he could touch her. Picking up the bottle and glass, he went over to the low table in a corner of the other room, motioning for her to come sit beside him. She trotted over and sat next to him on the tatami. The moment she reached out to put ice in his glass, his hand slipped inside the top of her yukata. She drew back; but with his hand now cupped firmly around her breast, he wasn't about to let go.

"Behave," she said. She tried modestly to pull her neckline together, but he only slid his hand in deeper. Soon the two of them were rolling on the floor, tussling. Inch by inch he dragged her over to the futon, and then lay on top of her with his arms around her, kissing her. Smothered by his kisses, she twisted her head from side to side to feebly protest this sudden attack. Soon, as the fight drained from her body, he could sense her first relax and then begin to respond.

When he was sure she wanted him, he got up and closed the sliding doors to the veranda, turned off the room light, and switched on the lantern at the head of their futon. Rinko lay with her eyes closed, as if to minimize the effects of her drinking. He pulled apart her yukata at the neck and gently slid his hand over the white breast beneath. At this snowbound inn on the shores of the old lake, the only one watching them was the bedside lantern. Emboldened by the thought, he pulled the garment further apart and gazed at her breasts, then laid his face between them.

He supposed he had had too much to drink; all he wanted was to lose himself in her softness.

As he lay still, scarcely breathing, she said softly, "I tried burying my face in the snow." At the outside bath, she must mean. "That's what you said, isn't it? That if you're dying in the snow, you should bury your face in it?"

"That must have felt cold."

"But it didn't. Little by little, the snow all around my face warmed and melted away; but then when I lifted my face up again, the air was really cold."

"So it was warmer in the snow?"

"Yes. It was a little painful, but the snow around me kept melting, more and more, and then I thought, if I fall asleep now I'll die."

Was that what she'd been doing in the outdoor bath, amid the falling snow? Disturbed, Kuki propped himself up on an elbow. She was gazing dreamily into space.

There were times when he couldn't tell what she was thinking. Here he'd been assuming that she went in the outdoor bath for the sheer fun of it, and all along she'd been sticking her face in the snow, pretending to die! Of course, she was only playacting, but the fact that she could do it at all gave him the willies.

"What did you do a thing like that for?"

"I felt like it."

She shifted over onto her side, her back to him. He fitted himself around her, sliding his hands over her breasts.

"Quiet, isn't it," she said, letting him hold her.

By the snowy lake there was no sound of traffic, nor could they hear any footsteps or voices. Listening intently, the only sound they could make out in the enveloping stillness was the whisper of falling snow.

"What time do you think it is?" she asked.

"Not yet ten."

City night life would just be getting under way.

"Smooth as silk." He slid his hands slowly down her belly. Ordinarily he wouldn't have stopped there, but tonight he'd had a bit too much to drink. He wanted nothing more than to drift off with his hands on her soft skin. "Fresh as a peach." He felt the swell of her hips against his body.

"I'm not young any more."

"Only thirty-eight."

"An old lady."

"Ha."

"No, I am." She added in a muffled voice, "This is enough for me."

"Enough?"

"I've lived long enough. I don't need anything more."

"You mean you're ready to die?"

"Yes. I'm not greedy."

He must have gone to sleep. At what point in the conversation he'd drifted off, he couldn't say, but clearly he had succumbed to his drunken lassitude and shut his eyes. When thirst woke him a bit later, he found the lantern switched off and a dim light from the adjoining room filtering through the transom. Before he went to sleep the lantern had been on, so Rinko must have roused herself and turned it off. They had been lying close together, but now they were slightly apart, both still on their side.

He reached out, switched on the lantern, and checked the time. Three A.M. Still the middle of the night. But since they had gone to bed around ten, that was a good five hours' sleep.

Thirst drove him out of bed. He got up and took a bottle of mineral water from the refrigerator, poured a glassful, and took it out to the veranda, where he nudged open the curtains. The sky was still black, the snow still coming down as hard as ever. It was piled as high as the window. That evening, Rinko had buried her face in the snow, he remembered. He couldn't understand at the time why she would do such a crazy thing, but now it came back to him: he'd said that the faces of people found dead in the snow were beautiful. He took another swallow of water and kept looking steadily out the window at the falling snow. Gradually his mind cleared.

Yes, and just before he'd fallen asleep, she'd called herself an old lady, that was it. Something about having lived long enough. He turned around and looked into the bedroom. Surely she wasn't thinking seriously about dying.

With some anxiety, he went back in and saw her sleeping peacefully on her side. He bent down for a closer look in the lamplight. Her long lashes were closed, and her small, well-molded nose cast a slight shadow on one cheek. No one lying asleep with so peaceful a look on her face could possibly be entertaining thoughts of death. Telling himself this, he gently slid shut the doors to the veranda and crawled back into the futon.

As before, he eased his arms gently around her, cupping his hands over her breasts and letting his fingers graze the nipples. She stirred and gave a fretful little cry, hunching over as if to avoid him. She needed more sleep. He left off and closed his eyes again, still pressing close to her smooth skin from behind.

What was as wonderful to touch as human skin? Everyone had their likes and dislikes, the chemistry had to be right, yet for both men and women, the sense of skin on skin was deeply soothing. As long as two people could lie like this, irritation and impatience, anxiety and fear all simply melted away. If only people could maintain this essential contact, strife would cease; but the pressures of work and daily life made that impossible. Going to the office, meeting with other people—all of that pulled lovers apart. Morals and "common sense" got in the way, too, cutting drastically into the amount of time people could spend like this.

Fortunately, right now he could revel in her softness everywhere. He lay pressed to her like a spoon, his chest against her back, his belly and loins fitting snugly around her hips, his legs bent exactly parallel to hers from knee to ankle and his arms encircling her, one hand on her breast, one on her belly. Surely a body this warm, this comforting, could never grow still and cold. Reassuring himself yet again, he drifted back into a deep sleep.

When he awoke, he thought he heard her calling to him. Half asleep, he opened his eyes at the sound of her voice. She was sitting up in the futon. "Look at that snow."

He lifted his head and looked toward the veranda. "What time is it?"

"Still only six."

He looked around, sat up, and went over to the veranda. The curtain was slightly open. It was still dark out, not only because sunrise came late but because of the snow. Against a solid black background, the snow struck the windowpane like tiny white arrows before vanishing.

"It's pretty wild out there." He remembered that on the way up, Rinko had been concerned about what time they would leave. "It's bound to stop by noon, though."

No hurry about getting up, under the circumstances. He went back to bed and invited her to join him. She readjusted the neck of her yukata and slipped in beside him without a sound.

Savoring her delicious warmth, he untied her obi and pulled the robe open. Last night he'd been too drunk to do anything but fall asleep with her in his arms; now, as if to make up for lost time, he began to caress her, waiting for her to grow moist, catch fire. After a good sleep, he felt full of renewed vigor.

In no time she was wet, and he moved closer. As if on cue, there was a low, moaning gust of wind. Simultaneously, he was seized by a wild impulse and tore off the sheet.

"What's the matter?"

Ignoring her surprise, he peeled off the thin yukata, leaving her completely naked. Inside this old inn, amid a swirling blizzard, lay a woman without a stitch on, every curve of her bewitching body open to his view—but no one else knew it, neither the people in the inn nor the whipping winds.

Another rush of snowy wind went by with a low roar.

In complete contrast to the blizzard outside, their room was warm and snug. The low lamplight played upon her naked figure. Kuki knelt at her feet and gazed down at her white, rich flesh, then slowly bent over and placed his lips on her breast. Anyone peering between the sliding doors just then would have seen what appeared to be a man genuflecting in worship before a naked woman. And indeed, at the time he felt profound gratitude and reverence toward the creator of this beauty, and toward Rinko, for her generosity in displaying it.

He remained for a while with his face on her breast, then gradually let it slide down her smooth belly until he reached the light thicket below, where again he pressed his lips. She responded with a tiny sigh and a wriggle that prompted him to look up as if just noticing her.

Kisses were all very well, but she yearned now for physical connection.

With a practiced hand, he reached for a pillow and slid it under her hips. She understood, and cooperated by arching her back and raising her pelvis, thighs slightly parted. Of all the positions a woman might assume, this, he thought, was the most erotic, the most provocative. His desire inflamed, Kuki drew his hips closer, lightly hoisting her legs and parting them wider before he slid himself between and slowly entered her.

Just then, another gust of wind tore past with a groan, and his body seemed to move in response. His loins fast against hers, he moved gently to and fro. The secret here was for Kuki to keep his hips slightly lowered, repeating the rhythmic motion again and again until her body, at first a bit hesitant and restrained, began gradually to twist in excitement. Again and again he drove into her, pushing and kneading, always from below, until she was overwhelmed with pleasure. Her mouth was open, her breath coming faster until she was panting.

No longer lording it over her now but joined to her, he felt himself losing control as they thrust and shook, thrust and shook, until he exploded inside her … and then collapsed—a limp rag, draped across a body that had the sheen of glossy silk.

Whether a woman can still find a man lovable in that rag-doll state depends on how ardent he has been, how sweetly suffused with love she is. Here in the winter inn, Rinko sensually snuggled up to the man lying spent beside her, enfolding his body with hers, and slowly rubbed his shoulder with one hand. She was now doing to Kuki exactly what he'd done to her before they made love. The banquet over, she was floating on a sea of abundance while he lay wilted and drained, in the calm of the dead.

Yet he managed to rouse himself from that state. If he continued to lie still with his eyes closed, sleep would overtake him, he knew, and that would mean leaving a physically satisfied woman feeling lonely, perhaps, and vulnerable. Overcoming an immense lethargy, he summoned all his strength to reach for her and draw her near. This time, of course, no fresh pleasure or thrill would arise from her nearness. But the cycle was completed only when they lay touching again, at peace. To accomplish this he put his arms around her, offering his chest as a pillow, and together they fell into a doze amid the swirling blizzard.

More time passed before Kuki woke up again and rolled over, rousing Rinko in the process.

"What time is it?" she asked.

He checked the clock and reported that it was past nine. Unwilling to get out of bed just yet, they lingered as they were, lightly dozing. Again, from beyond the veranda came the low roar of the wind.

"It's still snowing, isn't it?"

He nodded, and after a brief interval got up and opened the curtains.

Nothing but a swirl of white. After coming down all night, still the snow showed no sign of abating. It was coming down harder, if anything. Just before dawn, the window had appeared black. Now in the light of day it was solid white, the outside scenery all but invisible, only the eaves under the veranda showing up dark.

"Is it going to stop?" She too got up and peered out worriedly.

Earlier, he'd predicted it would stop by noon, but even then he had lacked conviction. As they stood there looking out at the driving snow, a voice called out, asking if they were awake. It was one of last night's maids. They had ordered breakfast for ten, and she was here to ready the room.

"Quite a snowstorm," Kuki commented, his arms folded.

Opening the veranda curtains all the way, she replied, "You know, this hardly ever happens, but today the newspaper couldn't get through on account of the snow."

"Is the road closed?"

"It's so steep, they might not be able to get up."

He remembered the hairpin curves on the Iroha Driveway. "We'd like to leave by eleven."

"The manager is getting in touch with the people below, so please wait a little longer." She bowed and left.

Rinko rubbed the window with her finger in obvious concern. Watching her, it struck him for the first time that they were trapped here at Lake Chuzenji. Snowbound. One of the main reasons he'd chosen Nikko for this outing was its proximity to Tokyo, and the convenience of the transportation. Naturally it would be cold at this time of year, he'd expected that—but not that the road would be closed.

Worried, he switched on the TV to catch the local weather report. A strong low-pressure area was in place all the way from the northern Hokuriku districts down to Tokyo, with continuing storms predicted for the remainder of the day. As they watched the report, a man came and put away the futon, while another woman poured tea and laid out their breakfast. Here in the room it was warm and pleasant, but outside it was snowing so hard they couldn't have kept their eyes open had they dared to step out.

"Snow like this happens once a year at most," the woman said apologetically. Her sympathy was not enough to clear the skies.

"What about chains?"

"The wind makes such high drifts on the road that they don't work."

Going down that twisty road in this weather would be a nightmare, anyway. He began to eat in resignation. Rinko seemed too upset to eat.

"What time did you have to be back, again?"

"Three, if possible."

To reach Tokyo by then meant leaving within the hour. "An appointment of some kind?" She only looked troubled, and said nothing. He let it drop. Sadly, there was no way to get her back on time.

They finished eating and were watching television again when the manager came in to explain that all traffic between Chuzenji and Nikko was halted. Would they be so good as to wait here in their room for a while?

"When do you expect the road to reopen?"

"Nothing can be done till the snow stops. That might not be till this evening."

Kuki turned around and looked at Rinko. She was pale, and her head hung down.

An hour later, it was still snowing. The flakes were small and powdery now, not coming down as thickly, but driven hard in the wind. Here and there, snowdrifts had formed.

"I'm afraid it's hopeless," she said. Getting back to Tokyo by three seemed out of the question.

"You should call."

Thinking she might find it awkward with him in the room, he went down to the big bath for another soak. On the way, he passed by the front desk, and saw seven or eight guests all packed and ready to leave, staring outside. They all appeared frustrated at being held up by the snow.

After bathing in the deserted bath, he went back upstairs and found Rinko sitting in front of the mirror, rubbing the corners of her eyes.

"Everything okay?"

She shook her head. "I told them I couldn't make it."

"Make what?"

"My niece's wedding reception."

"You have a niece?"

"It's his niece, actually."

Missing such an important family event would be a disaster. "What time does it start?"

"The ceremony is at five, but I was only going to attend the reception afterward."

It was almost noon. Even if the road opened up this minute, by the time they got to Tokyo it would be nearly four. Adding in the time it would take for her to go home and change, there was no hope.

"Does he know you're here?"

"Yes, I told him…"

"Is that okay, then?" The moment he said it, he could have bitten his tongue. The day of her husband's niece's wedding, she was off at a hot spring with another man, snowbound, unable to return. There was no way things could be okay.

They avoided the subject as the afternoon wore on, the snow showing no sign of abating. Watching the hour hand on his watch crawl from two to three, Kuki considered what to do. Even if the snow stopped now, it would be another hour or two before the snowplows were out and the road cleared. That meant an arrival time in Tokyo of eight or nine. If that was the best they could hope for, it might make more sense to give up and spend another night here.

Rinko was upset, but Kuki would have problems of his own to face if they stayed another night. He'd told his wife to expect him back sometime today, saying nothing about a trip to Nikko. As far as she knew, he was in Kyoto doing research. It would be a little awkward to have her find out he was stuck in the mountains somewhere. And even if he managed to smooth that over somehow, tomorrow was Monday, and he had an important meeting at ten. They'd have to leave awfully early in the morning for him to make that.

Still, for Rinko it would be worse. On top of missing the wedding, if she stayed out another night, what would happen? Things had not been going well at home. In all probability, the situation would just get uglier.

As he mulled these things over, three o'clock came and went. The maid served them some hot coffee. After she left, Kuki asked Rinko what she wanted to do. She said nothing, slowly stirring her coffee.

"Eventually it's got to stop, of course, but it could end up with us having to spend another night here."

"What about you?" she asked.

"I'd rather get back if I could, but if I can't, I can't."

"I don't mind."

"But you—"

She cut him off, raising her head. "We've no choice, have we?"

He couldn't argue with that.

"I've given up," she said in an undertone.

After four o'clock the snow began to let up a little, but evening came on fast. Lake Chuzenji was dark and silent.

As Kuki stood gazing at the scene, the manager came in and explained that temperatures would fall below freezing after dark, making the road even more impassable. He invited them to stay a second night at no extra charge. They had no other option. The other guests had all reportedly resigned themselves to the inevitable, and Kuki likewise gave in and nodded.

Rinko listened to the exchange standing beside him. She had seen it coming, and said only, "I'm going to take a bath," on her way out the door.

Alone, Kuki looked out on a single light at the edge of the lake, floating up in the darkness. He was remembering their two nights in Hakone last fall. That time, they were not forcibly detained, but had chosen to stay the second night on their own. There had been the pleasant thrill of embarking together on a mad adventure. Tonight, it was an uncontrollable natural event forcing them to stay on. The situation was devoid of any sense of fun or playfulness. He felt oppressed, cornered. Changes over the past few months were clearly to blame.

When they went to Hakone, the knowledge that their respective marriages were strong enough to withstand a couple of nights away from home had given him an inner security and sense of well-being. Spending an extra night together would make no ultimate difference, he'd been sure then, but this time it was different. His failure to go home tonight would have dire consequences.

He got up and went back to the table for a smoke, thinking of what Rinko had said: "I've given up." Given up on what—on going back tonight, or on maintaining the semblance of a normal relationship with her husband? The latter, more likely. Had she made up her mind to leave him? Then he, Kuki, would be compelled to make his own tough choice. Watching the windows become steeped in blackness, he faced the fact that he and Rinko were being slowly driven to the wall.

Night came on and they sat down to dinner, both having bathed. Outwardly everything was the same as the night before, but their mood was altogether different. Then they had just arrived at the inn; the view of Lake Chuzenji from their veranda, the big hot-spring bath downstairs with its outdoor section, all had been fresh and exciting. Tonight there was nothing to lift their spirits. They felt resigned, even slightly defiant.

No use brooding, Kuki told himself, and she evidently reached the same conclusion. At dinner, the pace of their drinking increased, as if that would help them forget this unpleasantness. She helped herself to the lightly chilled saké, drinking it boldly down.

In Tokyo, by now the reception would be under way. Her husband would be studying the empty chair next to him with suppressed rage, while his relatives looked on with mounting suspicion. Just imagining it made the blood rise to Kuki's head. He took another drink.

They'd begun dinner around six, and by eight, as they were finishing, the corners of Rinko's eyes were red, her cheeks flushed. The alcohol seemed to be having its effect. Suddenly she staggered to her feet.

"I know—I'll put my face in the snow again. Want to come?" She started for the door, but Kuki quickly restrained her.

"You're drunk. It's not safe."

"So who cares?—I'll die anyway sometime." She tried to shake him off and go. With her hair tousled, her eyes burning, she was strangely seductive. "Come on, you come with me."

"Wait." He put his hands on her shoulders and forced her to sit down.

"It feels so good. Why are you stopping me…"

She was disgruntled, but he ignored her and phoned for someone to clear away their dinner dishes and lay out the futon. Plainly, she had her limits with alcohol, and she'd had way too much, downing glass after glass of cold saké right after her bath.

"I said let's go. Why won't you?"

She wouldn't let go of the idea of going out into the snow, but Kuki went ahead and had them lay out the futon. As long as the maids were in the room, she sat quietly in a corner, but as soon as they were gone she staggered to her feet.

"No." He moved to stop her, and as she struggled to get past him, their legs became entangled and they fell in a heap on one corner of the futon, Kuki supine with Rinko draped across him. She picked herself up and straddled him like a rider on a horse. For an instant, she looked down at him in triumph. Then, with a glitter in her eyes like a panther eyeing its prey, she put her hands around his neck.

"What now? Okay, okay." He assumed she was playing around, but perhaps because she'd had so much to drink, she had unusual strength. "Damn it, Rinko, cut it out." He tried to get the words out, but his voice was muffled. Unable to breathe, he choked, but instead of releasing her grip, she pushed harder. He felt himself slipping toward unconsciousness. Above him, her eyes burned bright.

What the hell was she doing? Doubt brought sudden fear. Struggling to get hold of her hands, he tore them from his throat. After a fit of coughing, he drew one long shuddering breath and said hoarsely, "I thought I was going to die."

"Well, yes," she said coldly. "I thought I was going to kill you." Then, still straddling him, she commanded, "Give it to me now, the way we are."

She on top, he supporting her from below: they had made love in this position more than once, but always at his request, she with some diffidence initially. It was hard for her at first to be so fully exposed to his gaze, but gradually, the more they tried it out, the more he sensed her starting to enjoy it. These more unconventional positions were no less fun for her than for him. Even so, such a straight-out request was something new. Was it the saké, or the accident of finding herself astride him—or the knowledge that it was too late to go home?

He resettled her above him, gazing up at her nakedness as he took hold of himself with one hand. She had her eyes closed, but she bent back as she was told to do, hands placed lightly over her breasts as if to hide them. He drew her arms away so that nothing covered her, and then, parting her flesh with his hand, he slowly entered her. She gave a tiny sigh and twisted her body, but he plunged deeper until she let out a long, low cry that seemed to come from her very bowels. He was fitted snugly inside her now, all of him.

She arched backward slowly as far as she could, then gradually leaned forward, repeating this rocking motion several times until she hit upon the point of sweetest pleasure, her movements suddenly accelerating.

With his hands lightly on her hips from below, he gazed up at her blissfully, taking it all in: the growing flush on her face, the swaying of her breasts, the hollows and shadows of her belly. Soon her hair fell in greater disarray, half covering her face, and her features were contorted, as if she were on the point of weeping. This was it, her moment of supreme pleasure. Even as the thought came to him, like black wings her hands came out and wound around his neck.

He had never come this way before. Flat on his back while she mounted the heights of pleasure, astride him … that in itself was not unusual, but now she was gripping him tightly by the neck. They had crossed a line. This perhaps was a perversion.

His consciousness dimmed. He thought he might die.

Another minute, another twenty or thirty seconds, and it might have been the end. He felt as if he'd caught a glimpse of the world of death. The next moment, his consciousness returned with a spasm of coughing, and he knew that he was still alive.

It was some time before he grew aware of Rinko, lying slumped sideways. Yes, he had seen her crumple, hair flying as she cried out—

he couldn't remember the exact words. There was no doubting one thing: both of them had come at exactly the same moment.

As he traced his slowly returning memories, Kuki tentatively moved his arms and legs. Everything worked, knees included. No damage done. He gazed at the lantern, and it came back to him: this was a room in a suite looking out on Lake Chuzenji.

Rinko turned toward him, nestling close. "My God, that was incredible."

For Kuki it had been no less so. "I almost died," he said. "Just a little more…"

She nodded. "Now you know what I mean, when I say I'm scared."

Yes, she sometimes did say that. So this was what she meant. He retraced the contours of the experience in his mind, then thought of something else. "Kichizo said the same thing."

"Who?"

"The man strangled by Sada Abe." Images of the two lovers floated through his mind, based on what he'd read.

Rinko's interest was caught. Her voice still sounding exhausted, she repeated, "Sada Abe? The woman who did that grotesque thing?"

"It wasn't especially grotesque."

"She mutilated her lover and then killed him, didn't she?"

She knew only the sensational aspects of the case. Kuki, having read up on it in some detail, saw it rather as a deeply human incident between a man and a woman hopelessly in love. "She was misrepresented in the media." He nudged away the lantern, and added quietly in the half-light, "She did cut it off, but that was after she strangled him, not before."

"A woman strangling a man?"

"She'd done it often enough before, during sex. Like you, just now."

Rinko immediately shook her head and clung to his chest. "I only did it because I love you, I love you so much I can't stand it, I almost hate you…"

"She was the same. She was crazy about him. She didn't want to share him with anyone else, ever, and so she made up her mind to strangle him."

"Going as far as killing him?"

"Yes." He rubbed his own neck. "That was close, just now."

"No, don't you remember? I did it once before, for fun. I was remembering that, and I just tried it again."

"Sada started out the same way, for fun. The two of them would take turns choking each other during sex."

"With their hands?"

"She took to using her kimono cord. When she pulled on it hard, he would swell up inside her, and that felt good."

"Tell me," she said, winding her legs around his: "What about when I had my hands around your neck? Did it feel good?"

In the beginning it had been excruciating, but then he'd stopped caring. Everything had ceased to matter. "It was rough at first," he admitted, "but later I guess it might not be so bad."

"I knew it. Next time, I want you to do it to me, all right?"

"Choke you?"

"Yes. Just before I come. You know what I mean. Right then."

Gently he slid his hands around her neck, so slender that it fitted completely in his grasp. He applied pressure, and quietly she closed her eyes, her compliance endearing. He pressed still harder, feeling the cartilage in her throat and the throb of her pulse, continuing to press until her chin came up and she burst into violent coughing. Alarmed then, he pulled away.

She coughed a few more times and, when her breathing was quiet, said, "It's scary, but I think I understand." Her eyes were distant. "Sada used a kimono cord, you say? That would hurt more, wouldn't it?"

"They were fooling around the night before it happened, taking turns half-strangling each other, and she went too far and very nearly killed him. The cord left a red welt around his neck, and his face swelled up and turned bright red. She cooled it off for him and went out to get some medicine, which gave him some relief, but later that night as he was lying in a stupor, he told her, 'You're going to do it again tonight, aren't you? This time, don't stop. Go all the way. Letting go halfway hurts too much.'"

"But if he died, it would be the end."

"Maybe that's what she wanted, for it all to be over."

"Because she loved him?"

"And didn't want anyone else ever to have him."

A gust of wind swept by in front of the veranda. The lamplight flickered. Outside, the snow had stopped, but the wind was as strong as ever.

After a pause, as if she too had been listening to the wind, Rinko said, "What did Sada do for a living?'

"Kichizo ran a restaurant in Nakano, Tokyo, and she worked as a waitress there."

"So that's where they met."

"She was thirty-one, and he was eleven years older, forty-two. He wore his hair in a square, flattop style, and he had an oval face. A dashing, handsome guy. Sada had worked as a geisha from the age of seventeen or eighteen, so she must have matured early. She had beautiful skin, and apparently she had a strange power over men."

It was six months since he had looked into the case, but last December he happened to have reread a contemporary newspaper account, and the details were clear in his mind.

"Then maybe it was she who seduced him."

"No, he made the first move, but she was already in love with him then."

"Was he married?"

"Yes, to a fine wife, but one look at Sada and he was lost."

"They couldn't have been alone at work, though."

"That's why they stayed in a succession of inns and teahouses." As he talked, Kuki began to feel as if he were telling their own story.

"Did his wife find out?"

"Of course. That made it all the harder for him to go home, so they went from place to place. The day of the incident, they'd spent an entire week in the same teahouse."

"Without once going home?"

"They might have wanted to, but once they missed their chance, they couldn't."

Another burst of wind came. Both of them felt how the plight of the trapped lovers, Sada and Kichizo, had a close bearing on their own.

"Neither of them suggested it to the other, did they?"

"Of course, the reason they stayed on day after day was they couldn't bear the thought of saying good-bye—and for her, letting him go home meant sending him back to the arms of his wife."

"I know." She grabbed him suddenly by the elbow, and instinctively he drew back. "A woman can't help feeling that way."

Somewhat disconcerted by the intensity in her voice, he said, "I doubt if he wanted to go back, anyway." This bit of self-defense, disguised as Kichizo's imagined state of mind, seemed to placate her.

"Then it was more like a double suicide than murder, really."

"She did mean to kill herself, too."

"But before that, she cut off his … private parts."

Kuki nodded, remembering the newspaper account. "They found him with her kimono cord wrapped around his neck, and bits of him cut off and gone. Not only that, she'd written 'Sadakichi us two' in big letters on the sheet, in bright red blood. She wrote the same thing on the man's left thigh, and on his left arm she'd carved just her name, 'Sada.'"

"It's scary." She clung tighter to his chest.

"She killed him around two in the morning. That same morning she went out by herself, and when they found his body around noon, all hell broke loose. But the thing she wrote gave away their identities, and I don't think she had any mind to escape."

"What happened to the parts she cut off?"

"She wrapped them up carefully in tissue paper, then wound his loincloth around her waist and tucked them inside. She went around wearing them next to her that way."

It was not a pleasant bit of the tale to relate. He'd drawn close to her for comfort, but now all of a sudden he was aware of her hand lightly holding his penis. When had that happened? They were lying naked, face to face, so it wasn't altogether unnatural for her to be touching him, but given the present topic of conversation, he found it unnerving.

He drew back a little, but she maintained her grip, sliding down under the sheet. What was she up to now? He felt her lips encircle his flesh, followed a moment later by her warm breath. "Hey..." She had kissed him there before, somewhat shyly, but never had she taken him so far into her mouth. With a sudden surge of pleasure, his body jerked, and she let go. Holding his hardened flesh in one hand, she asked, "Is this where she cut?"

Unable to answer, he only shook his head.

"It wasn't only this, was it?"

"No. There, and behind..."

"Here," she said, lightly touching his scrotum. "And where did she go with them?"

"She wandered all over the city, planning to die. But she couldn't bring herself to do it. Three days later they found her in Shinagawa, in another inn. The newspapers made the most of it, with sensational headlines: 'Devil-Woman Laughs at Blood,' 'Acts of Perversion,' 'Grotesque Murder.' That sort of thing."

"That's kind of too bad."

"They laid it on thick at first, but gradually, as Sada's real intentions came out, the write-ups became a little more favorable. When they found her, she was carrying three notes, one of them addressed to Kichizo. It said, 'You, the one I love best, are dead, and now you're finally mine. I'll be coming soon.'"

"I can understand that."

"She was also carrying a night ticket to Osaka. She couldn't bring herself to die in Tokyo, so she was going to go to Mount Ikoma, where she'd been before, and kill herself there."

Rinko said curiously, "What happened to her after she was arrested?"

"I think it was a relief to her to be caught. When the detective asked her who she was, she said calmly, 'I am Sada Abe, the one you're looking for.' And she answered all their questions as calmly as could be. At her trial six months later, the prosecution asked for ten years' imprisonment, but the judge reduced it to six."

"Would that have been a light sentence back then?"

"For murder? Absolutely. She was a model prisoner, and got another year off for good behavior, so she spent only five years in jail."

Rinko nodded in apparent relief.

"That February there was the attempted coup by young army officers, when three government leaders were killed—the famous February 26 Incident. A time of huge social unrest. After that came the wave of militarism, starting with the Manchurian Incident and leading straight on to the Pacific War."

"So that's when it happened."

"Yes. The mood of the country was dark, people sensed the coming of war. I think one reason Sada's story made such a huge impression is that it was the opposite—a young woman risking all for love. Eventually, some reporters even wrote her up as if she were a crusader for moral reform."

"So public opinion was on her side."

"Yes, and that helped shorten her sentence, but her lawyer also put up an eloquent defense."

"What did he say?"

"He caused quite a stir by claiming that Sada and Kichizo were so deeply in love, so perfectly matched for one another physically, that they were one couple in a million. He said it shouldn't be treated as an ordinary murder case at all. That it was passion that was to blame, because they couldn't bear to be separated."

"One couple in a million?"

"Meaning that sexually, they were ideally compatible."

Rinko was silent. After a moment she slid her loins closer to him and said, "What about us?"

"We're one couple in a million, too, of course."

"We are, aren't we?"

"That's why we're here right now."

Love's spiritual side was powerful enough, but physical chemistry was no less so. Physical love alone could make separation unbearable.

"You can't tell in the beginning, though, can you?" she said thoughtfully.

"Not by appearances, no."

"It's terrible to end up with someone incompatible." This sounded like a jab at her husband. "What do people do when that happens?"

"Probably a lot of them put up with it, even if they feel a bit miserable. A lot of people probably don't know any better."

"Perhaps it's better not to know."

"That's not what I…"

"It was my bad luck to have you teach me so much."

"Come on now," he said, uneasy about this tack.

"Who could I have gone to? Who could I have told?"

She had a point. When sex caused problems in a marriage, it was hard to tell anyone else, and if you did, people were likely to tell you to be patient, or accuse you of having a roving eye.

"I'm jealous of husbands and wives who are perfectly matched. If all marriages were like that, no one would have to suffer this way…"

"Just because it's so rare, if you do meet someone who's right for you, isn't that good?" They could take comfort in this thought, anyway.

He looked at the clock. It was already after eleven. Somehow they'd gotten sidetracked and forgotten the time. The wind was still strong, but the snow had stopped. Tomorrow they would be able to get back to Tokyo. They hadn't yet decided what time to leave, but for him to get to work by ten, it would have to be fairly early.

He turned over, ready to get some sleep, and her hand reached out imploringly from behind, touching him between his legs. He laid his hand over hers and said in a chiding tone, "Shall we call it a day?"

"You don't mind if I just keep my hand here, do you?"

Before talking about Sada, they had made red-hot love, but Kuki now lacked the energy to respond. He let her smooth hand do as it liked. After a pause, she said hesitantly, "I wonder if Kichizo was especially good as a lover."

For a second, Kuki felt uneasily that he was being compared with the other man, but he told her what he remembered. "They say he was. That he had such energy, and such self-control, that he could go on pleasing a woman forever. Sada herself said he was far and away the best lover she'd ever had."

"Is that why she did … what she did?"

"When they asked her, she said, 'That was the part of him that meant the most to me, and I couldn't bear to think that when they laid him out, another woman would touch him there. I couldn't let anyone do that. Besides, even if I left the rest of him in the inn, I thought as long as I had that part, it would feel as if he were still with me, and I wouldn't be lonely.'"

"She was honest, wasn't she?"

"About writing 'Sadakichi us two' in blood on the sheet, she said that after killing him she felt he belonged completely to her, and she wanted everybody to know, so she combined their names."

"Did you read that somewhere?"

"It's all in the statement she made to the police."

"I'd like to see it."

"I'll get it for you, after we get back."

And then, her hand still holding him, he closed his eyes.

In the middle of the night, Kuki dreamed about Sada Abe. On the way back from Nikko or somewhere, he saw her standing in Asakusa at the end of a little shopping street, looking his way. She was rather old yet strangely alluring, with a creamy white skin. As he stared in fascination, she slipped into the crowd.

Remarkably, Rinko dreamed about her, too. In her dream, a crowd gathered, hoping for a glimpse of the famous woman, but a policeman chased them all away.

Kuki thought he understood why in his dream she had appeared in the crowded streets of Asakusa. A senior colleague had once told him that, soon after the war, she ran a small restaurant near there. Even in old age she was smartly dressed and attractive, he'd said, showing traces of her younger self. Word eventually got around that she was working there, and since apparently she didn't like the idea of being exposed to everyone's prying eyes, she soon disappeared. What happened to her after that, no one knew.

"How old would she be now, assuming she's still around?" asked Rinko.

She had been thirty-one in 1936, so that would put her in her nineties.

"Then she could still be alive!"

If so, Kuki would have liked to interview her for his social history, but on the other hand it struck him as unnecessary. "She's been avoiding the public eye, so who am I to drag her back into the limelight? Besides, her feelings are on record in the deposition, in full detail."

He sat up then, as if to call a halt to this talk about Sada. Throwing on a bathrobe, he went and opened the curtains, and there lay Lake Chuzenji, sparkling in the morning sunlight. Yesterday's snowfall had stopped, and the light reflecting off the new snow was dazzling.

"Look."

After learning last evening that they couldn't get away, he and Rinko had made love again and again, locked in the darkly intense world of Sada and Kichizo. Following on top of that, the beauty of this scene had an otherworldly quality.

As they gazed at it together, the maid came in and reported that the road was now open. Last night they had worried and fretted, hoping against hope for a way to go home, but now the news that traffic was restored only made them think absently how bothersome the trip home would be, how nice if the road had stayed closed forever. The moment they told themselves it was time to go, the gloom of the real world descended with crushing weight. What should he do about that meeting, wondered Kuki. Try to make it, or skip it and show up in the afternoon? And what to tell his wife? Rinko's dilemma was even greater: she had not only missed her niece's wedding but stayed away all night. How was she to explain that?

They knew how depressed they both felt, but said nothing, precisely because they recognized the seriousness of the situation.

They finally had breakfast some time after eight and left at nine, taking a taxi to the station and boarding a train that would get them to Tokyo before noon.

With no chance of making the meeting on time, he called his office to say he was staying home with a cold. He put off contacting his wife. Rinko seemed to feel a similar reluctance, giving no sign of having tried to call home that morning.

They arrived in Asakusa around eleven-thirty. Unable to face saying good-bye, they went to a nearby noodle stand for a light lunch, finishing just after twelve.

"What do you want to do?" he asked.

"What about you?"

There was something so forlorn in her expression that he said impulsively, "Let's go to Shibuya." Once back in their apartment, they would linger and get home even later, making a bad situation worse. Well aware of this, he asked her if it was all right, and she nodded. They hailed a taxi. Taking her hand, he whispered, "Now we're really no different from Sada and Kichizo." They both sensed what would happen after they walked in the door.

In less than an hour they were at the door of the apartment, and hurried inside. They hadn't traveled terribly far, but in relief at being back, combined with mild fatigue, they stretched out side by side on the bed. Neither had an immediate desire to make love. Comfortable, lying close together in their familiar bed, they went to sleep.

When they awoke, it was three. Evening was hours away, but as they cuddled in bed with the curtains closed, the room dark, they felt again the stirrings of desire. This time there was none of the fierceness of the night before. He stroked her gently until she became aroused and fondled him in return. The need grew and became irresistible, and he entered her. Forgetting the demands of work and family—or rather, seeking to forget them—they poured themselves into the getting and giving of pleasure, and once again fell asleep.

When they next awoke, it was after dark. The clock said past six. Rinko threw together a simple supper, and they drank beer with it while watching a bit of television and chatting about this and that. Not a word was spoken about the pressing issue of going home. After dinner they drifted back to bed together, not actively seeking one another but dallying, exchanging intermittent caresses and enjoying one another's responses. This was the land of pleasure, beyond day and night. At odd intervals the thought of going home would cross their minds.

Finally, at ten o'clock Kuki got up to relieve himself, and when he came back he said, "What do you want to do?"

That was all, but immediately Rinko seemed to know their time was up. "What about you?"

She had asked the same question that noon in Asakusa. This time

Kuki said, "I'd like to stay forever, but I suppose we can't." Even now, he didn't want to be the one to urge departure.

Rinko combed her hair, looking pale. Neither a shower nor makeup could erase the lingering traces of their liaison. It was the same with him: even with his coat on, the languor of love clung to him like sediment.

Finally they were ready. She had on her wine-red half-coat, black turtleneck sweater, and gray hat. He grabbed her and held her close. There was nothing to say. All he could do was hold her tight, and pray: *If her husband should get angry or abusive or, God forbid, violent, please let her be safe. Let nothing stand in the way of her seeing me again.*

She seemed to understand. "I'll go now," she said decisively, but quickly averted her face in apparent fear, her eyes filling with tears.

He took out a handkerchief and wiped at her tears. "Call me if anything happens," he said. "I'll stay awake all night." His own troubles awaited him at home. His wife had been relatively forgiving up to now, but this might be the last straw. This might be the night she blew up and they had it out. Still, he would keep his promise. "I won't let you go through anything bad alone."

His assurances seemed to give her heart. She repaired her makeup and put her hat on again. Then they looked at each other, nodded, and walked out the door.

It was after ten at night, the building silent. They skirted a cardboard box in the corridor, took the elevator down to the lobby, and went outside. If they took the same taxi, parting would again become impossible, so they hailed separate taxis, waving good-bye to each other as the vehicles pulled up.

"Don't forget," he said, and she nodded.

Seeing Rinko off, he waited until the taillights had disappeared. Then, realizing that their long, extravagant feast of love was finally over, he closed his eyes.

Spring's Shadow

Seasonal changes have a subtle yet profound effect on human affairs. The transition from winter to spring, when the whole world begins to swell with new life, can also place a particular strain on the human mind and body.

Just at that time of year, in late February and early March, a number of unexpected events took place—one being the hospitalization of Kuki's old friend Mizuguchi with lung cancer. The diagnosis was a double blow for Mizuguchi, coming on the heels of his sudden and demoralizing transfer to a subsidiary. Since the cancer was detected early, he underwent immediate surgery, and was resting comfortably. Kuki wanted to visit him in the hospital, but the family had asked that he wait until his friend had regained his strength.

Was Mizuguchi another victim of the energy drain of spring? Or was it linked to his removal from the company's front line, as seemed more likely? It sounded absurd that a job transfer could trigger the growth of a tumor, yet Kuki had seen that people who lost their position and their will to work often came down with a sickness, so perhaps there was some link after all.

News of his friend's illness gave rise in Kuki's mind to uneasy thoughts about his own mortality. Fortunately, he had no physical ailments to speak of, unless you could call his obsession with Rinko a disease.

It was interesting to him that their relationship did not deepen slowly over time but grew in sudden spurts, triggered by specific events. There were the two times they went to Kamakura; their trip to Hakone; and the night of Rinko's father's wake. Each of those risky rendezvous, and the deceptions they involved, had taken them to a deeper level of intimacy and inseparability. Most recently, being stranded at Lake Chuzenji in that February snowstorm had strengthened the bond between them even more.

But Rinko had committed two sins that society found hard to forgive in a wife: missing a family wedding, and just disappearing for two days running. Kuki couldn't sleep for worry after she went back home, not knowing what sort of reception she'd be given. Yet when she appeared two days later in their apartment, she seemed quite cheerful. Her good spirits, though, were all on the surface. Apparently, there was major trouble.

Haruhiko, her husband, had still been up when she got back after eleven that night, but even when she announced her return he had remained silent, not even glancing up from his book. She knew then that he was seething with anger, but she went ahead and told him how sorry she was that bad weather had kept her from attending his niece's wedding. When he still said nothing, she abandoned the effort and turned to go upstairs. The moment she did so, he said "Wait," his voice like a knife in her back.

"I know all about what you've been up to."

Stunned, Rinko turned around.

"I know exactly who you were with, and where."

Hearing this later from her in person, Kuki felt an almost physical shock, as if he'd been slammed in the head. According to bits and pieces he'd picked up from Rinko and Kinugawa, her husband was in his late forties, slim and handsome, faultless in appearance but, like many clever men, somewhat cold and dogmatic. No ladies' man or man of the world. Would someone like that go to the trouble of tracking down his wife's lover? Kuki could hardly believe it.

Rinko said simply, "He knew your whole name: 'Shoichiro Kuki.'"

"How on earth...?"

"He has a jealous nature."

Yet digging up his name couldn't have been easy. "Do you think he's been following us? Or did he hire a detective?"

"There are other ways of finding out. I've got your letters, remember? And sometimes I wrote your name, or the name of your company, in my appointment book."

"Did he see it?"

"I hid the book so he wouldn't. But I wasn't always as careful as I might have been, and lately I did wonder if he hadn't seen something."

"You're at home more than he is."

"Yes, but don't forget, at the end of the year I was away…" Following the death of her father, Rinko had gone to stay with her mother in Yokohama. Maybe her husband had gone through her things then. "Besides, this one time I told him the name of the inn, remember? If it had just been the one night it might not have mattered, but when I didn't come home the next night either, I'll bet he called the front desk and started asking questions."

There had been few other guests the night of the snowstorm, and in that emergency situation the manager might have given out personal information that he otherwise wouldn't have done.

"He really knows who I am?"

"Why would I make it up?"

Kuki felt strange, as though some formerly docile house pet had turned on him in savage fury, fangs bared. "What else did he say?"

"That I could play around all I wanted, for all he cared. That I was filthy and indecent."

Kuki remained silent, in pain, as if the words were aimed at him.

Rinko took a deep breath. "He said he hated me, but he would never let me go."

That made no sense. If he hated his wife, why not tell her exactly what he thought of her and send her packing? Why go on masquerading as a married couple?

"I don't get it."

Rinko nodded. "I know, it's crazy. But that's his idea of revenge."

"Against you?"

"He hates me too much to divorce me. He'd rather force me to stay trapped in this marriage forever."

A perverse kind of revenge. Still, Kuki was baffled. "Most men in his shoes would yell, get physical, raise the roof."

"Not him."

"Are you telling me that from now on, no matter what you do, he plans to say nothing, look the other way?"

"Oh, no. He plans to shut me in the house and watch me like a hawk. Even if he *were* willing to look the other way, I'd hear from a long line of other people: my mother and my brother, his parents, all his relatives … because, as long as we're not divorced, a wife has to act wifely, you see."

The nature of his revenge came into clearer focus.

"But if that's the way he feels, why would he even want to be under the same roof with you? God, meals would be a real ordeal."

"His mother lives in Nakano Ward, and he eats with her pretty often. Besides, he has his room at the university—and we already had separate bedrooms."

"Separate bedrooms? Really? Since when?"

"It's been over a year."

This time last year was when things had started heating up between Kuki and Rinko. Her marriage had already been foundering, then.

"Now what?" he said. "Do you want to keep on as we are?"

"Do you?"

Hearing his own question turned back on him, Kuki caught his breath. He couldn't glibly say the words that would satisfy her, but deep down he knew there was no going back.

He thought back to his own homecoming after Lake Chuzenji. He too had gotten in after eleven. His wife Fumie had still been up, but as she failed to come out to greet him, he went straight to his bedroom and changed into a dressing gown. If he went back and faced her in the living room, there would be tension and inevitable bickering. Why not plead tiredness, and turn in? Then again, if he just avoided the issue, he would have to deal with it the next day. He decided it was better not to put off the inevitable, and say he'd had a lot of extra work to do, or something.

Kuki collected himself, rose and looked in the mirror, checking to make sure his appearance was normal, before venturing into the living room, where his wife sat on the sofa watching TV. Seeing him come in, she said quietly, "Hello. You're back." Kuki nodded, relieved at her calm manner, and dropped into the adjacent chair.

"God, I'm bushed," he said, and yawned. "I meant to come home last night, but I couldn't finish my work. Took me all day today." So far as she knew, he'd been gathering research material in Kyoto temples and museums. It nagged at his conscience that he had used that excuse more than once before. "Yesterday I was going to call you, but I had too much to drink and fell asleep." He gave another slight yawn and was reaching for a pack of cigarettes on the coffee table when his wife switched off the TV and turned toward him.

"You really needn't go to so much trouble."

"Trouble?"

Slowly she nodded, picking up a teacup from the table and wrapping her hands around it. "Why don't we separate?" she said. "Wouldn't that be better?"

It was a bolt from the blue. These were words he had never dreamed of hearing from his wife.

"It would be a great deal easier on me, and I imagine it would simplify life for you, too."

She was joking, he thought, playing with him. But she went on gravely, "At our age, there's no point in trying to fool ourselves."

His wife never had been one to scream or carry on. When something was on her mind, she would get straight to the point, discuss it briefly and without elaboration, then resume her normal air of unconcern. Kuki had always chalked this behavior up to her natural self-possession, but tonight was different. Something in her manner, even calmer and more soft-spoken than usual, suggested this had been a difficult decision requiring intense thought.

"What are you talking about?" he asked, neglecting to light the cigarette in his hand. "You can't throw something like this at me out of the blue."

"It's hardly out of the blue. You of all people know the reason."

Under his wife's steady gaze, Kuki faltered and looked away. So she did know about Rinko. She had never given any sign, apparently content for them to live their separate lives, which had suited him just fine. He had seriously underestimated her: she had seen through his charade all along.

"But why now, why all of a sudden?"

"This discussion is not 'all of a sudden.' If anything, it's way over-due. If you don't leave me soon and go live with her, you're not being fair to her."

"Fair to *her*?"

"Yes. From the way you've been carrying on, you must be devoted to her." Her voice was maddeningly reasonable and dispassionate. "You don't need to worry about me. I'll be fine."

The thought of divorce was by no means new to Kuki. He had first toyed with the idea seven or eight years into their marriage, when the novelty of being a husband was wearing off, and later when an affair with another woman had made the prospect of bachelorhood enticing. Now that he was involved with Rinko, he'd thought about it seriously enough to imagine himself married to Rinko some day.

But, realistically speaking, a host of problems stood in the way. How could he divorce a woman who had been an excellent wife and mother—how could he make their only child, Chika, understand? Did he really want to destroy the home, the fabric of the life he and his wife had built up over the years, and start all over again from scratch? Wasn't he too old for that, and too used to the status quo? Most of all, would Rinko really leave her younger, more successful husband for him? His earlier eagerness to leave his wife had cooled. He truly believed that going on as he was, bearing the shackles of his marriage and seeing Rinko whenever he could, was the course of action that would cause the least pain for all.

For six months, he had been torn between an intense yearning to leave his wife and marry Rinko, and a cool determination not to act irresponsibly. In the midst of his private struggle, he had been forget-ting one critical factor: his wife's feelings. He had clearly miscalculated in assuming her feelings were fixed, unchangeable. His primary reason for not asking her for a divorce was his conviction that she loved him unconditionally and would never agree to end the marriage. A demand for a quick divorce from his wife's own lips suddenly turned his world upside-down.

"All right?" Her voice was untroubled, without a shadow of doubt or hesitation.

She might have thought this through in her own mind, but Kuki was so shocked he couldn't respond. And he decided to go to bed, leaving the matter unresolved.

The next morning he got up early, and studied his wife's face as she made breakfast. Outwardly, she looked the same as always. Perhaps her remarks last night were meant in jest, in retaliation for his crossing the line once too often. He was actually beginning to think this, but as he finished his meal and stood up to leave for the office, she said lightly, "Please don't forget our discussion last night, will you?"

He turned quickly around, but she was innocently carrying the dishes to the sink. He almost asked, "Are you serious?" but she immediately turned on the faucet and began running water to wash the dishes, so he headed for the front door. After stepping into his shoes he turned back, looking for her, but as she showed no sign of coming to see him off, he opened the door and went out.

The sky was blue, the air faintly moist—a sign, along with the budding branches, of approaching spring. As he walked slowly through the dewy morning air toward the train station, Kuki thought back over his wife's request. Divorce had always seemed foreign to him, yet here he was about to become a party to it. While still reeling at her seeming about-face, deep down he still wondered if she really meant it.

As the train jolted him toward his office, he became more and more perplexed, and as soon as he got off at his station, he headed toward a public phone to call Chika. She had been married for over a year now, but was not working and would undoubtedly be home. He stepped into the booth, collected himself, and dialed the number. His daughter's voice sounded immediately in his ear.

"Dad? What's up? What are you calling this early for?"

He hemmed and hawed, then blurted out the news: "Your mother is talking about us separating."

"Oh, she told you."

Kuki had expected surprise in her voice, not equanimity. Obviously, her mother had confided in her. Feeling like the odd man out, he said stupidly, "You mean you knew?"

"Yeah. Mom's told me a lot of things. What are you going to do?"

"What am *I* going to do?"

"She's not kidding, you know."

His daughter's matter-of-fact tone only made Kuki more flustered. "Doesn't it mean anything to you that your mother and I might get a divorce?"

"Well, of course I wish the two of you could always be happy together. But you don't love her any more, do you? There's someone else that you're in love with, and you'd rather be with her, right?"

It appalled Kuki to think his wife had said all this to Chika.

"There's no point in staying married to someone you don't love," she concluded.

She was probably right; yet in reality, how many couples were passionately in love, or even fond of one another? Many had long since lost interest, or were sick of the sight of each other. Still, it wasn't always possible to walk away, even from a bad marriage. That was part of what it meant to be married.

"Then you're in favor of the idea?"

"You'd both be better off, wouldn't you?"

"It's just that … we've been together such a long time…"

"Well, the problem is you, so think about what you're saying."

Kuki had no answer.

"Mom's worn out."

"Is she willing to make a go of it on her own?"

"You'll give her the house and as much money as you can, won't you?"

That was only fair, yet Kuki realized with some bitterness that his daughter was completely on her mother's side. He felt betrayed.

"I thought you'd argue against it."

"Why? It's between you and her." To a married daughter, the question of her parents' feelings for one another was perhaps not a pressing one. "I'll be fine. Don't worry about me."

Apparently, while he was out running around, his wife and daughter had been getting tougher-minded, deciding to take a stand.

Kuki and Rinko, after hearing one another's stories, found they could neither weep and wail nor laugh at their troubles; the only thing they could do was smile wryly and a bit sadly.

They found themselves at a crossroads, with opposite situations at home. He'd thought that when Rinko went home, her husband would blow up, perhaps threaten divorce. She, too, had been resigned to such a reception, and perhaps secretly hoped for it. Her husband, however, had not lost his temper, and had only mentioned divorce to say he'd never give her one. He was determined to keep her bound to him in wedlock forever, to never grant her her freedom, since that was obviously what she wanted. Neither she nor Kuki ever imagined such a reaction.

Just as Rinko was startled by her husband's intransigence, Kuki had been confounded by his wife's levelheadedness. Half expecting a shouting match when he got home late, he was astonished to hear her ask quietly for a divorce. He'd doubted his ears, taken it as a joke or, at best, an empty threat. He knew now that divorce was inevitable, as his daughter had corroborated on the phone.

"It's weird…" That was all he could say. "The way our situations have reversed." Rinko, expecting to be thrown out by her husband, now found herself shackled to him, while Kuki, despairing of ever getting free, was being rushed into divorce by his wife. "I mean, who would have thought it?"

Quietly, Rinko asked, "You're not sorry?"

"What do you mean?"

He could hardly answer that with a casual "Of course I am." He was in too deep to back down now. Objectively, however, he knew that he was feeling rather dejected and unnerved. After longing so intensely for his freedom, now that it was his for the taking, why the confusion and hesitation? Did it come down to anxiety at stepping outside the bounds of the socially approved married state? Or was it because his wife was the one to propose separation instead of him, shifting the balance of power?

As if sensing his indecision, Rinko murmured, "If you are, you can always go back, you know."

"Back where?"

"Home."

"Now?"

"You feel guilty about your wife, don't you?"

"I have no wish to go back."

"Is that true?"

He nodded hastily, to reassure her. "I will never go back."

"Neither will I."

Even as he nodded, Kuki reminded himself that she was tied fast to her husband. "But you—"

"I'm staying put. There's no point in going back now."

"He won't give you a divorce."

"I don't care. My body is free."

"What if people talk?"

"Let them. I don't care."

Impressed by her resolution, Kuki told himself she was right.

In late February and on into March, Kuki was restless in the extreme. Even after his wife suggested divorce, he would now and then return home, but there was never any squabbling or name-calling. On the surface, everything seemed the same as ever, so apparently normal that he sometimes forgot she had ever said anything. He even imagined she might be having second thoughts. For all her surface amiability, however, she had clearly undergone no change of heart, for one day early in March he came home to find an application for divorce on the table. She must have picked it up from the government office herself. In one corner of the page she had written her name, "Fumie Kuki," and affixed her seal. All that remained was for him to write in his name alongside hers and stamp it with his own seal. Then it would be official.

The simplicity of the procedure appalled him. Merely by signing his name, he could sever the connection. Then what was it they had spent twenty-five years working to build?

Unlike Kuki, who was quietly agonizing, his wife remained outwardly cheerful and businesslike. "I left the form on your desk, so sign it, will you?" she said over her shoulder the next morning on her way out the door. Her lack of emotion rankled. Had she no lingering regrets, no shred of wistfulness at what might have been? Was she so devoid of feeling—had her heart turned to ice?

In a state of some agitation he phoned Chika again, only for her to side again with her mother: "She struggled with this a long time before making up her mind, Dad."

Apparently, all his wife's suffering had gone on while he was out running around. She'd long ago decided she'd had enough. He ought to have been at least sensitive to her misery during that long stretch of time. Now the damage was irreparable. Kuki turned the matter over and over in his mind, unable to bring himself to sign the form. It lay untouched in a desk drawer as day after day slid by.

He still hadn't told Rinko that his wife had served him with divorce papers; he kept putting it off, feeling rather like someone on death row whose sentence could be carried out at any time. At work, he couldn't concentrate, and he was often tempted to sign just to end the pain. He scolded himself for shilly-shallying and hanging onto the past when it was clear that his wife wanted out. This was no way for a grown man to behave. Resolutely, he would pick up the document to sign it, only to lay it down again, thinking, "It couldn't hurt to wait one more day."

Ever since the divorce talk began, his life had undergone a steady change. Before, when he and Rinko had spent the night in their apartment, he had always made up an excuse, feeling vaguely guilty about it. Now he made no effort to explain his absence or to spare his wife's feelings. If they were separating, what the hell difference did it make?

Little by little, his underwear and socks, not to mention shirts, ties, and other belongings, began piling up in Shibuya. The same was true for Rinko. As their wardrobes grew, they needed somewhere to put their clothes, so they bought a chest of drawers, then a washing machine, a kitchen range, and other appliances. On his way home from work, more and more often he found himself gravitating to Shibuya, turning the key in the lock and entering their private domain.

With Rinko not yet there, he would sit alone, looking at the furniture and possessions that seemed to multiply daily, and feeling a mixture of contentment and unease. Once, without realizing it, he murmured "What in God's name will become of us?" Filled with anxiety over their unknowable future, he found himself giving in to a sense of fatalism. What would be, would be. And so, with Kuki in this somewhat reckless state of mind, the days continued to slide by.

With March already half gone, his restlessness lingered. In part this was due to his nagging inability to respond to his wife's request for a divorce, but it also seemed connected with the weather, with the languid look of the spring sky. On top of that, he was eager to see his friend Mizuguchi in the hospital.

So it was in mid-March that Kuki made his long-awaited sick call, the time when peach trees traditionally come into blossom. Around the hospital entrance, pink and white plum blossom was out instead. Arriving at three, the hour stipulated by Mizuguchi's wife, he found her there in the corridor waiting to usher him into a nearby visitors' room. He would have come sooner but for her.

"The surgery is over, and his strength is coming back," she told him, trying to sound matter-of-fact, but there was a shadow on her face. Sensing bad news, Kuki asked about the status of his friend's illness. The doctors had operated for lung cancer, but it seemed the tumor had metastasized. They'd told her he had, at most, six months to live.

"Does he know?"

"I can't tell him. He thinks they got it all, that he's in the clear."

That must be why she'd brought him into the waiting room: she wanted to make sure he understood before going in to see him.

"Thank you for coming," she said, and he bowed briefly before heading in to find a more chipper Mizuguchi than he'd imagined, nodding in welcome.

"Well, well, look who's here! Come on in !" he exclaimed with a smile. Although his skin had the pallor of straw, he looked almost like his old self.

"I wanted to come sooner, but I heard you'd had an operation."

"I've been through the mill. I'm okay now, though, so don't worry."

Kuki drew closer to the bed, at his friend's urging. "You look great," he said.

"The operation alone wouldn't be so bad, but the chemotherapy kills your appetite. I should be able to get out of here next month."

The tumor has metastasized. Six months to live. The words flashed into Kuki's mind, but he banished them and went on as if nothing were the matter. "Hurry back, will you? Marron can't get along without you."

"Oh, I doubt that. It takes more than the absence of one or two people to derail a company." After delivering this sober opinion, he went on ruminatively, "You know, sickness is a funny thing. It hits when your spirits are low, your defenses down."

"The end of last year…"

"Like I told you then, I was down in the dumps. Feeling rejected. First I was depressed, then I started feeling lousy, and when I had myself checked out they told me it was cancer." It was last December that Mizuguchi had been sent on loan to that small subsidiary, Marron. No sooner had he been installed there at the first of the year than he fell sick. "Could have been the transfer that did it."

"Come on, you don't really think that, do you?"

"There was never anything wrong with me before."

His enthusiasm for his former job, the sense of being in the thick of things—had that hindered the growth of the tumor?

"You seem to be in great shape," said Mizuguchi, looking up intently at Kuki from his bed. "You look like you've got it made. I should have enjoyed life, the way you do. Should have had more fun."

"You still can."

"Not any more, not like this. Everybody gets old and dies in the end, so you've got to do the things you want to while you still can."

In the corners of Mizuguchi's eyes, where there were more crow's-feet than before, Kuki could make out the faint gleam of tears.

Leaving the room after a half-hour visit, Kuki felt his mind was on fire. Before his eyes had lain a man his own age felled by cancer, a man for whom death was near. Kuki had been touched by the deaths of people his own age or younger before, but this was different. This was an old friend, someone whose life and career paralleled his own. He was badly shaken. The realization that he too was getting on filled him with a sense of urgency.

Besides that, his mind was burning with the advice Mizuguchi had given him: "You've got to do the things you want to while you still can." Faced with death, Mizuguchi now clearly regretted the way he had lived. To all appearances, his life had been meaningful and satisfying, yet apparently his mind swirled with thoughts of what might have been. Whether his regrets had more to do with work or with women, there was no telling, but they were undoubtedly genuine.

Perhaps at the end, looking back, even the most eventful life would strike one as mundane. No matter how one chose to live, a final sense of wasted opportunity might be unavoidable. He hoped not; he didn't want to curse his stars at the moment of death and dwell on what he'd left undone.

Kuki couldn't erase the image of those tears in Mizuguchi's eyes as he'd voiced his regrets. Terrible to end your life in such emptiness. The moment the thought crossed Kuki's mind, there flashed a picture of Rinko's face.

His love for Rinko was certainly the main thing, the only thing that made his life worth living. Some might sneer at the idea of pouring all one's passion onto a woman, but work and love were *both* of great value, well worth a lifetime of devotion. All his energies, he decided, should now be directed toward one single enterprise: loving and gaining sole possession of this woman. The thought brought on a rush of hot yearning, and eagerly his thoughts ran ahead to her.

This was the sort of weather known in literary language as "spring's shadow," a hazy afternoon in the cherry blossom season. It was early for them to flower, but in this warm weather the swollen buds seemed ready to burst. Kuki traveled past streets ripe with sweet promise, leaning against the leather strap as the train sped him toward the apartment in Shibuya.

It was 4:30. He'd left the office early to visit Mizuguchi in the hospital, and there was no need to go back now. That morning, when he told Rinko his plans, she'd said she would stop by her mother's house in Yokohama and be in the apartment by five. Their "date" would therefore begin before sunset—a luxury possible only because they had their own private apartment, a place safe from other people's eyes.

Kuki got off the train and headed for their building, then walked down the corridor with a spring in his step—almost a skip—until he came to their door. He opened it, but there was no Rinko inside. It was already five. Maybe she was running a little late.

Kuki opened the curtains, turned on the heat, and stretched out on the sofa. At this hour, everybody else in the office would still be at it, bent over their desks. He alone had escaped, to wait for a woman in a room no one knew about. Relishing the aura of secrecy, he switched on the TV and found a rerun of some drama showing. It came as a novelty to him that they showed steamy romantic dramas at this hour. He watched absentmindedly until 5:30 … then 5:45.

Where was she? It wasn't like her to be late. Maybe she was shopping for dinner on the way. Kuki began thinking about what he would do when she did finally show up. Since she was so late, going on an hour now, he ought to come up with an appropriate penalty of some kind. He could hide behind the door, maybe, then grab her and kiss her the second she walked in. Or force his hands under her clothes and grab her breasts. Or topple her immediately onto the sofa.

As he lay there alone, planning all the lascivious things he would do to her, the doorbell rang and the doorknob turned. At last. Nearly an hour late. Despite his plans to administer a swift penalty, his relief was so great that the best he could manage was a mild reproach.

"You're late."

"Sorry, I got held up at my mother's." She was wearing a suit of pale yellow, just the color for spring, with a floral-print scarf at the collar. Over her arm she carried a white coat and a big paper bag.

"What about dinner? You want to go out and get something to eat?"

She opened the bag and said, "I picked up a few things at the department store by the station, so let's eat here."

He certainly had no argument there. Far easier to stay here than wander around outside—and besides, here they could fool around.

"You're a whole hour late," he said, going up behind her as she stood in the kitchen and putting his arms around her. But she stopped him with a hand.

"I left my cat with her."

"With your mother?"

She nodded, and began taking things out of the bag. "She hit the ceiling."

"About the cat?"

Rinko had already told him that being away from home so much, she hated to leave the cat alone; and not wanting to ask her husband to look after it, either, she had decided to take it to her mother in Yokohama.

"No, she likes cats too, so that was all right, but she wanted to know why I would do such a thing."

"There's not enough room here and, anyway, pets aren't allowed."

"No, she wanted to know why I had to spend so much time out."

True, it was rather strange to entrust your cat to someone else when you had a home of your own.

"She knows I'm away a lot. The other night she called, and there was no answer. Where *was* I at such an hour, she wanted to know. I've been meaning to tell her, again and again, but somehow I can never bring myself to do it." With the loss of her father still so recent, it would be only natural if Rinko found the topic of her failed marriage difficult to broach. "Still, she knows."

"About us?"

"She's had her suspicions since last fall, and after I saw you at New Year's that time, she even said something to me."

"What was it?"

"'Surely you aren't in love with another man.'"

"What did you say?"

"'No,' of course. But she knew it in her bones."

Kuki had never met Rinko's mother, but from all he had heard she was a woman of refinement and exacting standards, as befitted someone from one of the old merchant families of Yokohama.

"She clearly wasn't pleased that I missed the wedding, but when she called three nights ago and I wasn't home…"

Three nights earlier they had spent the night together.

"She said Haruhiko picked up the phone."

"Haruhiko who?"

"My husband. He told her I would probably be back late again."

"He said that?"

"He didn't say anything about my staying out all night, but from the way he spoke, she put two and two together." Rinko took down some tea leaves and a teapot from the shelf. "She's always liked him anyway, and she told me if it turns out I've been unfaithful to him, she won't be able to look Dad's picture in the eye."

"But..." Nonplussed, Kuki went back to the sofa. "You can't keep it hidden forever. Telling her won't be easy, but once you do, she might understand."

"I did."

"So it's all out in the open?"

Rinko nodded. "I hated hurting her so soon after Dad died, but I went ahead and told her everything."

"And?"

"At first she listened quietly, then she got angry, then she burst into tears..." From the short, fragmentary description, he could still picture her consternation when she heard the news. "Even though she'd had her suspicions, being told straight out was still a shock. She said she never raised her daughter to be a slut."

Kuki said nothing, but only listened, head bowed.

"She said she was so ashamed she could never bear to tell my brother or any of the relatives, and my father was surely rolling over in his grave. That's when she started to cry. Then she wanted to know what I have against my husband." After a short pause, she continued, "But there's no point in my saying anything about that, since she'd never understand, so I kept quiet. Then she asked who I was having the affair with."

"And did you tell her?"

"Yes. There's nothing to gain by hiding it, is there?" Rinko turned to face him, tears in her eyes. "Now I've lost everything."

Kuki gathered her in his arms. For him Rinko had given up not only home and husband but also her last bulwark, her mother. All she had left was him. Kuki vowed to himself that he would protect her at any cost.

She, too, recognizing that he was all she had left to rely on, pressed herself flat against him. Bound in a sense of their isolation, wrapped tightly around each other, they moved into the bedroom as if it were their last refuge and sank onto the bed.

Bouncing lightly from the impact, he sought her lips, then, as if changing his mind, pressed his mouth on her wet eyelids. For a moment she turned her face away in surprise, but he persisted, keeping his mouth there until the trembling of her lashes quieted and her tears were transformed to a slight taste of salt on his lips. By sipping the teardrops from her eyes, he meant to heal her sadness. He might be powerless to change the circumstances facing them, but he knew he could at least ease her heart's pain. After slowly licking the tears from her eyes, his mouth next sought her nose, and covered it. She wriggled as if this tickled, but again, as the tip of his tongue traced the flare of her nostrils, she relaxed, and again he tasted her tears.

After he had pressed his lips against those three places—the mouth, the eyes, the nose—and kissed away her last tear, she seemed to recover at last from the sadness of parting with her husband and her mother, and her body began to reassert itself. Kuki helped as she took off her skirt and wriggled in evident impatience out of her bra and panties, becoming naked as a newborn child.

Then she murmured, "Now ... wipe me out."

It was clear she was throwing herself at him bodily in the hope of numbing her pain. Her words had the effect of stripping him of all pretense, all civility, and releasing the animal side of him—a wild and hungry animal.

He began by ripping away the sheet that covered her naked body. As she flinched, he grabbed her legs and swung them aloft, then forcibly spread them wide. It was after six, and no lights were on in the room, but there in the lingering dusk by the window, Rinko's graceful white legs hung in the air.

"What are you doing?" she said, flustered, but he paid no attention, dragging her by her still-open legs closer to the window. Only then did she seem to realize that she was exposed. "Someone will see!"

In practice, it was impossible for anyone to see into the room. Still, the possibility apparently aroused a new excitement in her.

"Stop it!" she cried, madly trying to fight him off, while he fought to subdue her in what became an all-out wrestling match, two sweaty, panting bodies trying to get the upper hand. All of this was necessary, all part of her request: to wipe her out.

At last her strength gave out and she came to a shaky rest, thighs slightly parted, as if she were accustomed now to the lewd position he had often forced her into. Kuki sensed that she even took a perverse pleasure in this posture now, in thinking that strangers' eyes might accidentally see it all. And, knowing this, he entered her, and started pumping hard to reach the goal she'd set.

A woman's body may be weak, but her sexuality is colorful and strong; a man's body may be strong, but his sexuality is linear and fragile. It was Kuki's sense of this difference that often led him to begin by shaming and exhausting her, treating her harshly before he settled on the moment of penetration. Once they were joined, one flesh, the woman's apparent handicap was eliminated.

Again and again he plunged into her, his breath coming in hot rasps, ramming her, raining kisses on her ears and neck, leaving the imprint of his teeth in her skin. Rinko responded by growing wilder and wilder too, until, with a long drawn-out cry, she went into a convulsive orgasm. Yet even now he doubted whether this was enough for her. Far from disintegrating, she was still burning like a fireball, pushing on and on in search of pleasure.

How he *loved* the look on her face at the point of climax! It wasn't a face with strongly defined features: her eyes, nose, and mouth were small, evenly spaced. But as her passion erupted, that heart-shaped face, changing constantly—now laughing, now ready to weep, now suffering in agony—captivated him. It was to go on looking at that face in all its tenderness, its throes, its deep sensuality, that he focused all his remaining energies, trying his utmost not to lose control as he went to the very limit.

When, inevitably, it came to an end, it wasn't because of her: it was he who was "wiped out." If it had been in her power to linger on in that state of bliss, she would, he felt, have chosen to, even if it meant toppling over the edge into a final oblivion and carrying him with her.

As if echoing this thought, Rinko, limbs spread-eagled, said softly, "That was wonderful," then added: "You can kill me when I'm like that..."

How different it was for a man... It was the sense of utter emptiness afterward, as if one's very soul had drained away, that made one think of death... Was the difference because women presided over the birth of new life, while a man's role in procreation ended with ejaculation?... If you thought about it, in many species the male fell gasping for breath after copulation, to hover a while on the border between life and death before finally expiring.

Rinko, her skin still incandescent, snuggled up to him from behind and said: "It makes me scared."

"I've heard you say that before."

She nodded. "Yes, but this is different. It's as if, somehow, I really will die..."

"Just like that?"

"Yes, but you see, it doesn't matter. Dying that way would be wonderful, not scary at all. It's my thinking that that frightens me the most."

What she said was contradictory, but it was clear that death held some strong appeal for her in the throes of orgasm.

"I can't have you dying now," he said.

"I wouldn't mind, though. Not now, not with all this." Her voice rose as she went on, "Now is the best time of my life. It will never ever be better than this." Seeing his incomprehension, she said, "Well, it's true. I love you so much, and my body is so completely alive ... having all this, I really feel that I could die with no regrets."

"You're only thirty-eight."

"That's enough. That's plenty."

Rinko had always been preoccupied with her age, and had said before that she felt old, ready to die. To Kuki, who was past fifty, she seemed still a young woman with her life ahead of her, but apparently she took a different view. He tried to convince her that growing old had its advantages, but she shook her head.

"That's what they say, but this is as far as I care to go. After this, it will all be downhill for me."

"Appearance isn't everything."

"Of course it isn't. But growing old is painful for a woman. No matter how hard you try, after a certain point you can't keep up the illusion of youth. Right now I can still pull it off, but just barely. I'm at the edge."

"Does it matter so much?"

"I don't like to dwell on it, believe me. But every day, you see yourself in the mirror, and there's another crow's-foot. Or you think, my skin's so baggy it's hard to put on makeup any more. A woman knows these things herself better than anyone, but she doesn't want to let on that she does. Especially not to the man she loves."

"But you just did."

"Only because I want you to know that I'm at my peak right now."

He turned back to find the sheet draped over her lower body.

"It's funny for me to say it, but I do think I'm at my most beautiful now. Thanks to you, my skin is nice, and my breasts are still okay..."

Yes, he thought, her skin was creamier than ever, soft and smooth, with a sweetness and a luster hardly seen in a twenty-year-old.

"Making love to you has changed me."

Impulsively Kuki reached out and cupped one hand around a breast. As if she'd been waiting for him to do that, she said softly, "Don't ever forget me as I am now."

Her talk was full of contradiction: claiming she was at her most beautiful now, and happier than ever before, then turning around and saying she could readily die; telling him she was getting more wrinkled and baggy every day, then saying she was at her best now so take a good look and don't forget. If she really thought that right now she was at her best, her most beautiful, shouldn't she be thinking of how to hold on to that?

"Why are you so obsessed with the here and now?" he asked.

In a casual tone she answered, "I don't mean to be. It's just ...

maybe I *am* too bound up in the moment."

"I'd say so."

"But to me, now is all that really matters. If this moment, *now*, is no good, then even if things improve later on, it won't matter. Don't you think?"

"Maybe. Still, I never knew you to be like this."

"It's your doing."

"Is it?"

"I changed after knowing you, and discovering my body."

"Changed so that you care only about the moment?"

"Yes. During sex, all your energy is directed toward the moment, the *now*, isn't it? *Now* is what counts, *now* is everything."

So the deepening of their sexual commitment had changed her philosophy of life. As Kuki was mulling over this revelation, she murmured, "If we forget about right now in favor of tomorrow or next year, we might end up with nothing. I don't want that kind of regret."

Kuki thought of his friend Mizuguchi. If setting a premium on the pleasure of the moment was so important, what of the life Mizuguchi had led, devoted entirely to work? Briefly he described Mizuguchi's condition to her and said, "When I went to see him, he said he was sorry he hadn't played around more."

"I know exactly what he means." She gently pressed her cheek against his chest. "Are you sorry?"

"No."

"Good." She rubbed her forehead against him. "We won't ever be sorry, will we?"

"Of course not."

"And *now* is important, isn't it?"

Kuki nodded, thinking of his age. He was past the half-century mark, considerably older than Rinko. Maybe for a man, this was the last hurrah. Any increase in status or income after this would be minimal, barely worth mentioning. And this was undoubtedly his last chance to pursue romance, to savor the sensation of living for love.

"I've changed too," he said.

"In what way?"

"In every way."

Rinko almost certainly had been changed by loving him, he thought. She never used to be so insistent, so frank about her desires. Originally, she'd had little interest in sex; although married, she had been indifferent to the pleasures of the flesh. Now, a little sheepishly, she accused him of having caused her transformation.

He understood that her previous indifference had been due entirely to sexual inexperience and rigid thinking. If she wanted to charge him with causing her body to blossom and learn the deepest joys of sex, it was a charge he would gladly accept.

Looking deeper within himself, however, Kuki had to admit that he was no less transformed. He'd imagined himself playing mentor to Rinko, awakening and shaping her latent instincts, but before he knew it, he himself was in thrall to their lovemaking, addicted to it and to her. He had begun by fancying himself her teacher, but along the way he'd been lured into the pupil's seat. And now there was no going back.

The change had gone beyond the realm of sex to affect his work and home life as well. His very approach to life—the longing to give himself completely to the moment, the realization of the importance of *now*—showed Rinko's unmistakable influence. As the older of the two, he had assumed he would naturally take the lead in most things, but in fact, as he thought it over, it was the opposite: he was the one being led along. He took a deep breath and let it out.

"What is it?" said Rinko immediately. "Something wrong?"

Nothing was especially wrong. Only, little by little, the two of them were becoming isolated, driven deeper and deeper into their own world. It was he dragging her along, he'd always thought, only to find he'd gotten it backward. Not that he was lamenting their lot; there was nothing to do but let natural events take their course. He was both unnerved and pleased by his own cavalier attitude.

"No, I feel great."

It wasn't yet nightfall. They lay naked together in bed, in the same twilight that had marked the start of their affair. It was oddly satisfying to be so debauched and unproductive. He fingered her nipples; her hand rested lightly in between his legs. Their playful reverie was interrupted suddenly by the ringing of the telephone.

Instantly, Rinko threw her arms around his neck and clung to him. No one knew the number here. Neither of them had passed it on to anyone, family or friend. Why was the phone ringing? Who knew they were here? Kuki's mind flashed back to earlier this evening, with Rinko naked in the light of the window; but no one outside could have seen anything, he was certain.

On the fifth ring he sat up, but Rinko caught him by the arm. "Don't answer it," she begged. It rang an even ten times before stopping.

"Who could that have been?"

"God knows," he muttered, thinking of his family. Surely his wife hadn't found out about the apartment, and yet he couldn't help wondering if something had gone wrong at home. Each time he stayed away, he worried. What if someone fell ill while he was gone, or had an accident? As long as he could be reached, there was no problem, but lately he'd invented destinations and hotels. If anything did happen, if he was needed and couldn't be reached, he'd never be able to live with himself.

A cell phone was the obvious answer, but with Rinko he tended to turn the damn thing off, unwilling to have their little time together interrupted by calls from his wife or from work. The only way for him to keep in touch with his family was to call home. But what if this really were an emergency?

Rinko seemed to feel the same anxiety. Relations between her and her husband were icebound, but if anything happened to her mother, she would have no way of knowing unless she called home. This enforced one-way style of communication was the biggest burden they faced when staying out all night at undisclosed locations. If they had truly turned their backs on the past, it shouldn't matter, yet it did. Was that because they couldn't isolate themselves completely, after all?

When the phone stopped ringing, Kuki said, "Did you give anyone this number?"

"No, no one."

It must be a wrong number, Kuki told himself, allaying his own anxiety, but there was no denying the telephone had shattered their self-indulgent mood.

"Want to get up?"

Rinko looked at him wistfully and said, "Let's go away somewhere again."

This apartment was the easiest place to meet, but having the phone ring like that was nerve-racking, as if they were being spied on.

"I know—it's almost the cherry blossom season, so how about going somewhere we can enjoy it?"

"Yes, let's! That's a wonderful idea!" She pummeled him on his chest for joy, then slid her fingers up to his throat. "If you don't take me, I'll strangle you."

"You might be doing me a favor."

"Okay, here goes." She put her hands all the way around his neck and pretended to choke him, but quickly relaxed her grip and said, "That reminds me. The book about Sada Abe. You haven't shown it to me yet."

The book containing Sada's statement to the police was popular in the reference section, and a colleague had taken it home to read.

"I'll bring it along on our cherry-blossom trip, okay?" He added, "I've got a favor to ask you, too."

"What is it?"

He whispered in her ear. "Bring a red under-kimono."

"To wear?"

"Yes. Bright red." She looked surprised. He added in a commanding tone, "That's my condition for taking you."

"All right," she said docilely, nodding, after a brief pause. Her voice held a touch of indolence and her lips remained slightly parted, like falling cherry petals on a cloudy day in the shadow of spring.

Falling Petals

For over a thousand years, the flowers of the cherry tree, or *sakura*, have occupied a special place of honor in Japan. Sen no Rikyu, founder of a sixteenth-century tea ceremony school, dubbed them "first among flowers," and the title held. Most Japanese consider the sight of sumptuous masses of cherry blossom in early April a glorious thing, but their hearts are moved even more by their fragility, their short-lived beauty.

Although the flowers last barely a week, they nonetheless possess enormous presence. Traditionally, when they are used in floral arrangements, they require special treatment: "Cherry blossom must be placed alone in the alcove; or, when other flowers are present, it must be given the dominant position."

For this very reason, there are some people who dislike *sakura*, considering them a bit of a floral prima donna. Sen no Rikyu himself dictated that they should not be used in the tea ceremony, pronouncing them "too grand for a teahouse." Because the essence of his tea ceremony was *wabi*, the beauty of austerity and simplicity, his rejection of the showy blossoms is understandable, while seemingly at odds with his outspoken praise.

Clearly, *sakura* have infused the Japanese aesthetic sense and are hugely popular. Part of Kuki had always been drawn to the blossoms' beauty, while another side of him found them loud and oppressive. It occurred to him that a lack of serenity in his own life might have kept him from following their fleeting lives with more enthusiasm.

Every spring, as the season approached, TV newscasters tracked the "cherry blossom front," detailing the progress of the phenomenon across the country. Cameras relayed glowing images of cherry trees at famous sites across the nation, reporting where the flowers were mere buds, where they were half open, and where at their peak. Still, unlike many Japanese who make *sakura* viewing an annual rite, Kuki had never really taken time to enjoy the flowers properly. The idea of specifically going off somewhere to relax and look at cherry trees in full bloom, tempting as it sometimes was, had always given way to the pressures of work, confining Kuki's scope of appreciation to the cherry trees lining his neighborhood streets and scattered trees around the city.

An old *waka* poem describes the "restless heart" of the falling blossoms, and every April, Kuki himself felt restless and flurried. It was always a relief to him when the season ended. After years of this, he had built up a certain resentment toward the lovely blooms, but this year things were different. Ironically, his demotion would be responsible for his fully enjoying cherry blossom for the first time in his life. He and Rinko planned to spend a weekend immersed in their beauty.

But where? For Kuki, cherry blossom meant Kyoto. Aside from the hanging blossoms of Heian Shrine, and the pink and white trees lit up at night along the riverbanks, there were Godaiji, Ninnaji, Jonangu, and countless other temples and shrines famous for *sakura*. In the past, Kuki had taken advantage of meetings or other business in Kyoto to grab a hurried look at a few of these spots, each beautiful in its own way—sometimes breathtakingly so—and yet it struck him at such times that everything was a tad too perfect. Kyoto cherry blossom blended delightfully with the setting of ancient temples and gardens backed by green hills, the surrounding scenery enhancing the flowers perfectly; yet something about this very perfection put him off, like a brand-name product in expert packaging. Everyone raved about these famous, picture-postcard views, but why not admire the flowers for themselves? The idea of enjoying them in a quiet spot untrampled by hordes of sightseers appealed to him strongly.

Kuki finally came up with the hot-spring town of Shuzenji, on the Izu Peninsula. Not far from Tokyo, it lay tucked in the mountains, so the lodgings and scenery would be quiet and peaceful. It was the second Sunday in April when he and Rinko set off—too late for cherry blossom, normally, but a fortuitous spell of chilly weather had kept it at its peak across the peninsula. It was a glorious spring day, full and bright.

They set out from their apartment with Kuki dressed lightly in a beige open-necked shirt and a slightly darker jacket, and Rinko in a pale pink suit with a floral-print scarf, wearing a gray hat and carrying a big purse. The day before, she had gone home for her spring clothes. Kuki wondered if she'd run into her husband, and what generally was going on between the two of them. He diplomatically refrained from asking about it, and she said nothing, which he took as a sign that she preferred not to discuss it.

After a recent visit to her mother, however, she revealed that she'd been told to "lay things on the line" with her husband and to "get her life in order." Since learning that her daughter was having an affair, and that her marriage was collapsing, Rinko's mother had been after her to stop bringing the family into disrepute and work out some sort of solution. But Rinko claimed her husband was refusing to grant her a divorce, as a form of revenge. When Kuki asked what her mother had to say to that, all she would say was, "I tell her, but she doesn't understand." For a woman of such old-fashioned standards as Rinko's mother, a man's refusal to divorce an openly adulterous wife must be beyond comprehension.

"She says the three of us should meet and talk it over," said Rinko. He assumed she meant Rinko, her husband, and her mother. "She likes him, and thinks she can patch things up between us, but I'd never agree. For one thing, how could I possibly broach the subject of sex?"

Rinko's dissatisfaction with her marriage was based on general incompatibility, including sexual incompatibility, and she had no intention of spelling matters out in detail in public or for her mother. She was, essentially, a very private person.

Kuki's marriage was equally in limbo. He had yet to sign the divorce form. Given the depth of his involvement with Rinko, his wife's request was reasonable, yet the idea of divorce evoked a tangle of feelings. He felt remorse for his own selfish behavior, misery at the thought of breaking the news to colleagues, friends, and relatives, and unwillingness at the prospect of explaining what had happened. Also, he was afraid to leave his marriage before Rinko could extricate herself from hers, as though he might be left hanging on a limb. Above all, he shrank from overturning a lifestyle that had endured for nearly thirty years.

Divorce was so final a step, he felt the need to take it slowly, saw no need to hurry. But what of his wife? On his rare visits home they spoke very little, he hurrying away after a minimal exchange of words. Yet neither did they quarrel. It seemed people were capable of adjusting to almost any situation. Their love had cooled completely, yet there was a strange calm between them. This implied no softening of his wife's stance, however, as she made clear one day in early April by confronting him again.

"You haven't forgotten, have you?"

He knew she was referring to the unsigned divorce form, but he only shook his head without saying when he would get around to it. As he started out the door, she came after him.

"After tomorrow, I won't be here, either."

"Where are you going?" he asked automatically, realizing as the words left his mouth that he was in no position to quiz her.

"It doesn't really matter, does it?"

Her answer was cool and unapologetic. He should have known. She was always like that, firm and plain, never more so than now when she was leaving him. Like Rinko, his wife wasn't likely to be deterred once she had resolved to end her marriage. His own stance seemed vague, wishy-washy by comparison. Men were like that, irresolute and prone to get cold feet. All right, he thought, maybe the time had come to act.

Telling himself this, Kuki went to Tokyo Station and took his seat beside Rinko on the "Kodama" bullet train headed for Mishima. From there they would transfer to the Izu Hakone Railway and go on to Shuzenji.

It was the height of the blossom-viewing season, but the train was empty. That was because they had chosen to leave on a Sunday afternoon, for once, and return on Monday to avoid the crowds. He owed the luxury of this trip to the meaninglessness of his job. Lately Kuki felt less like griping than celebrating his newfound freedom.

The train from Mishima was also empty, and as they headed south onto the peninsula, the number of houses dwindled and the mountainsides pressed in close around them, covered with cherry trees in full bloom. The trees were the common variety called *somei yoshino*, bearing large, single-petaled flowers and standing out against the green hillsides like pink garlanded hats.

"I always wanted to ride in a train like this," said Rinko of the poky local train that paused occasionally between stations, waiting for the conductor's whistle before it moved on. The leisurely pace of their progress was in keeping with the peaceful spring afternoon.

Parallel to the tracks ran a clear mountain stream where here and there a fisherman dangled his line. They gazed intently at the mountains, blossoms, and stream, a kind of scenery denied them in the city, and after about thirty minutes the train pulled into its final destination, Shuzenji Station.

The hot springs at Shuzenji are said to have been discovered in the eighth century by the itinerant hermit-monk Kukai, founder of the temple from which the town takes its name. Perhaps because of the springs, here the blossom was beginning to fall: a few scattered petals landed softly on Kuki's and Rinko's shoulders as they set out to see the historic temple before going on to the inn.

After a short ride from the station, they mounted a steep flight of stone stairs and went through the temple gate, entering the bamboo-encircled grounds where the main hall stands. Some eight hundred years earlier, Minamoto no Yoritomo, founder of the Kamakura shogunate, imprisoned his brother Noriyori in this temple, where after being attacked by Yoritomo's vassal, Noriyori took his own life in 1193. After Yoritomo's death in 1199, his eldest son Minamoto no Yoriie, the politically inept second shogun, was stripped of political power, banished, and eventually murdered here in a conspiracy led by his grandfather, Hojo Tokimasa. His mother Masako, grieving for her son, later set up a memorial for him in the nearby foothills.

In contrast to the grisly stories connected with the temple, the oblong main hall with its gently rolling roof, well set off by the trees in the mountains behind, had something of the charm of a graceful, high-born lady.

After visiting the temple, Kuki and Rinko paid their respects at Yorie's grave and memorial before returning to the car. It was past five by then, the sunlight fading, yet the brightness of spring lingered in the air. They made their way along a narrow riverside street lined with bath-houses until it widened and a rather imposing old inn came into view.

At the entrance was a massive gate and, further in, a wide porch with a peaked gable. The car pulled up in front, and a maid waiting to welcome them ushered them straight inside. The lobby was spacious, with a table of beautifully grained wood and rattan chairs set overlooking a pond.

Catching sight of a Noh stage seemingly afloat on the water, Rinko gave a low murmur of delight. From the far side of the large oval pond, the stage cast a delicate image on the surface; behind it, the steep hillside was thickly forested. She stood staring, eyes wide and unblinking, at this sudden vision of beauty at the end of their journey through the mountains and up the river.

The maid showed them to a suite in a rear corner of the second floor with two tatami rooms, one medium size, the other quite large; there was also a wooden-floored area next to wide windows looking out on the pond below.

"Come and see this tree—it's in full bloom!"

Kuki went over to the window as summoned and saw, just off to his left, at eye level, a blossom-heavy cherry tree close enough to reach out and touch.

"I told them we were here to enjoy the cherry blossom. That must be why they gave us this room." Kuki had never been here before. A friend from work had once told him about a quiet old inn in Shuzenji with a Noh stage, and he had written down the name and telephone number.

"Look, there!" exclaimed Rinko. "See the petals falling?"

A slight breeze had come up as evening fell. A single petal landed on her outstretched hand, then fluttered to the pond below.

"It's so quiet," said Kuki. Work, family, divorce, all belonged to some other, distant world. He breathed in deeply the mountain air, then stood behind Rinko and softly folded her in his arms as she gazed out at the flowering branches. She turned away as if shy of being seen, but the only witnesses were a tree in flower and the silent pond.

Kuki kissed her and whispered in her ear, "Did you bring it?"

"Bring what?"

"You know. The red under-kimono."

"You told me to. Of course I did," she said simply and, pulling away from the window, slipped into the bathroom.

Alone in the room, watching cherry petals drift down, Kuki lit a cigarette. The window was open but he felt no chill. Traces of the brightness of the season lingered in the air, both inside and outside. Savoring the pleasant, indolent mood, Kuki recited to himself in an undertone, "'If I may, let me die in spring beneath the cherry blossom in the month of rebirth when the moon is full.'" This short poem was one of his favorites, and was written by Saigyo, a twelfth-century poet who gave up a government post to spend his life wandering among the beauties of nature.

After resting a while and sipping some tea that the maid poured out, they went to try the hot-spring bath. Separate baths for men and women opened off the corridor on the first floor, but Kuki went past them to see about the open-air bath further down.

It was after six, the sky just turning from blue to indigo, not yet ink-dark. In these last moments before nightfall, the open-air bath was deserted. Evidently guests were few on a Sunday evening. The sound of water trickling over rocks could be heard in the hush of the empty bath.

"Let's go in together," he proposed. She looked hesitant. "It's okay," he insisted. Anyone coming in would see the two of them alone and decide to come back later. At his urging, she relented. Standing away a bit and with her back turned, she began peeling off her clothes.

The wide oval bath had a ceiling of woven reeds and was enclosed in reed screens, allowing bathers a measure of privacy as they relaxed in a natural environment. Kuki leaned back against a large rock, stretching his limbs in the hot water. Rinko stepped in, towel in hand. She was cautious, entering the steaming water almost one toe at a time.

Kuki waited for her to submerge her entire body before beckoning her to join him where the bath ended and the pond began.

"Take a look."

Stretched out lengthwise at the edge of the outdoor bath, without the wicker ceiling overhead, they could look straight up into the night sky. Hanging above them were branches of flowers in full bloom from the tree by their room, and beyond was the sky, washed in pale indigo.

"I've never seen a color like it," she marveled.

Out of the moonless, starless sky, a single cherry petal fell toward them, pirouetting. Rinko held out her hand to catch it, and another came fluttering down. Beneath the sky where evening shadows gathered, her white body curved in pursuit like a butterfly in the night, strange and beautiful.

After their bath, they had dinner in their room. There was a chill in the air now, so they closed the window, and each put on a warm padded jacket over one of the cotton yukata provided by the inn. They could still see the cherry blossom outside, lit from one side.

The meal offered other tangible signs of the season: stewed butterbur greens, *udo* in sesame sauce. Kuki started out drinking beer but soon switched to hot saké, the dry local brand. The maid poured his first drink, but after she left, Rinko attentively kept his cup refilled. During the next course—a hotpot of hairtail fish and dropwort in a clear broth—she kept an eye on the flame and ladled out a bowlful for each of them when it was piping hot.

Watching her brisk and efficient movements, Kuki thought of mealtimes with his wife. Years before it might have been like this, but not any more. Years of indifference and cross purposes were to blame and the contrast was amazing. What a difference love made! But what about Rinko's home life, he wondered. When she and her husband ate together, did she ignore him? Did they never eat together at all?

Kuki poured some saké for her. "Everything tastes good when we eat together."

"I know. No matter how fancy the food is or how nice the surroundings are, food only tastes really good when you're with someone you love."

He nodded, thinking how terrible it was that love should ever change. Once upon a time he had longed for his wife, his heart had pounded at the thought of her, but now the flame was dead. Rinko too had presumably trusted her husband and sworn to love him, yet now they'd drifted far apart. In their experience of marriage he and she were the same, a man and a woman alike in being sobered by disillusionment. And now they had found together a new intoxication.

Kuki had drunk only one glass of beer and several small flasks of saké, but he felt a bit tipsy. Maybe having Rinko near him hastened the effect of the alcohol.

Beyond the window, bunches of cherry blossom were still visible, off to one side. "Shall we go downstairs for a while?" he suggested. In the lobby, they would be able to see the Noh stage across the pond.

They waited for the maid to remove their trays before going out and down the stairs, past the entrance to the outdoor bath, then down another flight of stairs to the lobby. On their right, open doors led out to a wooden balcony overhanging the pond. They sat down side by side and breathed sighs of admiration. They had sighed before, upon arriving and first catching sight of the stage hanging over the water, but this was different.

Lights were fixed at either end of the balcony railing, their beams illuminating the Noh stage across the pond. The stage was about twenty feet square, the floor mirror-bright. On the large panel at the back was a painting of an old pine. To the left of the stage was a dressing room behind white *shoji* screens, connected to the stage by an oblique bridge over the waters of the pond. The entire scene was reflected in perfect symmetry.

It was like a wonderful painting. Originally built on the Maeda estate in Kaga, the stage was moved at the turn of the century to Tomioka Hachiman Shrine before being reconstructed here. Ever since, Noh plays had been staged here at night by the flickering light of bonfires around the pond, along with other traditional performing arts; there might be evenings of Japanese dance or lute-playing or *shinnai-bushi*, a form of dramatic narrative chanting associated with puppet plays. Tonight there would be no performance, but in the cold mountain air the stage lay silent with a mystery and beauty all the more profound. Kuki sat shoulder by shoulder with Rinko, staring untiringly at the Noh stage, experiencing the fantasy that at any moment there would emerge from the darkness a man and a woman wearing the masks of the mad.

It was last fall that they had watched a Noh play together by firelight at that Kamakura shrine, going afterward to a beachside hotel for the night. They had been passionate lovers then, but their link wasn't nearly as intense or significant as now. Back then, after a night together, Rinko still used to go back to her husband, and he too would go home out of concern for his wife. Barely six months later, their marriages were empty shells.

"That time, there was a Tengu mask," he said, recalling the long-nosed goblin mask in the Kyogen farce they'd seen in Kamakura. "Kyogen doesn't seem to belong here." Deep in these mountains, this stage with its delicate, solemn beauty seemed to cry out for drama that probed the human heart, bringing out its most subtle and profound emotions.

"I wonder ..." Kuki spoke in an undertone, studying the reflections of light swaying on the surface of the water. "Do you suppose that, long ago, people came here thinking no one would ever find them again?"

"Runaway couples?"

"Lovers..." Kuki looked up at the dark and silent mountain behind the Noh stage. "You know, even if you and I lived here together, it might not work."

"We'd eventually get tired of each other, you mean?"

"Laziness sets in, little by little, like a disease." Kuki was in fact a cynic, no longer innocent enough to believe with adolescent assurance that any two people who really loved each other would stay in love forever. "Love can only stay passionate for so long."

"I know. I think so, too."

Her assent took him aback. "You do?"

"That's why I'd like to die now, while our love is still passionate."

Under the spell cast by the light-encircled stage, her words had an eerie, hypnotizing sound. Suddenly chilly, Kuki tucked his hands inside his yukata. The temperature had dropped since nightfall. "Shall we go?" He felt that if he stayed any longer, he might be pulled back to a long-vanished world, under the sway of the old Noh stage.

They rose, turned back for a last look, and left the veranda. On returning to their rooms, they found them pleasantly warm, their futon laid out for them alongside the window. Kuki lay down on his back and glanced over at the blossoms peeking in at the window. Whatever happened here tonight, they would be silent witnesses.

He called to Rinko. No answer. He closed his eyes and lay without moving, limbs stretched out, until she came out of the bathroom. She was wearing only her cotton yukata; her hair, pinned up after their soak, swung loose about her shoulders.

"Aren't you going to wear the red one?"

She stopped short. "You really wanted me to put it on?"

"You brought it, didn't you?"

Persuaded, she disappeared into the other room. Kuki turned out all the lights except the lamp by his pillow, and looked back at the night window.

Here at this inn tucked away in the mountains, after looking at the mysteriously beautiful Noh stage, he lay in bed waiting for his lover to change into a red silk under-kimono at his request. There seemed something incongruous in the juxtaposition of the two experiences, the one so ethereal, the other so hedonistic; yet they shared a certain correspondence. After all, the five traditional categories of Noh drama— god, man, woman, madwoman, and demon—encompassed all of human passion. And certainly, a little while ago, the solemnity of the wooden stage had gradually given way to a kind of sensual enchantment. Everything had its two sides, front and back: the lascivious behind the sublime, the crazy behind the serene, the immoral behind the virtuous.

Just as he was having these thoughts, the door slid open and Rinko reappeared, swathed now in scarlet silk. He sat bolt upright, his eyes popping. In the low lamplight, her figure cast an immense shadow that stretched all the way to the ceiling. He felt at that moment as if the female protagonist in a Noh play had materialized before him. As he stared harder, her features seemed little by little to take on the look of a Magojiro mask, a mingling of youthful beauty, grief, and seductiveness. Unable to speak, he watched in fascination as the masked woman in scarlet slowly advanced, then opened her arms to clasp him by the neck.

Instinctively he flinched, shook his head, and gasped as if returning only then to himself. "Incredible."

The figure smiled slightly, the mask-like features reverting to the usual gentleness of Rinko.

"I could have sworn you stepped out of a Noh drama."

"Because we were looking at the stage before."

"Still, it really got me going."

Kuki remembered a painting of a Magojiro mask set against a ground of black. Lurking within the mild expression of the mask he had seen, or thought he'd seen, a powerful eroticism. Rinko's face just now had been the same.

"It's quiet, closed, but charged with eroticism."

"What's that?"

"A Noh mask...," said Kuki, and all of a sudden he pulled Rinko to him. Caught off guard, she tumbled face forward. He lay across her on the futon and whispered in her ear, "I'm going to rip off your mask tonight."

The under-kimono was a deep, bright red, the color of blood, with the power to evoke immediate excitement. Red silk was in a category all its own: worn by a demure-looking, fair-skinned woman, it couldn't fail to excite.

Kuki now pinned Rinko to the futon and slowly pressed his face against her, feeling like a beast tearing into blood-red flesh. He was openly excited by the scarlet garment, grateful for her readiness to play along with him. For a while he held her close, reveling in the cool sensation of the silk on his skin, then gradually loosened his grip and thrust his hand into the valley between her breasts.

"Wait—" She knew of course that the garment must in the end come off, but at the suddenness of this gesture she drew away, holding down his invading hand. "I want you to know something. I had a terrible time with this."

His hand fondled her breast. "How? Having it made?"

"I was out when it came, so he signed for it instead."

"Did he know what it was?"

"He must have glanced at it, and then been livid when he realized what it was. He insisted on knowing what I needed it for."

"You do wear one sometimes under your regular kimono, don't you?"

"Yes, but he figured it out. He said, 'You're going to wear this to bed with another man, aren't you.'"

Rinko claimed not to have slept with her husband for years. The sight of this red silk undergarment must have blinded him with fury.

"And then?"

"And then he called me a whore."

The moment the word left her lips, Kuki removed his hand from her breast, as if he were the one given a stinging rebuke. Prostitutes did wear such things to entice men, it was true. Still, "whore" was uncalled for—although it was understandable why her husband would feel driven to say such a thing: after years of avoiding him and refusing all his overtures, suddenly his wife had had this bright red thing made to satisfy another man's sexual fantasy. No wonder he blew up.

"What happened then?" Curiosity got the better of apprehension. "Did he hit you?"

"No, but he announced he was going to rip it to shreds, and—"

"This?"

"Yes. I told him to stop, and then all of a sudden he grabbed me and tied my wrists together." She broke off and rolled her head from side to side in revulsion. "I can't … begin to tell you."

"Go on. Tell me," Kuki begged.

She bit her lip and went on. "He tore my clothes off, stripping me naked."

"Did he force himself on you?"

"He wouldn't, not with a woman he'd just called a whore. Instead, he left me like that…"

Kuki held his breath.

"He knew just the punishment for a slut like me, he said, and brought in a camera."

"He took pictures?"

Rinko nodded. It struck him as indecent, and Kuki felt for a moment as if he were looking at a hard-core pornographic photo. What her husband had done to her was cruel and bizarre, but it showed the depths of rage and hatred a man's jealousy could drive him to.

Suddenly she cried out, "I can't bear it any more! I'm never going back there again!" Tears glistened between her closed lashes.

Even if he had stumbled on evidence of infidelity, for a man to punish his wife by stripping her naked and tying her up was degrading and vicious. True, technically her husband didn't lay a finger on her, but he humiliated her with the eye of his camera. It was just the kind of cruel stunt that a scientist in a cold rage might pull. No wonder Rinko wanted out. She could never go back to a man like that. He, Kuki, would make sure of it.

His mind racing, Kuki felt himself possessed by a vision. Unforgivable as her husband's behavior was, the thought of Rinko tied up and violated that way made his head feel strangely hot. He fingered the silken robe that covered her body. This single garment had the power to drive two men into a frenzy—one a frenzy of love, the other of hate.

As if thinking about what the man had done were a bizarre kind of turn-on, he couldn't help feeling a new stirring of desire. Whatever her husband had done to her, he would do more. Telling himself this, he slowly sat up and stared at Rinko lying wrapped in the red silk. Then he pulled open the neckline of the garment.

Rinko had finished talking. She lay quietly face up, eyes closed. With her husband, she must have fought like a hellcat, but with him, the man she loved, she was willing and compliant. Knowing this bolstered his confidence, and flattered his ego. He untied her sash and pulled the robe all the way open.

The minute he did so, an image of Rinko's husband and his camera flashed into his mind. Between folds of red silk were her slender white legs, laid bare. Had all this, even the secret place between her legs, been exposed to the camera's prying eye? The thought made him catch his breath. He lunged forward and pressed his face between her legs.

Just as there is an intimate connection between bullying and being bullied, so perhaps tenderness exists on a continuum with torture. Kuki's face lay buried in Rinko's flesh, his lips on the pink bud inside her secret place. The tip of his tongue criss-crossed it lightly back and forth, barely touching it, his infinitely soft, infinitely gentle caresses seeming only to distress Rinko until she began to whimper and writhe.

At first she uttered soft little cries, with tears in her voice. Then she began panting, her body arching and shaking with tiny tremors while the bud wrapped in his tongue swelled hot and ripe. She was near her bursting point, he knew, but still he clasped her legs, kept his lips clamped where they were. "No, too much!" she cried, pleading with him to stop, begging for time. But once they began, his lips and tongue never stopped their sucking and probing.

Kuki wanted to punish her for carelessly allowing her husband to find the scarlet under-kimono. All her weeping, pleading, and writhing wouldn't let her off the hook. The moment he knew with certainty that her senses were concentrated on this single point, that she was on fire, near the point of climax, he ceased the movements of his tongue as if struck by a sudden revelation. To keep on, allowing her to come so easily, would be no sort of punishment at all. He must be far crueler than that. He must not be satisfied until she'd suffered and wept for a very long time, until her breath grew faint.

Confused by the sudden lull, Rinko twisted as if to ask what had happened. Her body, lit with desire, wriggled sinuously, seeking greater satisfaction. When her excitement had ebbed slightly, his tongue began to flicker again, sending her into delirium, quickly wrapping her in flames. Driven back again and again from the shuddering edge, she wandered lost in a hell of no limits, suffering the torment of one con-demned never to find release. Again and again she would start to come and stop, only to begin again. Neither of them could have counted the times.

When he stopped prolonging the agony, allowing her to come, she did so with a low howl of anguish, her body rigid as a stick. Kuki looked at her face. Her eyes were closed. Only the trembling of her eyelids and the slight up-and-down motion of her chest, showing through the open folds of the disheveled red silk, reassured him that she was all right.

His cruelty had had the desired effect. Best of all, in contrast to her, he was hardly spent at all. If necessary he could attack her over and over again.

Flush with triumph, he said, "Did you suffer? Had enough?"

In answer, Rinko suddenly raised her fists and pounded him madly on the face, the chest, and wherever she could reach, then threw herself on him, straddling him with her body. She was screeching, her hair a wild jumble, the very image of a demoness. Thanks to his long, tormenting kiss, her bud alone had caught fire and reached climax; the core of the flower had been left out.

She sought him with her whole body, and Kuki started to respond but then caught himself: if they were fused together now, all the suffering she'd endured till now would be wasted. Before they were connected, he had to do one more thing.

He held her in his arms, dropping kisses on her mouth, her ears, wherever his lips happened to fall. On down her throat, her shoulders, and her breasts, he attacked her with his kisses, branding her everywhere with visible signs of their love, now sucking hard, now leaving the imprint of his teeth. Only then did he enter her, still chasing her husband's shadow in his mind.

Having never laid eyes on the man, he could only imagine what he looked like from Rinko's description, but he fancied now that he was battling him through the medium of her body. The outcome of the battle was obvious: the husband was the inevitable loser, he the victor. He wanted to obliterate him, annihilate all trace of him from her flesh.

Nothing is so exhilarating as to carry on a struggle in the expectation of imminent victory, knowing one's opponent to be dangerously weakened. Especially in the realm of sex, knowledge of superiority stirs male confidence and doubles male stamina. Kuki's extravagant determination communicated itself wholly to Rinko, and even after they were coupled, she rode wave after wave of passion, sometimes murmuring, sometimes pleading for release. He ruled her, mastered her like a male animal its mate. Only after he had fully had his way with her was his own passion spent, and the insane love-feast over.

The only witnesses to this madness were the cherry blossoms at the window. But both Kuki and Rinko, lying sprawled across the twisted bedding, had long since forgotten their existence.

Lying prone on the futon, Kuki was first to revive. He sat up slowly and, seeing Rinko close beside him, bent down and spoke softly in her ear.

"Was it good?"

She nodded, eyes still closed. "Incredibly good…"

He wanted to know how she felt about it all—the prolonged intimate kiss, the biting caresses, the joining of their bodies—but she only nodded as before.

"I tell you no, stop, but you never do…"

"You were naughty. I was teaching you a lesson."

"Lately you never stop when I tell you to. I think maybe, little by little, you've gotten me used to being handled that way."

There was a kind of lassitude in her tone and, somewhere, a touch of the spoiled child. Kuki was struck again with wonder. Moments before, she had been writhing, suffering, begging him in delirium to stop. Now that their lovemaking was over, she showed no resentment, only satisfaction, even saying she liked his ignoring her pleas to stop.

"I don't get it," Kuki sighed again. "Just a while ago you said you'd die if I kept it up."

"That's right."

"But you liked it?"

"I like everything you do to me."

Rinko had absorbed virtually the whole gamut of sex and was still going strong, with no sign of faltering. She was like the surface of the ocean, vast, with hidden depths. Pain, cruelty, sublimation: she took all these into herself, and promptly dissolved and blended them into a sea of pleasure.

Kuki slowly sat up and rested his forehead on Rinko's chest, then slid a hand across her bare shoulder until he touched the sleeve of her open shift. He tugged at it lightly, and found a tear running from the side all down the length of the sleeve in a tangle of loose red threads.

"Oh no, it's ripped," he said, poking his hand through the opening.

Rinko pushed his hand back and explained, "He did it."

"He did it?"

"When he was angry, he tore it apart. I sewed it up again, but I was in a hurry."

Kuki touched the broken cloth again, feeling that it somehow represented the gaping wound of Rinko's marriage.

Bothered by the torn sleeve, Rinko got up and went into the bathroom. A few seconds later she came rushing back out. "Oh no! What am I going to do!"

He turned around in surprise. She had both hands at the neck of her under-kimono.

"These awful kiss-marks. You bit me! Look at this!" She sat in front of him and opened the under-kimono, exposing her throat and chest. "Here, and here. See?"

The left side of her throat and the area around her collarbone and breasts were covered with blood blisters.

"I can't go back like this!"

"You said you weren't going back anyway."

"Not home, of course, but I can't even go outside looking like this!"

"It's all right," he said, laying a finger on a red mark on her neck. "They'll be gone in no time."

"How long?"

"A couple of days. Four or five at the most."

"That's terrible. I have to see my mother tomorrow."

"Can't you cover them up with foundation?"

"She'll know. What made you *do* such a thing?"

Easy. All over her body, from her throat to the pit of her stomach, he had left marks that were unmistakably the result of passionate kisses—first, to keep her from going back to her husband, and second, out of envy at the sexual voracity that took her to the peak of passion over and over again. His plan had worked—and yet, hearing her say she would never go home again forced him to admit that the situation was coming to a head.

"There's no way I'm going to see her tomorrow."

"You promised you would, didn't you?"

"She wants me to try one more time to talk things over with him. I'll just have to tell her it's out of the question." Rinko seemed to have lost every shred of nostalgia for her marriage. "What about you? You aren't going home either, are you?"

"Of course not."

"You do still go there sometimes, though."

"Just for a change of clothes and a look at my mail."

"Well, you can't any more. I'm not having it," declared Rinko. Her face swooped down to his chest, and she bit him just above one nipple.

"Ow!" he said, and drew back, but she clung fast.

"I'll fix it so *you* can't go home, either."

"Don't bother. I said I'm not going."

"Men always say one thing and do another."

Again her lips pressed against his skin, again her teeth sank into him. As he bore the twinge of pain, he told himself that there was nothing to do now but go with this love all the way, wherever it might lead. After a little while, Rinko slowly drew back and traced the mark in his skin with a fingertip. "And I bit you so hard!" She sounded put out at the faintness of the mark compared with the vivid welts all over her own soft skin. Still, bright red teeth-marks showed above the nipple.

"Lie back," she instructed him, and Kuki obediently lay face up on the bed, as she took the sash of her red under-kimono and passed it beneath his neck. "Don't move." She crossed the ends of the silken sash and slowly pulled on them.

"Hey!" Kuki still thought it was a joke, but Rinko calmly went on drawing the sash tighter around his neck. "What are you trying to do, kill me?"

"This much is nothing."

All at once she straddled him. Still gripping the sash ends in her hands, she demanded: "Do you swear never to go home again?"

"I told you I wouldn't, didn't I?" He managed to poke a finger between the sash and his neck, to keep her from tightening it further.

"You go home without saying anything to me and I'll kill you, so help me God."

"I won't, I won't," he swore. Then, coughing, he said, "Lay off. Who do you think you are, Sada Abe?"

Instantly she relaxed her grip, then knotted the sash loosely around his neck. "You were supposed to show me that book, don't forget."

"I brought it, just as I promised."

"All right, show it to me now."

"Like this?"

"Yes."

The red sash trailing around his neck, Kuki crawled naked over to his briefcase, took out the book, and crawled back. "Can I take this off now?"

"No. Read it to me just the way you are." Still holding the ends of the sash in her hands, Rinko told him sternly, "I want you to lie there and read to me out loud the parts that interested you the most."

It was a bizarre scene. Late at night in a room at an inn in the hot-springs town of Shuzenji, a man and a woman lay side by side with a book between them. The man, stark naked save for a red sash wrapped around his neck, held the book, and the woman listened to him read from it, the ends of the sash tight in her grip. The book contained the verbatim account given to a detective by a woman who, after an intense love affair, killed her lover by strangling him, then cut off his genitals and fled with them in her possession.

"It's long, but I'll read from the beginning."

The account was about seventy pages long. The frank, unflinching testimony by Sada Abe provided a vivid picture of the relationship between one man and one woman. Kuki shifted onto his side and turned to the first page, as Rinko settled herself close by.

It began with a reminder to the defendant that, based on the facts, she was charged by the public prosecutor with murder and mutilation of a corpse, and a question as to whether she had any statement to make concerning the facts. She answered by saying that the facts were just as they had been read to her. After that a question-and-answer format was used.

Q: What made you decide to kill Kichizo Ishida?

A: I loved him so much that I wanted to keep him all to myself, and we weren't married so I knew as long as he was alive he'd have something to do with other women. But if I killed him, he could never lay a finger on any other woman, so that's what I did.

Q: Did he return your feelings?

A: Yes, but I loved him more. It wasn't fifty-fifty with us, more like forty-sixty. Ishida always was clear that I was one thing to him and his family was another. He had two kids and he was getting on, he said, so he couldn't be running off with me. He said he'd set me up in some cheap sort of place somewhere, so we could go on meeting and enjoying one another for as long as we liked. But that sort of arrangement sounded so half-hearted to me that I didn't take it seriously.

Kuki read in an utterly plain and matter-of-fact tone, but Rinko listened intently, scarcely breathing. Aware of her keen interest, he read on, coming to the part about how they fell in love.

Q: What made you so devoted to him?

A: I can't say for certain, but I must say there was nothing you could fault about the way he looked. I never saw a handsomer man in all my life. He was forty-two but he didn't look a day over twenty-seven or -eight, and inside he was a simple man, delighted by the littlest things. He was quick to show his feelings, as innocent as a baby, and whatever I did pleased him and made him more loving. Also he was very considerate in bed. He always understood a woman's feelings, holding himself back so I had plenty of time to enjoy it too. He had plenty of energy too, always getting hard again right after we made love.

One time I tested him to see if he was really sleeping with me because he was in love with me or not. Pardon me for mentioning such a thing, but on April 23 when we ran away from the Yoshida place, I was having my period, and he touched me there and licked me there just the same. Around the twenty-seventh or twenty-eighth, when we were at a teahouse, I ordered some shiitake mushroom soup and I told him, "They say when two people really love each other, they'll eat mushrooms and raw fish from the woman's crack." Ishida said, "I'll do it," so I picked the mushrooms out of the soup and stuffed them up my crack, and then I put them back in the soup on the table. After fooling around for a while, Ishida ate half and I ate the other half. Then, I felt so crazy about him, I hugged him as hard as I could and I said, "I'd like to kill you so you could never make love to anybody else," and he said, "I wouldn't mind dying for your sake."

Q: During that spell together did you stay all the time in tea-houses?

A: Around the fourth or fifth of May we were in the Masaki, but we ran out of money and he said he was going home so I said I was going to cut off his cock, and he said, "Even if I go back I won't do it with anybody. You're the only woman for me." But after he was gone and I was all alone, I went wild with jealousy and frustration, and on the night of the tenth, I went all the way to Nakano, where his restaurant was, to see him. He brought out twenty yen with him, and we used that for drinks at a little stand by the station, and then we went back to the Masaki and ended up staying there for the night.

As he read, Kuki began to feel hot all over, and so, apparently, did Rinko. At first they'd lain facing one another, not touching, but before he knew it she was pressed up close beside him, saying throatily, "It's so real." Sada's testimony was so matter-of-fact, so straightforward that it brought the distant past to life, as though they could actually hear her voice.

"She certainly wasn't dumb," said Kuki. Her statement was taken well after the murder, but she spoke unhesitatingly about the details of the affair and her feelings about it. Throughout, her manner was cool, quite objective.

"What did she do before all this started?"

"Originally she was from Tokyo, from the Kanda district. Apparently she was a bright, lively girl. Her father's business went under and she became a geisha at an early age, moving around from place to place. She worked as a waitress at Ishida's restaurant under the professional name Kayo."

"I'd like to see a picture of her."

Kuki turned to the frontispiece, a photograph of Sada taken just after her arrest. Her hair was done up in the old-fashioned *marumage* style, and her rather long face had neat, even features. She looked calm, with a trace of loneliness in her eyes.

"She's nice-looking."

"She looks like you." Kuki said it half facetiously, but there was in fact a softness and a subtle sensuality about her that did bear a faint resemblance to Rinko.

"I'm not as pretty."

"You've got much more class," he added quickly. Looking at the picture, he felt that Sada's particular beauty embodied the mystery of women in general.

"When it happened, she was thirty-one," he pointed out.

Holding the book in one hand, Kuki flipped back to where he'd left off and began to read aloud again. The investigator's questions began to probe the heart of the matter.

Q: Describe what happened on May 16 as you were strangling Ishida.

A: Before that, on the twelfth or thirteenth, he told me he'd heard that being choked during sex was exciting, so I said, "Is it? All right, then do it to me," and he tried. But he said he didn't like hurting me like that. On the night of the sixteenth, he was making love to me and I was so crazy about him I didn't know what to do. I was biting him and this and that, and then I thought of doing it with my arms around him so tight he couldn't breathe. Then I told him I was going to choke him with my cord, and I took the kimono cord by my pillow and wrapped it around his neck, loosening it and tightening it while we made love. At first he joked around, playing tricks like sticking out his tongue, but when I pulled hard, his stomach would stick out and his cock would jerk inside me. It felt really good. I told him so, and he said if I enjoyed it he didn't mind putting up with a little discomfort. But I could tell he got tired right away. His eyelids drooped. "You don't like this very much, do you?" I said, and he said, "No, I don't mind, you go ahead and do what you want with me."

We went on that way for another couple of hours, me alternately loosening and tightening the sash, just enjoying myself till around two in the morning on the seventeenth. I was only paying attention to what went on down below, so one time I pulled too hard and jerked it tight around his neck. He groaned and just like that his cock went soft, so I undid the cord right away. He said my name and put his arms around me, whimpering, and I rubbed his chest for him. His neck was bright red and his eyes were kind of popping. "My neck hurts," he said, so I took him to the bathroom and splashed cold water on it. By then his face was all red and swollen too. He looked in the mirror and said, "Damn, would you look at that!" But he wasn't angry, not one bit.

Q: Did you have him looked at by a doctor?

A: I was going to, but he thought we'd better not or the police might get involved. I wiped his face with a cold towel and gave him a massage but it didn't help. In the evening I went to the pharmacy and said a customer had been in a fight and gotten strangled and his neck had turned bright red. They gave me some pills called Calmotin and told me to be sure he didn't take more than three at a time.

Impulsively, Rinko reached out and began to untie the sash around Kuki's neck, frightened perhaps by the graphic testimony. Kuki waited for her to finish and then went on reading.

Q: The night of the incident, did you spend all night in the teahouse?

A: Ishida's face was still swollen, so he couldn't go out. We'd had nothing to eat that morning except a little fish hotpot with egg in it, so at night when I went out for the medicine I bought some watermelon and fed it to him. After that I ordered noodles for him and riceballs for me. I gave him three pills right away, but they had no effect so I gave him six more. His eyes got heavy, but he didn't go to sleep. "I can't let the maids here see me with my face all swollen like this, I've got to go home," he said, and he told me to go somewhere and wait for him. I told him I couldn't bear to go anywhere without him, and he said, "You can't be so fussy, sweetheart. You've known all along that I've got kids, and we can't be together every minute of the day. If we're going to go on seeing each other, I'm sorry but you're going to have to be patient." I knew he was ready to leave me for a while, and I started crying, and he cried too and began saying all sorts of sweet things. But the more he did, the more I couldn't stand the thought of him taking off. All I could think was, "How can I stay with this man?" I was listening to him, but it was as if I was in a trance.

Q: And you ended up spending the night there?

A: Yes. Time was going by, and then the maid brought in some chicken soup I'd ordered. I fed that to Ishida, and around midnight we went to bed. His face was still swollen and he didn't have much pep. But I was kind of sulking so he licked my crack to keep me happy, and we did it together for a little while. But right away he said he was tired, he was going to sleep. He asked me to stay awake and watch over him so I promised I would, and I told him to sleep as long as he wanted. Then I put my cheek down next to his, and he began to nod off.

Kuki felt a sudden urge to touch Rinko, and reached out for her hand. Holding it tightly, he went on reading the deposition.

Q: When did you make up your mind to kill him?

A: From May 7 till about the tenth when I was alone, doing

nothing but thinking about Ishida and feeling terrible, I started to think maybe I should just finish him off. At the time, I put the thought right out of my mind, but on the night of the seventeenth, when he told me that after his neck was better it would be best for us in the long run if we split up for a while, I looked at his face while he was sleeping, and I thought about how once he was home his wife would nurse him the way I had, and how we wouldn't be able to meet again for at least a month or two. It had been hard enough to bear the last time, and I knew this was more than I could stand. I was just determined to not let him go. Until then, whenever I told him I wanted us to die together, or run away together, he'd never take me seriously. All he ever said was that he would set me up in my own teahouse some day so we could spend a nice long time together. I decided that the only way to make him mine forever was to kill him.

Q: Describe in detail what happened on the night of the seventeenth when you tied your kimono cord around Ishida's neck and strangled him as he lay sleeping.

A: As he was drifting off, I kept my eyes on his face, cradling his head in my left arm. Suddenly he opened his eyes and saw I was there, then he closed his eyes again like he was relieved. "O-Kayo," he said, "after I'm asleep, you're going to strangle me again, aren't you?" "Yes," I said, "I am," and I smiled. He said, "Well, do me a favor. Don't quit halfway, will you, because afterward it hurts like hell." Maybe he *wants* me to kill him, I thought, but I quickly changed my mind and turned it into a joke.

Before long he looked like he was sleeping, so I reached out and picked up the cord by the pillow, passed it under his neck, and wound it around twice before pulling on the ends. His eyes popped open and he said "O-Kayo," and raised himself up to hug me. I rubbed my face against his chest and said, "I'm sorry," crying, and then I pulled on both ends with all my might. He gave a long groan, and his arms shook, but then he went limp so I let go. I couldn't stop shaking. I drank down the rest of the saké on the table straight from the bottle, and pulled the cord tight, one more time, so he wouldn't come back to life. Then I hid the ends under the pillow. After that I went downstairs to see what was going on. Everything was as quiet as it could be, and the clock on the wall said a little after two.

Rinko let out a great sigh after this description of the murder. Kuki paused briefly before going on.

Q: Now state how you proceeded to sever Ishida's genitals, carve your name on his left arm, and write in blood on the body and bedding before fleeing the scene.

A: After I killed him I felt relaxed, even lighthearted, as if a heavy load had rolled off my shoulders. I drank down a bottle of beer and then I lay down next to him. His lips looked dry so I wet them with my tongue, and wiped his face. It didn't feel like I was beside a corpse. He was almost dearer to me then than when he was alive, and I stayed by him till morning, fondling his cock and putting it between my legs. All the while I was thinking, now I've killed him, I have to die too, but first I've got to get out of here. And then while I was touching his cock and holding it, I got the idea of cutting it off and taking it with me. The butcher's knife I'd shown him once before, the time I threatened to cut it off, was hidden behind a picture frame on the wall, so I got that out and pressed it against his tool, right at the base of it, but it didn't cut very well and it took me a long time to do it. One time the knife slipped and cut him on the thigh. After that I tried to cut off his balls too, but that was even harder and I don't think I got everything. I laid the things I'd cut off on some tissue paper, but so much blood came out that I stopped the wound with more tissue paper and then I dipped my left forefinger in the blood and smeared it on the sleeves and collar of the under-robe I was wearing. I wrote "Sadakichi us two" on his left thigh, and on the bedding. Then I took the knife and carved my own name, "Sada," on him, washed my hands in the metal washbasin at the window, and tore out some pages from a magazine at the head of the bed to wrap those precious things in. I took Ishida's six-foot loincloth from the basket where he'd put it when he took it off, wrapped it around my middle, and tucked the package inside. Then I put on his undershirt and drawers, put my kimono on over that and fastened the obi, straightened up the room, and threw away the bloody tissue in the second-floor toilet. When I was all ready, I wrapped the knife in newspaper, kissed Ishida good-bye, and covered his body with a blanket and his face with a hand-towel. Around eight o'clock I went down and told the maid I was going out shopping, and please to let him sleep in till noon. Then I got in a taxi I'd sent for.

Kuki had told Rinko the same story in outline once before, when they were snowed in by Lake Chuzenji. There was some redundancy, but he continued to read aloud from Sada's statement.

Q: Why did you cut off Ishida's penis and testicles, and take them with you?

A: That was the part that meant most to me, and I knew that unless I did that, when his body was washed, some other woman would be certain to touch him there. Also I thought that as long as I had to run off and leave his body, if I at least had that part of him with me I'd feel he was with me, and I wouldn't be so lonely. The reason I wrote "Sadakichi us two" on his thigh and on the bedding was because once I'd killed him, he belonged completely to me, and I wanted people to know that. So I took one character each from our two names and combined them, and wrote "Sadakichi us two."

Q: Why did you carve "Sada" on Ishida's left arm?

A: I wanted his body to have me attached to it, that's why.

Q: Why did you wear Ishida's loincloth and underwear next to your skin?

A: They had a man's smell, Ishida's smell, so I took them as keepsakes.

Q: Describe the escape route you took after the crime.

A: About eight in the morning on May 18, when I left the Masaki, I had about fifty yen on me. I decided to change my clothes before I did anything else, so I went to a secondhand clothing shop in Ueno, sold what I had on, and bought an unlined kimono and a big wrapping cloth to put the knife wrapped with paper in. I also changed my wooden sandals for a new pair. After that I telephoned the Masaki and said I'd be coming back at noon, so to be sure to let him sleep till then, and the girl just said "All right," so I relaxed, knowing they still hadn't found out. Then since I knew Mr. Omiya [former principal of Chukyo Business High School] was staying in the Mayokan, I phoned him and arranged for us to meet in Nihombashi. But when I saw him I got all choked up and started crying. "Whatever happens," I told him, "it's got nothing to do with you." Then I said good-bye. My unlined kimono wasn't warm enough, so after that I went to Shinjuku and bought another kimono made of serge and a Nagoya obi and changed into that. Then I took a one-yen taxi to the park in Hamacho, and decided while I was there that if I was going to die anyway, I might as well go back to Osaka where I used to be, and jump off a cliff on Mount Ikoma.

The record then moved on to events immediately preceding Sada's arrest.

Q: The night after Ishida's murder, where did you stay?

A: I wanted to die in Osaka, but I didn't have the courage to die right away and I also wanted to spend some time just thinking about Ishida. At about ten P.M. I went to a hotel in Asakusa called the Uenoya, where I'd been before. When I got there I took a bath, taking my precious bundle into the bathroom with me, and then went up to bed in my room on the second floor. On the bed I opened the bundle, and while I was looking at his cock and balls I would kiss them and hold them up between my legs, and the more I thought about it, the more I cried. I hardly got any sleep all night. Early the next morning I borrowed a newspaper from the front desk, and there was a picture of me, much younger, with a big article about the Masaki. I was afraid the people there would recognize me, so I quickly paid my bill. Because it was raining heavily, I borrowed an umbrella, and left.

Q: Tell us what happened from the nineteenth until the time of your arrest.

A: Since it was raining, I decided I'd take the night train to Osaka. I went to Asakusa and watched a motion picture before going to Shinagawa, where I bought a third-class ticket to Osaka. There were still two hours before the train left so I bought five different newspapers at a station kiosk and packed them away to read later. I had a drink at a place in front of the station, and that made me woozy and sleepy. After five, I went to an inn close by called the Shinagawakan and had a massage and dozed off. During it I dreamed about Ishida, and I was afraid I might have talked in my sleep, but the masseur said I didn't, so I felt better. After that I had a meal there and looked at the evening papers.

They had my name as O-Den Takahashi, and they'd printed all sorts of terrible things about me. It also said there were detectives staked out at every station, so it looked like I wouldn't be getting to Osaka after all, and I made up my mind to die right there where I was. The balcony was too low for me to jump off of, though, so the best I could do was have the maid move me the next morning to a room in the annex where I thought I could hang myself by letting myself drop down toward the garden. I borrowed a fountain pen and paper and wrote three letters, one to Mr. Omiya, one to Mr. Kurokawa, and one to my dead Ishida, and then I drank two beers and went to sleep, meaning to get up and die during the night. Around four A.M. a police officer came in, so I told him I was Sada Abe. And that's how I was caught.

Kuki had grown a little tired of reading, but he moved on to the finale, Sada's description of her mental state following her arrest.

Q: The defendant will now state her present feelings about this incident.

A: While I was in the police station it still made me happy to talk about Ishida, and at night I looked forward to dreaming about him. It made me feel good and loving. But as time went by my feelings changed. I wish now I'd never done such a thing. I'm doing all I can now to forget about it. From here on I don't want ever to talk or think about this again, so if possible, rather than a trial or a big interrogation in front of a lot of people, I'd prefer if the authorities could just talk it over among yourselves and decide on a proper punishment. I won't complain. I'm ready to go along with whatever you decide, so I don't think I need a lawyer, either.

Q: Is there anything else you wish to say?

A: What bothers me most about all this is that people have gotten the mistaken idea that I'm a sex maniac, so I'd like to say something about that. I think you can tell whether I'm one or not just by looking at my past history. I never did anything with another man like what I did with Ishida. Sometimes I'd get fond of a man and sleep with him for no money, but I never got carried away and I'd break up with him easily enough when the right time came along. That's how normal and in control of myself I always was. Sometimes men would resent it, in fact. But Ishida was just perfect. He was a bit of a rough diamond, so maybe "perfect" isn't the right word, but to me that was part of his charm. I loved him body and soul. Now that all of this has come out, people are going crazy, saying any old thing they want to about me just for the fun of it. But I think it's only natural for a woman to love her man's cock. It's like this: a woman who might hate the taste of raw fish, for example, learns to like it if her husband does. The smell of his clothes makes her happy. Leftover tea in the cup of the man you love tastes delicious, and if he pops some food from his own mouth into yours, that's fine too. Why do men pay a whole pile of money to buy out a geisha? Because they want the woman all to themselves. I've no doubt in my mind there are other women out there who love somebody so much they think about doing what I did too, they just don't go through with it. Of course it takes all kinds to make a world, and some of them may care more about material things than love, but let me say this: just because somebody is so much in love she can't stop herself from doing what I've done, that in itself doesn't make her a sex maniac.

Kuki finished reading the deposition and turned to Rinko. Her face was slightly flushed. Feeling thirsty, he got up and took a beer out of the refrigerator. Rinko got up too, and came and sat across from him at the table.

"Well, what did you think?" he asked, pouring beer for them both.

"That was amazing," she murmured. She paused, and went on, "I had completely misjudged her. Until now, knowing what she'd done, I'd always assumed she was weird and nasty, but it's not true. She sounded honest, even likable."

Hearing her say that made Kuki feel rewarded for the effort of reading it aloud.

"I'm amazed you ever found it."

"I was determined to get my hands on it. First I went to the Ministry of Justice, but they turned me down on the grounds that it was private information. They said they could only release it for academic or scientific purposes."

"Wouldn't that include you, since you're doing social research?"

"You'd think so, but I got turned down again and again."

"They ought to clear Sada's name by having the whole document made public."

"Yes, but you're up against the petty bureaucrat's love of secrets. When I got to poking around, though, I found it was already public property."

"Where did you find it?"

"There are so-called 'under-the-table' books containing sensitive information like this, things that are usually kept secret."

"Then other people must have seen it."

"Probably the investigating officer, or whoever took down what was said, smuggled a copy out and started circulating it behind the scenes."

"Then what's the point of hiding it any more?"

"That's the bureaucratic mentality for you."

Rinko seemed thirsty, too. She gulped down her beer, then picked up the book and opened it at the front. First were the head shots of Sada and Kichizo that ran in newspapers immediately after the murder, then a group photograph of Sada, the arresting officer, and the local police backup, taken after her arrest. Strangely enough, they were all smiling pleasantly, as if celebrating something.

"It must have come as a relief to her to be arrested."

"And she was an attractive woman who surrendered to them easily: that would probably be enough to make them smile."

"But wasn't this a time when the police and the military used to throw their weight around, terrorizing ordinary people?"

"It was 1936, when Japan was sliding into militarism. The country's mood was grim and anxious. Who knows? Maybe Sada's total commitment to her lover aroused people's sympathy. Maybe it just took their minds off other things."

Rinko nodded, flipping through the pages. "The whole thing strikes most people as macabre, but it's not as extraordinary as they might think. I bet she's right: there *are* other women who think about doing what she did, they just don't go through with it."

"That's something you can relate to, is it?" he said, joking, but she nodded without a second's hesitation.

"Of course it is. If you're very much in love, it's only natural to feel that way."

"Killing the guy seems going a bit far."

"It depends on how intense your love is. If you loved someone very, very much, so much you had to have him all to yourself, what else could you do?"

Kuki for a moment was nonplussed. "But carrying it out would be another matter, I assume."

"Yes, but if you cared about someone enough, who knows what you might do? I think that urge is always there, deep inside a woman."

Under Rinko's straight-on gaze, Kuki unconsciously looked away. Suddenly finding the room stuffy, he stood up. The moment he opened the window, a cool draft of spring night air pleasantly skimmed his cheeks.

"Come here," he said, and she came and stood beside him at the window. To their immediate left was the blossom-covered cherry tree and, beneath it, the pond, lit up by lights. The pond continued on around the tip of the outdoor bath to connect with an area where the dark surface reflected the mysterious beauty of the old Noh stage.

"It's so quiet..." Kuki drew in a deep breath, as if to clear his mind of the events he'd just been relating. Here in this tranquil mountain enclave, Sada's story seemed something from a distant world. They lingered, looking up at the night sky spreading far beyond the black, curving line of the mountains confronting them.

"The cherry blossoms...," murmured Rinko.

Turning his head, Kuki saw petals drifting down from a branch of fully opened flowers. One floated past them and landed on the surface of the pond below. Another rode toward the window ledge on a faint stirring of the night air.

"They come down even at night, don't they."

Her comment jolted Kuki. It was an unexpected revelation. All the while they had been in the open-air bath, all the while they had been making love, all the while he had been reading aloud, the petals had continued to fall. "Even while we're asleep, they'll go on falling," he said.

"Shall we stay up and watch, to keep them company?"

It was a nice thought, but he was feeling a little tired. It might have been the ferocity of their lovemaking, or the excitement of their reading. One by one, cherry petals went on drifting soundlessly into the blackness of the night.

Kuki laid a hand lightly on Rinko's shoulder and whispered in her ear: "Let's turn in."

It was faintly embarrassing to go back to rumpled bedding, this time to sleep peacefully and nothing more.

Kuki got into bed first, while Rinko lingered by the window. "I'll leave it open a little," she said. The cool would be refreshing, he thought, nodding with his eyes closed. She turned out the light and got in beside him. He reached out for her, missing the soft touch of her skin, but she intercepted his hand, lightly holding it down as she murmured, "Still, you have to feel sorry for her."

For a moment he didn't understand.

"And I'd never do what she did. No matter how much you loved someone, it wouldn't make any sense to kill them, would it?"

Kuki had to agree. "She killed him to have him to herself, but that was no guarantee of happiness. She paid the price for what she did. She was still a murderer."

After serving her time in prison, Sada had gone back to work in a restaurant in Asakusa. Some people reported having seen ads for "The restaurant where Sada Abe works," a clear sign that whether she liked it or not she was prey thereafter to the eyes of the curious.

"It would be worse to be the one who survived," said Rinko.

Yes, but it was bad enough to be murdered and have your genitals lopped off. "There's not much to choose, either way," he observed.

"You think so?" After a moment, she added, "The whole problem is that one of them survived."

"Problem?"

"Yes, they should have both died together. That way they could have been together always, and neither of them would ever have been lonely."

Kuki turned slightly away from Rinko, suddenly short of air. Her declaration that the lovers ought to have shared death shook him to the core. Surely she wasn't suggesting outright that the two of them should die? Surely she was still talking about Sada?

He turned back as if reconsidering and pressed his cheek against her breast, looking up at the ceiling.

Ishida had lain with his cheek on Sada's breast, just like this, when Sada strangled him. Kuki lay against Rinko's softness in the same pose, his heart slowly calming. After a while he searched for her nipple with his mouth, his lips traversing the gentle slope of her breast until they found it and fastened around it. Slowly he moved his tongue to left and to right, then curled it around the nipple, thinking of nothing, his mind blissfully at rest. Breast and mouth form a bond between mother and infant from the time of birth, and in the same way, breast and tongue bind women and men for all time.

As he lay half-dreaming in the stillness of the night, his tongue winding around her nipple, a light, gossamer sensation brushed the corner of his mouth. What was it, he wondered, still suckling, then felt it again. This time he pulled slowly away and turned on the bedside lamp to see what it was. Two petals of palest pink lay on either side of the nipple.

"Cherry petals," he murmured.

Rinko was looking at him strangely. "There's one on your mouth, too."

It was true. He picked the petal off his lips and laid it on her breast with the others.

"They came right in through the window," he said, looking in that direction. "And they'll keep falling all night." At this rate, the blossom would be gone in a day or two. "Don't move." He laid a hand on her bare shoulder peeping through the folds of red silk.

Driven by the breeze, cherry petals came fluttering in one by one until her soft white skin was covered with pale pink.

Early Summer

Each spring, for many people in Japan, the fall of the cherry blossom stirs a sense of poignant loss, like that felt for someone who dies too young. Soon enough, however, the sadness ebbs, as the lengthening days of spring and early summer bring a profusion of new and colorful life: wisteria, azaleas, tulips, poppies, peonies, and rhododendrons coming into flower as a diversity of trees put out leaves of every shade of green.

Kuki reacted to the arrival of this season intensely, but as everything out of doors seemed to explode and expand, the walls of their Shibuya love nest seemed in contrast to be closing in on them. It was their only home, as they each had sworn never to return to where they'd lived before, but the hastily assembled haven now felt depressingly small and poorly equipped. Kuki wanted to move to a roomier apartment, even though money was in limited supply. It also weighed on him that if they were to live together officially, he'd have to have her name entered in his family register. The next-door neighbors assumed they were husband and wife, but others had clearly reached a different conclusion.

All this he'd been over with Rinko, who was in the apartment most of the time and must have been only too aware of its limitations. It was too cramped: the kitchen was tiny, and their little chest of drawers wouldn't hold all their clothes, so she had bought plastic storage boxes to accommodate the overflow. She practiced her calligraphy daily and conscientiously, but it was painful to see her laying out brushes, paper, inkstone and other equipment on the same table where they ate their meals. It seemed such a comedown, and all because she had chosen to leave her husband and live with him. He longed to provide her with a bigger place, but no matter how often he brought up the idea she always brushed it aside, insisting they stay put. At first he had assumed that her reasons were financial, but he came to suspect that she was actually quite satisfied with the dinky, dingy apartment after all.

"The only thing that matters is that you come home to me here every day," she would say with her head held high, making his heart swell with such affection for her that he couldn't help giving her a hug. And one thing would lead to another, so that almost every time he broached the subject of their moving, they would wind up back in their usual routine, naked in each other's arms.

Kuki remembered Sada Abe's statement to the police. In it she had said that, for several weeks before her crime, she and her lover had spent nearly every waking moment in physical contact with each other. It seemed more and more that way with him and Rinko: not constant sex, but a continual affectionate touching or twining of limbs. He might fondle her breasts, while she played with his penis, the two of them trading tender looks and endearments. Sometimes this would lead to coupling, but just as often they would doze off peacefully in each other's arms.

On weekend afternoons it got so that they began to feel they were prisoners of sex, trapped in a narrow cellar. It occurred to Kuki that the real reason for Rinko's opposition to leaving the tawdry little apartment was that she was now steeped body and soul in what went on inside it.

Her curiosity about sex had plainly gone up a notch. One Sunday early in May, they went out shopping late in the afternoon and stopped on the way back at a little furniture store. Kuki went in intending to get Rinko a bigger table for her calligraphy, but while looking around he spotted a mirror display: stout full-length mirrors with props enabling them to stand alone, others with simple wooden frames for hanging. Looking them over, he'd said impulsively, "What if we put one of these by the bed?" He was teasing, remembering the time in Yokohama when he had stealthily looked at her naked in the mirror. Rinko, however, took it seriously.

"A big one like that would show both of us," he added, nudging her on.

Quite calmly, in a low voice, she told him "Let's take it."

They arranged for delivery the same day. When the mirror arrived that evening, they promptly set it alongside the bed and lay down, eager to try it out. They brought up a lamp for extra light, adjusting the mirror so that they were both clearly illuminated from the waist down. The sight in it of Rinko's white body with its black tuft was enough to excite Kuki on the spot, and she was equally aroused. When he entered her, she moaned with pleasure, raising her head again and again to gaze at their reflection.

Not for the first time, he found her intense receptiveness to new experiences both appealing and a little frightening. Where would this take her, take them, and how far would it go? He felt responsible for her transformation, and yet her irrepressible eagerness made her now seem a different person altogether. With the new mirror by the bed, their little hideaway seemed even to him more sultry and seductive than before.

There was another place he and Rinko visited for the first time: an "adult" toy shop in an alley in Shibuya. They hadn't set out intentionally to go there, but when they happened to find it, Kuki suggested they take a look inside. She followed, unsuspecting, only to be startled by displays of gaudy underwear, leather whips, penis rings, and vibrators. She tugged at his sleeve in embarrassment, rooted to the spot, her eyes downcast; yet she made no move to leave. Slowly she looked around in the shelter of his back, her interest evident. She pointed to a vibrator and asked what it was for. Kuki picked it up and explained, showing which part went where, and she showed surprise, reaching out hesitantly to touch it. He thrust it at her playfully, but she quickly backed off, both hands in the air, shaking her head.

"You might like it. You never know."

"Don't you believe it!"

Seeing her turn away, he yielded to a naughty impulse and bought the thing.

Rinko only eyed it skeptically when he produced it later at home, asking dryly, "Is this the sort of thing you men get a kick out of buying?"

"What do you mean?" he protested. "The whole store was full of things for women."

"No gizmo could ever be an improvement on you."

It was nice to hear her say this, but eventually the new toy did in fact become a permanent fixture in their bedroom. Although it was he who had stumbled on the mirror, and had impulsively bought the electric dildo, it was she who became engrossed in these erotica and adept in their use. And in their lovemaking she became more and more insatiable, allowing it to end only when he was utterly consumed, unable to go on a second longer.

By this stage, for him to say that he'd initiated and guided her, while true enough, meant very little. The pupil had outstripped her teacher, gone beyond his control. Perhaps this was why so many husbands hesitated to go further with their wives, to explore the deeper secrets of sex with them. Did they fear their power, the unleashing of a greedy monster, the struggle to satisfy a growing appetite?

Many men dream of sexually transforming the woman they love, but the average man probably holds back for fear that her increased voracity might become a burden on him. Was it only outside marriage that they dared try to bring about such a transformation? Was it only there that they could be free enough to reap the benefit of those hidden riches, like digging a well from which they could drink their fill and then depart?

But for Kuki that "freedom" was now out of the question. Far from petering out after a year or so as many romances do, his and Rinko's affair seemed only to grow deeper, as both of them were swept along together by a powerful current through a world that neither had ever seen before.

When he asked himself why he still loved her so much, he knew it was partly because *only* he knew the prodigious awakening that had taken place in her. To most people she appeared ladylike and reserved, someone whose sensuality was hard to guess at. The reversal of that dignified image in private was still intensely exciting to him.

At times, though, he did sense that her other side showed itself in subtle and unconscious ways. Occasionally, when they were out together, men would give her sidelong looks, and when she walked alone in the park strange men would speak to her. Quite recently she had told him that two young men, in different places and at different times, had approached her that day and asked her out.

"Do you suppose I'm attractive to men?" she asked with feigned innocence.

Provoked, he told her, "We men have an instinct. We can sniff out a hot-blooded female a mile off."

"It's you who made me what I am," she snapped, placing the blame back on him.

"Well, from now on when we go out, I guess I'll have to keep you on a leash," he laughed.

He could joke all he wanted, but the one on a leash was him, and he knew it. At times, this awareness made him chafe against it: having managed to win the woman of his dreams, why couldn't he keep setting the pace, maintain a semblance of control, instead of being made to follow her agenda, manipulated at her whim? At other times, he took a perverse pleasure in the situation. No use brooding. Might as well let things take their course, see just how low he could sink. Defiance was mingled with resignation as he surrendered to his own instinct for debauchery.

Rinko was sensitive to his moods. When he heaved a sigh, or gave some other sign of discontent, she would say gently "Never mind, don't dwell on it," helping to cushion him from reality.

He knew eventually he would have to give some serious thought to their future, to how they were going to live. This indolent way of life couldn't go on forever. Somehow things would have to be sorted out, their respective marriages dissolved. But for the moment he was disinclined to deal with such hard, unpleasant facts. He ought to move swiftly to divorce his wife and see to a hundred related matters, but the thought was tiresome. He was prepared to sign the form the next time his wife brought it up, but if she never did, he was just as prepared to go on as they were.

With Rinko it was much the same. She had dropped all communication with her husband, and showed no sign of starting negotiating for a divorce on her own. She and Kuki had burrowed deep into their own world, with little thought for anything but each other. That this was an evasion of social responsibility they were prepared to accept, but what was to be gained now from any attempts at reconciliation? It was too late for them to come to their senses now.

While others might see their behavior as debauched and scandalous, they themselves did not. They floated along as their desires led them, seized intermittently amid the surrounding darkness by moments of prolonged, intoxicating rapture as they pushed their bodies to the limit, seeking the apex of pleasure.

For Rinko, who seldom left the apartment, this might have been enough, but for Kuki, still commuting to the office nearly every day, an inevitable breakdown occurred between reality and a life suspended between waking and dreaming. In the reality of daylight he saw his colleagues in the office and sat working at his desk, while his disordered private life receded to a half-dream. To travel back and forth between those separate worlds was disorienting; to reconcile them, all but impossible.

In fact, signs of the dissolute life he was leading in Shibuya began surfacing at work without his realizing it. The secretary made sly little comments about how tired he looked. If he happened to doze off at his desk, she was quick to tease: "You're pushing yourself too hard, Mr. Kuki."

His male co-workers never said anything outright, yet they did pick up on his general lassitude and sense of preferring just to let things slide. Muramatsu, with whom he was on close terms, asked him occasionally if he was feeling okay. Kuki would always shrug the question off, but finally, in mid-May, word got out that he was no longer living at home.

It happened when Muramatsu, needing to talk to Kuki for some reason, dialed his home number. His wife answered airily that he hadn't been home in quite some time, and no, she didn't know where he could be reached. So, there it was. "We had a little spat. Nothing serious," Kuki lied to save face, but it was no use. The news soon spread that he had a mistress with whom he was spending all his off hours.

In theory, whatever might be going on in an office worker's private life shouldn't matter as long as the work got done—but, in fact, a scandalous sex life couldn't help having an adverse impact. Should a man's mistress come storming into the office, or his wife appeal directly to his superior, the repercussions would be huge. Compared to banks or investment houses, the publishing business was relatively flexible and tolerant, but unsavory incidents were definitely taboo.

To be sure, Kuki's job was essentially a sinecure, the usefulness of his work marginal, and no obvious trouble had occurred. A chance phone call had uncovered the fact that he was living with another woman, that was all.

A few days later, happening to be alone with Kuki, his section chief Suzuki broached the subject indirectly: "I understand you've had your hands full lately."

Kuki quickly understood this to be a reference to his love affair with Rinko, but he couldn't think of any appropriate response. "I have?" he stammered.

"I wish I had your stamina," said Suzuki sardonically. That was it. No warnings, no advice. It seemed he wanted Kuki to know that he knew what was going on, nothing more. But if Suzuki knew, everyone else must know too.

At first, Kuki told himself this was no cause for alarm. Sooner or later, word was bound to get out anyway. Having it out in the open was all to the good. Nonetheless, he couldn't help wondering what the others really thought. Of one thing he was sure: revelation of his personal "situation" killed whatever chance he might have had for a professional comeback.

With his job in this depressing state, Kuki tended more and more to stay away. He wasn't guilty of any particular misconduct at work; it was only that everyone now knew about his private life. The sight of colleagues whispering made him apprehensive, even paranoid, and with people from other sections he was self-conscious, alert to any gossip. His doubts and suspicions served only to weaken his already tenuous position. Weighed down by anxiety, he sought refuge at home. The only one who could distract him and ease his mind was, after all, Rinko.

Back in their tiny rooms in Shibuya, alone with Rinko, he could escape the demands of convention. There, in their own little world, outside rules did not apply and he could relax. As long as he was there, away from shaking heads and disapproving looks, he could do exactly as he pleased—lie back and do nothing at all, or indulge in a frenzy of sex, with no fear of censure or blame. Indeed, with a beautiful, accommodating woman always there waiting for him, it seemed only natural to shut himself away with her.

Nevertheless, he couldn't shake off the sudden onset of misgivings. If they went on as they were, in time they would find themselves disconnected from outside society in general, totally isolated. Cutting themselves off from the world, even to avoid criticism, meant allowing the breach to expand until return became impossible—a fact brought home to Kuki while seeing Kinugawa again.

As usual, Kinugawa phoned him and they arranged to meet at the same tavern in Ginza. It was their first get-together since Rinko's calligraphy award the previous fall, nearly six months earlier. In the interim, increasingly preoccupied with his love affair, Kuki had neglected his friend. Embarrassment had played a part in his silence, while Kinugawa had apparently made himself scarce out of tact.

Kinugawa seemed heavier, more physically imposing than before. He spoke with more energy, too, starting with a breezy, "How's it going?"

"You know—same old thing," Kuki answered vaguely.

Kinugawa drained his beer glass. "How's Rinko? Is everything okay between you two?"

Put off by his friend's probing look, Kuki averted his eyes, but Kinugawa persisted.

"She's a real treasure, my friend," he said. "Whatever you do, don't let her get away." Despite the seeming encouragement, the words were tinged with sarcasm. "I mean, who ever would have thought she'd have the guts to walk out on her husband and move in with you?"

"Who told you that?"

"A little bird," he said smugly. One of the calligraphy teachers at the Culture Center must have said something, someone Rinko had confided in, Kuki thought.

"She still doing calligraphy?"

"Sometimes…"

"It would be a shame to let that talent go to waste. She didn't enter anything this spring, did she?"

Rinko had decided to skip the spring show because she felt unable, with all that had happened, to concentrate.

"She talked once about leaving her husband and setting herself up independently."

Kuki nodded vaguely, remembering that Rinko had asked Kinugawa to make her a full-time teacher at the Center.

"But if she's with you, she won't be working any more, will she?"

Kuki took this to mean Kinugawa no longer intended to act as intermediary.

"It'd be a shame for her to bury her talent," said Kinugawa again. He gave an exaggerated sigh. "If it happens, it'll be your fault."

Barely thirty minutes after sitting down with him, Kuki felt stifled and uncomfortable. Last year when they met, there'd been none of these undercurrents. Why now? Was it because he'd spent the last six months engrossed in an extramarital affair, while Kinugawa had gone on being a solid citizen, the embodiment of common sense?

Unaware of what was passing through Kuki's mind, Kinugawa leaned forward and asked, "So, how are things at work?"

"Could be worse." Again, Kuki was noncommittal.

This time Kinugawa looked obviously annoyed. "You never give a straight answer, do you?"

Kuki remembered then that at the end of last year, Kinugawa had asked if he was interested in working for the publishing division of the newspaper company where he, Kinugawa, had formerly been employed. Unable to make up his mind, Kuki had been deliberately vague. Kinugawa had never brought it up again.

"Maybe the job you have now is right for you, then," he said, which suggested an oblique withdrawal of his previous offer. Kuki remained silent, having no desire for any transfer at this point, and Kinugawa changed the subject. "How'd you like to come and lecture at the Center again?"

"No thanks." No point in going back there for the sake of a small honorarium.

"We're nothing to sneeze at, you know. There are more new classes, and enrollments are way up. We're rated one of the best in the city."

"That's great."

"Matter of fact, I just won the President's Award. Starting in July, I could become general manager of all the Culture Centers in Tokyo." That might be the real reason Kinugawa had arranged this get-together, to share this piece of news.

"Congratulations."

Kuki refilled Kinugawa's glass, thinking that this explained the uncomfortable feeling he'd been having. Put it down to the difference in style between a man on the rise and one on the way down.

Seeing Kinugawa was depressing. Not because of the news of his upcoming promotion, which could have no direct effect on Kuki since they worked for different employers. What bothered him was that Kinugawa was plugging away at work while he, Kuki, did nothing but pursue his relationship with Rinko. It made him feel thoroughly uneasy about his own flagrant self-indulgence, about behavior that, to put it bluntly, made him afraid to show his face in public. He felt ashamed.

Was this any way for a man to live? Ever since moving into the Shibuya apartment with Rinko, he had never stopped asking himself this, and seeing Kinugawa only intensified his doubts. Then two weeks later came still more depressing news, as if triggered by the start of the June rains: two days after the official start of the rainy season, his old friend Mizuguchi had died in a Tokyo hospital after a long illness.

Kuki stared at the interoffice memo: "At 5:20 this morning, Goro Mizuguchi, president of Marron, Inc., passed away." After that came his age: fifty-four. Looking at the figure, Kuki recalled his single visit to the hospital three months ago, when Mizuguchi had told him, "Everybody gets old and dies in the end, so you've got to do the things you want to while you still can." Had such thoughts been on Mizuguchi's mind right up until the end?

The wake was at six P.M. the next day, at a temple near Mizuguchi's home in suburban Tokyo. Funeral arrangements were the province of junior colleagues; by the time Kuki arrived, shortly before six, a crowd of mourners had already gathered and the sutra reading was under way. The picture of Mizuguchi in the center of the altar, surrounded by masses of flowers, had evidently been taken two or three years earlier. It showed him smiling slightly, with the sparkle in his eyes of a man in his prime.

Since he had been a company president at the time of his death, the room was lined on both sides with huge wreaths from heads of publishing companies as well as editors, managers, and clients. As Kuki looked at the flowers, the words "untimely death" came into his mind. A fifty-four-year-old man was no stripling, yet from the perspective of someone the same age, it was certainly too young to go.

In any case, Mizuguchi had been single-minded in his devotion to his job. How strange and ironic it was that someone like that should have died while a useless leftover like himself went on living.

After a while it was time to offer incense, so Kuki got in line with the other mourners, many of whom he recognized. He found himself next to Nakazawa, now head of the sales department. They exchanged silent greetings.

Step by step as they approached the altar, Kuki was struck forcefully with the realization that his friend was dead. He gazed at the photograph, palms pressed together in a gesture of respect. *What did you go and die for?* That was all he could think. Rather than grief, or prayer, that one question consumed his thoughts: why the hell did he have to die so suddenly? It was unthinkable, unacceptable. Sickness comes without warning, yet this was too extreme, as if Mizuguchi had carelessly stepped on a land mine called cancer. All that separated Kuki in the land of the living from Mizuguchi in the land of the dead was the simple matter of which of them happened to set foot on that mine.

Still struggling to understand and accept, he finished offering incense, said his condolences to the bereaved family, and was heading out the door when Nakazawa proposed they stay on for a few minutes. Outside the building, to the right, was an anteroom where close friends of the deceased were gathered. Kuki would have liked to go in and share in the reminiscences, but once inside he knew he was likely to encounter former colleagues. His loss of status weighed on his mind. Perhaps he was making too much of it.

"Come on, just for a little while."

Succumbing to the repeated invitation, Kuki went along, finding twenty or thirty people inside, all drinking beer. He nodded to those he recognized and took a seat, and Nakazawa lost no time in striking up a conversation.

"Mizuguchi used to say he envied you."

"He did?"

Wiping foam from his mouth, Nakazawa said, "He was a fiend for work. Work, work, morning till night."

"He liked it, though, didn't he?"

"Yeah, but his transfer got him thinking, wondering what the point of it all was. Then just when he was getting ready to loosen up a little, *boom*. Cancer."

Mizuguchi had told Kuki much the same story in the hospital.

"He said he wished he could be like you."

"Like me?"

"You don't have to pretend. You're living with somebody, aren't you?"

So even Nakazawa had heard. Kuki felt a weight descend on him.

"Work's okay, but romance is important, too. Especially at our age."

"Yes, but he had a good marriage. He loved his wife…"

"Anyway, it was too late for him. But when I think how he died, I get this hunted feeling. My life seems dreary, like something's missing…"

Coming so soon after the death of his friend, Nakazawa's remarks were no doubt sincere, but to love a woman in earnest wasn't something you just pulled off in your spare time. It could become a serious burden in itself. Did Nakazawa have any idea? Again, Kuki found himself feeling out of step, isolated.

What Nakazawa doubtless had in mind was to keep his home life intact while romancing an attractive woman on the side; to keep a nice balance between the security of family and the excitement of a fling. Most men of a certain age doubtless fantasize about an adventure of that kind. Kuki himself had started out thinking it would be fun to meet Rinko now and again for meals, to revel in the heady atmosphere of a flirtation. Even after taking the next step and becoming intimate with her, he had never supposed it would affect his marriage. Yet that marriage now teetered on the edge of oblivion. How had it come to this? Unknowingly, he had passed an invisible point of no return.

Under the circumstances, Nakazawa's confession was the last thing he needed to hear. Nakazawa might envy him and Rinko all he wanted, but behind the scenes lay suffering and pain unimaginable to any but those concerned. Clearly, Nakazawa had no idea that Kuki's marriage had collapsed, or that he and Rinko were so deeply lost in one another. Instead, he seemed convinced it would all unfold like the latest TV drama, where characters lightly wound and heal one another with their words, and in the end sincerity and kindness lead to general happiness. If some smooth and superficial plotline of that kind was what he had in mind, he was dreaming.

Frankly, Kuki had no interest in living in a world of such sweetness and light. Or rather, he would if he could, but they had come too far for that, he and Rinko. They were in too deep to be swayed by appeals to reason or conscience, too possessed by that raw impulse which every living creature is born with and bears deep inside him like original sin. It wasn't sweetness and light but ruin and the mutual shortening of their lives that was a more likely ending. With this preying on his mind, such ignorant expressions of envy were not merely irritating but maddening.

The number of mourners in the anteroom had increased; there now appeared to be forty or fifty of them.

"Die before retirement and you get a big turnout," observed Nakazawa wryly. It was true. Even as head of a subsidiary, Mizuguchi had maintained his affiliation with the main company, and people in publishing had come in droves to pay their respects, alongside representatives from the worlds of broadcasting and advertising. "It's a shame he died so young, but if he'd lived to retirement age, half these people wouldn't be here."

Remembering all the funeral wreaths around the altar, Kuki murmured, "He knew a lot of people."

"This many wouldn't have come."

"You really think so?"

"People can be heartless when someone's no longer any use to them."

"But surely coming to pay your respects to the dead is one sign of being a real friend."

"Anyway, you have it made." In answer to Kuki's puzzled look, the other man added mischievously, "You've got a girlfriend to mourn you. I haven't got anyone like that."

"Oh, now…" Kuki realized as he spoke that he'd never thought about the matter at all.

"When the time comes, you be sure to let me know. It would be a shame if the poor girl came only to be stuck off in a corner somewhere."

"Come on, stop it, will you?" Nakazawa was obviously imagining a scene in which Kuki's wife was chief mourner and Rinko came to offer her respects. Nothing like that could ever happen.

"Or maybe in your case your girlfriend will end up being chief mourner." Nakazawa was evidently enjoying himself, but this too was a novel idea to Kuki. "Anyway, a funeral is a kind of comment on a person's life, so you'd better be careful."

New people were coming in, so Kuki got up. "It's about time for me to be going."

"Where to, her place?"

Since Nakazawa wouldn't have believed him even if he denied it, Kuki said nothing.

"You're not going to marry the girl, are you?"

"What do you mean?"

"Yokoyama and the others are worried."

So that was who'd told him—Kuki's colleagues in the reference section. "Can't say I've ever thought about it."

"Good. But then there's never any telling what you'll do."

"No?"

"Well, that was a long time ago."

As Nakazawa gave a forced laugh, Kuki remembered the incident alluded to. Three years earlier, as head of the editorial department he had opposed the issuing of a certain religious book. It would have sold well, but in Kuki's opinion it reeked of self-aggrandizement on the part of the leader of the sect, and didn't fit the company's image. Never one to put sales first, Kuki had fought the book's promoters. In the end, publication had been permanently shelved. Nakazawa had acted as intermediary back then.

"And of course, that was different," added Nakazawa.

You bet it was, Kuki wanted to reply. For one thing, he no longer had the passion for work that had motivated him then.

"Okay, I'm off," he said, and left the room with a wave. From there he was going to walk straight to the station and take the train to Shibuya.

He had done no work to speak of that day. All he'd managed to do was go to the wake, offer incense, and drink a little beer. Why was he so tired? One reason was obviously his despondency over Mizuguchi's death, but there was also the sense he had after meeting Nakazawa and the others that he was somehow set apart from them, in a different world. That feeling of not belonging might have increased his fatigue.

After eight P.M., the train heading into the city was nearly empty. Kuki took a corner seat and thought back over Nakazawa's remark: "You're not going to marry the girl, are you?" He'd said it casually, but perhaps marriage *was* a legitimate option. Both he and Rinko had left their spouses to live together in the same apartment, ignoring public opinion and the wishes of parents and offspring alike. If they were willing to go that far, the next step might just as well be marriage. With or without the blessing of other people, the thing to do was to start over, build a new home together and a new life.

Strangely, the idea of marrying Rinko and formally setting up house with her had never really occurred to him before. The desire for more space or a place to put his books had crossed his mind, but never thoughts of embarking on a new life. Equally oddly, it was apparently the same for Rinko. The words "Marry me" had never crossed her lips, nor had he ever said them to her. When they were so drawn to each other, so passionate, why had the idea of marriage never surfaced openly?

Certainly Rinko's husband showed no sign of agreeing to a divorce any time soon, and if they forced the issue by getting married anyway, she would be guilty of bigamy. Meanwhile, even if Kuki's wife was agreeable to a divorce, when the time came, there would be messy details having to do with property distribution and disposal of the house. Until all that was settled, he couldn't jump into marriage with Rinko.

It had been hard enough just to leave their respective spouses and move in together; they'd scarcely had time to think about going a step further. No wonder the idea had slipped their minds, he was tempted to say—but was that true? They spent an unlimited amount of time together, and whichever one had said the word "marriage," the other might have been quick to agree—yet the subject had never come up. Why not?

As Kuki puzzled over this, another voice whispered, *Maybe you're both too scared of marriage.* There in the night train, Kuki asked himself what it was he feared deep down that kept him from proposing to Rinko. As he faced the question, an image from the past crossed his mind: his wife and he, though now estranged, had once been lovers. While their feelings for each other had never been as tumultuous and undivided as his and Rinko's were now, still they had loved one another and married, each thinking the other an appropriate partner in life. Yet twenty-five years later the marriage was a shambles, irretrievably broken down. The main cause was his affair with Rinko, but even before that, signs of rupture had been there. The love they had placed such confidence in, that everyone around them had given their blessing to, had vanished all too quickly and easily. Why?

Two words floated into his mind: "routine" and "inertia." The sheer routine of married life was perhaps enough to make any love become automatic and ultimately expire. In just the same way, then, the love he shared with Rinko, a relationship so intense it ate away at the very core of their lives, might well die out, too. Perhaps that was the real reason neither of them had spoken of marriage in all this time: they both knew from experience that marriage contained within it the germs of two afflictions, laziness and dullness, offsetting any benefit that security might represent.

Sada Abe murdered her lover, Kichizo Ishida, barely three months after they'd met, he suddenly recalled. Their mad affair had ended with her strangling the man in an access of affection, the crime facilitated perhaps by timing: it happened when their passion was at its hottest, like a flower madly in bloom. Had they gone on seeing each other and married, it was likely that six months or a year later Sada would not have felt the same degree of affection for him, or the same desire to keep him all to herself. The intensity of their passion might even have yielded to an equally intense hatred, causing them to part company before long.

Love, too, had its seasons.

It was nine P.M. when Kuki arrived in Shibuya, having mulled these things over on the way. As usual, the station was packed with home-bound commuters and young people heading for the entertainment areas. Avoiding the throng, he headed up the gentle slope of a wide avenue and turned into the sudden quiet of a small lane. On the next corner stood the apartment house where they lived. It was five stories tall but not very big, only some thirty apartments in all. When he signed the papers he'd been told it was fifteen years old, but it had a rather rundown appearance, and the cement-block wall at the entrance had partially collapsed.

For some reason, unlike the house in Setagaya where Kuki had always had a sense of homecoming, here it still felt like getting back to a secret hideaway. Before going in, he glanced furtively around. After making sure there was no one else about, he went in and took the elevator to the fourth floor, then rang the bell at the second door from the end.

When Rinko was in, she usually came flying to the door as if she'd been waiting impatiently for him, but tonight she took her time. He rang the bell again, and was about to open the door with his key when finally it opened from inside, and Rinko's face appeared. "Welcome back." It was her usual greeting, but spoken with a subdued voice and downcast eyes.

"What's wrong?" he asked quickly, but got no reply. "Did something happen?" he asked again as he started removing his black suit.

279

Putting it on a hanger for him, she said, "My mother just called." Rinko had given her mother in Yokohama, and no one else, the telephone number here. It was clear from her expression that the phone call hadn't been a welcome one.

"What'd she have to say?"

"Lots. And then she told me she never wants to see me again." Overcome, Rinko raised her hands to the corners of her eyes, now wet with tears.

Kuki changed into a dressing gown, sat down on the sofa, and took a deep breath. He knew that Rinko had already been given a talking-to by her mother more than once. It was only natural for a parent to lash out at a married daughter who'd left her husband and taken up with another man, but as far as he remembered, this was the first time anything had been said about severing relations with her.

"She telephoned you out of the blue?"

"You know how I've been staying here, not contacting anyone, even her? She decided she had to do something."

"And she really said she never wants to see you again?"

"Yes. 'You're no daughter of mine, so don't ever come back again,' she said."

Kuki knew how strict and old-fashioned the woman was, but this was going too far. "Then she's still opposed to your getting a divorce."

"No, I think she's given up on that. It's just the idea of my taking off before things were settled and starting living with another man. She says it's unforgivable, that she never raised her daughter to be a slut."

"A slut…," Kuki muttered. Yes, what went on between these walls every day was pretty hot and steamy, but there was a passionate love behind it, don't forget. "You explained things to her, didn't you?"

"She won't listen. She says I'm naïve, that I'm being led along. That our relationship is purely physical. That it's pathetic to go off my head like this."

Kuki said nothing.

Rinko sighed. "I told her there was more to it than that, but she doesn't understand. Nobody could, unless they'd been through it themselves."

It must have been a difficult conversation: the mother accusing her daughter of being attracted to a man for purely physical reasons, the daughter denying it, insisting that her mother knew nothing about real love. And now, perhaps incongruously, after standing up to her so forcefully, Rinko was crying her eyes out at the prospect of being cut off from her—as any loving daughter would.

Kuki felt how much to blame he was for pulling this once inseparable mother and daughter apart and forcing them into bitter confrontation.

"Now there really is nowhere else for me to go," said Rinko, her head drooping.

Gently, Kuki laid an arm around her shoulders. "It's all right. She'll come round."

"No, she won't. She can't. She's never loved anybody this much, she'll never understand."

"The point is that you *have* loved more deeply than she has." Surely she knew that she'd surpassed her mother as a woman.

"Mother likes everything to be nice and calm… But I don't care if she doesn't understand me. As long as you do…"

"Of course I do."

The moment he said this, Rinko clung to him, pleading, "Hold me. Hold me as tight as you can." Obediently, he embraced her with all his strength; but then she cried out, "Hit me, hit me hard!"

"What?"

"You heard me, hit me. I mean it. I'm bad, I'm a bad girl, so hit me…"

Abruptly, she sprang up and began tearing at the buttons of her blouse, ripping off her clothes, with Kuki just sitting there uncertain what to do. His heart went out to her as he sensed the deep shadow of loneliness in her. It was the loneliness of someone who, after pitching headlong into the most emotional experience of her life, found herself shut out by other people and now even by her own mother.

In the end, a man and a woman set apart in this way had nowhere to turn for comfort but each other, drawn together in shared isolation. That healing contact was all they had to offset their loneliness.

"Go on, hit me, hit me as hard as you can!"

She lay face down, stark naked, in the dark hollow of the bed. She looked strangely out of place, like a white butterfly that had somehow found its way into a dank prison cell. Kuki still felt uncertain. If he did as she asked, what should he use? Looking around, he realized he was wearing a belt. He took it off and let it dangle from one hand.

"You really want me to hit you?"

"Yes. Do it."

His hesitation seemed to further distress her. Kuki gazed again at the white skin, gulped as if to ask her forgiveness, and then swung the belt over his head and down in one motion. The room rang with the high, dull crack of the belt against her flesh, and she let out a sound that was half groan, half scream. Though she'd brought this on herself, Rinko quickly shrank away and tried to escape, knowing for the first time the full force of a whip. Kuki paid no attention, bringing the belt down on her twice in a row as she crawled about on the bed, crying out in pain and begging him to stop. She must have miscalculated. In asking him to hit her, she'd imagined not so much the pain of a whipping as the figure she would cut and the sense of punishment she would get from the touch of the lash. The pain of the actual experience was now too much to bear.

The next time she said "Stop!" Kuki tossed the belt aside.

"Does it hurt?"

"Of course it hurts! It's awful… How does it look? Is the skin broken?"

He turned on the bedside lamp for a look. Her back was crisscrossed from shoulders to hips with red welts.

"It is a bit red."

"You hit me so hard!"

"You told me to."

"I didn't think you'd really do it."

Her remarks seemed to him arbitrary and contradictory. "It'll go away," he said. With a finger, he traced the outline of one red welt on the white skin.

Rinko murmured, "That part is numb. I can't feel a thing there."

Then she said resolutely, "Okay, now it's your turn, now I get to pay you back."

"No. There's no point."

"I want to watch you try to get away."

There was something provocative in her voice. Kuki moved away from the bed and looked down at her back. "You know, it's almost beautiful…" Red lash-marks from his belt covered the clear white skin like an abstract painting. Again, he traced a welt from her shoulder to her hip.

"So hot…" Apparently the marks burned and stung. She wriggled and said again, "It feels like I've been burned, it's so hot."

As Kuki hesitated, unsure about what she wanted him to do next, she drew his hand down. "Hold me, hold me tight." Obligingly, he lay down on the bed, and Rinko pressed herself against him. "There's something wrong with me today. There is, isn't there?" she groaned. Then she told him point-blank, "Take me now, I want you."

Kuki mounted her, careful not to hurt her back.

The belt-lashing had been all the foreplay she needed. Her wet thighs clamped down on him. He wasn't leading her, she was off and running, transported, moaning "I'm on fire," then "I'm burning," until finally Kuki was aroused beyond the point of containing himself and exploded, and in response she howled, "I'm *dying!*"

Like the wind sweeping through open space, the last vowel was followed by utter stillness.

As he lay beside her, struggling to regain control of his breathing, Kuki thought back over the brief storm that had just engulfed them. Strange. Rinko had asked for the beating apparently because she wanted to punish her body. Shocked at hearing her mother call her names and say she'd disown her, she must suddenly have felt that the only way to expose and purge the dirtiness in her was to undergo a beating. And while he was doing it to her he himself had had the illusion that, all over her body, little worms were being forced from all her pores. But when it was over, the result was the direct opposite of what had been intended. Rinko had moaned in anguish, yes, but she had also cast aside all anxiety and shame, and experienced a more violent form of pleasure than ever, apparently. What use was the beating, then? Had it served only as a stimulant, to inflame her body and rouse her to new levels of desire?

She was lying on the bed face down, arms outstretched, in the same position she'd lain in for the beating; but now in addition to the long red X extending down to her buttocks, her whole body was suffused with a rosy glow.

"I'm so hot," she murmured again, without moving.

Small wonder. The beating would have opened all her capillaries, speeding the circulation of blood, and on top of that, they had had urgent sex. Her body radiated heat from head to toe.

Touching her flushed skin, Kuki continued to let his thoughts roam. What *was* it like for a woman? He could only wonder, but her orgasms seemed far deeper than anything a man was ever capable of. Of course, the moment of ejaculation was one of intense pleasure, but it was over so soon, in a split second. For a woman it must be many times stronger, like the moment of ejaculation stretched out indefinitely...

Maybe there was a more concrete way of comparing: by experiencing anal sex oneself. Homosexuals did. It seemed a likely way to approximate what a woman felt during sex. Supposedly, once used to it, some men became so addicted to the pleasure of anal intercourse that they couldn't give it up. It involved a transformation: from the sex of insertion to the sex of reception. Men under the spell of that particular sexual practice could never go back to the other way, or so he'd heard.

So the pleasure of being on the receiving end of things must be considerable. But women didn't have to use such an unnatural body cavity, they came supplied with one that was undoubtedly superior. On top of which they had their bud, corresponding to a man's phallus. In fact, they had it awfully good, really.

Not that all women were capable of making the most of their bodies, by any means. Some never opened up fully to their own potential, others felt only disgust or shame. How many ever repeatedly attained a truly intense erotic experience? There was no way of knowing, but those who did were surely in a small minority.

Rinko was now one of them. She lay on the bed as if afloat, buoyed up by the fecundity, confidence, and satisfaction of a woman who had experienced a full and palpitating climax.

"It's just so strange," Kuki murmured to himself.

Rinko edged nearer. "What is?"

"For us to be doing this on the night of Mizuguchi's wake."

"Is it wrong?"

"No, I didn't mean that. It's just that life and death seem separated by such a fine line..." He recalled the photograph of Mizuguchi on the flower-massed altar, taken when he was healthy. "Here we are, alive and well now, but sooner or later..."

Rinko nodded, still lying with her back to him. Then she reached for his hand and laid it on her breast. "Let's die together," she said.

"Together?"

"As long as we've got to die anyway, let's do it together. I've lived long enough."

A longing for death had clearly taken root in Rinko. Yet her idea of death was dying at the peak of happiness and satisfaction, whereas his was tinged with nihilism, the effect of going to his friend's wake. There was a distinct difference. Kuki pursued the issue.

"You really think you've lived enough?"

"Oh, yes. I'm ready to die any time."

"Don't you want to go on living?"

"Of course that would be okay too, but I just feel so sure that I'll never be happier than this. Being with you every day, knowing how much you love me..."

"There could be something even better just ahead."

"Or something dreadful. The one thing certain is that I'll be getting old."

"You've still got a long way to go."

"Not really. Like I told you—from now on, day by day my skin will get baggier and more wrinkled, and little by little I'll wither away."

A pessimistic view, he thought, yet for him, too, life offered only the certainty of aging, loss of work, and increasing irrelevance. Maybe it would be better just to fade away as he was now, wrapped in this flower of a woman—Rinko.

"Maybe this is as good as it gets," he mused.

"It *is*; no two people can love each other more than we do."

Kuki nodded as Rinko turned slowly to face him.

"I'd like to go away somewhere again," she said. "It's depressing to stay here all the time."

He agreed.

"Shall we go to Karuizawa?" she suggested. "My father built a summer house there. We'd have it all to ourselves."

"Nobody else uses it?"

"No, not now. We can do as we like there."

Rinko's thoughts were already fixed on the deep, quiet groves of Karuizawa.

Rain

In mid-July, Kuki took two days off to go to Karuizawa with Rinko. Although the rainy season was almost over, heavy thunderstorms showed no sign of tapering off. He would have preferred delaying the trip until the weather improved, but he had meetings scheduled at the end of the month, making it hard to get away. In addition, the dismal prospect of spending more gray, oppressive days cooped up in their tiny apartment made him anxious to leave.

He was also swayed by Rinko's insistence that Karuizawa in the rain had a charm of its own. The foliage would be deep green and glistening with moisture, and since the summer vacation was still to come, there wouldn't be many sightseers about. A long weekend there would give him just what he needed, a cleansing of mind and body.

They were both feeling more than a little depressed. Kuki was upset because his daughter Chika—not his wife, from whom he hadn't heard recently—had told him outright to "stop wasting time and get on with the divorce." He didn't need his daughter to tell him what to do, and he certainly had no intention of going back to his wife after all this time. Yet he couldn't bring himself to put his seal to the form, either, feeling a reluctance that only a person who'd been married for years would understand. He knew that it was frustrating, possibly nerve-racking for Chika to see her parents trapped in this limbo, but having her pressure him in this way only left him feeling more isolated than ever, cut off from any sense of family or support.

Rinko, meanwhile, hadn't recovered from a startling discovery she'd made during a recent trip back to her married home, to retrieve the key to the summer house. It had been a weekday afternoon in early

July. Her husband always left for work by eight, so he was long gone, the house deserted. She went straight to the upstairs room that had always been hers and removed the summer house key from the dresser drawer. She was about to leave when she sensed something odd about the house. Her husband was naturally tidy for a man, and particular about housekeeping matters, but even so, the study and living room were just too clean. Not only was his morning coffee cup washed and put away, but the kitchen cloth was wrung out and neatly folded, the sink wiped clean, and on the desk in his study was a vase containing some hydrangeas from the garden. Her first thought was that either his mother had come and tidied up or that he'd hired a housekeeper. Then she found a red toothbrush and an unfamiliar floral-patterned towel in the bathroom. And it hit her: *another woman had moved in.* The realization drove her quickly from the house.

"It's awful!" she'd said to Kuki in a tone that was half complaint, half amazement. She wasn't really angry. After all, she had been the one to leave him, so if someone else had now taken her place, she knew she had no right to object.

"I'm glad he's off my back," she went on, still unsettled. "If he has found someone else, I hope he'll hurry up and give me a divorce." If Rinko's suspicions were correct, her husband was refusing to let her go even though he himself was involved with another woman. "Now I've got no ties left anywhere," she added with a wan smile. There was a sadness to her profile.

They'd hoped for a break in the weather, but the day they left for Karuizawa turned out rainy, after all. The weather report predicted heavy rain throughout the Kanto and Tokai regions, with the rainy season front stalled along the southern Pacific coast and a typhoon near the Ogasawara Islands. Despite the chancy outlook, they set off immediately after dinner.

They went in Kuki's car, with him driving, although when they got to Karuizawa, Rinko was going to take over, being more familiar with the roads. Traffic was heavy on the city highway, but as soon as they reached the expressway, they began to make good time. The rain wasn't coming down in buckets, but neither was it drizzling. Kuki stared out the windshield past the moving wipers, feeling as though they were two people in a movie.

"Not a gangster movie, I hope," said Rinko.

"No, nothing to do with crime. A pair of lovers fleeing the city, heading for parts unknown."

After a pause, she said, "Maybe we are criminals in a way."

"Did you kill somebody?"

"No, but we're causing so many people so much pain. Your wife and daughter, for example, and the people around them…" She had never so much as mentioned his family before.

"Well, as far as that goes, your family is just as—"

"I know. We're hurting the people around me, too."

She sounded so contrite that he wanted to comfort her. "Falling in love is a selfish thing to do—it can't be helped. At our age, it's hard to find happiness without hurting others in the process."

"So what are we supposed to do?"

"It all comes down to whether you've got the courage to hurt people or not."

"You do, don't you?"

Kuki gave a slight nod. Rinko stared out the rain-spattered windshield and murmured, "Love is frightening." From then on she was silent, brooding.

In the surrounding darkness, the sudden silence inside the car created a void. To fill it, Kuki put a tape on, and the languorous sounds of a piece by Erik Satie floated in the air.

"It's only natural to love someone you've fallen for, isn't it?" she ventured.

"You can't love someone you hate."

"And yet once you're married, it's no longer allowed. If you love anyone but your husband, you're a slut." Her pent-up anger was beginning to show. "Of course, after marrying someone you thought you'd always love, it's not right to stop loving them, but feelings do change, don't they?"

"Absolutely. Music or books that might have been all right when you were twenty can seem boring or unbearable at thirty or forty. It only stands to reason you could easily fall out of love with somebody you liked fine when you were twenty."

"If your taste in music or books changes, nobody cares. They'll even tell you you're making progress. So why is it bad to develop an aversion to a person you once loved?"

"Because when you marry someone, you swear to be constant in your feelings toward that person, and people expect you to live up to that. When you can't, the only thing to do is pay whatever it costs and split up."

"That's all *I* want to do. So why is everybody giving me such a hard time?"

Pressed for an answer, Kuki did the best he could. "Because the bond between a man and a woman, or, I should say, between a husband and wife, goes beyond subjective feelings, likes and dislikes. It's a contract."

"But to stay with someone you don't even like isn't fair to them, either. That too is a betrayal. It makes so much more sense to be with the person you care about—but then you're accused of being *un*caring, of causing other people pain."

The murmur of Satie only added to her gloomy mood. The car sped on; the rain showed no sign of letting up. To try to raise her spirits, Kuki reached over and laid his hand on hers. She responded to his touch by drawing closer.

"Tell me," she said, "what is it you like about me?" After the hard realities they'd been discussing, she seemed to want to switch to something lighter.

"Everything."

"There must be something you could single out."

"I can't sum you up in a word or two."

"Try!"

Her insistence made Kuki feel like saying something perverse. "You were extremely self-possessed, and a bit distant. I couldn't take my eyes off you. Then when I finally got to know you, I realized…"

"What?"

"What a little sex fiend you are."

Rinko hit his knee with her fist. "You made me one."

"You were as wild in bed as you were dignified out of it."

"That's all you like about me?"

"Okay, I'll tell you all the things I love about you. You put yourself heart and soul into everything you do, you've got real spirit, you're surprisingly daring but a little bit of a crybaby too; and beautiful as you are, your features have a kind of nice irregularity to them…"

"Irregularity? Nobody's ever told me that before."

"Look at us both, what we're doing here. Highly irregular."

Rinko touched the windshield with a finger. "All right, should I tell you what I love about you?"

"Is there anything?"

"It's the irregularity in you, too."

"Oh?"

"From the time I first met you, I thought you were different. I knew you worked at a big publishing house, so I expected you to be rather stuffy, and then you didn't put on any airs at all. When you started talking about the thing you were working on, you were as excited as a little boy. When you approached me later, you seemed clumsy. Then you surprised me, coming on to me and saying you wanted to see me again."

"Well, that was because—"

"Just listen." She stuck a mint in his mouth. "If you want to know, I underestimated you."

"You did?"

"Yes. I thought you were the consummate gentleman, so I let down my guard, and the next thing I knew, you'd whisked me off to that hotel." They'd first made love three months after meeting, having spent the earlier part of the evening at a restaurant in Aoyama. "I remember during dinner you grabbed the salt shaker and, not knowing the top was loose, shook it hard and got salt all over your plate. You seemed to need somebody to look after you, so I went with you to that hotel room—and then you turned and grabbed *me* the moment we got there."

"You make me sound like a gangster."

"That's it, there *was* something of the gangster about you. You kidnapped me. I never stood a chance."

"Anybody would think you meant this."

"Gangsters use drugs to keep their girls in line, don't they? Instead of drugs, you used sex. You bad, bad man."

He wondered if he should find the characterization flattering or upsetting. "Come on, now. Gangsters keep girls to make money. Not this gangster. I fell for you. I loved you so much I couldn't bear to let you go. Maybe that *is* a kind of bondage, but I didn't hold on to you with drugs, I did it with love."

"I know, that's the trouble. There's treatment for drug addiction, but there's no cure for love. You just get in deeper and deeper."

Kuki turned this over in his mind, feeling miffed, but she brought her face close to his and murmured, "You may be a gangster, but you're a sweet one."

They were approaching Usui Pass, on the Gumma-Nagano border. The rain had eased up a little, but now the road was foggy and the beam of the headlights dimmer than before. Kuki drove silently and cautiously as the road wound steadily uphill. After a series of tunnels the fog suddenly thinned, and they were in Karuizawa. The car clock read ten. They had left Tokyo at seven-thirty, so the trip had taken two and a half hours.

The roads were deserted, it being a weekday before the start of the summer vacation. The only light came from the odd vending machine shining bleakly in the rain. Rinko had been visiting Karuizawa since childhood and knew her way around, so she got behind the wheel. They went via the new road to Manpei Avenue and after five or six hundred yards turned right into the old section of town, a peaceful enclave of summer homes surrounded by larches.

"We made it," she said.

They left the car at the edge of a dense grove of oaks, amongst which the triangular roof of a Western-style building with a light on in the porch could be seen. They had informed the caretaker, Kasahara, that they would be arriving tonight, and he had apparently left the light on for them.

"Cozy, don't you think?" As she indicated, it wasn't big, but the grounds were extensive, with a luxurious growth of trees surrounding the house. "It was built almost twenty years ago, so it's not new."

"It's got style."

At night it was hard to see clearly, but the outside was done in light beige brick, and just inside the entryway was a stained glass window.

"My father wanted a European-style place, so he had it designed this way." Her father had been an importer in the cosmopolitan city of Yokohama, and the summer house reflected his taste. From the hallway they stepped into the living room, where the grain in the wood paneling showed to advantage. At the left end of the slightly oblong room was a fireplace with a sofa and chairs grouped around it. Beyond was the kitchen and an oak dinner table; in the right-hand corner was a small bar.

Rinko showed him around the rest of the house. To the right of the hallway were two other rooms, one Japanese-style and one Western with two beds in it; upstairs was a study with a big desk, and a bedroom with a dresser and double bed. "Nobody's been here for a while, so the damp has settled into things." She went around opening windows and letting in the night air.

"Doesn't your mother come?"

"She has a touch of arthritis, so she doesn't like to come during the rainy season." She took off the bedspread. "Nobody will bother us here."

It did seem that they could stay hidden away there almost indefinitely.

After a quick tour they went back to the living room, and Rinko lit a fire in the fireplace. Even though it was almost the middle of July, there was a definite chill in the air, perhaps from the rain. Next to the fireplace was a big pile of firewood which the caretaker had thoughtfully laid in. As the wood caught fire, flames danced in the heat, and the sense of being in a cool summer resort grew stronger.

"You didn't bring any pajamas, did you," said Rinko, holding out a pair that had been her father's. "We'll have to get you some."

Obediently, he put on her father's pajamas, laughing because they were a bit big.

"I'll change too. Be right back."

Kuki sat down on the sofa and gazed at the fire for a few minutes until she reappeared, wearing a white silk dressing gown.

"Shall we have some champagne?" She took out a bottle from the front of the bar, opened it, and poured some out into slender Lobmeyr glasses. "Here with you at last," she said, offering him one. "Here's to Karuizawa and us." They clinked their glasses and drank.

"Where shall we sleep tonight?" he asked.

"The upstairs bedroom, I think." There had been a black lacquered chest of drawers and a big double bed there, he remembered. "My father used to stay there when he came, but it's been three years since his last visit, and the sheets and bedspread are new. Would it bother you?"

"No, but it might upset your father."

"Don't worry. He was a lot more understanding than Mother. When I got married he told me if it didn't work out I could come back home to live any time I wanted." The year before, she'd been devastated by her father's sudden death. Perhaps there had been a special closeness there, hard for outsiders to imagine. "It was such a shock to me when he died. I wish I'd been a better daughter to him."

Abruptly, Kuki remembered the night of her father's wake, when he had taken her so violently. Apparently she was thinking of the same thing. "That was the night you called and I went to see you in the hotel, remember? I couldn't forgive myself at the time, but now I think that seeing you then may have given me strength."

"What if he knew we were here like this?"

"He'd understand. He always used to say the greatest happiness in life was to be with someone you love. If I'd told him you and I ran away here from Tokyo, he'd have said 'Fine, stay as long as you want.'" Her voice caught, as if the memory of her father was painful.

They were silent for a while, both staring into the fire. Then she said, "There are so many shapes of flames, aren't there?" It was true: the same log produced big red flames and little yellowish ones. "I'm that big flame," she said, pointing. On her forehead, a reflection of the flickering firelight shone faintly red.

That night, Kuki dreamed about Rinko's father. He was leaning back in the chair in the study next door, his large, bulky frame visible only from behind, face hidden from view. "That's my father," Rinko whispered, so he went over to say hello, but then to his surprise the figure disappeared. A cremation was in progress. Kuki looked down at the fire burning at the bottom of a black pit, and Rinko told him they were cremating her father. He placed his palms together in prayer, and the flames gradually died down. Someone said the firewood was damp. Then the flames vanished.

Kuki awoke feeling chilly, perhaps because the fire had gone out. He looked at the room in the pale light of the Lalique lamp on the nightstand, then at Rinko sleeping beside him. Realizing where he was, in the Karuizawa house for the first time, he tried to retrace his dream. The scenes were fragmentary, disjointed, but he thought he recognized a connection: before bed Rinko had talked about her father, and it was her father's pajamas he'd been wearing as they looked into the fire. The last part, about the flames consuming her father's body, was so spooky that he glanced around the room, but there was nothing unusual about it.

What time could it be? He'd left his watch downstairs, so there was no way of knowing, but it was probably around three A.M. The rain was still coming down. Raindrops pelted the window by the head of the bed.

Still feeling chilly, he moved closer to Rinko, who lay sleeping on her stomach. He put an arm over her and pressed up against her, feeling her warmth. Last night when they went to bed they had embraced, then gone to sleep as they were. He'd been tired from driving to Karuizawa after work, and she'd bustled around opening up the house and putting it in order. Above all, they took comfort in the idea that they had three full days together here, with no need to hurry. Now, having slept a little, he felt the first stirrings of hunger for her, but it seemed a shame to wake her from a deep sleep. Secure in the knowledge that they had plenty of time, he contented himself only with the touch of her soft skin before falling back into sleep and the continuation of his dreams.

When he next woke up, Rinko still lay beside him on her stomach, but she was awake. He slid over to close the gap that had developed between them during sleep, and she immediately snuggled up in response.

As they embraced, enjoying the warmth of one another, he wondered aloud what time it was. "There's a clock on the nightstand," she said. Still cradling her in his arms, he craned his neck at the clock: eight A.M. Surprised he had slept so late, he looked wonderingly at the window, where he could hear the rattle of rain.

"Are you getting up?"

"No." There were a few places he wanted to see in Karuizawa, but that could wait.

"It's still raining."

Heavy curtains covered the window, so the room was still fairly dark, but from the muffled sound outdoors he could picture raindrops striking the leaves and running down the windowpane. "Let's stay like this."

It had now been raining for three days straight; even here in Karuizawa, there was no sign of a letup. Ordinarily, the unrelieved gloom would have been depressing, but not now. What could be more enjoyable than a rainy morning in bed with the soft body of a woman beside you?

"Are you cold?" He pulled her closer still, opening the front of her silk gown.

The room was neither too warm nor too cold. With the rain beating in a steady monotone, he pressed his mouth to her white, round breast and slid his right hand down to the tuft between her legs. As he gently caressed her, she murmured, "Do you want me now?"

"Yes. Last night we went straight to sleep…"

She was silent a moment, then twisted her upper body a little and said, "Can I say something crazy?"

"What?"

Another short pause. "Once you start, go on and on."

"On and on?"

"Yes. Don't ever stop."

Kuki froze and stole a look at her face. In the faint light Rinko lay with her eyes closed, lips slightly parted like the mouth of a morning glory. As he studied those lips, he thought about the impossibility of what she asked. "Don't ever stop": that might be the straightforward request of a woman seeking prolonged pleasure, but from a man's point of view it was a cruel demand, a quest in which he was bound to fail.

Yet he decided to oblige her. How long he would be able to continue he didn't know, but he was determined to go on as long as he could. As if she were a queen and he her slave, he felt it was his duty to strive to please her as long as he lived.

He took her hardened nipple in his mouth and curled his tongue around it, twirling it in his mouth, his breath hot. At the same time, the hand below gently found her bud, barely touching its tip while slowly moving back and forth, back and forth in an unbroken rhythm until the different parts of her body resonated together like a bell, her cries of pleasure intensified, and she wrapped both arms around his head while his lips went on sucking at her breast.

From behind, his dark head must have looked as if it was held immobilized by fingers with manicured nails of light pink, but he wasn't to know, absorbed as he was in arousing her with his fingers and mouth, his caressing touch at once pleasurable and a form of slow torment, until the woman lifted her hips, sighing, moaning, her cries hot with urgency. The next instant she was shaken by a series of rippling spasms, allowing the man his first respite.

But this was only the beginning. Seeking new stimulation, she arched her back, and in response he changed his position too, burying his face between her legs where only now she had burst with passion. Lying flat on the bed, he used his tongue and lips to excite her again, bending her more and more to his will until again she was in a frenzy, begging and pleading with him. Only then, after waiting till he felt the moment was just right, did he slip inside her.

This, though exactly what she wanted, marked the end of his ascendancy. Once he was in the supple grip of her inner flesh, advance and retreat alike required her consent and concurrence. Ready for a long haul, he fitted himself against her sideways and wrapped his legs in a leisurely way around hers. His left hand was on the small of her back, his right hand reaching for her breasts. This way he could make free use of all his limbs and reach every part of her as he plunged forward and drew back, forward and back, in a sensual, measured rhythm. Now and then he would hoist her buttocks upward just enough for his hot flesh to be able to trace the surface of her sweetest inner spot, and she would gasp, breathless at the throbbing onslaught of pleasure. Then he would pull away, withdrawing the tip till it barely remained within her. Afraid of him leaving, impatient for his return, she became even more desperately inflamed.

His goal was for her to peak and ebb, again and again, time after time without end. How long could his own passion be sustained? With no way of knowing, he strove for all he was worth until finally she gave a long, full-throated groan that seemed to sink down somewhere deep beneath her, and she dissolved. His features strained in grim desperation as he held on to the very limit. To give in to his body's bidding now would be to defy a queen's command. The moment he did that, he was lost.

Sensing that her passion had crested, he waited anxiously for her permission to find release as well, panting like a faithful dog. But this cruel queen wasn't about to let him off so easily. Seeking only further pleasure still, she spurred him on, allowing him no time to rest, no chance to disobey.

The morning rain and the sense of being sealed off from the world had helped fuel his passion, but by now, after about an hour of this, every last bit of strength in him was gone and so, inside the woman's still-incandescent body, he collapsed, forced finally to withdraw in dejection. Even then she gave a little cry, reluctant to let him go, but he just couldn't go on. He might not have fulfilled his promise, but at least she'd soared up high above the clouds—not once, but again and again—and surely must be satisfied. That had to count for something.

He stretched out on the bed, hoping to hear how good it had been for her. After a while, she raised herself and slid in close. Touching him, she murmured, "You didn't come."

He gave a little start, but with her hand around his flesh there was no escape. "I don't have to, every time."

If he devoted himself to her pleasure and also allowed his own passion to play itself out each time they went to bed, he would soon wear himself out. Lately, he had acquired the knack of keeping himself on hold for long periods of time.

"But you said you wanted me."

"It doesn't have to be all at once." Even if he didn't share her satisfaction every time she scaled the heights, little by little his vitality was sapped. "There's still tonight."

Rinko seemed to accept this, but then said suddenly in a serious tone, "You really must think I'm a sex fiend."

"No."

"I myself think I'm bad. But I can't help it, it feels so good." As if remembering something she wanted to say, she laid her hand lightly again on his penis and asked, "How can you stay so detached during sex?"

"Who says I'm detached?"

"But you're able to hold yourself back."

"Only because I try as hard as I can to make it good for you."

"For me?"

"I want to make it wonderful for you."

"Me too—I want to make you feel so good you could die." The degree of their pleasure might not be the same, but in general the more two lovers had sex, the more pleasurable it became for both of them. "If there's ever anything you want me to do, tell me."

"You're fantastic. No woman could ever compare to you."

"Do you mean it?" she asked, but he didn't have to reply. It was true. He had always had a strong sex-urge, but never in his life had making love been so fully charged and exciting as now. It seemed to him that he'd never known anything before but the most humdrum sort of pleasure. Since Rinko, his enjoyment was richer by far, and he had learned to make it last longer and longer. Beyond any doubt she had fired him up, taught him, illuminated him.

"I'll never let you go, my darling," he said tenderly.

"Nor I you. I couldn't live without you."

Her voice was softened by the morning rain. Listening, Kuki lightly closed his eyes.

After floating for a while somewhere between sleeping and waking, they got up sometime after ten. Rinko looked in the mirror, running her hands through her hair, and said, "Being here does make a difference. I was really turned on…"

The apartment had become too familiar. There, they were in some ways just coasting, going through the motions. For Kuki too the change of scene had been invigorating.

"It's no good letting yourselves get in a rut, is it," she said.

That would apply to any love affair, he thought, not just an illicit one like theirs.

"Let's always try to be fresh and new together."

Easy for her to say, but could they do it? Wouldn't inertia steal in and cast its inevitable pall over them?

"Okay if I shower first?" she said, and went downstairs to the bathroom. In her absence, he stayed in the bedroom and opened the window. It was still raining, though not as hard as last night. It was almost eleven o'clock, but their surroundings were still. Rain skimmed the leaves and sank into the mossy ground.

Alone with the quiet rain, Kuki realized that he had turned fifty-five that day. Nothing much to celebrate. It seemed like an achievement of sorts, if rather a dubious one. If anything, he was amazed he'd kept going all this time.

Suddenly he thought of his family. Had he stayed with her, today his wife would have wished him happy birthday, and his daughter would have at least phoned.

Just as he was thinking these things, Rinko called up cheerily from below: "How about eggs and toast for breakfast?"

He went downstairs and showered before taking a seat at the table. She had prepared a simple meal of fried eggs and sausages, with a small salad, toast, and coffee. By the time they finished, it was noon. She quickly did the dishes and then got ready to go out, changing into some light blue clothes.

Kuki had been to Karuizawa several times on business trips to visit writers, but not for a few years. This was a place of some nostalgia for him, a reminder of days when he'd taken an active part in the publishing scene. Rinko asked him where he would like to go, and immediately a place with literary associations sprang to mind. "What about the site of Takeo Arishima's suicide?" he suggested.

Rinko got out a map. "It's somewhere near the old Mikasa Hotel. His summer house is down by Lake Shiozawa, though."

They went to the summer house first, since that was easier to find. The old, Japanese-style villa on the lakeshore was still standing. According to the guidebook, it was called "Pure Moon Retreat," and had been restored and moved here after years of neglect. The present location enjoyed a wonderful view of the lake, but they decided they might as well go and see the original site, too. After another consultation with the book, they went back to the old part of the resort area, heading north on Mikasa Avenue between rows of larch trees. They turned right just before some rental cottages and quickly found themselves on a slope thickly overgrown with trees. Pressing on down a narrow, wet path, they came to an oblong stone monument surrounded by tall grass and knew this was it: the site of Takeo Arishima's death.

Then the darling of the literary world, Arishima had died here in 1923 inside his summer house in a love suicide with Akiko Hatano, a good-looking reporter for a popular ladies' magazine. He was forty-five, a widower with three small children; Akiko was thirty and childless, the wife of another man. They committed suicide by hanging themselves side by side, their bodies going unnoticed for an entire month in the rainy season, from mid-June to mid-July. When finally discovered, the corpses were fully decomposed. In the words of the person who found them, "They were covered head to toe with maggots; it looked like two fountains of maggots coming down from the ceiling."

The love suicide had been a glamorous scandal in its day, affecting not only the literary world but society at large; the reality of what had happened, however, was grim. Rinko, frightened to learn that their bodies had been found putrid and maggot-infested, put her palms together in front of the stone monument in silent prayer. Standing in the rain in this grove of trees that was dark even in the daytime, it was easy to feel that they, too, would belong soon enough to the land of the dead.

"Now I'll take you to one of my favorite places," said Rinko, driving back south on Mikasa Avenue and turning down a little lane before the forest of Kajima till they came to a pond. It was not very big, but looked deep. "This place looks lovely even in the rain," she said, and it was true: ringed by dense greenery, the pond was half hidden by the soft rain, alluring and mysterious as a lost marsh.

"See that swan over there?" She pointed to a flock of wild ducks with a lone swan in its midst. "It's always here alone. I can't imagine how it got here." It distressed her that the swan had no mate, but the bird floated nonchalantly on the water, looking like a figurine.

"It might not be as lonely as you think." Kuki put up his umbrella and drew her closer; thus protected, they walked on further around the pond. The rain was still falling lightly, still with no sign of stopping. Not another soul was there by the quiet pond. They went as far as they could, until the track became so wet they had to stop and turn around. There was a restaurant nearby offering a view of the pond, and they went in and ordered some coffee.

"You know, I feel sorry for them, not being discovered for a whole month like that," said Rinko, her thoughts wandering back to the dead lovers. "They had to stay there dead, all that time, in that godforsaken place."

"No one thought to look for them there."

"Even if they did do it together, what an awful way to die." Rinko spoke in a low voice, looking out at the rain-misted pond.

That night they ate out, at a hotel near their house. It was a fairly old hotel, a two-story structure whose white facade and wood trim blended well with the surrounding greenery in an atmosphere of cool serenity.

Shortly before sunset, they sat face to face in a section of the dining room looking out on the garden. Rinko was wearing a silk sweater with wide white pants. Before dinner, she decided they should have champagne, and when the sommelier had poured out the pale amber liquid for them, she picked up her glass and touched it to Kuki's.

"Happy birthday."

Momentarily flustered, Kuki managed a nod and a smile. "So you knew?"

"Of course! Did you think I'd forget?"

It was only this morning that he had realized it was his birthday, and when Rinko failed to mention it, he'd assumed she had forgotten.

"Thanks. I never expected a celebration here."

"I knew today was your birthday before we left Tokyo."

This time it was Kuki's turn to raise his glass in a gesture of thanks.

"Presents are always a bit risky," said Rinko, taking out a small package from her purse. "Here, open it." Inside the wrapping was a black case and, inside that, a white gold ring. "You may not like it, but I want you to wear it."

Kuki tried it on his left ring finger. It fitted perfectly.

"I knew how big your finger was. And I had one just like it made for me," she said, showing him her left hand. Sure enough, on her ring finger was an identical ring. "You've got to wear it all the time, just like me."

Having never worn a ring before, Kuki felt slightly uncomfortable about it, but how could he take off something that meant so much to her?

They decided to order à la carte. For appetizers Rinko chose salad and cold consommé, and a main course of rainbow trout *meunière*. Kuki ordered tuna carpaccio and soup, and grilled lamb with herbs.

After another round of champagne they had some red wine, and Rinko's cheeks began to glow. "I was thinking of ordering a birthday cake for you tonight, too," she said, "but you wouldn't want one here, would you?"

The idea of putting on such a spectacle in front of other people didn't appeal to him at all. "Fifty-five candles would take a lot of blowing out."

"But you're so young. Not a bit old."

"In bed, you mean?" he asked in a debonair tone, his voice lowered.

She squirmed. "Yes, that too. But what I mean is, you're not set in your ways, like most men your age."

"I have you to thank for that."

"No, you were like that from the first time I met you. So much younger than that Mr. Kinugawa, more playful, more fun…"

She meant it as a compliment, he knew, but being told he was young aroused mixed feelings. "One time I interviewed an eighty-eight-year-old businessman. He told me that one of the problems of being his age was that he felt as young as ever. Now I have an idea what he was talking about."

"Why—is it bad to stay young?"

"No, I think he was talking about how hard it is when you still feel young but your body can't keep up. It would be easier to have your spirit decline at the same rate as your body."

"Then it wouldn't be long before you were totally useless."

"As a matter of fact, I *am* totally useless at work these days," he said with some bitterness.

"That's only because of decisions other people made that have nothing to do with you. Who cares about job titles, anyway?"

She was doing her best to cheer him up, but a man's morale and physical appearance are subtly affected by his situation at work. Kuki was determined not to let it bother him, but there was no guarantee that his comedown in the company might not take a gradual toll.

More wine drove off his momentary depression and restored his appetite.

Rinko's rainbow trout looked so good that Kuki had her share a little of it with him, transferring some of his lamb to her plate in return. "The advantage of dinner for two," he said, "is getting to try more kinds of food."

"Surely not just *any* two."

"Well, of course, it has to be me and you."

For a man and woman to share their food was an unmistakable sign of physical intimacy. Kuki knew that the other patrons in the restaurant might well be looking at them furtively with this in mind, but by now he didn't care. At the beginning of their affair, even on the train to

Kamakura, he'd been acutely conscious of other people's eyes. Now such worries were behind him. If anything, he felt defiant: if people wanted to be nosy, then fine, let them.

After a year and more of this relationship he'd developed a thick skin, but there was more to it than that. The crucial thing, he knew now, was to spend the rest of his life—however long or short—doing what he wanted to do. If that wasn't possible, he could always choose to end it prematurely. Some such defiance, or resolve, or better yet single-mindedness of purpose, had taken root in him.

By a simple adjustment in values, people could adapt to any way of life. Sometimes a slight shift in viewpoint was all it took for what had loomed large to fade away, and what had seemed insignificant to become supremely precious.

"Maybe I should quit my job." The words popped out of his mouth. Startled by the sudden notion, Rinko appeared doubtful, so he offered an explanation: "If I quit altogether, it would wipe my slate clean, mentally."

"You think so?"

"As long as I go on working there, I have a feeling I'll never be really free."

She seemed unable to understand why he should leave. Well, that was only natural: never having experienced the life of a company man, how could she?

In point of fact, Kuki had no very clear reason himself for wanting to quit. It came down to something like a vague tiredness. Anyone who worked in the same company for thirty years was bound to feel a certain fatigue; what made it worse lately was the sense of alienation he felt from his co-workers.

"If you're sure, I don't mind," said Rinko, puzzled yet sympathetic. "But don't go turning into an old man on me just yet, will you? I want you full of life."

"I know."

"You're sure about this?"

"Not completely, but it's about time I did the things I want to do, for my own sake." Frankly, the work he'd done until now had always been low-profile. Behind the scenes, he worked on things other people had written, collecting and touching them up without ever stepping into the limelight himself. He was like the black-robed attendant on a Kabuki stage, meant to go unseen.

"I can understand that." Rinko had spent a large chunk of her life in her husband's shadow, an inconspicuous figure in her own right. "As a matter of fact, I don't want to go on the way I am, either. I know it sounds a bit dramatic."

"Not really." The red wine in the clear wineglass was the color of blood; perhaps that was why, somehow, as he gazed at it, he felt courage rise up inside him.

"Why don't we do something radical?"

"Radical?"

"Yes. Something to blow people's minds. Something we can point to and say, there, how about *that*!" Rinko too was holding her glass and staring at the red liquid inside, her eyes shining.

When they finished off the wine, feeling now buoyed up by it, it was after nine o'clock, so they had some dessert and then left the restaurant. On reaching the front desk, they found that the rain had stopped. "Want to walk a bit?" asked Rinko. From the hotel back to the house was a twenty-minute walk. Kuki nodded and stepped outside with her, holding the unopened umbrella.

Fresh after the rain, the night air felt pleasantly cool against their wine-flushed cheeks. The pavement lit up by streetlamps was a glossy black, and no moon or stars shone overhead, as if the sky were still covered with thick clouds. They crossed the open space in front of the hotel and came out onto the larch-lined road, where Rinko slipped her arm in his. It was ten P.M. Everything was quiet, with only a trickle of light like an afterthought here and there in the dense foliage. Who might that be? People who came early like them because they enjoyed the peace before hordes of summer vacationers arrived?

As they made their way down the glistening pavement, the sound of their footsteps was swallowed up by the night sky. Finally the trees thinned out and a lane leading off to the left came into view. There would be another cluster of summer houses down that way, but now all they could see was the light of a single streetlamp.

After they had passed a T-junction and were again walking between rows of larches, Rinko said softly, "This is how quiet it was for those two when they died here." Takeo Arishima and Akiko Hatano. She must mean them again. Walking down this dark and silent road must have turned her thoughts back to their love suicide. "In such a remote villa…" She was picturing to herself the rain-soaked woods on the hill they'd visited that afternoon. "It must have been so cold."

Another tiny ray of light showed ahead in the distance, among the leaves.

"Did that summer house belong to him?" she asked.

Kuki had read up on the incident in the course of his study of the Showa period, so he had some knowledge of what had happened. "Apparently it was his father's, and he inherited it."

"So when they went there, it wasn't being used, was it?"

"His wife had already died, and his children were still small, so usually it was empty."

Headlights appeared in the distance as a car approached. Rinko waited till it had gone by, then asked, "Was it the beginning of July when they died?"

"It could have been as much as a whole month earlier, around June 9. They found the bodies July 6."

"How can you be so sure?"

"Akiko went to work till the eighth of June, and they were seen heading from Karuizawa Station to the summer house on the ninth."

"They walked?"

"Apparently someone saw them."

"It must be a good two or three miles." That was about right. It would have taken them nearly an hour to get there. "Wouldn't they have stayed a few days in the house first?"

"I don't know about that. But when they were ready, they tied some rope to the lintel, put chairs underneath, and then kicked them away."

"How awful…" Rinko clung tightly to him for a while, then pulled away and murmured, "Still, it took quite a lot of energy to do all that."

"What do you mean?"

"They walked for an hour to get to the villa, then they had to hang up the rope, set up the chairs, and put the nooses around their necks. All so they could die."

Kuki agreed that it required a good deal of effort to plan and carry out your own death like that. It would be different if you were sick, but both of them had been perfectly healthy, not a thing wrong with them. To take the life from your own healthy body by your own hand could only be done if you were intensely focused on doing it.

"Still, I wonder why they died?" Rinko murmured to the sky. "Why did they have to?" Her words were lost in the dark larch forest.

"They didn't really have to, did they?" Takeo Arishima had been a best-selling, acclaimed author, and Akiko, at thirty, a reporter with the glamor of an actress. Everyone had envied them. Each was at the pinnacle of life, so why choose the path of death? "One thing set them apart from most people, though."

"Only one?"

"They were intensely happy." A line from Arishima's will came to his mind. "He said so himself, in the note he left behind: 'I go to my death now right at the peak of happiness.'"

Abruptly Rinko stopped and stared straight ahead into the darkness. "You mean, they died because they were happy?"

"That's what his will strongly suggests."

In the cool of the rain-washed night, a breeze swept through the larch trees.

"Ah… So that's why they died." Rinko began walking again.

"Maybe they were afraid of being too happy."

"I can understand that," she said. "When things are that good, you do start to feel scared, wondering how long it can last."

"Maybe they wanted it to last forever."

"How could it?" Softly, Rinko asked the question of the surrounding darkness, then nodded to herself. "Dying was the only way, wasn't it?"

Back at the villa, they had some brandy, both of them still thinking about what they'd said on the way there. Rinko bent over to look at the fire in the fireplace, nodding to herself and repeating softly, "Dying was the only way." Kuki was not inclined to disagree. As happiness crested and waned, the desire to prolong it might turn inevitably into the desire to die; spooky though it was, the idea struck him as true.

"Shall we turn in?" Thinking about it any more seemed morbid. He showered first, and while Rinko took her turn he went on upstairs to the bedroom. That morning they had made lingering love in this room, to the accompaniment of the sound of the rain. Now the rain had stopped, and all was dark and silent. He lay on the bed without turning on the light, and presently Rinko opened the door and came in, wearing a silk nightgown. She paused in the doorway as if hesitating, and stole noiselessly to the edge of the bed. When Kuki took her in his arms, she clung to him fiercely, and without moving whispered again the same words: "Dying is the only way, isn't it?" It sounded as if she were seeking affirmation of this new idea, and also telling herself it was so. "The only way to hang on to happiness."

"Happiness comes in all varieties."

"To love the way those two did, deeply and permanently, without any possibility of change..." He understood her wanting that sort of constancy, but no one could swear undying devotion with any certainty. "Isn't it possible for two people to go on feeling the same way about each other—always, on and on?"

"Maybe," he answered, "but life is unpredictable. It might be asking too much. There's no ultimate guarantee."

"Then you're saying it can't be done. It can't be done in life." Rinko's voice sank into the darkness.

Far away, they heard what sounded like the cry of a bird. What sort of bird would be awake at this hour? Or was it some other sort of creature? As Kuki tried to work out the direction of the sound, Rinko spoke again.

"I know how she felt."

"Who, Akiko?"

Slowly she turned over on her back. "No, that woman—Sada—the one who killed her lover. She said she did it because she didn't want to hand over the man she loved to anyone else. If she hadn't killed him, he would have gone back to his wife, almost certainly. Once she decided she couldn't give up the happiness they had together right then, she had no choice but to kill him."

"Which would end his life, but, more to the point, prevent him from ever betraying her."

"So loving someone more and more intensely means you end up killing them… Love really is a frightening thing." She seemed finally to be convinced of this. "Loving someone makes people want exclusive possession. But you can't get that just from living together, or from marrying."

"No, because there's always the possibility of betrayal. To prevent that, you could end up with no choice but murder."

"So the love that consumes one person ends up consuming the other one, too. It ends in destruction." For the first time, it almost seemed, the vicious side of that soft word "love" was becoming plain to her: egotism, pain, wreckage.

The more they talked about love and death, the more wide awake Kuki became, and apparently so did she. Turning back toward him, she laid her fingers on his chest and asked, "Will your feelings always stay the same?"

"Of course."

"Will you always love me, and only me, and never ever love anyone else?"

As he began to answer "Of course" again, two slender fingers pressed down on his Adam's apple. He choked, unable to breathe, and in the darkness her eyes bore down on him. "It's a lie. It's a lie that you'll always love me."

"It's not a lie," said Kuki, rubbing the place where she'd attacked him.

She shook her head. "Just now you said it might be asking too much, that there was no ultimate guarantee."

The fact was that Kuki felt unable to swear with certainty that his feelings would last unchanged till the end of time. "All right, then, how about you?" he said, placing his fingers on her left collarbone. Women with slender necks and firm neck muscles had a small hollow at the base of the throat, right above the collarbone, just deep enough to hold the tip of a man's forefinger. When the woman was naked, that hollow, in which a pulse beat, was very attractive somehow. "You'll never change?" he asked, his fingers alongside the hollow in her throat.

"Of course not," she said.

"Never ever, no matter what happens?"

"You're the only man I'll ever love, absolutely."

Now Kuki pressed on the hollow above her collarbone, and Rinko gave a little scream of pain.

"You shouldn't say 'absolutely.' You might change sometime, too."

"That's a horrible thing to say. Then you don't trust me."

"As long as you're alive, you can't swear with absolute certainty that you'll never change."

"Then you and I will have to die, too. Now, when we're at our happiest. It's all we can do." Rinko said this in a rush, and then fell silent.

Not a sound was to be heard. It was night in the deserted resort and its surrounding woods. Yet just as there is white in the deepest blackness, there was a kind of sound embedded in the silence. Clouds moving in the night sky, trees in the garden dropping their leaves to the earth, the contents of the room slowly eroding and turning to dust: perhaps all of these motions came together with a hundred others to form the slightest sound imaginable. As Kuki lay listening intently to the sound of the silence, Rinko slid close to him and asked what he was thinking.

"Nothing."

There was another short silence, and then Rinko said under her breath, "But I don't want that kind of death." Kuki turned to her inquisitively, and she repeated, "I don't want to die like that." She was thinking again of the condition of the lovers' bodies when they were found, two fountains of squirming maggots from the lintel to the floor. "No matter how perfectly happy you were, that way of dying would be just too grotesque. I couldn't bear to be found looking like that."

"The message he left urged people not to look for them."

"Even if no one had, it was only a matter of time before they were discovered. As long as you were going to be found anyway, I'd much rather be presentable."

That was ideal, but when you really thought about it, she was only talking about what those left behind would want. "Someone about to die might not think that far ahead."

"But I couldn't bear it, I couldn't!" In obvious distress, Rinko propped herself up in bed. "I don't mind dying. If I were with you, I could die any time. But not like that."

"Anyone's body would start to rot if it took too long to find."

"That's not the same as being covered in maggots. You'd at least want them to find you before that happened, wouldn't you?"

Kuki had never given any thought to the reality of his own death, let alone to what figure he might cut afterward. He knew that those who were given life must sometime lose that life, but he'd never felt like pursuing the thought; it was too unsettling. Yet for some reason, talking it over with Rinko now, he didn't feel the same fierce attachment to life as before; death seemed less frightening, more intimate. Why was it that, when he was with her, the prospect of dying became so unalarming?

Slowly he removed her gown and underwear. When she was fully naked, he wrapped her tightly in his arms, his chest and belly and groin flat against hers. They each lay with their arms around the other's back and neck, their legs firmly entwined, his flesh and hers pressed together without any space between. They were so close and such a perfect fit that their very pores seemed to overlap.

"I love this, it feels so good," breathed Kuki, the words a sigh of contentment from the surface of his whole body. As he savored the sweet pleasure that seemed to well up from deep within him, he saw that the sensation of skin on skin gave not only a sense of peace but a certain resignation. As long as he could feel the smooth softness of her body, so round and warm, he felt no fear of losing consciousness or dying. "That's it," he murmured into her soft skin. "I could die happy like this."

"Like this?"

"In your arms."

Cocooned, at peace, he became once again a boy in his mother's embrace, a fetus in her womb; next he would become a drop of semen, and so vanish. "Now I'm not afraid to die," he told her.

"Neither am I, when I'm with you."

To banish the illusion of fading into nothing, he hugged her tightly again. She drew back after a moment, as if she found the tightness of his arms suffocating, and took a deep breath.

Lying there motionless in a half-embrace, his body still touching hers at the chest, belly, and thigh, he closed his eyes again. "It's so quiet…" They gave themselves over to the stillness of the night, the blackness of it deeper than he ever remembered. "I'm so glad we came to Karuizawa," he said. "I feel washed and clean."

People tended to avoid Karuizawa in the rainy season, but Kuki liked it now. Not only were there few other visitors, but the serenity of the moist landscape was refreshing to a heart tired and parched from city life. There, the rain had only seemed oppressive; here, it made the trees luxuriant and nourished the moss growing between them.

Of course, in the long run the continual rains had a dampening effect on people's spirits, making them inward-looking, morbid. Heavy clouds and steady drizzle might well explain why, after seeing the place where Takeo Arishima and Akiko had died, Rinko had been preoccupied by the image of death and talked of little else.

"Then shall we stay on here, just as we are?"

As Rinko said the words, a vision of Tokyo streets and his office passed slowly through Kuki's mind. "I suppose we can't…" Any longer here, and all desire to return to work seemed likely to fade away.

"It's so crowded in the summer. I'd like to come back in the fall," she said, clinging to him. Feeling the round softness of her breasts, desire overcame him. After so much talk about death, some strong affirmation of life was needed. If they could lose themselves in an act that would bring pleasure and consume their energy, then surely any lingering fear of death would subside, leaving only a radiant sense of being alive.

In the silent night, hoping for some such comfort, there in the tree-encircled house they sought one another with quick animal urgency.

Cicada Shell

In late July, the heavy summer rains are followed by a week to ten days of clear skies and scorching heat. It is the hottest time of the year, when the midsummer sun beats down from early morning on the asphalt city, sending midday temperatures soaring into the nineties. Even at night, the thermometer seldom dips below eighty. People barely done moaning about the oppressive rains are punished with the fierce onslaught of the sun. Panting in the sweltering heat, they mop their brows and droop like wilted flowers.

Most newcomers are amazed that the Tokyo summer divides neatly into two mini-seasons so categorically different. For many people, the dramatic change of weather causes a corresponding emotional shift. During the rainy season, the constant downpour and overcast skies have a depressing effect on everyone, but the moment the rains end and the sun pokes through, people throw off their sense of oppression, becoming more upbeat and active almost overnight.

This change of mood is easiest to spot in children, since a major characteristic of adult life, at least on the surface, seems to be "business as usual," whether skies are gray or blue. With the coming of midsummer, company workers put on short-sleeved shirts and carry their suit coats over one arm, dabbing their faces with handkerchiefs as they sway in overcrowded trains on the way to work. By mid-morning, the mercury is around 90°, the heat making its presence felt everywhere— in the stairwells of underground promenades, in the advertising banners hanging down building facades, on the bare shoulders of women in sleeveless blouses.

It was late in the afternoon of just such a day that Kuki found himself summoned to the managing director's office. Obata, its occupant, said, "This came in the mail the other day."

Kuki picked up an open letter off the desk and examined it. It was done on a word processor on several sheets of stationery, beginning with these words in large type: "A Report on Shoichiro Kuki."

He was dumbstruck. What was this, some sort of report on his personal affairs? Why would anyone write such a thing? Baffled, he began to read, and the first words leaped out as if to bite him: "Offenses of the Past Two Years." With a sharp intake of breath, Kuki plunged on.

> Two years ago this December, Shoichiro Kuki, former head of the editorial department of your company, took advantage of his temporary appointment as a lecturer at the Tonichi Culture Center to force his attentions on Rinko Matsubara, then a calligraphy instructor at the same institute. In the full knowledge that she was a married woman, he called her repeatedly at home and used all his wiles to seduce her.

Kuki felt his heart pound and his palms grow sweaty. Who the hell could have written this? It was a deliberate smear. He shot a look at Obata, who remained seated behind the desk smoking a cigarette, his face impassive. Then curiosity drew Kuki's eyes back to the page in front of him.

> Ever since the following New Year's, Kuki has done nothing but chase after Mrs. Matsubara, arranging secret meetings on any number of occasions. Finally, in April of last year he lured her to a Tokyo hotel and forced himself on her, engaging in obscene sexual behavior.

Kuki got that far, and clenched his fists. What rotten, lowdown slander! He would have liked to rip the letter up and burn it, but his superior was there in front of him—and besides, he had to know what the rest of it said.

> He then took advantage of the woman's naïveté by threatening, when she refused to see him again, to tell her husband everything. He also forced her to participate against her will in a variety of sexual acts. Finally, in April of this year he dressed her

in a red silk under-kimono and performed various acts of perversion, took a number of photographs, and forbade her ever to return to her home.

This had gone beyond slander to outright intimidation. It was a cowardly attack by someone who really hated his guts.

The document went on to declare that Kuki had inveigled her into living with him, renting a small apartment in the city where the two of them now resided as man and wife, thus causing the woman's marriage to collapse and her husband to suffer incalculable emotional and physical distress. It ended with these words:

> One can only question the ethics and integrity of a company that would maintain a man of such disreputable character on its payroll. There must be a full accounting.

The moment Kuki finished reading and looked up from the letter, Obata came around and sat in a chair across from him. Kuki waited till he was seated, then bowed his head and offered a deep apology. After all, there was no denying that it was his actions that had resulted in this stinking letter crossing his superior's desk, even if it was made up of gross distortions and downright lies. Accuracy aside, it was his responsibility to apologize for the trouble he was causing.

"As you can see, it came addressed to me," said Obata, evidently embarrassed that he'd opened and read the letter at all. "Of course," he went on, "I certainly don't take what's written here at face value." He lit another cigarette. "Looks to me like the work of someone with a personal grudge." The fact that the letter was addressed not to Kuki himself but to a company director certainly suggested a serious desire to do harm. "Do you have any idea who's behind it?"

Kuki thought of people close to him. The only one who knew for certain about Rinko was Kinugawa, but Kinugawa would never do something like this. His other colleagues might have some inkling of what was going on, but none of them could have known so many of the details. Besides, why bother making a power play against someone who'd already been demoted?

"I do have some idea," he said. Only two people in the world could know this much about Rinko and him, with a strong enough motive to use such knowledge against him: his wife, and Rinko's husband. As he was thinking this, Obata spoke again.

"As I say, I personally give no credence to any of this, but since it's forced the issue into the open, I'm afraid we can't very well ignore it, either."

What was that supposed to mean? Kuki glanced up, and Obata looked away.

"Your private life is, of course, your own affair, but the company's integrity is being called into question."

"And?"

"And so, first and foremost, I wanted to hear your side of it."

"Certainly." Kuki paused to clear his head. There was no doubt that the letter was extremely unfair, and if necessary he and Rinko together could dismiss it as pure rubbish. However, regarding its basic claim, things were a little more complicated. Though he had by no means forced himself on her, or done anything against her will, as the letter alleged, he had indeed become intimate with Rinko, a married woman. "It's completely one-sided," he said finally. "Everything is blown out of proportion and twisted to make me look bad."

"The whole point of this kind of harassment is to stir up trouble for the victim, so I'm sure that's true."

"I never used coercion, never locked anyone up."

"I know that. You're hardly the type," Obata said with an ironic smile. "But you do admit having become intimate with this woman?"

When Kuki failed to respond, the director quickly stubbed out his cigarette. "Look, I did a little asking around in your section, off the record, when this came up."

"About me?"

"Don't worry, I didn't give out any details of the letter. But I did hear that you've left your wife and are living with the woman in question." Suzuki or somebody else must have revealed at least that much. "Is that true?"

Kuki remained silent. The facts were open to all kinds of interpretation. As he saw it, the love he shared with Rinko was so intense they could die happily for one another at any time; so pure, God himself couldn't come between them. But from a different perspective, one could just as easily say their affair was wicked and adulterous, the kind of immoral behavior that undermines society and offends decent people. Using highly charged words like "force," "seduce," and "perversion" made their love for each other seem filthy, sordid. Perhaps he and Rinko *could* only see things from their own point of view, ignoring how it appeared to others.

While Kuki was considering this, Obata suddenly grinned. "You're a sly one, though, aren't you?"

"No, I—"

"God, I envy you. I'd like to be on your end of a letter like this, once in my life." He covered this with a laugh, but there were traces of real jealousy as well as mockery in his expression. "Anyway, I'm turning this over to you." He held out the letter in its envelope. After watching Kuki pocket it, he added in a more formal tone, "Now, on a quite unrelated basis, we've decided to ask you to transfer to Kyoeisha."

Kuki repeated dumbly, "Kyoeisha?" This was a subsidiary that handled freight and distribution.

"Yes, starting in September."

"You want me to go there?"

Obata nodded slowly. "I know it's sudden, but as it turns out, your Showa history project has been put on hold."

"It has?"

"Without that to work on, you'll be freed up."

The decision hit Kuki like a lightning bolt. To steady himself, he looked out for a moment at the puffy clouds floating in the summer sky, then shifted his gaze back to Obata.

"What exactly do you mean, 'on hold'?"

"Of course, the board is still behind it, and we did go over the schedule you submitted, but the economy is in bad shape, as you know yourself. There's no guarantee it would sell, and with publishers everywhere struggling to stay on their feet, the majority of directors felt it should be shelved."

Granted, readership was steadily declining, and putting out a huge twenty-volume history at this time did have its risks; but the retrospective Kuki envisioned was something no one else had ever done, focusing on personalities and key players of the Showa period.

"Is that definite?"

"Unfortunately, yes, as of our last meeting. I did everything I could to save it…"

Obata sounded sincere, but how far out on a limb had he really gone? Kuki was growing more and more resentful. "And that's why I'm being sent to Kyoeisha, because the Showa project died?"

"No, that's not all. We thought it was time you had a look at distribution anyway."

"I see. But all I've ever been is an editor, you know that. That's not my area of expertise."

"Well, it's a good idea to familiarize yourself with every aspect of the business."

This sounded reasonable enough, and yet why should Kuki be singled out this way, sent off to a place he had no connection with whatsoever? "It's because of this letter, isn't it? That's what's really behind all of this, isn't it?" he demanded. Obata denied it, but he didn't believe him. "Let me think it over," he said finally, then left the room and returned to his office.

Oddly enough, when he got back to the reference section he found everyone from Suzuki on down sitting there as if waiting for him. To offset the unnatural quiet in the room, he announced in a deliberately cheerful, matter-of-fact voice: "Looks like I'll be leaving you all." The moment the words left his mouth, Muramatsu and Yokoyama turned and looked at him, but Suzuki, the section chief, kept his eyes downcast.

"Obata just called me in and told me I'll be transferring to Kyoeisha come September."

Slowly Suzuki raised his head, still avoiding Kuki's eyes.

"He said it was because the board of directors decided to put the kibosh on my Showa history project." Sensing everyone's eyes on him, he added quietly, "Suzuki, you must have known about this."

"No…" Suzuki shook his head, then said apologetically, "There was talk, but I had no idea the decision would come so soon. Anyway, it was an executive decision."

Summoning his resolve, Kuki took the letter out of his pocket and placed it in front of him. "Somebody sent this crazy letter to the boss."

Suzuki barely glanced at it before looking away again.

"I'm afraid my private life has become a company problem."

"I wasn't aware of it."

It might well be true that Suzuki hadn't actually read the letter himself, but as head of the reference section, he must have been grilled by the managing director concerning what he did know.

"Someone did this to expose an affair I'm having with a woman, and that's what's behind the transfer, too." It went without saying, yet Kuki needed to say the words out loud.

That evening, Kuki went straight back to Shibuya as soon as work was over. Normally, after such a blow, he would have gone out drinking with a couple of buddies to let off steam and talk over what lay ahead. But Kuki no longer had any friends close enough for him to open up to. Of his fellow editors in the reference section, Suzuki was in league with the higher-ups, and Muramatsu and Yokoyama were both a bit distant; his old friends and classmates, meanwhile, were all in management or general affairs by now, not editing. He felt Mizuguchi's loss all the more keenly. If Mizuguchi were still alive, things might have gone differently, but there was no point in dwelling on that now.

The situation was hard to talk over with male friends anyway, involving as it did an extramarital affair. The only person he could open his heart to was, in the end, Rinko.

When he walked in, she was just starting to get dinner on. She seemed surprised to see him back so early. "I'll have it on the table in a jiffy," she said, but Kuki stopped her by holding out the letter.

"My boss gave me this today."

With a bewildered look, she started to skim through it where she stood, blurting out almost immediately, "What *is* this?"

"Just read it."

She went on reading, her face stiffening visibly. When she'd read it to the end, she was pale with anger. "Of all the nerve!" she spat out, and demanded to know who had written it.

"Who do *you* think it was?"

"Someone with a terrible grudge against you." Then, staring into space, she murmured, "Oh my God … could it be him?" She didn't say "my husband," but Kuki knew perfectly well who she meant.

"There's one other possibility."

"Her?" Again, she avoided saying "your wife." Briefly she considered the idea, her eyes distant, then shook her head. "I don't see it."

Certainly Kuki's wife had every right to resent him, but in reality she was more appalled than embittered, and besides, she wanted the divorce. What had she got to gain by exposing him to his company? Rinko's husband, on the other hand, was still "attached" to her, and no doubt blind with anger and hostility toward Kuki.

"Whoever wrote it," he went on, "knows that you taught at the Culture Center, and that that's where we met. Anyway, *he's* the only one who knew about the red under-robe."

"It says here you took obscene pictures, but that's what *he* did."

"I'm afraid it all points to him, what it says and how it says it."

"That *bastard*! Who does he think he is!" Distraught, Rinko clutched the letter in both hands.

"He might at least have sent it to us directly."

"He wanted to make trouble for you at work. It's not *fair*. How mean can you get!"

For some reason, the more agitated Rinko became, the more Kuki relaxed. Until now he'd been alone in his anger, but now that she was angry, too, he was able to calm down.

"I'll get him for this," she said. "He's not going to get away with it."

Kuki laid a hand on her to prevent her from flying off to the phone that instant. "Hold on," he said. No matter what she told her husband, it could do no good now. He got her to sit down on the sofa before telling her the rest of his news.

"Listen. Today they told me I'm being transferred to a subsidiary."

"You're what?"

"It's called Kyoeisha. It handles freight and distribution."

"What do you have to go there for? You're working on a project."

"That's been shelved. Permanently."

"They can't do that! Besides, what would you do in a place like that?"

"I don't know. I've never done that kind of work before, so it's hard to say. It might not be easy."

"Don't do it." Rinko looked him in the face. "You don't want to go, do you? You hate the idea, don't you?"

"Of course."

"Then say no."

Easy for her to say. Kuki knew all too well that a company worker like him did not have the option of turning down a transfer.

"Why can't you?" She looked at the letter. "Wait. Surely it's not because of this?"

"They said not, but who knows?"

"Well, is it?"

"I can't prove it, but yeah, I'm sure there's a connection."

"That's not fair!" She took his hands in hers and shook them. "Don't you see, they're playing right into his hands. He gets exactly what he wants, and you end up paying the price. You can't let that happen."

He didn't want to, but what choice did he have?

Rinko said firmly, "You've got to turn it down. If you can't, just quit."

Kuki looked her straight in the eye. "Do you mean that?"

The minute she said "quit," he knew the idea had been rattling around in his head all along, from the moment he'd first heard about the transfer. Or even before. From the time he was shunted to reference it had been there, gaining strength even as the notion of parting from Rinko grew more unthinkable. Now that she'd put it so clearly and simply, the idea was almost irresistible.

"Maybe I will," he said. "All right, I will. I'll quit my job." He sought her approval once again. "Is that really okay with you?"

"Of course it is."

Kuki nodded, even though somewhere inside he'd been half hoping she would say no. He was nine-tenths persuaded, but one tenth of his mind still wavered. Had she argued the other way, he could have rebelled and declared he was going to do it no matter what she said. As it was, he felt he had to point out the obvious. "Things won't be easy, you know."

"I suppose my offering an explanation would do no good."

"What do you mean?"

"Say, if I met with your boss and told him my side of things."

"Forget it." That would only amount to a public admission of how deeply involved he was with her. "Once something like this happens, you've had it. You can't go back."

Suddenly, Rinko bowed her head in contrition. "I'm sorry. It's all because of me."

"No, no, you're wrong..." There was no point in assigning blame. If anything, it was falling too deeply in love that was responsible.

Kuki's feelings continued to waver. He was disenchanted with the company, no longer felt like going to work—yet to walk away from the place where he'd worked for nearly thirty years was no easy matter. If he were retiring, it would be one thing, but to quit in his mid-fifties, a few years from retirement, seemed a waste.

All through the rest of July he weighed the pros and cons of resigning, without giving any indication that he was thinking of walking out. But as August came along and the day of his impending departure grew near, he learned the details of the arrangement and his heart sank. He had assumed he would be going on loan from the main company, but now it seemed he was to be a full employee of Kyoeisha, at a thirty percent cut in pay. After such callous treatment, what did he owe this company? He was more inclined than ever to walk out the door. What held him back was fear of the future. Until now, he'd been earning nearly a million yen a month, half of which went to his wife. The moment he quit, that income would drop to zero. There would, of course, be severance pay, but that came in a lump sum, and wouldn't last forever. How could he and Rinko manage? The more he thought about it, the more afraid he grew of handing in his resignation.

One day, as if reading his mind, Rinko said, "You're worried about our finances, aren't you?" Her words hit the nail so squarely on the head that he could only stammer a reply. She went on unconcernedly, "I have cash reserves of my own, you know, so don't worry." Perhaps her father had left her a small inheritance. "Even if you quit your job, we'll make out somehow."

Once again she was proving herself tougher and more determined than he was. Not dragging him into anything, but strengthening his resolve. Early in August, just before everyone's summer vacation, Kuki strode into Obata's office and announced his intention to resign, effective immediately.

"What's this all about?" asked Obata, a look of bafflement on his face.

Kuki felt a surge of satisfaction at the man's evident astonishment. "I can't allow myself to go on imposing on the company's goodwill," he said, at pains to express himself politely.

Flustered, Obata said, "What are you talking about? We're moving you to freight and distribution because we know a valuable individual like yourself will come up with some new ideas."

"I appreciate your saying so, but all I'm good at is editing. I'd do nothing there but get in the way."

"Don't underestimate yourself."

"I'm not. Others have."

Obata's eyes opened wide at this, but Kuki paid no attention. "Well, good-bye," he said. "Thank you for everything."

"Don't be so hasty. Take your time, calm down, think it over."

"I have given it plenty of thought, believe me. Nothing you could say would make me change my mind. Good-bye."

Kuki recognized that he was more worked up than was good for him, but there was no backing out now. He got up, made a deep bow, and with a sidelong glance at his former boss, walked out of the room. Out in the corridor, he took a deep breath. In all his life, he had never talked so bluntly to a boss, nor would he ever do so again. He savored the exhilaration of the moment, sensing all the while that he had taken an irrevocable step.

"So be it," he told himself, and with one more look back at Obata's office, he headed toward the elevator at the end of the corridor.

Kuki's resignation brought about a great change in Rinko's life.

First, she quizzed her husband over the phone about the anonymous letter, but with unsatisfactory results. He insisted he knew nothing about it. "It's so obvious he did it, and yet he just goes on playing dumb!"

Despite Rinko's fury, there was no hard proof that her husband had written the letter. He had the motive, and the letter's contents pointed to him, but because it was written on a word processor, there was no way of identifying the print. The stationery and envelope could probably have been tracked down and identified, but since no criminal offense had been committed, who would do the tracking?

Besides, what kept Kuki from pursuing the matter was this: even if they established that Rinko's husband was the culprit, it wouldn't alter his decision to resign. "Let it go," he advised, wanting to calm her down, but she was implacable. "I never thought he was such a snake!"

The more she lashed out, the more dispassionate Kuki became, able finally to see the situation from her husband's point of view. Yes, sending the letter was a lousy thing to do, but Matsubara was up against a man who had stolen his wife, was living with her openly, and had no intention of returning her. Why shouldn't he be so full of hate that he would try to get Kuki fired?

"That does it. My mind's made up. I'm divorcing him."

"He'll never agree to it."

"I don't care. I'll send him the papers myself."

"Do you really think he'll—"

"It doesn't matter. I just want to make a statement, to let him know I'm through with him."

As usual, Rinko's decision was swift, her reasons clear. Her decisiveness spurred Kuki to do something about his own divorce, which he'd been allowing to hang in abeyance. Now was the time to settle it.

"I'll get a divorce, too," he told her.

Rinko turned around in surprise. "You don't have to do that!"

"I'd feel a lot better if I did."

"Then you will?" Despite her previous disclaimer, she was all smiles. "So we'll both be single again."

"Ex-adulterers."

"I'll go to the ward office tomorrow and get the forms. All we need to do is fill them out and put our seals on them, right?"

It seemed to Kuki there had also been spaces for the names of two witnesses, but those they could just leave blank.

"Anyway," she said, "if I send him the form, he'll be forced to face reality—that I want to end our marriage."

The following day, she brought back two sets of divorce papers from the ward office. They each signed one set, affixed their seals, and put them in envelopes, one for his wife and one for her husband. And that was that.

Along with this document, Kuki enclosed a short letter to his wife. He still hadn't told her of his decision to resign, so he wrote that he was leaving his job at the end of August, and apologized for not having sent her the form sooner. Then he added one more line: "I know I've caused you pain, but I won't leave you destitute. Take care of yourself." Somehow, writing that brought back to him all the years they had shared. Tears stung the corners of his eyes. Telling himself that it was over now, he stuck the packet in the mailbox and immediately felt a sense of liberation, as if an actual physical weight had been removed.

Freed at last from the confines of family, he was a husband no longer, a man on his own. Not that family life had ever been particularly burdensome, or the status of husband particularly trying. There had been mild annoyances, but that was the same for everyone; that was life. Still, knowing that his divorce would soon be a reality helped to blunt the pangs of conscience about repeatedly betraying his wife and family. Suddenly, he felt as light as a bird taking wing.

Leaving the company where he'd spent so many years was part of the sense of liberation. Starting tomorrow, there was no more setting off for work with one anxious eye on the clock. Never again would he have to face the people above him, or fake an interest in their unimaginative projects and stupid little schemes. He and Rinko could go arm in arm anywhere they liked now, without a care.

But there were times when he fell back to earth with a bump. This freedom had come too easily. What had he done but tell his boss "I quit," and send a form off to his wife? How could actions so simple be enough to rid him of all the usual shackles? And why had he never known how simple it all was? One moment he felt ashamed of his own shortsightedness, but the next, he saw how lonely the road ahead might be. True, what time he got up, what he wore, where he hung out no longer mattered. But the cost was severance from colleagues and friends, as well as his wife and daughter.

Rinko felt no less isolated. With typical resolution, she had sent the divorce form straight off to her husband and let her mother know. A reaction wasn't long in coming.

It was barely a week until the mid-August O-Bon season honoring the souls of the dead. As this would be the first O-Bon since her father's death, Rinko had planned to go home for the occasion and join in the family visit to his grave. When she called to ask about arrangements, her mother said coldly, "Oh, were you intending to come?"

"How could she talk to me that way?" said Rinko, in shock that her mother had effectively ordered her to stay away. "She's upset because I signed the divorce form. But what's that got to do with me visiting my father's grave?"

Limiting her access to her father's grave did seem a bit extreme.

"Nobody wants anything to do with me now." After she moved in with Kuki, not only Rinko's mother and brother but all her relatives, from her sister-in-law on down, had begun treating her as a "loose woman." "What sin have I committed?" she asked sadly.

Kuki had no answer.

"Now I'm completely cut off," she said softly.

Kuki gripped her tightly by the hand. "You're not the only one."

In the last half of August, Kuki savored the full flavor of freedom—and of solitude. His resignation would take effect at the end of the month, but in addition to the usual O-Bon holiday, he had paid leave coming, so he was on extended vacation already. It was nice to be able to relax for once, but at the same time, it only emphasized his isolation.

Spending the days alone with Rinko in their tiny apartment, Kuki realized how tired he was, mentally and physically, after years of going to the office. He could sleep now all he liked, not only at night, but in the morning and at midday too, if he chose. Sometimes he forgot when it was time to eat. Even so, when he awoke in the morning his first thought was still, "Gotta get up." The next moment he would remind himself, "Not any more."

He rejoiced then, luxuriating in the freedom to stay in bed, but he also felt a strong sense of being out of step with the world. The sensation was all the more vivid when, each morning, he looked out the window and saw crowds of workers heading briskly for the station. It made him only too aware that, as long as a man was part of that daily parade, his income and his family's future were secure.

The days slid by in this curious interweaving of serenity and unease. Kuki's one foray into the outside world was a trip to the Culture Center to see Kinugawa. For once, the meeting was at Kuki's instigation. He still hadn't told his friend the news of his resignation and imminent divorce. He knew he had to get around to it eventually, but wasn't looking forward to the prospect.

Since quitting work, he found himself strangely loath to show up at the restaurants and bars he had formerly frequented. He had always paid cash, so he had no reason to stay away, but he felt intimidated, afraid he would be unwelcome. After some hesitation, he took Kinugawa to the little pub in Ginza where they'd been before. They sat down side by side at the counter.

It was late August, and the searing heat of midsummer had somewhat abated, but the place was no less crowded with thirsty customers for all that. They raised their beer glasses to toast each other, then talked for a while about mutual friends. Finally Kuki came out with it: "Guess what ... I left my job." Kinugawa set down his glass in surprise, but Kuki went on without waiting for a response, filling his friend in on all that had happened.

Kinugawa listened right to the end without comment, then said only, "Are you sure about this?"

"What do mean, am I sure?"

"You won't regret it?"

He couldn't deny having regrets, but there was no point in getting into that. Instead he gave a faint smile, and shook his head.

Kinugawa lowered his voice and asked, "So, have you got something new going?"

"Not really."

"How are you going to survive?"

"We'll make out somehow." The minute he said it, Kuki realized that these were the very same words that Rinko had used.

"Once the divorce comes through, there'll be alimony to pay, too, you know."

"I figure the house in Setagaya will cover that."

"You're handing it over to her?"

Kuki nodded. Over the past month, his attachment to money and possessions had diminished.

"You know something? You're not acting your age."

"Think so?"

"By our age you're supposed to think a little about the consequences of your actions. Who doesn't want romance in his life, who doesn't see a good-looking woman and dream about making his move? But to lose your head, throw away your position and your work on a woman's account, that's giving up the whole game. You might as well be a cat or a dog."

Kinugawa was telling the truth as he saw it, but his tone and manner were too severe. He made it sound as if any man with a wife and family who fell in love with another woman and devoted his time to her was crazy, no different from an animal in rut.

Since Kuki remained silent, Kinugawa seemed to realize he'd gone too far. "There's nothing wrong with falling in love," he said. "You've just got to keep it in bounds." He took a sip of cold saké and added, "You never struck me as being that naïve."

"Me, naïve?"

"Yeah. To think you had it all—job, money, family—and threw it all away for the sake of a woman."

That wasn't naïveté, Kuki wanted to say, it was far more: the result of an aching passion they felt for each other with body and soul. But he said nothing, knowing he couldn't express the idea adequately in words.

Then Kinugawa said in a low voice, "Or maybe I'm just jealous."

"Of me? Why?"

"She is a really beautiful woman. If you hadn't gone after her, I might have. That's what gets me." He had never made such a confession before. "But you swept her off her feet, so what could I do?"

After a short silence, Kinugawa had a sudden thought. "Oh, yeah. She came to see me the other day."

"At the Center?"

"Four or five days ago. She showed up and wanted to know if she could have her old job back again, teaching calligraphy. Now I see the connection." Kuki hadn't known this. "You've got to hand it to her, she's tough. She must have thought that with you out of a job, she should go back to work."

After a slight pause, Kinugawa said something else unexpected. "She asked me where your wife worked." Kuki had mentioned once to Rinko that his wife was a design consultant to a chinaware maker. "She asked twice, so I gave her the name of the store in Ginza. Was that bad?"

"No, that's all right." His wife hadn't made any complaint, so it seemed unlikely that there had been words between the two women —but why would Rinko want to know?

As he was chewing this over, Kinugawa leaned toward him and said, "I'm no one to tell you this, but she's gotten even better-looking."

Unable to agree or disagree, Kuki looked down at the wooden counter.

"She's definitely changed. Granted, that could be your doing, but before, she had a kind of iciness, like she wouldn't give you the time of day. And now she's poised, and confident, and ultra feminine." Apparently the saké had started having its effect. Kinugawa stared off into space. "You see her every day, so you probably don't notice it much, but her chest is so white, and her skin—God forgive me—her skin looks like it must be so soft to touch."

What on earth could Rinko have had on? Most of the time she dressed modestly, but in the blistering heat she must have worn something like a low-cut sundress.

"Even the receptionist commented on it. Said she was more than beautiful … that she had the kind of aura that gives even other women goose bumps."

Kuki had never heard him praise any woman at such length before. He looked down modestly, as if the praise were for him.

"She did look a bit thinner. Her neck was slender, but that only added to her charm."

It was true. Lately Rinko's appetite had fallen off, perhaps from the heat.

"It reminded me of the old saying that beauties don't live long."

"How's that?"

"As she was leaving, she lowered her head in a certain way, and there was something about the sight of her walking away … something sad and unsettling." Kinugawa downed the last of his saké, as if to drown his sorrows. "Be sure you take good care of her."

After they'd had something to eat, they went to another drinking place, but all Kinugawa did was go on about work, forcing Kuki into the position of listener. Perhaps once a man lost his job, he'd gradually have less and less to contribute to a conversation. Kuki was feeling rather low as they walked out.

In parting, Kinugawa said softly, "Take care, buddy." His tone was oddly heartfelt. Kuki gave a slow nod, and Kinugawa stuck out his hand. After a brief handshake they went their separate ways. A few minutes later, it dawned on Kuki that it was the first time he had ever shaken Kinugawa's hand.

What was that all about? Kinugawa had offered his hand quite naturally, but his last words had such an odd warmth to them that Kuki couldn't get them out of his mind. He mulled it over in the taxi on the way home, but arrived at Shibuya without reaching any conclusion. It was then eleven o'clock.

He went straight to the bathroom and soaked in a hot bath Rinko had run for him, put on a bathrobe, and lay down on the sofa. The TV news was on, but he turned the volume down and took a swallow of beer before remarking to Rinko, who was standing in the kitchen with her back to him, "I was out with Kinugawa." For a second she turned toward him, but quickly recovered and went on making some coffee.

"He said you're even prettier than ever."

"Oh, you know him."

"You went to see him about a job?"

"Yes. I'd asked before and never gotten an answer, so I thought I had nothing to lose by going to see him in person." She brought over a cup of coffee and joined him on the sofa.

"I told him I'd quit work, and he told me I was a fool."

"That was nice."

"He has a sharp tongue, but I know what he means." Eyes on the TV, he added, "You asked him where my wife works in Ginza?"

Casually, as if she'd been expecting this, Rinko said, "Actually, I went to see her."

"You did? What for?"

"Nothing. I'd always wanted to see her, that's all."

What would prompt a woman to pay a call on her lover's wife, he wondered. He could see the temptation, but to go through with it was another matter. Much as he might like the chance to size up Rinko's husband, he wouldn't have the nerve.

"I only looked at her from a distance." Since his wife was helping out at the shop in Ginza, all Rinko had to do was mention her by name and someone would have pointed her out. "She seemed like a lovely person."

He had no idea what to say to this.

"I mean, I could see why you would fall in love with her. She's still so slim, and she has such energy."

Getting a job had had a rejuvenating effect on his wife, but she was over fifty. Rinko was nearly fifteen years younger. His wife might be young for her age, but there was no comparing them.

"Yet even someone like her ends up alone," she murmured, half to herself. "Of course, I know it's my fault things turned out this way, but still, looking at her, I got scared."

"Scared of what?"

"Of time passing. After ten years, or twenty, a person's feelings change. After all, when you married her, you must have loved her and wanted to make a home with her, yet now see what's happened."

Why bring up this now, for God's sake?

Her eyes on the curtained window, Rinko said, "Sooner or later, you could get tired of me."

"No. Never."

"You don't know that. Or it might be the other way around."

She might as well have held a dagger to his throat. It was true. If a man's feelings could waver, why not a woman's? They might be deeply in love now, swear eternal devotion, but who was to say the years would take no toll? What guarantee was there that their love, too, would not slowly erode and crumble?

"When you met your wife, you were just as sure, weren't you?"

"No." There was no comparison with the way he felt about Rinko now. Yet there was also no denying that he'd made a pledge to love Fumie for life.

"I know *I* was," she said. "I never dreamed things would turn out this way." Kuki sat dumbly, arms folded. She leaned over and touched the ring on his left hand. "You will get tired of me one day, won't you?"

"No. I love you far too much for that."

"Even so, I'll get old. Every day, little by little, until one day I'm an old crone." Despite her admiration of his wife's youthfulness, perhaps she had detected signs of aging, after all. "How can you say your love will never change? Nothing is absolute, is it?"

She'd said the same thing in Karuizawa, he remembered; but just as he was thinking this, she suddenly threw herself against him, saying "Hold me! Hold me tight!" With her full weight pressed up against him, he was knocked off balance, but she only buried her face deeper in his chest. "I'm scared! So scared!" Encircled in his arms, she added in a softer voice, "Now is our best time. This is tops. However long we're together, it can only go downhill from here."

"That's not true." Even as he denied it, deep down he suspected she was right.

Rinko found release from her increasing fear of the future in the throb and quiver of sex. It did for her what a hundred endearments, a thousand assurances could not. It was her deliverance; there was nothing so honest, so self-forgetting as the body. And now her mood took hold of Kuki, too, and the spark of desire he'd been suppressing all evening, from the time he was with Kinugawa, burst into flame again as she straddled him, the ends of her long hair streaming and catching in her mouth, their bodies soon glistening with sweat on that midsummer night.

But when, as had happened already more than once, he heard her cry out at the height of joy that all she wanted was to die, it sounded more urgent than ever before. And later, looking up at him with eyes moist with tears, she said: "Can't I die like this? With you … with my breasts, my belly against you … and you inside me… If I could die like this, I wouldn't be frightened one bit. Don't you see?"

Kuki nodded, conscious that they were still joined together.

"Let's die together like this," she said.

He felt only a flicker of concern, almost reconciled by now to the idea. If it was meant to be, then so be it. Perhaps the languor after sex or the sensation of still being anchored inside her, had reduced his range of thought. Anyway, he hadn't the strength to resist her.

"Will you die with me?"

"Mm."

She pressed him. "You really will?"

"Sure." He thought of Kichizo, the man mutilated by Sada Abe. He wondered if she had said, "Is it okay if I strangle you?" and Kichizo had answered "Sure," caught in the grip of the same kind of languor.

"I'm so glad." Rinko hugged him, the slight movement making him slip out of her. "No!" she said, but he paid no attention, rolling off and stretching out on his back.

"Are you sure it's okay if we die together?"

"Yes." As he spoke, it occurred to Kuki that he had never been this gentle, this docile before.

"That way we'll always be together."

She was like the bird of legend that led men to their deaths, he thought, yet the idea of setting out on a voyage to the land of death, borne on her wings, was not unattractive.

"Bite me here, as a pledge," she said, thrusting at him a breast still flushed and hot from their lovemaking. Kuki obediently did so, leaving the red imprint of his teeth in her flesh. Then she did the same to him. As he bore the twinge of pain, he told himself that he was now well and truly hers.

"Let it stay there always," she said.

He lay on his back, her bite tingling. She had bitten him hard, but it was a token of her love. He lay still, eyes closed. Rinko murmured in his ear: "It's true, this *is* the best time of our lives, right now."

He considered this. Yes, financially he was still in good shape, and he still had a measure of youth. Above all, he had the overwhelming love of Rinko, this one-in-a-million woman. Living longer was unlikely to bring any golden age capable of eclipsing the happiness he felt now. Death would inevitably come, but of all the possible deaths he might die, none could be as appealing, as special as dying with her.

"From the time I was a little girl, I always thought that dying at the peak of happiness would be the best way of all."

He thought of Akiko Hatano, the woman who had lured Takeo Arishima to his death. The circumstances were different, yet there was a fundamental similarity: they too, a couple in the prime of life, had chosen death at the woman's instigation.

"What will happen after we're gone?" she asked.

"What do you mean?"

"What will people say, how will they react?"

He saw the faces of his wife and daughter.

"It gives me a little thrill just to imagine it." She seemed less eager for death than taken with the idea of double suicide. "We'll die with our arms around each other, all right? Never letting go."

"Is that possible?"

"We'll have to figure out a way." She spoke as if they were setting off on a treasure hunt. "Everyone will be so surprised!"

Hearing the lilt in her voice, Kuki too felt the stirrings of a covert enjoyment as he pictured the general astonishment it would cause.

"Nobody knows we're going to die."

Kuki nodded, slowly accepting the invitation that hovered over Rin-ko and the bed, full of wonder at his doing so.

Paradise

Autumn came early to the streets of Tokyo. In the Ginza, the windows of women's boutiques displayed dozens of outfits in shades of wine and brown, while the clothing of the jostling pedestrians showed similar hues. The season itself, slow to arrive, was now definitely in the air, the sunshine bright yet nothing like as strong as before.

It was just after five P.M., with a mild breeze stirring as the sun sank golden in the west. Kuki made his way up to a coffee shop on the second floor of a building with large windows through which one could look down on the Ginza as darkness fell. The working day was just ending, and mixed in with the drab suits of company men whose work was done were the brighter, more fashionable, more varied colors sported by the younger women.

As he gazed at this late afternoon scene, a waitress in pink and white came up behind him, making him jump. "Here you go," she said, setting down his coffee with a little nod. For some reason Kuki kept his eyes lowered, as if he'd been caught doing something wrong. After she was gone he let his breath out slowly in relief.

He was by the window at a table for two. Except for one couple and a party of four, the establishment was empty: it was a tad too early for the after-work crowd. What made Kuki so sensitive to the clientele, and the movements of the waitress, was the item he had stashed in an inside pocket.

That afternoon he'd gone to a chemical laboratory in Iidabashi to get it. He'd had the idea because of the promise he made to Rinko. He and Rinko had spent the last couple of weeks trying to answer the question of how they could manage to die together, with their arms still around each other. After doing a good deal of research in everything from medical texts to mystery novels, they had decided only two days earlier that this was the only way.

Having made his decision to join Rinko in their planned escape, Kuki felt as if he'd broken through a barrier. The thought of death was naturally frightening, yet one could also see it as merely the beginning of another journey. Since it was a journey that every creature on earth had to embark on eventually, what better way to do it than accompanied by the person one loved most?

Rinko said that if she could die in his arms, she wouldn't be afraid. She wanted death to come in the course of sex, at the height of pleasure. If they were each to draw their last breath at that special moment, as their bodies experienced release, then perhaps death really wouldn't be frightening at all. In fact, even Kuki now felt a sort of yearning for it spreading slow and hot inside him. A brilliant, intense, fully satisfied ending, an act of consummate happiness such as only two lovers dying together could know: how many couples in all the world were capable of wanting and carrying it out? He was willing to bet they were one in a million: the chosen, the "love elite."

The traditional image of double suicide in Japan was one of doomed lovers with nowhere left to go, the man perhaps turned thief for the sake of his beloved, both suffering from society's rejection of their relationship. But this was no longer the Edo period, the age when writers like Chikamatsu and Saikaku had imprinted that image on the national consciousness. The time was long gone when only the wealthy had relative freedom; when the lowborn, burdened with poverty and debt and fettered by rigid social obligations, chose death as their only escape.

For the first time, Kuki felt he understood why, when the police found her with her lover's genitals tucked inside her obi, Sada Abe had been smiling. She must have felt the same way as Akiko Hatano, who on the day before her double suicide with Takeo Arishima had gone to work as usual, parting from her colleagues at the end of the day with a quiet smile. Kuki came to think that people regard a love suicide as something tragic or crazy because they see only the outer shell, when the souls of the man and woman involved have moved elsewhere.

Thinking this way, Kuki's fear of death had gradually changed to something positive. Nonetheless, difficult problems had remained in planning how to pull the whole thing off. Two people in good health were seeking to cast off the body's natural inclination to go on living. To defy the ethics of common sense was not terribly hard, but to defy the rules of biological life was no easy task. In addition, the death he and Rinko wanted would be particularly their own, no simple ending.

If it were only a question of dying together, there were any number of methods. They could hang themselves side by side like Arishima and Akiko, or throw themselves off a cliff, or go to sleep in a gas-filled room. As long as "together" meant simply "at the same time," there was no great difficulty. But what Rinko wanted was for the two of them to remain in an embrace even after death.

Any two people who loved each other enough to commit double suicide no doubt longed to stay together, but usually, when the bodies were found, they were apart. Even if two lovers tied their hands together and jumped from a high precipice, for example, both they and the material that bound them would be ripped apart and scattered by the time they were found. If they slept together in a gas-filled room, not only would they end up apart, but there was risk of an explosion, causing not only trouble but perhaps danger to others. It could also leave them burned to a crisp.

For two people planning suicide to concern themselves with their appearance after dying was in itself odd. But the death that Rinko envisioned went still further: she wanted them to die locked in a close embrace, their bodies firmly joined at the base. Could such a thing be done? If so, Kuki also wanted it, besides wanting to grant Rinko her heart's desire.

Kuki had done his share of thinking about life, but always in the forward-looking context of how to live. Now he had to do a complete reversal, focusing instead on the question of how to die. Nor was he searching for measures to deal with the slow approach of death from old age or sickness, but for a way to interrupt and stem with his own hand the tide of life within him. Books about how to live were legion; books on the significance of suicide and the necessary steps involved, all but nonexistent. Under the circumstances, it was tempting to say that carrying out a perfect death took much more energy and concentration than living a full, positive life.

As he thought about how hard it was to die, Kuki felt a glimmer of understanding as to why some people chose to hang themselves, jump in front of an oncoming train, or otherwise commit suicide in a way no one could call aesthetically pleasing. Presumably, their priorities were certainty and painlessness. The average suicidal person seemed to opt for jumping off a cliff, a rooftop, or a train platform. Death by hanging was a more complicated matter requiring careful preparation and a cool head, while toxic gas also called for a certain ingenuity. Poisons, on the other hand, were often difficult to come by, and their effects uncertain.

Kuki spent the latter half of September absorbed in the problem, until one day he recalled a casual remark once dropped by his old friend Kawabata—something about there being a lot of potassium cyanide where he worked.

Kawabata was an old high school classmate who went on to major in science at college, and now worked as a researcher at the Environment Analysis Center in Iidabashi. The last time they'd seen each other was at a high school reunion the previous fall, nearly a year earlier, but Kawabata had been his closest friend in high school and they were still on good terms.

Kuki dredged up his friend's phone number and dialed it. Kawabata said he'd be in his lab that afternoon, and could spare some time. On the spot, Kuki made an appointment to see him. Casting about for a reason to explain this sudden visit, he said that a novel he was editing contained a scene involving poison, and he wanted to check its accuracy.

Kawabata's speciality was chemical analysis. He was now chief researcher, with a private office on the third floor, where Kuki was ushered in and warmly greeted. For a while they talked about mutual acquaintances, and then Kuki got down to business. In the book, the murderer killed his victim by putting potassium cyanide in his tea; wouldn't the poison be detectable to the victim that way? If so, what ought it to be mixed with instead?

Kawabata, who was wearing a white lab coat, answered without any hesitation, clearly assuming that Kuki still had his old job. The poison gave off a bitter, acidic odor that tea would not disguise, he said, adding that in his opinion strong coffee or sweet fruit juice would work better.

Kuki then asked to see some of the stuff, if he had any on hand. Kawabata nodded, and promptly fetched a six-inch vial from a corner cabinet in the room. To shield the contents from sunlight, the vial was made of dark brown glass. The label said "Chemical Reagent," then "Potassium Cyanide" in both English and Japanese.

"Shall I shake a little of it out?" Kawabata laid a sheet of paper on the table, and on top of that put a smaller piece of paper used to wrap individual doses of powdered medicine. Then he put on some rubber gloves and removed the lid of the vial. When he tipped it over, out came two bean-sized lumps, followed by a white powder containing smaller lumps.

"How many people would this…?"

"It's so pure that a teaspoonful would be enough to kill off four or five."

Kuki took another close look at the white granules on the table. They appeared perfectly commonplace, easily mistakable for sugar or salt—yet just licking some off a fingertip could cause death. What in this immaculate powder gave it that hidden, magic power? As Kuki was staring at the stuff, the phone rang, and Kawabata got up.

The room was partitioned by a screen. Kuki sat in the front half, a reception area with sofas and a coffee table, and Kawabata was on the phone in the rear half, among desks and bookshelves. All of a sudden, the idea of stealing some of the white powder right now popped into Kuki's mind. All he needed was two or three little spoonfuls. He could carry it out wrapped in tissue paper. That would do it.

Go on, he told himself, but fear held him back.

Before long, Kawabata finished his phone call and returned. "Sorry, I have to step next door for a minute," he said. "Be right back."

Something urgent must have come up. As the sound of Kawabata's footsteps faded away, Kuki decided to seize his chance. He put on the rubber gloves, following Kawabata's example. Then, after making sure he was alone in the room, he transferred some of the white powder to one of the medicine papers on the table, folded the paper over, wrapped it around and around in tissue and quickly stuffed it in an inside pocket. By the time his friend returned, Kuki was innocently smoking a cigarette.

"Sorry to keep you waiting. Are we done with this now?" Kawabata put the powder back in the vial, obviously suspecting nothing.

Calmly, Kuki asked, "How much does it cost to buy?"

"It's not available to the general public, but we need it for our work, so if we order it they bring it over."

The label said "25 grams." It also gave the name of the manufacturer.

"Anyone ever swallow some accidentally?"

"No, but long ago they say there was a researcher who licked some off his hand without realizing it, and died."

"Just like that?"

"It's the most virulent poison there is. Destroys the breathing control center in the brain, so death is virtually instantaneous. A minute or so at most."

Listening to Kawabata made Kuki too uncomfortable to sit still any longer, and he stood up.

Without stirring from his corner seat in the coffee shop, Kuki patted the inside breast pocket of his suit, where the packet he had stolen only a while ago made a tiny bulge, barely palpable. Kawabata had said that a teaspoonful would easily kill four or five people. This must be enough to finish off ten.

Shaken by the realization that he was carrying such a deadly poison, Kuki had ducked into the coffee shop to catch his breath. Why had he come to Ginza of all places, with its crowds and constant activity? He didn't know for sure, but suspected he was seeking the comfort of mingling with people laughing and talking in the glitter of city lights.

Kuki took a sip of coffee to calm himself, his thoughts traveling back to the research facility he had just left. After pocketing the paper, he'd quickly taken his leave. Had Kawabata sensed anything amiss? He had made no comment when putting the potassium cyanide back in the bottle, so probably he hadn't noticed, but that abrupt departure might have seemed odd. Knowing what he'd just done, Kuki simply couldn't bear to sit and chitchat any longer. To tell the truth, he was amazed how easily this dangerous substance had fallen into his hands. Kawabata had had his guard down because of their longstanding friendship. He could have stolen even more if he'd dared. Of course, because the substance was so very deadly, it wasn't something most people were eager to get hold of, and if they did get some, they might end up unwittingly doing themselves great harm. Most people were not interested in killing themselves, so it was fairly understandable if Kawabata had been more than a bit remiss.

The question in Kuki's mind was, if he and Rinko used this stolen powder to kill themselves with, could Kawabata be held legally responsible? Kuki decided it was doubtful, since his friend was unaware that it had been taken. The cause of death would doubtless be ascertained, but the supplier and route would remain a mystery unless Kawabata came forward.

The more he thought about it, though, the more nervous he became. He picked up the bill and left. It was six o'clock. The streets were lit up by neon signs of every color and description, more brilliant than ever. He headed for the subway station, thought better of it, and hailed a cab. What if he took the train with a thing like this in his pocket and bumped into somebody—what if the paper somehow tore? Disaster. Anyway, since he'd already made up his mind to die soon, why scrimp on carfare?

He had the cab stop outside a supermarket, where he bought some gloves and a small lidded container before going back to Shibuya.

"I got it," he announced casually, and opened the packet on the table while telling her about his trip to the research lab. Rinko had started copying sutras a few days ago. She paused now to stare at the white powder. "All we have to do is mix this in some juice and drink it."

She looked hard at the powder before asking quietly in a dry tone of voice, "Are you sure we can die with this?"

"It stops your breathing a minute or two after you take it." Kuki put on the gloves and poured the powder into the small, round container he'd bought. Kawabata had explained that exposure to light or air would weaken it, so it seemed best to store it away in a dark place. He decided to put the paper packet and tissue in another bag and either burn or bury it somewhere. "This will be plenty," he assured her.

"Will it be painful?"

"Maybe a little, but hold tight to me and everything will be all right."

Rinko went on peering at the powder inside the container. Then, as if suddenly remembering something, she said, "Can't we put it in wine?"

"What kind of wine?"

"Red, of course, the best."

"I don't see why not."

"We'll drink it together, with our arms around each other. First you can take some in your mouth, and then transfer it to mine…" Rinko was fond of fine wine, and evidently intended to end her life in proper style.

"Let's do it." If that was how she wanted to set off on her journey, he had nothing against it. Now that it was settled how they were going to carry it off, he felt more peaceful and at ease, purged not only mentally but physically, in every corner of his being, as if his body were gradually becoming transparent.

The only question remaining was *where* to die, but that was easy. They agreed that it had to be Karuizawa. Of course, other places held unforgettable memories, including all the hotels and inns they'd stayed in over the course of their involvement. But to die where others were guests would cause trouble for too many innocent people, including the staff. The one place where they could die in peace without inconveniencing anyone, in just the way they wanted, was the summer house in Karuizawa.

It would be upsetting for Rinko's mother and brother, who would probably never be able to set foot in the place again. Still, they at least were family. With apologies to them, he and Rinko would have to ask their indulgence in seeking, this one last time, to have their own way.

With the decision to die in Karuizawa made, Kuki was inevitably reminded of what had become of Arishima and Akiko there. They had died in the rains of early summer, but he and Rinko would be going to Karuizawa in early fall—though the season might be at its height by then, since fall came early in the highlands. The bodies of those other two had quickly putrefied in the heat and humidity, but at this time of year, that wasn't likely.

"It will only be getting cooler from now on."

"Even in clear weather there's a chill in the air, and in October everybody's gone except the locals," said Rinko.

Kuki pictured to himself the summer house, silent amid foliage beginning to change color.

"The larches all turn yellow, and when you're going down that path, you feel you're stepping into a faraway world you've never seen before," she added.

Both of them were aware that when they followed that path, it would lead them on to the farthest world of all.

Everything was flowing slowly yet inevitably toward their death. With their minds and bodies inclined so strongly that way, they felt less and less of an attachment to life. And yet this was by no means a time of mutual inhibition and quiet withdrawal. Instead, their sex drive became steadily richer and stronger, their attraction to each other more intense in the last few days they took to get ready.

Each morning, on waking up to find her beside him, he naturally pressed close to her, caressing her breasts and every part of her until they found themselves making love. After making sure she was satisfied, again and again and again, he would go back to sleep with her. Toward noon they would resurface, and before long were enjoying one another once again. And at night they would fall back into each other's arms as if they'd been awaiting the onset of darkness all day. For them, day and night lost meaning, ordinary life receding to the point where anyone who didn't know better would have thought they were sex maniacs, with only one thing on their minds. Yet having thrown off the common human urges to be productive, acquire wealth, and enjoy a life of ease and comfort, they had very little left to concern themselves with. All that remained were their appetites for food and sex, of which the former was much the weaker, being little aroused by this indoor life, leaving them in the end with nothing but the shared passion of a man and woman in love.

Yet they were much more than a pair of tireless sex machines, champions of libido. They weren't out to prove anything; rather, by deliberately losing themselves in sex, they were burning off any jitters they had about approaching death.

The only way for two people of no particular religious conviction to give up their lives naturally, without regret, was to diminish the vital reserves within their bodies, to come as close as they could to a state of death-in-life; to consume every bit of the energy that, as creatures meant to live on earth, they naturally possessed; to burn it to ashes, so that their longing for life might diminish and they could slip easily, when the time came, into the realm of death. Their tireless devotion to sex was a way of preparing themselves, mind and body, for a tranquil and composed end.

As Kuki went about setting his affairs in order, one thing weighed on his mind: he wanted to see his wife and daughter again. Not because he had unresolved attachments or regrets, but simply as a token of respect and love for the two people with whom he'd shared the greatest part of his adult life. He was sure that, after months with no sign of him, they must have written him off entirely. Still, after so much selfish behavior on his part, he felt that seeing them again might be a final demonstration of good faith.

After thinking it over, Kuki went to see his wife the day before he and Rinko were to leave for Karuizawa. He called ahead of time and asked her to tell Chika to be there too. It felt ridiculously formal to sit with them, not in the family room, but in the living room. As ill at ease as if he were in a stranger's house, he asked how they were, but his wife avoided answering; instead, she said, "I've asked a lawyer I know to handle things. Will that be all right?"

He understood that she was referring to the division of his assets, but he no longer cared one way or the other about that; he wouldn't be alive to see it done. As long as everything went to his wife and daughter, he was content. He nodded in agreement, and drank the tea Chika served. There was nothing else to say.

"You look a little thinner," Chika said, and he told her, "You look good." The conversation flagged.

Then his wife brought over two big paper bags. "It's fall now, so you'll be needing these."

Peering inside, he found his thicker suits and sweaters, neatly folded. "You got these out for me?" It shook him for a moment to realize that she could do him such a kindness, when all along he'd been assuming she hated him. To do this for a man who'd left her for another woman might, he supposed, be a sign of lingering affection. Or was it only long-standing habit, after having been his wife for so many years?

"Thank you." He bowed his head in humility at this last show of generosity from her. Still, the whole situation was bizarre. They weren't yet divorced, but he had walked out, and another woman shared his bed. For that his wife despised him and treated him stiffly, but she had carefully sorted out the clothes he'd need at this time of year. His daughter was angry with him for being so selfish, but at the same time she had only wanted, at first, to reunite her parents. He planned to kill himself in a few days' time, but neither woman had any inkling of that. All three of them felt a certain amount of awkwardness, but wanted to stay on as they were a little longer.

After another cup of tea, Kuki pointed upstairs and excused himself to go and take a look at his old study. It looked exactly as it had in early summer, when he left home. The lace curtains were closed, and the pen stand and attaché case, for which he would have no further use, were in their old places. A thin layer of dust covered the desk. Kuki smoked one cigarette there for old times' sake, then went back downstairs and told them he was leaving.

His wife looked a bit surprised, but made no move to detain him. Chika looked anxiously back and forth between her parents.

"I'll take these with me, then." Kuki picked up the paper bags and went to the entranceway, then turned around to face his wife and daughter. "I'll see you." He meant to say something more, to apologize, but the words stuck in his throat. They seemed likely to ring very hollow. Instead, he gazed at the two women and said quietly, "Take care of yourselves." He tried to make it casual, but this was painful. Eyes down, he opened the front door.

"Don't go!" Chika called out from behind.

He turned back and saw his wife looking away, and Chika staring at him, on the verge of tears. Mentally filing their two faces away, he said a wordless good-bye and went out the door. When he stepped off the porch into the street he looked back again, but no one was coming after him.

The day after this visit to his old house in Setagaya, Kuki left Tokyo with Rinko. It was, at last, their final journey, and the thought that they were looking at everything for the last time made their cramped little Shibuya apartment where they'd lived for so short a time, and the noisy, crowded city streets, seem dear. But this was no time for sentimentality.

"We're off!" said Rinko gaily, and together they left the apartment.

To match the season, she wore a camel suit and matching hat, while Kuki had on a beige jacket and brown slacks from the bags his wife had given him. He was carrying one traveling bag. To a casual observer, they looked like a devoted couple, with a rather unusual difference in age, setting off on a short trip together.

Kuki took the wheel, driving through the city center to the Kan'etsu Expressway. That's the last of Tokyo, he told himself as he was handed the entry ticket to the expressway. Rinko took the piece of paper and, staring at it, murmured in English, "A one-way ticket." True, he thought. "Bound for paradise." She was being a bit silly, but her eyes were fixed intently on the road ahead.

His hands on the steering wheel, Kuki said the word over to himself: "paradise." Rinko believed in paradise—believed that after leaving this life their love for each other would continue unchanged forever there.

Long ago, a man and a woman ate a forbidden fruit and were banished from Eden. Now the same two, Adam and Eve, were trying to go back. Though they had been deceived by a serpent, they had turned against God and tasted the fruit. Could they ever go back to paradise again? Kuki had no idea, but even if access were denied them, he had no complaint. The reason they were here in this world of sin was that they had tasted the forbidden fruit of sex. Since that was why they'd fallen from grace in the first place, then why not make the most of it, and indulge in sex to their hearts' content? He and Rinko had satisfied this basic human longing to the utmost.

Kuki couldn't say whether the rosy picture she painted of what lay beyond was justified or not; but he knew that however much longer he might live, nothing in his life could ever surpass the joy that he'd known with her. He would die in joy's embrace, at its pinnacle, secure in the knowledge of Rinko's unswerving love. Armed with that unshakable fact, he could embark with her on this one-way journey with a peaceful heart.

When they arrived in Karuizawa, the Prologue to *The Wind Has Risen* popped into his mind. It was a meditation on love and death by novelist Tatsuo Hori: "One such afternoon ... all at once, out of nowhere, a wind arose." The lines were hazy in his memory. A bit later came a quotation from Paul Valéry: "*Le vent se lève, il faut tenter de vivre.*" The wind has risen, we must seek to live. Although a rising wind isn't a uniquely autumnal image, together the words perfectly conveyed an autumn scene. With its strong affirmation of life, the line seemed an inappropriate sentiment for two people on their way to die; yet hidden in the words, at odds with their superficial meaning, was a sense less of vitality than of something akin to resignation, a sense of autumn in all its ripeness, intent on life and death at once.

It was just such an autumn that they found in Karuizawa, with a cool wind blowing fitfully through the silent trees. They arrived in the afternoon, when the sun was still high, so they drove on through central Karuizawa, past Sengataki and all the way to Oni-oshidashi, enjoying the fall highlands to the full.

The weather was bright and clear, a far cry from the dampness of their July visit. Mount Asama, giving off its wisp of smoke, looked quite small under the high, wide sky. The mountainsides had already started to change color in places, and around their flanks long plumes of pampas grass shone in the autumn sun.

Neither Kuki nor Rinko spoke much, not because they were out of sorts, but because they wanted to imprint the glories of the fall scenery on their minds. With the setting of the sun, the ridge of Mount Asama glowed ever more brightly, and as they gazed at the changing sky, the mountain began to darken from the base up. For one dazzling moment, just the white of the clouds stood out, and then it was evening.

Oddly enough, whereas it had been the loneliness of autumn that had held an attraction for them when they were still full of thoughts of life, now that their thoughts had turned toward death, they were eager to avoid such sad scenery, and they hurried down the mountain. By the time they reached the summer house an hour later, it was completely dark. The light in the porch, left on for them by the caretaker, emphasized the blackness of the night.

"Back at last," said Rinko, and Kuki repeated the words under his breath as they walked in. They had agreed that they would spend one last night here, then, tomorrow night, they would drink the red wine together and so end their lives in this world.

That evening, they had dinner at a nearby hotel. The next day they didn't plan to go out anywhere, so this was the last time they would ever eat out. They had dined here in early July as well, toasting Kuki's birthday with champagne, never anticipating that barely three months later they would be back in the same place saying good-bye to the world. And yet, looking back, perhaps there had been signs even then. Kuki, for example, although unaware at the time that he was to be transferred to a subsidiary company, had already begun thinking of quitting his job, and had been filled with a sense of the uselessness of his life. Rinko, too, had been uneasy, thinking of the fickleness of love and the inevitability of growing old.

Mizuguchi's death, then the anonymous muckraking letter leading to Kuki's demotion and transfer—all of that had triggered his decision to leave his job, but there was no doubt that his obsession with Rinko, along with a sense of having lived life to the full, had given added impetus to this yearning for death. It was as if bullets stored up in the spring and summer were to be shot one fine fall day toward the skyline, the two of them disappearing forever in a brief but violent burst of gunfire.

As Kuki contemplated this unexpectedly sudden ending with some trepidation, the sommelier came over and poured wine into his glass. It was a Château Margaux. The wine swayed in his large, round wineglass. Blood-red, with a rich, swaying bouquet.

"It's good, isn't it?" Rinko had chosen it, feeling that something red and terribly expensive would be appropriate. It had a deep mellowness in the mouth, conveying centuries of European fertility and tradition as well as the allure of pure sybaritic pleasure underlying them. "Shall we ask for another bottle, for tomorrow?"

Simply by tipping their glasses, as they were so pleasantly doing now, they would be able to set off hand in hand for the rose-colored world beyond.

That night, Kuki and Rinko slept and slept. In part, they were exhausted from all the preparations of the last few days, but beyond that, they were exhausted by life itself. It was as if all the accumulated mental and physical fatigue of a lifetime weighed on them now like lead, inducing deep slumber.

Kuki awoke early to feeble rays of sunlight straggling through the window, but after making sure Rinko was there beside him, he fell back asleep. Rinko, too, awoke fitfully now and then, but Kuki's presence close beside her was enough reassurance for her to snuggle up to him and sleep again. By the time they were both fully awake, it was shortly after noon.

Rinko took her usual shower and put on some light makeup, dressed in a cashmere sweater and long chestnut-colored skirt, then began to tidy up the house while Kuki went out on the veranda for a smoke. It was too early for the full autumn colors, but here and there the foliage was starting to turn, and leaves that had fallen in the last few days lay thick on the dark soil.

As he stood gazing at the sky beyond the treetops, Rinko came up behind him. "What are you looking at?"

"The sky." He pointed, and they looked together at the deep blue sky beyond the grove of trees.

She murmured, "We need to write our wills."

He had been thinking the same thing. "Have you got a last request?"

"Just one. I want us to be buried together."

"That's all we need, isn't it?"

"Yes. That's all we need." Whether it would be granted or not, that was their sole dying wish.

Later that afternoon they sat down together and wrote out their final good-byes. First Rinko wrote with a brush, "Forgive us this last act of selfishness. Please bury us together. That is all we ask." Then they signed their names, first he, then she.

After that, Kuki wrote a separate letter to his wife and daughter. Rinko was writing to her mother, too. He not only apologized again for what they were about to do, but also added the words that had stuck in his throat the other day: "Thank you for everything, with all my heart." As he was writing that, Chika's parting cry rang again in his ears: "Don't go!" What had she meant? Was it a simple request not to leave their house, or had she somehow sensed his determination to go, and keep going? By tomorrow, both mother and daughter would know what had been on his mind.

When they had finished, it seemed suddenly as if all their tasks in this life were now done. They spent a while in meditation, Rinko leaning back in the sole easy chair in the house, Kuki stretched out comfortably on the sofa beside her with his eyes closed. They remained that way for some time, giving themselves over to the quiet until the autumn sun began to sink and, before they knew it, evening was near.

Silently Rinko got up, turned on the lights, and went into the kitchen to begin preparing their final meal. She had gotten all the ingredients earlier. In short order she produced a bacon and mushroom salad and a hotpot of duck and watercress, then summoned him to the table. As she began dishing out the salad in small bowls, he swelled with happiness to think that his last meal on earth would be her home cooking.

"Let's open the wine," he said. Uncorking the bottle of Château Margaux they'd bought the previous night, he slowly poured it out. They picked up their glasses and touched them together as he murmured, "To our…"

When he hesitated, Rinko quickly filled in, "… wonderful journey."

They drank to that, and looked into each other's eyes. Rinko said with deep emotion, "Life has been good."

It struck him, for a moment, as a strange kind of thing to say on the brink of a journey into death.

She went on, still holding her wineglass, "I got to know you, I got to learn all kinds of wonderful things, and I have oh, so many happy memories."

He felt the same way and nodded, full of gratitude.

Eyes shining, she continued: "Liking you, loving you, made me feel so good, and every day, day after day, it taught me what it means to be alive. Of course there was pain too, but a hundred times more happiness. Loving you so much made me able to feel things I never knew before. I learned to appreciate everything I saw, and to see that all other things have their own lives, too…"

"Yet you and I will die…"

"Yes. I'm full to the brim with wonderful memories. I can't hold any more. I'm ready. I can die without a single regret, can't you?"

It was just as she said. Kuki had loved and cherished this woman with all his heart, and he too could die without regret. "Life *has* been good," he murmured, unconsciously repeating her words, truly feeling that their having lived so fully and deeply in the past eighteen months did make it possible to die without fear.

"Thank you," said Rinko, holding out her wineglass again.

Kuki touched it with his. "Thank *you*."

Nodding to each other, they slowly drank the wine.

Later tonight they would repeat this simple ritual, and so begin their journey. Knowing this, reminding one another of this, they tilted their glasses again.

It was 6:00 P.M. when they finished their last meal. Outdoors it was now dark, only the light at the end of the veranda reflected in the nocturnal garden. No one used their summer homes in October; only here was there any sign of life.

Yet inside this house, preparations for death were under way. First, Kuki took a clean wineglass and filled a quarter of it with the remaining Margaux from dinner, then tapped potassium cyanide into it from the white container. There were only a couple of little spoonfuls, but since one was enough to take the lives of several people, it was plenty.

As he looked at the poisoned wine, Rinko stole up silently and sat down beside him. "When we drink this, it will all be over, won't it," she said. Carefully she reached out and picked up the glass by the stem, bringing it close to her face as if to taste it. "It smells all right."

"The wine will mostly cancel out the flavor, but there may be a bitter aftertaste."

"Says who?"

Said Kawabata, but now that she mentioned it, it did seem strange that anyone living would know about the flavor of a poison that caused immediate death. "Maybe somebody took a tiny amount by mistake and lived to tell about it."

"That won't happen to us, will it?"

"Definitely not," Kuki said confidently, and looked over at the telephone. "Why don't you ask Kasahara to come over tomorrow around one o'clock?" He had roughly calculated the time of their death. They wanted to be found locked in each other's embrace, as Rinko had proposed, and for that to happen, discovery had to take place between twelve and twenty hours after death, when rigor mortis is most conspicuous. "Tell him we need firewood and he'll come for sure." He felt sorry for inflicting this on the caretaker, but by the time he arrived, their bodies would already be cold, clasped tight together.

"Shall we?" These casual words were all he said to start them off. Rinko nodded, and hand in hand they mounted the stairs.

Upstairs in the bedroom, the window overlooking the garden had been open during the day, but now it was closed, the thermostat turned up a bit. Kuki switched on the bedside lamp and set the glass containing the wine on the nightstand, then sat down alongside Rinko on the edge of the bed. Night had not yet fallen, but they were enveloped in a deep silence underscored by the faint chirrup of insects. Kuki listened to it carefully, filled with a sense of peace that in the midst of such quiet there should be life.

Rinko said softly, "No regrets?"

Kuki answered her low whisper with a slow shake of his head. "None."

"Your life…"

"… had its ups and downs, but in the end I met you, and you made it wonderful."

"I have no regrets, either. Knowing you has made me utterly happy."

Swept by a sudden surge of tenderness, Kuki couldn't stop himself from holding her and kissing her. Not only her lips but her nose and eyes, all of her was dear to him, and he rained kisses on her until he stopped, needing now to look at her. "Take everything off, will you?" Before dying, he wanted to gaze at her body one last time, and fix the image in his brain. "Be naked."

Hearing him plead with her like a little boy, she nodded like a mother and, with her back to him, removed first her sweater, then her long skirt. After that she unhooked her bra and tossed it aside, then slid out of her panties before turning back. "Like this?" She stood before him naked, not a stitch on. Her hands covered her breasts in a last show of modesty, but the body facing imminent death was pale white, as graceful as fine porcelain.

As if drawn to his feet by the naked form in front of him, Kuki stood up, then took hold of the hands covering her breasts and slowly lowered them. "You're so beautiful…" Never before had he looked so intently and carefully at her body in the lamplight. As he gazed reverently at every part of her, over and over, from head to toe and back again, Kuki began to feel as though this female figure belonged to an Amitabha or a bodhisattva enshrined in a temple. Now for the first time he saw that all along what he had sought was this, an image of the Buddha, a sacred being, in the guise of the female form. Just as a faithful worshiper lays his hand on a Buddhist statue, touching it for a foretaste of bliss, so now Kuki extended both his hands and touched the slender neck, sloping shoulders, firm round breasts, and nipples. Next he slid his hands down to her narrow waist, across the gently flaring hips and richly rounded buttocks until he reached the small black thicket between her legs. Then he tumbled to his knees and said as if in prayer, "Show me this."

Rinko seemed taken aback, but she lowered herself slowly onto the bed, face up, and moved her thighs slightly apart. He took heart. Eyes gleaming, he caught hold of each knee and swung her thighs open as far as he could, then gradually brought his face closer.

Opened as wide as this, the black fuzz grew thin; between the curly tendrils there showed only the tip of her bud. Suppressing an urge to kiss it, he probed still lower. Placing his fingertips on the thicker, darkish folds, slowly pulling them apart, he found her central core, a shining salmon pink that no one could have guessed at from the outside, heavily moist and lustrous.

This deep fissure, at once elegant and obscene, was where his life had begun and also where it would end. Just beyond this soft and pinkly shining threshold lay unknown depths from which, captured and held in fold upon fold of soft flesh, he would not return alive. His premature departure from this world would be an atonement for the dark and splendid sin of prodigality, for having broken into this rich, fertile garden and partaken greedily of its store of joy.

Having feasted his eyes on her for the last time on earth, Kuki impatiently removed his own clothes and then put his lips directly inside her core, revolving his tongue in a lingering caress. Aroused by his boldness, Rinko in turn reached for Kuki's stem and stroked it with evident regret, then took it deep inside her mouth and held on tight. She too was feeling a sense of destiny at the thought of how it had changed her life, this part of him on which she had bestowed such ardent love, bringing her now to the point of cutting her own life short.

For a while they stayed that way, indulging in their loving attachment to one another's flesh. Then they righted themselves, lying face to face. Now it could begin, the final feast that would culminate in their taking leave of this life together. She turned face up and tucked a pillow under the small of her back so that her hips were thrust forward; then he stretched himself over her body as though to shield it, and in that position they clung to one another tightly, resolved never to part again.

From that point on there was nothing to fear. All that was left was to climb together to the heights of pleasure. Kuki's intentions communicated themselves to Rinko without words. When he gathered all his strength for a final surge, a ripple ran through her as, fully eager and aroused, her flesh condensed and converged until her whole body shuddered and she moaned "No," then cried out "I'm dying!" At that moment her flesh drew him in, embracing and entwining around him so that all the fire in him blazed up. "I'm so happy..." With this cry of rapture that seemed to come from the depths of Rinko's being, the fire in Kuki was sucked out of him and, with every last ounce of vitality, he released his passion.

When they had fully shared the moment, Kuki's right arm slowly reached out for the edge of the nightstand. While radiant pleasure still throbbed within them, he would pour the poison, first into himself, then her, to send them off. This was it: the start of the journey they had set their hearts on.

He didn't hesitate. His five fingers wrapped firmly around the wineglass and brought it to his mouth. He looked at the crimson liquid lapping the edges of the glass like a flame, then took it all into his mouth. He was surprised; there was no bitterness or acrid flavor. Or maybe there was, but his attention was focused solely on the need to swallow.

He took one gulp. A second after feeling it slide down his throat, he lowered his head and passed the rest of it from his own mouth down through Rinko's red lips, now parted in a beatific smile like a bodhisattva's.

Face up, her body curved into his, she clung to him and sucked the liquid eagerly from his lips without the least resistance, like a babe sucking milk from its mother's breast. As the red wine passed from his mouth to hers, finally it overflowed and ran down both corners of her lips and across her white cheeks.

Kuki stared, entranced, until all at once his entire being was seized by a massive suffocation. Shaking his head in a frenzy, he summoned the last of his strength and cried out:

"Rinko..."

"Darling..."

Their voices trailing like ships' brief signals in the mist, they each uttered their final cry, their final song, in this life.

Report of Postmortem Examination, Part 1

Date and time: October 6, 1996, 3:30 P.M.

Place: 2-450 Nashinoki, O-aza Karuizawa-ue, Karuizawa-cho, Kitasaku-gun, Nagano-ken.

Witness: Karuizawa police officer Takeshi Saito.

Name, Age, Address, and Occupation of the Deceased:
Shoichiro Kuki, male, aged 55.
2-15 Sakura Shinmachi 3-chome, Setagaya-ku, Tokyo.
Former employee of Contemporary Books.

Time of Death: approximately 7:30 P.M., October 5, 1996.
The body was 5'7" in height, somewhat heavy in build, and in average nutritive condition. Elapsed time after death, approximately 20 hours.

Coroner's Remarks

The deceased was found naked in a close embrace with his female partner (cf. attached report) beneath him. The genital regions of the two had adhered, the penis of the deceased remaining inside the vagina of the female. Discovery occurred when rigor mortis was at its peak, hence the two bodies were extremely difficult to separate. Separation was finally achieved by two police officers.

The skin of the deceased was pale, the hair black and somewhat coarse with some graying around the temples. Pubic hair was black and somewhat thick.

As the deceased was prone with his arms and legs around the female beneath him, dependent livor mortis occurred on the chest and abdomen. Rigor mortis was severe in all joints. The upper extremities were in the position of an embrace, bent sharply inward from the elbow. Both hands had reached all the way under the female's back, and were partially embedded in her skin. The lower extremities were bent sharply at the knees and hips.

As the deceased had lain prone, the facial region was reddish brown with severe congestion. Blood vessels in the eyelids and conjunctivae were engorged. In the conjunctivae several small petechial hemorrhages were present.

The back was generally pale in color, although along both sides, from the shoulders down, there were abrasions caused by the fingernails of the female, extending as far as the lower back.

The mouth had been firmly attached to the mouth of the female, with a small amount of bloody foreign fluid in the oral cavity. Mucous membranes of the mouth and lips were reddish brown and highly congested, and a foreign liquid had been disgorged from either side of the lips.

There were no other external injuries.

Cause of death: acute respiratory failure due to poison (potassium cyanide).

Type of death: suicide.

Certified by police coroner Ryosuke Hirata

Report of Postmortem Examination, Part 2

Date and Time: October 6, 1996, 3:30 P.M.

Place: 2-450 Nashinoki, O-aza Karuizawa-ue, Karuizawa-cho, Kitasaku-gun, Nagano-ken.

Witness: Karuizawa police officer Takeshi Saito.

Name, Age, Address, and Occupation of the Deceased:

Rinko Matsubara, female, aged 38.

6-3-10 Kugayama, Suginami-ku, Tokyo.

Unemployed.

Time of Death: approximately 7:30 P.M., October 5, 1996. The body was 5'2" in height, of medium build and average nutritive condition. Elapsed time after death, approximately 20 hours.

Coroner's Remarks

The deceased was found naked in a tight embrace with her male partner (cf. attached report), their genital regions conjoined. Discovery having occurred when rigor mortis was at its peak, the two bodies were extremely difficult to separate. Separation was finally achieved by two police officers.

The skin was generally pale in color, the hair black, pubic hair black. The man's penis had remained inside the vagina, and semen was detected in the vagina and environs.

The deceased had lain supine beneath the man holding her. Extensive dependent livor mortis was exhibited on the underside of the body. The upper extremities were shaped in an embrace, as both arms were found clinging to the man's shoulders and back, where abrasions from her fingernails could be seen. The lower extremities were bent at the knees and hips.

Due to the male's prone position on top and his added weight, the upper back and buttocks were pale, but other areas showed dependent livor mortis, reddish brown in color. Additional areas on the shoulders and back showed pale pressure marks from the man's arms.

The face showed mild congestion, reddish brown in spots. Engorgement of the eyelids and conjunctivae was mild, with several small petechial hemorrhages.

The mouth had been firmly attached to the mouth of the male. The tip of the tongue was behind the teeth, and a small amount of bloody foreign fluid was found in the oral cavity. Mucous membranes of the mouth showed intense congestion, and lines of red congestion extended from either side of the mouth down the cheeks, due to an efflux of foreign fluid.

There were no other external injuries.

Cause of death: acute respiratory failure due to poison (potassium cyanide).

Type of death: suicide.

Certified by police coroner Ryosuke Hirata

Observations on Circumstances Surrounding
the Deaths of Shoichiro Kuki (55) and Rinko
Matsubara (38), and the Coroner's Reports

Based on the presence of potassium cyanide in fluid inside
a wineglass found fallen at the bedside, the cause of
death for both is ruled acute respiratory failure due to
potassium cyanide poisoning. How the poison was obtained
remains unknown at this time, but the red wine is thought
to have contained a large quantity of the poison, far
above a fatal dosage.

The bodies were found in a mutual embrace so strong that
prying them apart was extremely difficult. The person who
first found them came upon the scene of the double suicide
after being summoned to the summer house at a specific
time and day. Kenji Kasahara, the caretaker, received a
phone call the day before the incident instructing him to
bring over a load of firewood at 1:00 P.M. the following day,
as their supply had run out. On the day of the incident, he
arrived at about 1:30 P.M. Receiving no answer at the front
door, he let himself in and witnessed the death scene,
which he then reported to the police. Because the caller
had emphasized repeatedly when Kasahara was to come, in a
voice which the caretaker easily recognized as belonging to
Rinko Matsubara, it is suspected that the couple calculated
the time when their bodies would be most difficult to
separate, and arranged for the caretaker to arrive then.

Just before death, the man and woman engaged in sexual
intercourse, and after death their bodies remained fastened
together with the genital areas conjoined, a highly unusual
state. Generally, initial slackening of muscles causes
the bodies to separate; they remained firmly together in
this case probably because the man imbibed poison immediately after ejaculation, and they endured the subsequent
agony with their arms tightly around one another. A slight
smile was detected on the woman's face.

Effects included two white gold rings of identical design worn by each on the left ring finger.

Three suicide notes were found at the head of the bed: one addressed to the man's wife, Fumie Kuki, and daughter Chika; one to the woman's mother, Kuniko Kudo; and one more addressed "To Everyone." The contents of the last letter are as follows: "Forgive us this last act of selfishness. Please bury us together. That is all we ask." The writing appears to be that of the woman, but at the end of it both signatures appear: Shoichiro Kuki and Rinko Matsubara.

Based on the above evidence, it is judged that this is a clear case of double suicide by mutual consent. There is no sign of foul play, and no need for autopsy.

Ryosuke Hirata
Police Coroner